THE WEDDING PARTY

ALSO BY REBECCA HEATH

The Summer Party
The Dinner Party

THE WEDDING PARTY

REBECCA HEATH

An Aries Book

First published in the UK in 2025 by Head of Zeus,
part of Bloomsbury Publishing Plc

Copyright © Rebecca Heath, 2025

The moral right of Rebecca Heath to be identified
as the author of this work has been asserted in accordance with
the Copyright, Designs and Patents Act of 1988.

All rights reserved. No part of this publication may be reproduced,
stored in a retrieval system, or transmitted in any form or by any means,
electronic, mechanical, photocopying, recording, or otherwise,
without the prior permission of both the copyright owner
and the above publisher of this book.

This is a work of fiction. All characters, organizations, and events
portrayed in this novel are either products of the author's
imagination or are used fictitiously.

9 7 5 3 1 2 4 6 8

A catalogue record for this book is available from the British Library.

ISBN (PB): 9781035913121
ISBN (XTPB): 9781035913114
ISBN (E): 9781035913138

Cover design: Simon Michele | Head of Zeus

Typeset by Siliconchips Services Ltd UK

Printed and bound in Australia by Opus Group

Head of Zeus Ltd
First Floor East
5–8 Hardwick Street
London EC1R 4RG

WWW.HEADOFZEUS.COM

To Mum.

Your belief lit something in me, and, still, it shines.

BODY FOUND IN SEARCH FOR GUEST MISSING OFF LUXURY YACHT

REFUGE BAY, South Australia – The overnight search by police and rescue personnel for a missing person is believed to have ended tragically.

Emergency services were called to the scene yesterday after a wedding guest was reported overboard from a vessel in the waters off Refuge Bay – around two hours from Adelaide. Preliminary reports are that police searching the area on jet skis found a body around midday. It is thought to be that of the missing guest, however there has been no formal identification, and the cause of death remains a mystery.

Police appear to be treating this as an accident; however, they are tight-lipped on exactly how the guest came to be in the water.

A young police officer was seen grey-faced and vomiting after coming off the assisting boat, and the divers involved in the search refuse to answer any questions. Locals say the rocks at the far end of the bay may be the cause. A fisherman, who didn't want to be named, said, 'hitting them would make a person damn near unrecognisable.'

Rumours are the group on the yacht are related to the young man who died in an accident at the local jetty twelve years ago. However, it is unlikely the two incidents are related.

Police continue to investigate. A report will be prepared for the coroner.

1

ADELE - THE BRIDE

SATURDAY – ONE WEEK BEFORE THE WEDDING

'Tell me again why you even have this Sophie-fucking-Rhodes chick as a bridesmaid?'

My best friend, and maid of honour, Katja, poses an excellent – but not simple – question. I have almost nothing in common with my dead ex-boyfriend's little sister, and I haven't seen her in person for at least two years, but we'll always be connected. Here, in this posh dress shop, under the glare of the outwardly polite, but obviously irritated fitting adviser isn't the time to discuss it. Especially as the playlist they've provided based on my favourite music is on its second rotation through the discreet speakers, and the ice holding the celebratory champagne is melting.

'She'll be here any moment,' I say, willing Sophie to walk through the door.

When that fails, I sneak a glance through the small section of window to the street outside. None of the figures hurrying past are my missing bridesmaid. Or, at least, I don't think they are.

I'd recognise her, wouldn't I?

Katja slicks back her long braid, the dark roots in stark contrast to the ash blonde tips, presses a glass into my hand and draws me away from the door. 'Are we really surprised? You should have cut her from the bridal party last time she was a no-show. Or the time before.' She grins. 'It's not too late. Ditch her now, by text.'

It would be easy to explain away Katja's bluntness by the long sips of expensive alcohol she's been gulping since I gave up on waiting for Sophie and opened the champagne. But she's always like this. Usually, I value her no-bullshit approach, but today she's prodding at an open wound.

Sophie has missed every fitting, only sending me her measurements after two emails and three texts. I didn't mind when it meant only Mum and Katja were there for my final dress fitting two weeks ago, happy to share the occasion with them alone. We'd all been teary as I stepped out wearing a designer's interpretation of everything I'd ever wanted in a modern princess dress. From its stunning neckline to the pockets within the voluminous skirt, the outer layers of which can be removed for dancing, it turned out even better than I'd imagined. But now Sophie's dress is hanging in its plastic sleeve, the wedding is only days away and the expensive creation might not even fit her.

That's if she even shows up. *God, what if she doesn't turn up to the wedding?*

'Breathe,' Katja orders.

I do as I'm told, not realising I'd stopped.

As I inhale the calming floral and citrus scents released by tasteful diffusers, the fuzziness in my head begins to dissipate. I sip champagne and glance once more at the door.

The shop assistant, whose name I've completely forgotten, clears her throat and adopts a polite smile. 'Will your other bridesmaid be joining us soon?'

I doubt it.

'Perhaps we'll go ahead without her for now,' I say. 'Unless that's a problem?'

'No problem,' Polite Assistant says.

It obviously is, but Polite Assistant is hardly going to say that to a customer, not in this store. My family has always had expensive taste, but this place... It's something else. Jason insisted only the best would do and, since he's paying, I could hardly argue. They're usually booked more than a year in advance and I feared the mere months of lead time would prove impossible, but it seems with enough money one can even buy time.

I gesture for Katja to try on her dress. When she's out of sight, I check my phone but there's nothing from my missing bridesmaid, only my grimacing reflection.

The heavily accented voice of my hairdresser at our wedding practice appears in my head. 'It doesn't matter that I have created for you a stunning, multi-tonal blonde, and styled it in waves that fall perfectly down your back, if you insist on creating these terrible frown lines.'

I relax my features and for good measure I press my fingers between my eyes, attempting to smooth the skin. Just a few more days and I can make all the lines I want.

'Dun dun dun.' Katja emerges from the changing room, arms wide and twirling for effect. The champagne-coloured dress falls from spaghetti straps in a shimmer, perfectly draping her tall frame.

'You look incredible.'

Katja comes to a halt in front of the huge mirror and narrows her heavily kohled eyes at her reflection. 'Not bad.'

Polite Assistant swoops in to fuss, muttering while checking a seam before standing back. 'If you are happy, then I, too, am satisfied.'

'It's great,' I say.

The assistant makes a note on her tablet, huffing dismay at the other dress still hanging up.

I down the last of my drink without tasting a drop.

Katja changes and returns with her dress in its bag, hanging over her arm. Concern shines from her blue eyes when she takes in the fact I'm still alone. 'What will you do?'

Polite Assistant lifts her head – not all that politely – to listen in, but I don't blame her. I bet places like this don't usually have no-shows in the bridal party.

'I'll bring Sophie's dress to the bay along with mine, and hope like hell it fits,' I say, for both their benefits. 'It's too late to change anything now.'

2

MELANIE - THE MOTHER

WEDNESDAY AFTERNOON – THREE DAYS BEFORE THE WEDDING

It happens when I turn my little hatchback off the main highway at the big, new sign that's replaced the faded piece of metal showing the way to the beach. Memories crush my lungs and make the gum trees arching over the dusty road ahead blur. With barely a flinch, I blink back the tears, gripping the steering wheel like a lifebuoy. I've gotten so used to pretending that, even alone in my car, I force it down.

Why do you come back to Refuge Bay?

I can hear Jim's question as though he's sitting in the passenger seat, can almost smell his old cigarette and laundry scent, despite it being years since my ex made this drive with me.

Before I can answer – *God, am I talking to myself now?* – a hint of brine comes through the air vents. I suck it in, making my memories go from sepia to technicolour. And hurt that much more.

This is why.

Because from the sand swirling across the road, to the bend of the straggly gum trees, to that first brilliant glimpse of bright blue ocean, Ollie's here with me. Nowhere else is my son more alive than here, in the place where he took his last breath.

Here, I can pretend I'm still a youthful mum, turning heads with my beach-tousled chestnut waves and tanned skin, making plans for the future, rather than the hunched-shouldered, greying, middle-aged object of pity I've become.

My hatchback rattles along the old road. It's petty, but the thought of all the fancy sports cars and four-wheel drives jangling along here brings a smile to my face. I'm sure there have been complaints but the council prides itself on being glacially slow.

I should know. I had a petition in front of them for more than a year. In the end, however, it only took five minutes for them to rule against me.

A few minutes of driving and the road curves around to run parallel with the arc of the bay. Once, I would have been able to see the ocean from here, but the build-up of beachside properties jostling for every inch of the shorefront makes for scarce gaps. Now, there are even taller houses on the inland side of the road, and some even further back on land that used to be native scrub. Unlike the original shacks, these new houses seem to crowd close to the road's edge, waiting impatiently to cross. Or perhaps for global warming to swallow those in front.

I slow to turn into the potholed drive behind number fifty-seven and park my car behind the huge, tin shed where Jim once kept his boat. After a day out in it, they'd bring back buckets of King George whiting. The boat was perfect for fishing, but not fast enough for Ollie. I can almost hear the complaints he made as I haul out my bag and cross to the screen door at the back. I lay awake so many nights worrying he'd hurt himself on that boat.

Foolish woman.

Although I try to ignore it, the shape of the new build on the block across the road has my jaw tight. The builders have moved along with the framing since I was last here. There's also some brickwork, building up like the first layers of flesh on the skeleton, blocking the view of the bush beyond.

Given the stunning beauty of Refuge Bay, development was always going to happen, but every change grates. Mostly because Ollie wouldn't even recognise it anymore.

It's been a couple of weeks since I was last here. After unlatching the screen and wrenching the key in the battered lock, I heave the reluctant door wide and stride straight through the living space to slide open the glass door leading out onto the rickety, old porch.

Breathing in deep, I take a few paces forward, kick off my shoes and step into the soft, white sand, letting tiny shells prickle my skin as sun-warmed grains envelop my feet.

Straight ahead, where the ocean meets the shore, waves dance gently. On either side, the bay sweeps around, into the distance. Reflections of the sun on the water and the curve of the land itself mean I can't see the boat ramp at the end of the line of shacks, nor can I see the twin jetties jutting out into the blue.

But every single part of me can feel them.

The old jetty, wrecked decades ago in a storm, stands alongside a newer structure – all white pylons and fresh wood. And in my head I see the dark, murky ocean between them where the currents are the most dangerous and the water unexpectedly deep.

Where innocent boys can drown.

The bang of a nearby door has me stumbling backwards. Sound travels strangely in the bay, perhaps due to the particular undulation of the land, the water or the swirling breezes. Whatever the reason, the noise could be from close by or several shacks along. I make it inside just in time.

Someone steps outside next door. 'Melanie is already here; I saw her car.'

Idiot.

I should have parked out of sight, but I didn't think anyone would be looking for me. Foolish of me when the note with the invitation said the bridal party and close family were welcome from Wednesday. And of course, that includes me. We've all known each other for so long we're practically family. Shared sorrow from the accident created bonds between us time cannot break.

In theory.

I, however, know grief can't be shared.

I ease the sliding door closed, not yet ready to make nice, but time is running out. Hiding in here until the ceremony isn't an option. They all think this is the beginning of happy ever after, but I've waited long enough for karma to have her say.

Now, it's time to take retribution for what happened to my son into my own hands.

3

ADELE – THE BRIDE

WEDNESDAY AFTERNOON – THREE DAYS BEFORE THE WEDDING

'What do you think of Refuge Bay?' I ask my maid of honour from the doorway of the guest bedroom, twin to mine across the hall.

She's taking in the views from a spot I know gives a spectacular vantage point of the sparkling ocean. 'This is incredible. It's like we're floating on the water.' She sighs. 'Maybe I should offload my worldly possessions and find something around here, live the simple life.'

I manage not to scoff. Only someone who's never had to go without could say such a thing. 'I couldn't live without the hustle of work and the city.'

She pouts. 'Why haven't you brought me here before?'

'We're here now.' My wrist buzzes and I check the notification. Jason's wondering where I am. 'I should probably head over to Jason's. Do you want to come?'

'Definitely. Just give me a minute to freshen up.'

As I shut the window of my room, a gust of wind swirls something off my bed and to the ground. I pick it up, battling an odd sense of trepidation. The hint of gloss and logo of a classic French perfume brand suggests the piece of paper is ripped from one of the gossip rags Mum insists she never reads.

I'm about to drop it in the wastepaper basket when I catch a glimpse of the other side. A bride. The dress is not the same as mine, but close enough in style that it defies coincidence. The shape ripped carefully around to outline every detail, except above the model's collarbone, where her head should be, there is a sharp, neat line across her graceful neck.

My neck.

No, creepy as it is, it's just a piece of rubbish. But when the sound of my friend in the hall outside my room gets me moving, I can't help myself. I slip the paper inside my compact mirror instead of putting it in the bin.

Katja and I make it down the stairs and out towards the beach without being stopped by Mum or Dad who've been preparing the place like I'm getting married here. We walked in on them arguing when we arrived and I'm hoping Katja didn't notice. They've been sickly sweet to each other since.

'Going to Jason's,' I call.

At the foot of our private boat ramp, I lead Katja down to the sand and as far as possible from the shack next door without wading into the sea.

Ollie's place.

Although, technically, it hasn't been that for twelve years. The shack is like a time capsule. Unchanged, other than the natural wearing from sun and sea.

As kids, we treated the three shacks in a row as extensions of our own. Ours at number fifty-six, then Ollie's, then Jason's grandmother's place. It used to be the last before the dunes, but Jason somehow got permission to build on the far side a few years ago.

When I began to notice Ollie as more than a friend, I'd get butterflies just stepping onto their porch. Then as we grew closer, they fluttered double-time with a new, heightened awareness of his bedroom. Of his bed. I can still picture the room in detail. From the window that could be silently lifted from its tracks, to the fraying patched blanket that was so much softer on my bare skin than it looked.

'Are we late?' Katja asks.

I make myself slow. 'That's Ollie's shack.' I take a shaky breath and I can almost smell him. Sweat, sea, sunscreen and some cheap deodorant. Ollie Rhodes.

My first love. I didn't know the connection we shared doesn't happen often. I couldn't have imagined it might never happen again.

'Ooh,' she says. 'Let me get this straight. You two were dating and he tragically died? Like Romeo and Juliet.'

'Except I'm alive.'

'Details,' she counters. 'And it happened here?'

'At the jetty, but essentially yes.'

'And Sophie, who theoretically is the other bridesmaid, is his little sister?'

We're almost at Jason's. 'Yes,' I say, hoping that's the end of it. Jason may want Sophie involved to honour his best friend's memory, but the past can be awkward.

Thankfully, she gets the hint from my clipped tone. 'If that's Ollie's, and Jason's grandmother's is in between, I'm guessing that makes that one our destination.' Her eyes widen at the impressive wood and stone two-storey structure.

I grin. 'That's Jason's shack.'

Katja splutters. 'Shack? It's more like a mansion.' She grins. 'And soon to be yours.'

I look up at it. From the pool lined with palm trees, to the massive enclosed entertaining space complete with kitchen, table, heaters and television, and the second floor with a main bedroom stretching the entire width of the structure, it has very little in common with Ollie's rundown shack. Pride surges through me that this will be mine. This is the future I'm choosing, married to a man who can afford this for a holiday house, and no silly memories of teenage love will derail that. 'It's not bad.'

For the first time, Katja appears nervous. 'Who did you say will be here tonight?'

'Jason said his best man, Rory's driving down today. According to the itinerary he sent me, Pip should be here already. Typical of my dear brother, I haven't heard anything since he landed in Dubai. And then there's Sophie. Who knows whether she'll turn up.'

Her face clears. 'Rory's a good guy and I adore Pip. Seeing your brother on stage from prime seats on Broadway is still a life highlight. And Sophie doesn't count. That's all?'

I nod. 'The crowd will be tomorrow night. Oh, and Dorothy, Jason's grandmother, will be somewhere.'

A deep-pitched yell comes from inside Jason's place. 'You little—' Jason cuts off like he's clamped his jaw shut.

A moment later, something small, brown and furry bolts out of the open door.

An older woman's voice floats behind it. 'You said you had her, dear.'

That's his grandmother, Dorothy, which means they must be talking about her tiny, designer dog.

'Laila?' I drop to one knee. 'Come here, girl.'

The dog swerves towards me, leaping into my arms. By the time Jason and Dorothy appear, I'm dodging enthusiastic attempts to lick my nose.

Jason's handsome features are twisted in annoyance. 'Adele has her, Gran,' he says. 'It's fine.'

Dorothy's craggy features light up in a smile. 'Oh, good girl. I told Jason to be careful, but he wouldn't listen.'

Jason rolls his eyes in a way that makes him more the bratty private-school kid me and my friends used to hide from as a practical joke, and less the suave, successful businessman I agreed to marry.

Dorothy props her walking stick next to her and takes a seat on one of the white, wicker loungers. The silver-haired octogenarian, with makeup my wedding stylist would be proud of, holds out her arms. 'Come to Mummy,' she murmurs.

I only let myself relax when the dog is safely on Dorothy's lap. Laila's big, brown puppy eyes are framed by her caramel fur, the picture of innocence.

'What happened?' I ask.

Jason kisses the top of my head. 'The little devil tried to have a piece of me for dinner.' Although it's said lightly, there's irritation in the clench of his jaw.

Dorothy tuts. 'I'm sure she didn't. However, I admit my little princess does not like men. Not that I blame her, given the rampant misogyny.' She smiles at Jason. 'No offence, dear.'

'Of course not, Gran.' He introduces Katja to her and then adds, 'Wait, Gran, I think you dropped something.' He bends over to pick up a white linen handkerchief.

She takes it from him. 'Thank you, Jason.'

His annoyance vanishes. 'And are you sure you won't join us for dinner?'

'Please do,' I add quickly.

'No thanks,' she says. 'I'm sure you youngsters have better things to do. Besides, I've got two episodes of *Outlander* to watch.' She lowers her voice. 'It gets quite steamy, if you know what I mean, girls.'

This is not the kind of conversation I want to have with my future grandmother-in-law. 'I don't think I've watched that one,' I reply.

'You should,' Dorothy says, her well-plucked eyebrows actually waggling.

I can hear Katja choking on her giggles behind me.

'Right, I'll be off then,' Dorothy announces. She's up on her feet with the little dog walking obediently at her side before anyone can react.

'Do you need any help?' Jason calls out after her.

Dorothy snorts. 'No, thank you. There's life in the old chook yet.'

When she's out of sight, Katja and I laugh.

Jason shakes his head and then grins suggestively. 'Maybe we should watch that show together.'

'I'm not listening,' Katja says loudly, covering her ears for good measure.

Jason chuckles. 'Sorry, you understand it's difficult for a guy when he's only days away from marrying the most beautiful woman in the world.'

I smile at the compliment. 'Drinks out here?' I ask. 'It's a gorgeous night.'

Jason nods. 'I think so.'

I make sure Katja is settled, and trail him inside. Once

the door closes behind me, Jason catches my hand and pulls me close, his pale-blue gaze searching before he kisses me. 'Adele Pippen, I can't wait to give you the life you've dreamed about.'

I swallow, stuck for words. Shouldn't I know instinctively what to say? I kiss him back, buying time. He's planned the perfect weekend, allowing enough media that we'll make the social pages, but not enough to dominate the event. Everyone important in our lives will be here. He's been so good to me.

'I don't deserve you,' I say, finally.

His smile is satisfied. 'You have me. Always.'

4

MELANIE – THE MOTHER

WEDNESDAY EVENING – THREE DAYS BEFORE THE WEDDING

I'm standing by the table when there's a knock on the sliding door.

'Drinks at the parents of the bride's place in ten,' Tammy calls.

Her heels – so impractical for the beach – click away. She doesn't need my answer; after all, we're all here for the same reason. The wedding. Her daughter, Adele's, wedding. I grip the chair in front of me.

Ollie's Adele.

Not that I believe anyone can own anyone else, but they were meant to be. Now, she's marrying *him*.

'Mum, what are you doing?'

I lift my head at Sophie's question. My glowering, black-haired daughter radiates disapproval, with her arms folded across her chest and heavy eyebrows knotted under her blunt fringe. The tiny stud in her nose glints in the afternoon light. She looks like she's on her way to some concert playing that awful music she got into after Ollie died.

'I didn't hear you arrive,' I say.

'Probably because you were off with the fairies.' Her gaze darts to where my nails have left tiny crescent indents in the vinyl chair. 'Is everything okay?'

Of course it bloody isn't okay. Nothing is okay, nothing has been since the day my precious boy didn't come home.

'It's fine,' I grind out. 'But shouldn't you have been here earlier?'

Not that she let me know her plans, but thanks to Tammy's incessant updates on the wedding group chat, I have the weekend itinerary saved.

She shrugs. 'I had work.'

I'll get no more of an explanation. As a location manager for some TV series I've never watched, she could have been anywhere, doing anything.

'I've made up a bed for you,' I say. I'd expected her to refuse to stay here, but I guess it's better than next door. 'You can have the main bedroom. Bigger bed and better mirror.'

She stares at me. 'Tell me you're not.'

I lift my chin. 'Not what?'

'Still sleeping in Ollie's room. It's not healthy.'

'Why?'

'Because he's dead.' Her tone is flat.

Sometimes I look at this young woman and wonder where I went so wrong. 'I'm surprised.'

She sighs. 'What's that supposed to mean?'

'You didn't seem to remember on the anniversary six weeks ago.'

Her shoulders slump. 'We deal in different ways.'

'Exactly. You can't judge how I "deal" with my beloved son being snatched from me.'

'God, Mum, I'm not going to do this.'

'Do what?'

Her arms spread wide. 'Any of it.' Her gaze seems to catch on the table and she moves closer. 'What the hell?' She drags a fingertip across the surface, close to the puzzle pieces. 'The same puzzle.'

If there was any starker a reminder of how she's avoided this place since Ollie died then this is it, because everything's been this way for a long time. From his room to the puzzle to the filleting knives Jim left on the outside sink to run to the jetty that day.

The end of her finger is black with dust. Without a word, she strides towards the bedroom.

'We all deal in our own way,' I repeat to her back.

A little while later, I knock on the partially open door of the bedroom I once shared with Jim. Sophie looks up.

'I'm heading to Tammy's. You'll let Adele know you're here?'

'Soon.' Her lips are a blood-red slash on her pale features. 'I need to unpack.'

'You can't avoid them forever.'

'Believe me, Mother, I know.'

'You won't mention anything to Adele about…' My voice trails off. The list of things I don't want Sophie to discuss with the bridal party is longer than the terrible train on my own wedding dress.

Sophie sighs. 'Trust me, I'll be speaking as little as possible.'

Her words aren't particularly reassuring but I don't have time to argue. If I don't turn up to Tammy's soon, she'll come looking for me.

On my way through the living area, I divert to close the window but the sound of Tammy's voice from her kitchen, just the other side of the fence, stops me.

'Poor Mel.'

I freeze.

The response of whoever she's talking to, likely her husband, Terry, is lost in the rustle of a cracker packet being opened. The two deserve each other with their fake tans and faker personalities. But then she laughs. 'Melancholy Mel. Oh, you are wicked.' More laughter. And then, 'She needs to move on. It was an accident.'

My stomach drops, but not going to drinks isn't an option. I can't miss this wedding. I fumble in my bag for the small bottle and take a sip. Let the liquid burn and soothe. Make myself *get over it*.

Jim threw versions of those words at me so many times while our marriage disintegrated, but I know I deserve this pain.

And, that Ollie's death was no accident.

It's a short walk next door to Tammy's place. There was a time when the kids would vault the railings dividing the wooden decks out front, but now there's a wall, behind which they've built their outdoor kitchen, and the glass fence isn't made for jumping. Neither am I.

I've left it long enough that the groom's mother, Laura, and her partner, Ruth, are already seated at the outdoor table.

'Mel's here at last,' Tammy says tucking back a strand of her bleached bob.

For all her talking about me moving on, I'm not the only one who remembers all that happened that summer. Tammy's still thinking about it, I can hear it in the edge in her voice.

Once, I would have gushed an apology. Now I say nothing. Over the last twelve years I've noticed people will rush to fill a silence.

Tammy's mouth opens and closes like a fish flopping for air. 'Bubbly?' she asks eventually. 'It's tradition.'

I nod. 'It's tradition.'

Relief makes her smile, showing coral lipstick smudged on her white teeth. I can practically see her thoughts. *Thank God, Melanie isn't going to ruin this weekend.*

I let her have her moment of relief, however misplaced, and turn to the others.

When we first spent summers here, Laura and Stephan were the third regular couple along with Terry and Tammy, Jim and myself. When Stephan died and Jason started high school, Laura suddenly had time on her hands. With no interest in the family business, she decided to find herself. She went back to university for her master's degree, finding her supervisor Dr Ruth at the same time.

Ruth inclines her head. 'Melanie.'

'Evening, Ruth,' I reply.

In the old days, girls' drinks on the deck meant the hubbies were fishing or down the pub. Now, Terry's popping out from the kitchen every five minutes. My Jim is, well, not mine anymore, and Ruth with her short grey afro, smooth dark skin and bright red-framed glasses is here with us. Don't get me wrong, I like Laura's new partner much more than Stephan but it's different to the old days.

'I'm so glad we finished the renovations in time for the wedding,' Tammy says with a sigh, as though she personally lifted a finger that didn't involve the pages of a catalogue. 'We waited ages for the backsplash tiles.'

Terry appears as though summoned. 'They were specially imported, you know. It didn't help that this one kept changing her mind.' He waves his finger at Tammy, with a smile for the others and a determination to pretend I don't exist.

Tammy sighs. 'I wanted it to be perfect.'

'You've done a marvellous job,' Laura says, ever polite.

I join Ruth in making a murmur that passes for agreement, although the house looks hardly different to Tammy's last round of renovations.

'How's work?' Ruth asks me, popping a peanut in her mouth.

Back in the old days, we connected over educational policy. She was climbing the ranks at her university and I was a school principal going places.

'It's nice to work one-on-one with the students,' I reply about my now part-time role.

It's my usual comeback when work comes up, but the truth is, after Ollie, I couldn't bring myself to care. For a long time after Ollie died there was no fight left in me for anything, but then I read those articles and I had an enemy I could do something about.

As I do now.

'I love the new lights around the balcony,' Laura says loudly to Tammy.

Her interjection breaks the silence that developed when I missed my cue to ask Ruth about her work. It's the kind of mistake that risks people questioning my mental state. The kind I can't afford to make.

5

SOPHIE – SUNDAY JANUARY 16ᵀᴴ

TWELVE YEARS AGO

'Jim? Are you even listening?' Mum asked Dad.

Sophie wanted to scream, 'No, he's not,' but knew she'd get in trouble. After their years of marriage, Jim Rhodes had virtual superpowers when it came to ignoring his wife.

His silence seemed to drive Mum on. 'You mark my words. Our unspoilt stretch of paradise will soon be like those rich people's places you see on TV.'

'What, like *Midsomer Murders*?'

Despite the walls separating them and the headphones covering her ears, Sophie could hear the smirk in Dad's voice. She turned up Taylor singing about being fifteen, and wished she was on stage. Eyes closed, she leaned back on the bed and pictured the curtain, the lights, the audience. But instead of the *Tangled* lead she'd played in the musical theatre camp she attended every summer, she was Sandy in *Grease*. She was singing opposite her best friend, Pip, and he...

'What are you doing?'

Sophie's eyes flew open at her brother, Ollie's, scathing

question. He stood in the doorway, all lanky and long limbed, nose peeling, brown hair tipped golden from the sun.

Her cheeks flamed. 'I was just listening to—'

'Actually, I don't want to know.' He shuddered. 'I'm heading to the jetty.'

It wasn't an invitation, exactly, but he knew he had a better chance of being allowed to go if he let her tag along. Maybe the boy who'd let her dress him up to play musicals when they were little was still somewhere under the grumpy teenager he'd become.

By the time she was on her feet, he'd already disappeared down the small hallway and she could hear him asking to go and meet the others.

'I want you back here by dinner time,' Mum said. 'And be careful.'

'This is Refuge Bay not the city. Nothing bad ever happens here. Because *nothing* happens here.'

'I'm just saying you need to be careful. I know what kinds of things those older boys do at the jetty.'

'Yes, Mum,' Ollie replied on cue.

'They're not a good influence.'

'Mum,' Ollie groaned. 'You're friends with Jason's mum.'

Sophie knew he'd be pink-cheeked and looking outside to make sure her voice hadn't carried to one of the neighbouring shacks.

'And take your sis—'

'I'm here,' Sophie said, stumbling over the raised bit of lino marking the edge of the hall, a sharp thrill of pain spreading from her toe. The sunglasses she'd gotten for Christmas clattered to the ground, followed by her iPod touch – Ollie's old one. He'd gotten an actual iPhone because he was starting year twelve soon. He used the distraction to escape, banging the sliding door closed behind him.

'And I'll be careful, too,' she promised.

Ollie had disappeared before Sophie made it down onto the sand, thanks to Mum's lecture about the dangers out there for nice girls.

Her best friend was waiting for her not far from the twin jetties at the end of the bay. Kyle Pippen, or Pip as everyone called him, grinned when he saw her coming.

Sophie's traitorous belly flipped in response.

'You made it,' Pip cried, jumping up from the sand and wrapping her in a quick hug.

When he let go, she stared at her pink toenails so he wouldn't see her flushed cheeks. A hug usually didn't mean anything, but ever since she'd seen him centre stage as Danny in *Grease*, nothing about being around Pip had been the same.

'You okay?' he asked.

She could hear the frown in his voice. He must have said something and she'd been too busy dying inside to hear. 'I'm fine,' she snapped, sneaking a look up.

Hurt flashed across his delicate, stupidly perfect features and she wanted to kick herself. Pretending everything was normal, she dropped her towel on the sand next to Pip's.

Refuge Bay never really changed. The single kiosk selling bait, and a few treats, kept the same brief hours, and the bottle shop was always open. The surf club beyond it was mainly closed, except for weekends. Up on the jetty, the ancient fishermen sat with their tanned leather faces. Grey whiskers and disapproving glances made them hard to tell apart. Except for Giovanni Valente, their neighbour next to the Pippens, because he glared longer and harder than the rest. Down on the sand, kids hung out in groups, the locations of which were dictated by age – with the space between the old and new jetty, behind 'STAY OUT' signs, the domain of the older crowd. There, Ollie was mucking around in the shallows, and Pip's older sister, Adele, was tanning with her friends as though oblivious to the boys.

As Sophie watched, Jason, whose parents had the shack next to theirs, tried to jump on Ollie's back. Ollie managed to flip him over his shoulder so Jason landed butt in the air, spluttering salt water out of his nose. Everyone laughed as Jason glowered and Ollie pretended to flex his muscles.

'They're like animals doing a mating ritual,' Pip observed, his tone scathing.

Last holidays Sophie would have agreed. But that was last year.

'I think he really likes her,' Sophie said, watching as Ollie stood over Adele, dripping water on her back until she jumped up to tackle him.

They didn't talk about Ollie and Adele dating, but Sophie thought it was so romantic that they'd now been seeing each other for a whole year despite living on opposite sides of the city and going to different schools.

'I think he looks like an idiot.'

Pip wasn't the biggest fan of her brother, having always been teased by the other kids for his love of musical theatre. Before, Sophie had been glad Pip didn't get along with them. Now, she worried about spending every day alone with him.

She'd hoped when he'd washed out the black hair dye he'd return to being the same old Pip she'd known forever. It hadn't worked. If anything, his natural blond brought out the summer blue of his eyes. She caught herself staring and dragged her gaze away. Her life was basically over. These feelings she was having could wreck everything. Pip was her friend, the only one who understood how much she wanted to be a star. They were going to New York together one day and would share an apartment and drink coffee, and now all she could think about was kissing him.

Something brushed her arm and she jerked away.

Pip frowned. 'Tell me what's wrong.' He leaned closer, so she caught a taste of his breath, sweet from the chocolate-mint White Knight bars he was addicted to.

'I can't,' she squeaked. 'I just can't.'

He studied her face. Maybe he'd see straight through her. Maybe he'd admit he was having feelings for her, too. He'd lean in close and then...

He snapped his fingers. 'I get it.'

Her heart pounded so loud it drowned out the crashing waves. 'You do?'

'Vagueness, distraction, romance talk. There's a guy, isn't there? You can't listen to me because you're mooning over him.'

'Mooning?'

'Yes, read a dictionary,' he teased. 'Who is it? My gosh, please don't tell me it's one of them.' He jerked his head towards the older kids.

She covered her face, unable to stop tears pricking at her eyes.

He lightly brushed her cheek. 'I am a heel. It *is* one of them, isn't it?'

She pictured the long days ahead, the two of them together, and her tummy churned. Maybe, if they were around the other kids, Pip would see her in a new light.

'It is,' she lied.

'The heart wants what the heart wants, far be it from me to judge.' He jumped up. 'Let's go.'

She stared up at him. 'Really? But you hate all that.'

He shrugged, holding out a hand. 'I like you.'

She let him pull her up. 'I just know this is going to be the best summer ever.'

They crossed the beach towards the other kids. Pip grabbed a football kicked to him by Ollie and kicked it back, while Sophie joined the girls on the sand, and tried to pretend she wasn't vibrating with nerves. Darting a look to Pip, smiling in the sunshine, she tried to keep hold of that certainty. But the shadows of the jetty looming above them sent a chill over her skin. She shivered.

6

ADELE - THE BRIDE

WEDNESDAY EVENING – THREE DAYS BEFORE THE WEDDING

'How could I have forgotten my phone?' I ask, looking though my bag again like it will materialise. 'It's my life.'

Katja shakes her head. 'It's not surprising with all that's happening.'

'I'll just duck back to Mum's. Tell Jason I won't be long.'

'Don't dawdle,' she says with a glance to where he's inside on a work call. There hasn't been much need for them to spend time one-on-one in the short months that Jason and I have been together.

I'm about to step up onto the deck at Mum and Dad's when I stop, my legs heavy. Part of me registers Mum speaking, but whatever she's saying becomes a distant drone. Recognition jolts through me at the sight of the woman at the table, the hunched set of her back as though she's permanently bracing for the worst. It's Melanie Rhodes. Or, as she'll always be to me, Ollie's mum.

She hasn't seen me yet. I could leave. But Mum is saying

something to the others that I can't hear over the rushing in my ears and it's just a matter of time.

Melanie turns.

I swallow a gasp at the grooves in her face, and the dark, smudged hollows around her eyes accompanying the streaks of silver left to sparkle in her dark hair. Her cheeks and the tip of her nose are red, like she's been out in the sun all day.

Hoping my face doesn't show my shock, I make myself approach her. But I can't help comparing her to the other women gathered at the table. Mum's bleached, botoxed cling to youth. Jason's mum, Laura, with her stylish grey bob and classic makeup, even the careful precision of her partner, Ruth, with her military eyeliner and distinctive glasses.

I struggle to reconcile the woman before me with the image I've held of her in my head. The truth is I've had opportunities to see her before now, but I've chosen not to look. The self-reproach souring the champagne I drank means I let her arms wrap around me. She holds me tight.

'Oh, Adele. It's so very good to see you,' Melanie says when she finally pulls away, emotion filling her gaze.

I mumble something. It's hard to think or form a proper sentence because the apple scent of her family shampoo slams me back to the past. Back to Ollie's hair near tickling my nose as he nuzzled my neck.

'Adele, darling.' The greeting from Jason's mum breaks through the cloud of memory.

'Laura,' I say, quickly going across the deck to lean over and air-kiss her on the cheek. It's still hard to believe that in a few days we'll be family. It's not that she hasn't been welcoming, but there's been none of the enthusiasm that Mum has lavished on Jason. In fact, Laura has been borderline uninterested in the whole wedding.

'What are you doing back here?' Mum asks, while I shake Ruth's outstretched hand.

'Forgot my phone.'

'That explains it. You can't miss updating the socials,' Mum says knowingly. 'She's an expert,' she adds to the others.

'Something like that,' I say. 'How was the drive across?' I ask the table in general, edging towards the doors.

'Good, thanks,' Melanie says. 'Although I wouldn't want to have left it any later.'

'We managed to beat the traffic, too,' Ruth says.

I'm about to step inside when I remember there was something I wanted to ask my future mother-in-law. 'Laura, did you get my message about the flowers?'

She frowns. 'What flowers?'

'The peonies.' I omit the swear word that usually comes when I mention the item that has been so painful to source, and really doesn't match the aesthetic of the rest of the wedding.

Laura blinks. 'I'm terribly sorry, but I have no idea what you're talking about.'

I try to remain pleasant. Jason said it was vitally important to his mother that we include peonies because it's a family tradition.

'Nothing important,' I lie. 'Just letting you know the table arrangements will include them.'

'That's nice,' she says of the decision that Jason and I argued about for what seemed like days. There's a definite 'I could not care less' vibe coming from her.

Annoyingly, my eyes prickle and the crush of all the decisions I've had to make so fast threatens to take my breath.

'I love peonies,' Melanie says with a fond smile. 'We had them at the church for Ollie.'

And suddenly, I remember. That's why they looked familiar.

'Well, these are going to be wedding peonies,' Mum says brightly. 'I'm sure they're very different.'

I raise my eyebrows at her.

'Flowers are flowers,' Ruth points out in her practical manner.

'I know,' Mum says. 'I just meant that this is going to be a special celebration. Now, tell them about the honeymoon.'

I hesitate. 'Jason will be wondering where I got to.'

'He can wait. And I know the girls all want to hear.' Mum emphasises her point with a wave of her glass, splashing liquid onto the table. 'That's why we're all here. All for my baby girl.'

With Melanie here, I'm aware of how much of what we've planned Ollie would have liked. 'It's just your run of the mill honeymoon,' I say eventually.

'Tell them,' Mum insists.

I sigh. 'We'll start in Canada, travel through New York to see Pip and we'll finish up in New Orleans. Right in time for—'

'The French Quarter Festival.' Melanie mouths the final destination along with me, and my stomach churns.

'I didn't know you and Jason were into jazz music,' she says softly.

Mum is raving about something and I use it as an opportunity to escape inside.

Phone retrieved, I take the longer way to Jason's via the

road, scrolling through the comments on my latest work post for Jason's hotel group. There's the usual glowing reviews, someone complaining that they only got two chocolates on their pillow on their last visit and then:

> You should never mix business with pleasure. Marrying it just makes it worse.

I stop, nearly at the door to Jason's. It's anonymous, of course, and my hands tighten on my phone. Is that a dig at me? Our relationship has nothing to do with me getting the job to manage the business's socials.

'Are you working?' I look up at the question to see Jason standing in front of me. 'I missed you,' he adds. 'Thought I'd come find you.'

'I was just check—'

His gentle touch on my lips halts my excuses and he smiles that smile that pushes away my worries and makes me feel safe. 'No more work from now on. It's our perfect weekend, agreed?'

I push aside the thoughts of the anonymous comment that probably isn't to do with me and Jason at all.

'Agreed.'

Nothing will ruin this for me.

7

MELANIE – THE MOTHER

WEDNESDAY EVENING – THREE DAYS BEFORE THE WEDDING

I watch the door for Adele but she doesn't come back out. After a few minutes, I realise she must have gone the other way. Probably to avoid her mother.

While she stood there in her simple but elegant summer dress and low sandals, her long hair flowing around her face, I couldn't help picturing a grown Ollie at her side. Imagined them taking the trip she described together. I didn't indulge myself for too long. Instead, I noted the shadows beneath her eyes. Usual pre-wedding weariness or something more?

Tammy is still gushing. 'Pip has promised them the best seats for any show they want to see while they're in New York. Do you think they'll choose *Hamilton* again?'

In contrast, Laura's trying to change the subject. 'Is this dip homemade, Tammy?' she asks, despite the obvious packaging.

There's a vagueness to Laura around the wedding, an apathy typical of her as long as I've known her. Perhaps when she's alone with Jason she's more enthusiastic.

The crack of wood on wood splits the conversation.

We turn as one towards the sound but I already know what we'll see. Or more like *who*.

Giovanni Valente is standing on his porch, resplendent in nothing but faded swim shorts and a scowl. As much a part of Refuge Bay as the salt in the air. He's been old for as long as we've been coming to the bay, with grey straggly whiskers on his jowls to match his chest hair and a tanned, shining, bald dome of a head. He's holding a chunk of wood roughly the shape of a human forearm, and he thuds it against the rail. 'Enough!'

'Good evening, Giovanni,' Tammy says, attempting politeness. 'We were just having a drink to celebrate my daughter's upcoming—'

'I don't care,' he snaps. 'You're disturbing my peace.'

Tammy flounders. 'The, uh, sun has barely set and I don't think we're being loud.' Her gaze goes around the group and we nod in confirmation.

Giovanni crosses his arms, resting them on the swell of stomach hanging over his shorts. 'This is my home. I'm not here on a vacation. You city folk think you can roll through the bay without caring what happens when you go back to your "real lives"'. The unexpected air quotes he adds with stubby fingers should be funny but the venom wipes away any amusement.

Tammy splutters some more and looks to the door as though she hopes Terry will appear to defend her, but I'm not surprised he stays inside.

'Well,' she says. 'What about your noise?' She points to the wood in his hand. 'You tinker in that workshop of yours at all hours.'

Giovanni glares. 'That's my work.'

From Tammy's sneer she's about to say something about the art that Giovanni makes from debris he finds around the bay, and I'm pretty sure it won't do anything to calm the situation.

I clear my throat loudly. 'We'll try to keep it down.'

He harrumphs. 'You'd better or I'll be making a complaint.' He stalks inside, slamming his door behind him.

'Lucky he's not invited to the wedding,' Ruth observes.

Tammy chuckles. 'Oh, Mel, that reminds me, Jason wanted me to let you know that you're welcome to ride with the family, since Sophie is in the bridal party.'

The unspoken 'and you're on your own' whispers in the back of my thoughts. No Jim and, of course, no son anymore.

Laura nods, but not in such a way that suggests she already knew. It needles me that she can be so distant. Doesn't she know how lucky she is to have a son? Tammy's wedding enthusiasm might grate like sand in my toothpaste, but at least it's understandable.

I was hoping to be involved this weekend but complete access to the wedding party is more than I dared dream. This time, when I smile, I don't have to force it at all.

'That would be nice,' I say. 'Please thank Jason for thinking of me.'

I drain my glass of champagne. He's going to regret it.

8

ADELE - THE BRIDE

WEDNESDAY EVENING – THREE DAYS BEFORE THE WEDDING

Sitting with Katja, I'm aware of Jason by the grill, likely checking again for a message from Rory, his best man, who's yet to arrive. I can't blame him when I'm on alert for not only my missing bridesmaid, but Pip too. At least my brother has the excuse that he's travelling from overseas.

They do say weddings can be one of the most stressful things a couple can do. Maybe we should have allowed longer to organise everything, but waiting comes with its own problems.

'Is there anything else we need?' I ask, moving over to him.

As well as the salads and freshly baked bread, there's dips and crisps and a stunning charcuterie board filled with prosciutto, olives, three different cheeses, sundried tomatoes, pita thins, blueberries and toasted almonds.

'It'll be fine,' he says, but he doesn't look fine.

'Then, is there something else wrong?'

He sighs. 'I just found Gran's reading glasses in the freezer.'

Sympathy flares. 'I'm sure she was simply absentminded.'

'Hopefully you're right.' He squeezes my hand.

It's maybe fifteen minutes later and Katja's talking numbers for a new client to me. 'The artisan gin distillery will practically sell itself. I know you're the media expert,' she says, 'but the owner's backstory makes for perfect branding.'

There's the sound of a door. 'Rory's here,' Jason calls.

I keep my focus on Katja. 'We're on holiday,' I remind her, not wanting to think about the comment on the hotel socials.

Katja's insisting she can't just switch off her brain, but I'm aware of the men heading this way. I prepare to offer Jason's best man an appropriate greeting. My stomach rolls with sudden nerves. With both our maid of honour and best man here now, the wedding feels frighteningly close.

'Good afternoon, ladies,' Rory says.

There's no touch of his lips on my skin as he kisses the air near me, but I can't miss the hit of smoke coming from him, mixing with the earthy notes of his aftershave. As far as I know he's not a smoker, and it makes me think of him pulling over somewhere off the highway, buying a pack and giving in to the cravings of a long-kicked addiction. The image in my head is all classic James Dean and moody Harry Styles, probably helped by Rory's passing resemblance to both. His tousled hair is pushed back like he's just run his hand through it, and he's wearing a white T-shirt that hugs his lean body, as well as worn denim jeans.

I'm about to give him my standard lecture on the horrible habit that took my grandmother young, when I remember that it's none of my business.

'Welcome to Refuge Bay,' I say instead.

Rory walks to the edge of the deck and looks out at the water before swivelling slowly to take in the expanse of the bay, his eyes locking with mine. 'It's gorgeous.'

'It is,' Jason says abruptly. 'Can I get you a beer?'

There's a beat where I think Rory is going to say more, but then he grins. 'Mate, I thought you'd never offer.'

'Don't forget us,' Katja calls after him. 'Two bubblies, thanks.'

Jason lifts his hand in acknowledgement as he steps through the door and disappears inside, already in conversation with Rory about the most recent extension to the shack.

They return with drinks, talking about some fishing expedition they have planned.

'For my bride-to-be,' Jason says, placing a glass in front of me.

'My hero.' I make a show of swooning gratefully.

'Where's mine?' Katja asks, when Jason keeps hold of the other glass.

'This is yours,' he says, holding it high in mock hostage. 'Well, it will be, as soon as you tell me more about the hen weekend.'

Katja shakes her head. 'Not telling. I'm sure you don't want an inquisition on your bachelor party. Although, I have plans for Rory on that front.' She smirks suggestively at the best man. 'He can tell me all about this golf trip. Surely you couldn't have played golf the whole time you were away?' She practically purrs as she leans towards him.

'Ask me no questions and I'll tell you no lies,' Rory fires back.

I laugh along with the others but I shoot Katja a questioning look. She holds my gaze. She's playing at something.

'Were you flirting with Rory?' I ask a few minutes later when the boys have headed back to the grill.

Katja shrugs. 'I tried. That night we all went out for drinks after the whole production asking us to be in the wedding.'

I think back. We'd had such fun taking our two best friends out to a gin-tasting masterclass and surprising them with custom bottles inviting them to be in the wedding. We ended the night at a bar near my apartment.

'What happened?'

'I cornered him in the booth after you left.' She grins. 'Quite literally.'

'And?' I sip my drink, hoping I don't look too interested. As far as I know, Katja hasn't dated anyone since her girlfriend dumped her a year ago.

She sighs. 'And he turned me down. Politely, but it was a firm no.'

'Did he say why? You're so stunning that I can't imagine anyone not being keen.'

'You weren't,' Katja teases.

'Not for want of a lovely kiss to make sure,' I remind her. Our mutual adoration is purely of the friendship variety, as we discovered one night after a terrible kiss.

Katja grins. 'Ugh, don't remind me. I've had better pashes from a street lamp.'

'Wait? You've kissed a street lamp?'

She mimes zipping her lips. 'Nice girls don't tell.'

I laugh and realise we've drifted away from the topic. Before I can work out how to redirect the conversation back to Rory, a figure slinks towards us from the beach. Sophie Rhodes has lowered herself to turn up after all.

I needn't have feared I wouldn't recognise her, although the bright colours I always associated her with are gone. Despite the warmth, she's dressed in heavy black. Her combat boots crunch over the sand, and thick bangs shield most of her pale face.

I jump up and cross to meet her, stopping short of a hug.

'Hi,' Sophie says, giving me a brief glance from under long eyelashes.

'You made it.'

She nods. 'I know I'm a bit late.'

Part of me wants to rant at her over all the ways she's messed me around, but more than that I want this weekend to be perfect. I owe it to Jason. And that means not starting off with a bitch fight. Luckily, my brother isn't the only one in the family with acting skills. 'You're here now.'

'I can't stay long.'

'Seriously?' I say. 'That's how you're going to begin this?' So much for my good intentions.

She gives me a cool look. 'I'm here, relax.'

'If you didn't want to be in this wedding, you should have pulled out months ago.'

She doesn't reply. No apology, no reassurance.

'You don't want to be in it?' I whisper, hating how it comes out all needy.

For a second the cool mask slips. Her eyes implore me, but she still says nothing.

And it's her eyes that kill me. They're just like Ollie's. At my dress fitting I'd had to force myself to think of Jason by saying his name every second sentence. *Jason will love this one. Do you think this will go with Jason's suit? What do you think Jason likes?*

Now Sophie's here, and Ollie might as well be standing with her. I drag my gaze away, not sure if I want to shove her or pull her close.

'I am sorry,' she chokes out. 'Really, I am.'

'You haven't even seen your dress.' I try to hold on to the anger. 'What if you hate it? Or it doesn't fit?'

'I'm sure it will be fine.'

Jason's hands come down on my shoulders. 'What's going on over here?'

Something I can't name flickers across Sophie's face, the sight of it setting my already anxious belly churning.

'Nothing,' I say. 'Just bridesmaid stuff.'

'Ah…' Jason lifts both hands in a gesture of surrender. 'I'll ask no more, I know my place.' Then he leans past me to lightly kiss Sophie's cheek. 'Little Sophie Rhodes, we're so glad you could be part of our special day.'

'Sorry I'm a bit late, traffic was a nightmare,' she says.

'No harm done,' Jason replies, stepping back.

'Pip isn't here yet,' I tell Sophie. 'He's been delayed.'

She gestures to her phone. 'I know.'

Of course, he'd have messaged her. They're still so close.

'We were just about to eat. Please help yourself,' Jason interjects, ever the smooth host. 'The girls are having bubbly, but I can get you something else if you'd prefer?'

'Thanks,' Sophie replies. 'Bubbly is fine.' She heads towards the table.

'Now everyone due to arrive tonight is here at last.' Jason sounds pleased.

I nod, but find myself watching Sophie cross to where Katja stands bristling, and I remember how annoyed she's been on my behalf. The moment stretches. Then Rory introduces himself and the tension evaporates.

As we eat, Jason carries the conversation, talking about some new series he's keen to watch. It lets me study Sophie.

This reserved woman is nothing like the girl who'd sought the spotlight.

Was it losing her brother that changed her? Or something else?

9

MELANIE - THE MOTHER

WEDNESDAY EVENING – THREE DAYS BEFORE THE WEDDING

It's not even midnight when a few conspicuous yawns from Laura have Ruth bluntly announcing their departure. I leave too; it's not like I can linger with the hosts, given our history.

I'm checking on Adele's social media updates before I'm inside my place. Each happy snap and gushing caption sours the champagne in my stomach but I need to know what I'm dealing with. I hadn't followed Adele or Jason on social media before their New Year's Eve engagement. Hadn't wanted to see their lives playing out while Ollie's ended so abruptly. Tammy's excited engagement post changed everything.

I'm all caught up by the time I flick the latch on the screen door behind me.

The moonlight makes a light unnecessary. It's bright enough that I can see every part of the puzzle that's still at the same stage of completion as it was that day when Ollie didn't come home. I was trying to place an edge with the beginnings of a pastel rainbow when it happened. Sometimes, holding it, I can almost smell Jim's deodorant wafting through the shack, and the hint of the King George whiting he'd caught that morning and gutted on the steel bench. Feel the warm evening air and hear the faint lap of the waves.

And, if I'm very lucky, my mind takes me back to the time before Ollie was betrayed by the people who were supposed to be his friends.

But tonight, it's too late and I'm too weary. Still, I go to pick up my little piece of rainbow from where I left it on the edge of the table. Small enough to hold between two fingers, or fit completely within my curled hand, I've held it so often since he's been gone that any rougher edges have been smoothed away.

It isn't there.

Nor is it anywhere else on the table. Turning on the light, a single old bulb, doesn't do much to chase away the shadows but shows it's definitely not there. I drop to my knees and scramble under the furniture, finding nothing but dust and cobwebs. The couch cushions prove equally barren.

Where is it?

I breathe deeply, trying to keep the panic at bay. Puzzle pieces can't get up and walk by themselves. Has someone been in here? Did they push at the door with its rickety latch? Slide open a window? Either would only take a little force.

No.

Nothing else has been disturbed. No one would break in and take only this. I must have forgotten I was holding it, carried it with me and put it down somewhere.

Besides, I was right there, on the deck next door. I would have seen or heard any disturbance. But logic doesn't help, because it still isn't here.

I widen my search.

Not left on the bathroom sink as I got ready to go next door. Not by the kettle or the fridge, and not in the room that used to be Ollie's. Back in the living area, the room wavers at the edges and I hold the back of the chair to stop myself falling.

'How much have you had to drink?'

Sophie's voice from the doorway cuts through the humming that has become vibrations in my skull.

My eyes close. I'd forgotten she was here.

'That's none of your business, young lady.' The words come out okay and the dismissive tone is bang on, but the slur at the end spoils the overall effect. My eyes will be glassy, too, and my cheeks flushed. Grief and menopause are an easy excuse for those, if she comments, but she probably won't.

Her nose crinkles in disgust. 'Too much, clearly.'

'For your information, I was feeling a bit dizzy.'

'Alcohol will do that.'

I'm about to argue when I remember the missing puzzle piece. I take a step towards her. 'Did you take it?'

'Take what?'

'My puzzle.' More slurring, as the reality of not being able to find it catches in my chest. 'There's a piece missing. Did you take it?'

'Why would I do that?'

'Maybe you just couldn't stand for me to have a little bit of something to cling to.'

'Like this?'

I squint, trying to focus on the paper she's holding but the text swims.

Her hand tightens, crumpling the edge. 'How to object at a wedding,' she reads out the top line. 'Seriously, is that your plan? Follow some internet instructions? You know most services don't even include that part these days?'

I grab at the evidence I must have left out here somewhere, the paper tearing as I take it from her. 'That's private.'

She shakes her head. 'You should go to bed before you pass out.'

'You don't understand,' I say. But I'm talking to myself, and a moment later her door clicks closed.

Fine, I don't need her help anyway. Not for the puzzle, not for the wedding.

My bag gapes open on the ground next to the table. I rummage through the contents until I find the bottle. My hands shake in anticipation as I unscrew the lid. One sip. Two. Just enough to steady me so I can keep searching. The burn down my throat sharpens the world around me while dulling the ever-present pain.

That's better.

10

ADELE – THE BRIDE

WEDNESDAY NIGHT – THREE DAYS BEFORE THE WEDDING

It's late and I'm momentarily alone on Jason's deck, my knees pulled up to my chest. My glass is nearly empty, but the fizz of expensive champagne lingers on my tongue. I shiver, suddenly chilled. Darting a look behind me, I scan the shadows between the shacks. The prickle in my neck insists someone's there, even as my eyes tell me there's not.

I close my eyes. Is that a headache forming?

'Are you okay?'

When I open my eyes, Jason's best man is standing way too close. I straighten, leaning forward under the pretence of picking up my glass and then keep a gap between us as Jason steps out the door, looks over and smiles.

'I'm great.'

The message is as much to the man across the other side of the deck as the one close by, not that Jason is likely to be jealous. The two have been close since university, with Jason head-hunting Rory for the family business

Rory's watching me. 'You look miserable.'

I take a sip of my champagne and it's all I can do not to

gulp the last mouthful. What is Rory playing at, with that intimate tone?

'How could I be?' I put all the pep I can muster into my voice.

Rory glances across the deck and, once he's sure Jason's back is to us, he touches my shoulder. Brief. Intimate. Goosebumps rise on my skin.

'You're cold,' he says. 'Do you want me to get you my jacket?'

A simple question on the surface but I'd swear the way he's staring at me, that he's asking for so much more than a decision about a jacket.

Jason appears behind Rory, his smile wide. 'What are you two doing then?'

I grip the base of my glass so hard my fingers grow numb. 'Nothing.' It's too bright, too loud, too guilty.

'Your fiancé was shivering,' Rory replies. 'I was simply being a gentleman.' There's something underlying the words as he looks at Jason.

I swing my gaze between the two men, not liking where this is going but not sure why. What is taking Katja so long in the bathroom?

'Are you cold?' Jason asks me. 'I offered to put the heaters on earlier,' he says to Rory, gesturing to the discreet appliances above. 'She refused; said she'd be fine.'

'I am fine,' I say. 'And I'm also quite capable of getting a jacket if I want one.'

Rory shrugs. 'Just trying to be nice.'

'That's so typical of you,' Jason says. 'Mr Nice Guy.'

It's said as a joke, but there it is again, that something unsettling beneath the surface. For the first time, I wonder about their history. Jason was definite he wanted Rory for his best man, but how well do they really know each other?

I stand. 'Excuse me, I might grab a jacket.'

Hours later, only the faint lap of the water on the sand breaks the quiet as I sit in the dark out on Mum and Dad's deck alone. With sleep proving impossible I'd come down here for fresh air, but so far it's not helping.

The clink of glasses has me turning towards the door.

Katja holds up a bottle of gin and ice-filled glasses. 'You look like you need this.'

Despite still feeling the effects of the earlier drinks, I don't argue as she sets the glasses on the outdoor table and fills them with practised ease.

'You're having doubts,' she says as she sits next to me.

It's normal, isn't it? To be a bit nervous? Perfectly normal. 'I might be feeling a little overwhelmed.'

Katja sips her gin. 'You can change your mind.'

'In theory, maybe.'

She grips my wrist. 'You can change your mind.'

She doesn't let go until I nod.

'But why would I? Jason's a catch. He's everything I want in a husband.'

She considers, then pulls out her phone. With a swipe of her finger, she opens the notes app. 'We make a list, then you decide.' Typical analyst. Despite her blonde bombshell appearance, Katja is happiest with logic and numbers.

'You don't want to talk about my feelings? Put it down to nerves?'

'Talk?' Her nose scrunches. 'No, we make a list. Pros and

cons of marrying Jason.' She angles her phone to show me that she's already written the title and underlined it.

I sigh. 'Fine. Then the first pro has to be that he's a good guy.' I say it even though that's never been my priority when imagining a husband.

'What do you mean by good?' Katja asks. 'You mean in bed?' she adds wickedly.

I focus on the first part of her question. 'Jason always calls me back, generally shows up when he says, remembers anniversaries and both my parents' names. Oh, and he doesn't go out and get hammered every night with the boys.'

'Ah, so we're giving credit for the bare minimum?' she teases. 'And he should know your parents' names, he's known you forever.'

'True, but I've dated plenty of men who don't meet that low bar.'

Her mouth twists. 'You're not marrying them. And in bed?'

I can't think of sex with Jason without thinking of the secret I promised not to tell anyone. There's so much at stake if I don't go through with this.

'You probably don't want graphic images,' I say lightly.

She snickers. 'Fair point.'

'He's generous,' I offer. 'There was that time he surprised me with a flight over Antarctica for our three-month anniversary.'

Katja writes down 'Rich'. She smirks and adds, 'and not stingy'.

'Security is important.' Somehow I manage to say it lightly, when the truth is it's everything. 'And it was an incredibly romantic gesture.'

Katja, though, has heard me rant about how such

excursions are a blight on the environment enough that she just raises her eyebrows.

'I know him so well,' I try.

Katja rolls her eyes. 'We all have secrets.'

That, I can't deny, but she doesn't know Jason and I share secrets that bind us. That single rash moment that doesn't need to be spoken about to unite us in a way no one else could ever understand.

Despite wracking my brains, it turns out I can't think of a single *con*. 'I've got nothing else.'

'Maybe it's simply too fast. You know there is such a thing as an actual engagement, taking time to adjust to sharing your entire lives together?'

She makes being married sound like a jail sentence. 'It's not like we've done this in two weeks.'

She looks like she's going to argue that a few months isn't much more, but sips her drink instead. Peering at me over the top of the glass she seems to set herself, take a breath and then change tack. 'Maybe it's being here,' she says gently. 'What really happened with Ollie? I know he jumped off the jetty and he died – may he rest in peace and all that – but there must be more.'

'Must there?'

'It clearly is still affecting you.' Her tone is light but her eyes sincere.

'It was a long time ago…' I begin. How to explain? How much does guilt and wishful thinking colour a memory?

She waits.

'We were young,' I say. 'So young. And we all thought we were invincible. Ollie was no different. The day he died, he jumped off the jetty at the end of the bay into dangerous waters and he got into trouble.' I force the words out like I'm reciting Ikea instructions. It's the only way I can say it without splitting open.

'Have you been back to the jetty?' she asks.

Something in her tone makes me think she guesses the answer even though it's been so long. 'No. I haven't.' Maybe it's not healthy, maybe not proper going through grief stages or whatever, but who the fuck gets to define that anyway?

'Maybe that's your problem.' She straightens. 'Let's go.'

'What? Now? It's...' I have no idea what time it is... 'Late.'

She's already on her feet. 'Come on.'

In the end, it takes only minutes to grab jackets and walk to the end of the bay and the twin jetties. The old and the new side-by-side. Minutes and twelve long years to go back.

I stand at the point where the new jetty meets the shore. My heart pounds a painful ache in my chest. Despite the silence of the night, I hear it all in my head. The splash as he hit the water.

'Ollie, this isn't funny.'

The cries. People running. The screaming refrain of the ambulance siren.

'Adele?' Katja says my name with concern in her voice.

I wipe a hand over leaking eyes. 'I'm good,' I lie.

We walk out onto the jetty. My breath hitches and I stop well before the jumping spot where we used to gather. We lean against the railing looking out across the stretch of water at the ruin of the original jetty, a ghostly shape of jutting wood and worn timbers.

I don't know what Katja's thinking, but I'm mentally reciting the seating chart for Saturday. Anything to stop my mind replaying the last time I was here. But, then, a memory sneaks past. 'We talked about marriage.'

Katja's eyes practically fall out of her head. 'What? You were babies.'

I chuckle. 'Not right away, but we talked about where we'd be, what we'd wear.' I remember being with Ollie. Lying on his scratchy blanket after I'd snuck into his bedroom, whispering about all the tomorrows ahead.

'And?' she asks.

'Barefoot, out on a boat on the water, our family and friends there. Cake.' I smile. 'He was pretty insistent there would be lots of cake.'

'What was it about him that made him so special?'

'He was hot,' I admit. 'Tall, and beginning to fill out across the shoulders, tanned and strong from playing sport. His sun-lightened hair fell over his face and his nose was always peeling. He made me laugh. He had this quick, goofy sense of humour and the best grin. Just seeing it chased all the shitty things happening at home away. And he'd talk. About articles, books, things he found interesting.'

'Not your normal teenage boy, then?'

'Yes and no. It's hard to explain.'

'Sounds dreamy.'

I can't tell if she's being sarcastic and suddenly I don't care because I don't want to do this anymore. Talking about Ollie won't change the fact I'm marrying his friend.

'It's late,' I say abruptly. 'We should get back.'

I should never have come here tonight.

11

SOPHIE – WEDNESDAY JANUARY 19TH

TWELVE YEARS AGO

Day four of hanging with the older kids and Sophie didn't feel as nervous walking with Pip and Adele to meet the others. Slowly she was working out all their names and who to avoid.

Daniel was the leader. The other boys copied his tough guy stance, his sneer and the way he smoothed back his black hair. He reminded Sophie of an evil Troy Bolton from *High School Musical* and she tried hard not to stare each time he disappeared out of sight with one of the others and they returned acting weird, or when he took money in exchange for something too small for her to make out. Instinct told her not to look too hard or ask about it.

She didn't want to out herself as a little kid any more than her tendency to snap photos on her iPod apparently already did. Just yesterday, Ollie growled at her to try to be a bit less lame even though he'd posted pictures online from his new phone.

Pip slowed, the wind tousling his blond hair so that Sophie wanted to reach out and touch it. 'Want to hang out just us two today?'

Her breath hitched. 'Just us?'

'Yeah, Jason tripped me in front of everyone yesterday, and Daniel applauded.'

Sophie hoped her dismay didn't show on her face. Pip needed to be able to take a joke. And he needed to see Sophie as a potential date rather than a safety net.

'Forget it,' he said when she didn't reply. He hurried to catch up to his sister with Sophie trailing behind. 'Who's she?' Pip asked, pointing at the girl next to Daniel.

The new girl seemed older than everyone, with lots of eye makeup and wearing a top like Adele's. What looked fresh and summery on Pip's sister, fit tighter and revealed more on the other girl. Her sun-bleached curls hung around her shoulders in waves like she'd stepped out of the surf.

Sophie found herself unconsciously trying to imitate the girl's bored pose, even as instinctive dislike fizzed down her spine.

Just then, the girl gripped Ollie's arm and simpered something right in his ear. Next to them, Daniel bristled.

'Kirsty or something,' Adele said with a scowl. 'She's staying in town with her sister.'

When Kirsty moved back to Daniel's side, his hand rested on her back then slid down, casually intimate in a way that made Sophie's cheeks hot. *They're probably doing it.* The unexpected thought made her look away.

'Yay, Adele's here,' Kirsty said too loudly. She muttered something else under her breath to Daniel and they both snickered. As Ollie took a step away from the group to come to meet Adele, Kirsty yelled, 'Last one to the jetty sucks ass.'

She tossed her hair over her shoulder and ran. As though she'd tugged on invisible leashes, both Ollie and Daniel took off after her. The three of them reached the nearest jetty post and hit the sand in a tangle of limbs.

'Do you think she's jealous?' Pip whispered, looking at Adele.

His sister was smiling but it looked forced.

'They're just mucking around,' Sophie assured him. 'Ollie, like, loves her.' But an odd feeling swirled in Sophie's stomach, like she was watching something important unravel.

As she passed a few of the older boys to join the girls, one of them said something. It was about her. She could tell by the leers and the snickers. He lifted his hand for high fives and a pungent jab of body odour rose from the group.

Sophie pushed down the silly urge to cry.

Later that evening there was a loud knock at the door leading out to the beach while Sophie and Ollie were eating dinner with Mum and Dad.

'I think young Jason from next door would like to speak with you, Ollie,' Mum said.

Ollie got up and crossed to open the door.

'Are you coming or what?' Jason demanded.

Ollie glanced back at us pointedly. 'In a minute, we're eating dinner.'

'Hurry up, man,' Jason whined.

Mum tutted. 'There will be no hurrying up for this *man* until he's finished his dinner.'

Ollie grunted something at his friend that Sophie couldn't make out.

Jason smirked then backed away from the door. 'Yes, Mrs Rhodes,' he called. 'We'll wait out here.'

In a couple of steps Ollie was back at the table. He set about inhaling the last of his barbecue. 'Can I please leave the table?' he asked, still swallowing.

Mum huffed through her nose and adopted her principal voice. 'It's important to spend time together as a family.'

From the snickers from those waiting outside, Sophie could tell that Mum's voice had carried. Ollie had to know it too.

Ollie's jaw set. 'What are you going to do, put me in detention?'

Mum's eyebrows practically flew up off her head. 'Watch your language.'

Sophie held her breath as the two locked gazes.

After a long moment Ollie dropped his and relaxed the hands that had formed fists around his cutlery. 'Fine, sorry. I've finished my dinner like you said. Thanks. Now can I please go?'

Mum sighed. 'Fine, but don't come to me looking for food when you get home, and be back before nine.'

'Seriously...' he began. But then her narrowed eyes registered. 'Yes, Mum.'

'Oliver,' Mum said when he reached the door and had it open and was almost free.

He turned back slowly. 'I'll be home later.' His eyes begged Mum not to make this worse in front of his friends.

She said nothing.

'And I'll get Sophie in half an hour if she wants.'

At the mention of her name, Sophie tried to play it cool, but inside she was cheering. She'd not been included at night before. What if Mum said no? What if Mum said yes?

'Okay,' Mum said.

Ollie flashed a grin. 'Thanks, Mum.'

He headed outside to high fives. As the older kids trooped towards the beach, Jason could be seen through the window looking back. His satisfied smile made it look like he thought he'd won some kind of victory.

From the pucker of Mum's mouth, Sophie thought Mum saw it too.

12

MELANIE - THE MOTHER

THURSDAY MORNING – TWO DAYS BEFORE THE WEDDING

There's a chilly edge to the early morning breeze despite the pink glow of the rising sun. I'm wearing a hoodie as I step out onto the porch and pull the sliding door quietly closed behind me, so I don't wake Sophie nor make my headache any worse.

Back when we first inherited the shack from a distant aunt, Refuge Bay was a virtual ghost town this time of year. That's all changed, but even with the differences, this end of the bay feels more private. There are fewer places advertised on those holiday sites and more family vacation homes.

Although I love the bay at this time of day, I walk quickly and without taking the time to appreciate the view. It will be light soon, and what I want to do is better not done with an audience.

Like any woman, I used to be afraid walking alone, but losing Ollie made me realise there was nothing left to take from me.

With my hair tucked under an old beanie, and my black leggings so old they nearly match the grey of the hoodie,

I blend into the shadows. I hitch my backpack on my shoulder and shove my hand in my pocket to find the softened edge of the puzzle piece I'd searched so long for last night. There it was this morning, on the edge of the table.

How could I have missed it?

I'd surfaced sometime after midnight from the familiar black oblivion with the ancient spring of the old couch digging into my spine. Realising I must have sat after Sophie left and passed out, voices drifting in on the night air woke me. Adele and her bridesmaid out on the beach, talking about Ollie.

I'd staggered to the door to peer out into the darkness, the silhouettes confirming the speakers' identities.

'Ollie was like, a bad boy, then?'

The question from Adele's friend was a punch to the stomach.

No, I thought. *He was an angel*. But I didn't cry it out, instead waiting for Adele's answer.

'He liked a good time,' she said eventually.

I wanted to go out there and shake them both. How dare she make it sound like he was a party animal? Like the local papers tried to do in the weeks after it happened, snide digs at my boy everywhere I turned. Those malicious lies broke through the fog that had gripped me. They gave me an enemy I could do something about.

I complained to the editor about the journalist spreading unfounded slander about a dead child, and when that didn't give me what I wanted, I went above them. I threatened legal action. The monster who'd smeared my boy's name in some attempt to make a news splash ended up fired but it didn't change that those horrible words were out there.

Now the puzzle piece beneath my fingers comforts me as I climb the stairs at the foreshore. At the top, the view that fills so many social media posts opens up before me in shadow form. As a backdrop there's the wide, stunning horizon of sea meeting sky with the silhouette of gorgeous palm trees and of course, the prime attraction of the twin jetties. One old and crumbling, the other relatively new. The past and the present stretching out into the water, side by side.

I pull out the contents of my backpack, then stride out onto the new jetty, trying to ignore my body buzzing at being so close to where my Ollie took his last breath. I don't have time to let myself get caught up in memories, but I can't help slowing and then stopping.

Can't help looking down.

Water churns around the pylons below me. The water is as black on this side of the jetty as I know it is turquoise on the other. There, the sand shows through, and on a still day it's possible to count shells on the ocean floor. Here it's all dark weeds and murky ripples.

This is the side of the jetty that takes young men from their mothers.

I didn't get here that day until he'd been pulled out of the water but I've pictured what must have happened so often it's almost a memory. Him launching from the railing on the side extension, hitting the water, slicing through those dark depths, disappearing beneath the surface.

I close my eyes and squeeze them.

He's not there.

But nonetheless when I open my eyes I imagine he's before me in the water. I reach out and one of the pieces of paper I'm carrying flies free. I see his smile, man-like but with a hint of my baby boy, and the last words he ever said to me echo in my brain.

Don't you worry about me.

Oh, Ollie, I should have worried more.

The scrape of sand between wood and shoe alerts me to the fact that I'm not alone – a heartbeat before the voice speaks.

'What do you think you're doing?'

I take my time turning around, using the delay to pull myself together.

Mayor Fiona Lewis, local GP and bane of my existence, stands a little further along the jetty. Lean and fit, she's in hot pink, name-brand activewear and her blonde ponytail swishes at me accusingly as she crosses her arms. I did not pick her as an early riser, but given her rapid climb within the council I should have realised she isn't the type to waste a second.

'I'm enjoying the gorgeous view,' I say. 'After all, this is public land, despite what you on the council seem to think, approving private developments.'

Her lips purse. 'I'm referring, as I'm sure you realise, to those.' She points to the wad of papers in my hand that are a match to the flyers I've stuck up along the jetty and along the foreshore. 'You failed in your motion. What do you hope to achieve?'

'People have a right to information.'

'That may be.' She's annoyingly calm. 'However, I'm sure you understand there are council rules about actions that amount to littering, vandalism and defacement of public property.'

'Littering?' I sputter. 'Defacement?'

'Yes.' Her voice is still level and she gestures at one of the flyers down on the sand. On cue the wind picks it up and the thin sheet cartwheels a little closer to the water.

'Let me see, the fine for littering is $210, so if we take each instance… well, it could add up pretty quickly.'

'You can't threaten me.'

'I'm not. I'm making you a promise. You will not win this battle. You lost at the vote. Let it go.'

I pull myself up to my full height so I can look down on the perky little upstart. 'Haven't you heard what they say about winning the battle but not the war? Don't forget that I've been around Refuge Bay a lot longer than you, and I'm not going anywhere.'

My longevity claim isn't strictly true. She did a rotation back at the local country hospital years ago, before moving here permanently. It makes my heart ache to wonder whether this woman may have been the one to pronounce my beautiful son dead.

'If you've been here so long,' she says, her smile saccharine. 'Then perhaps it's time for you to move on. For all our sakes.'

'You wish.'

'On the contrary, I don't think about you at all.'

She walks away. Dismissing me as though I'm nothing. My hands clench but I don't chase her.

This isn't over.

Although the engineer I paid handsomely to come out here and run his tests was more than willing to provide a report testifying to its structural flaws, it sometimes feels like the old jetty will outlast every attempt I make to bring it down. The council might have rejected my application for demolition, but Fiona Lewis is wrong if she thinks I'll let it go. Other families can't suffer like we've suffered, Ollie can't have died for no reason.

And I refuse to let that woman win.

13

ADELE - THE BRIDE

THURSDAY MORNING – TWO DAYS BEFORE THE WEDDING

I'm the first one up on Thursday morning and I move through the house on silent feet. It's almost muscle memory, from all the sneaking out I did as a teen.

It's a long day ahead so I figure I'll treat myself to an early coffee with Mum's fancy machine, before getting ready for breakfast with Jason's family. I'm at the foot of the stairs when there's a rap on the door that leads out to the road. The frosted glass shows a figure on the other side. I pull my dressing gown tight before opening the door a crack.

'Adele Pippen?' The gruff question comes from behind the largest bunch of flowers I've ever seen.

'That's me.'

'Then these are for you.'

'They're gorgeous,' I say, opening the door wider.

'Here.' The fragrant arrangement of stunning orchids, pink peonies, white roses and purple snapdragons is shoved in my direction.

'Thank you,' I manage, only just keeping hold of the over-sized glass vase. Water slops over the edge making a small puddle on the floor. Looking down, the corner of an envelope tucked under the mat catches my eye. Enough to see the red 'urgent' on the front. Another unpaid bill, addressed to my parents, my jaw tightens.

I can't do that now. I won't.

The delivery person is already walking away, head ducked. 'Wait,' I call. 'Is there a card?'

They're already at the van. 'Dunno.' They shrug. 'I'm just the delivery guy.' Then they're in the van and it's accelerating away along the dirt road.

I find a card tucked deep within the foliage.

It's small, white and nondescript. The message on it is printed in a typewriter font.

For you, baby girl.

The card slips from my fingertips and flutters to the ground.

A strong coffee and a hot shower clears my head. 'Baby girl' is common; it probably doesn't mean anything that it's what Ollie used to call me.

When Katja and I arrive at Jason's shack, only Rory is out enjoying the sunshine. His tanned, muscled chest is bare and navy shorts cling to his strong thighs. Memories play in high definition in my head and I almost forget to breathe.

'Morning,' I say brightly. Too brightly? I drag my gaze away as my cheeks flush. 'Is Jason—'

'He's inside,' Rory says, a smile lurking in his voice. 'His family isn't here yet.'

'Great.' I hurry towards the sliding doors, eager to get to my fiancé.

'I'll stay here, shall I?' Katja says behind me.

I nod my agreement before closing the door behind me.

Jason's by the bench, which is filled with platters for breakfast. He has his phone in hand, and he's staring out at the water with his mouth in a hard, flat line. He's not all hot surfer like Rory but he's handsome in his cream polo shirt and brown shorts. Freshly shaved and his hair perfectly in place. Though he doesn't look like a man eager to be married.

Dread pools deep in my stomach. 'What's wrong?' I ask.

He forces a smile. 'Nothing.'

'That's not what your expression said.'

'It's fine. Just some work stuff getting to me.'

It makes sense given the size of Ellingsworth Hotels, the family business he runs.

'Maybe we could cut the trip short?' I say, thinking back to Melanie's discomfort with our honeymoon itinerary, thoughts lingering on the flowers and the message.

'No.' Jason's face clears instantly. 'Forget I said anything.'

The sound of greetings draws us outside before I can try harder. There, Laila has her teeth bared and Rory – who has thankfully put on an ice-blue T-shirt – is backed up against the railing and has his hands up in surrender.

'Oh, she's not going to hurt you,' Dorothy says dismissively as she picks up the dog.

Jason places the platter he brought from inside on the table and holds out his hand with its faint red mark. 'I'm not so sure about that, Gran. I'm pretty sure she's scarred me.'

'Don't be such a wimp, dear,' Dorothy replies.

I meet Katja's gaze and struggle not to laugh, only saving myself by returning inside to help bring out more food.

The caterers have outdone themselves with a stunning array of fruit and pastries, complete with toppings and conserves and a variety of freshly squeezed juices. Jason's coffee machine allows him to fulfill everyone's coffee requests from lattes to macchiatos. Combined with the luxurious setting, it feels like we could be at a swanky hotel rather than a few shacks away from where I once made my little brother eat sand.

Thinking of Pip has me checking my phone for a message as plates are scraped clean and the conversation hums around me, but there's been nothing since Dubai. I fire off a quick message anyway, telling him to let me know when he lands in Australia.

I catch Dorothy, with Laila now settled sleepily on her lap, looking at me and I slide my phone away. He'll be here for the wedding; he wouldn't miss my big day. And in the meantime, I don't want anyone to think I'm being rude.

Of course, we're talking weddings. We've covered the romantic story of Laura and Ruth's Barcelona wedding and now, as Jason tops up drinks, Rory begins the tale of how his parents' boxer dog, Bear, took a bite out of the lavish three-tiered cake only hours before his sister's ceremony.

'Oh no,' Katja cries. 'What did they do?'

Rory grins. 'I was already at the venue because I was officiating the ceremony. I'd done the qualification as a gift to my sister. However, Mum is known for her quick thinking. The colour theme was pink and white, and she sourced enough rosebuds from the supermarket to make a floral addition that hid the damage. I wouldn't have known Bear had taken a bite if I hadn't—'

The screech of Dorothy's chair across the wood cuts Rory

off mid-sentence. 'Laila doesn't even like cake,' she announces, clutching her little dog close.

'I wasn't implying—' Rory begins.

Dorothy's chin lifts. 'And she's too little to reach the refrigerator handle.'

I'm sure my mouth is gaping and I'm not the only one as Dorothy snatches her walking stick, turns on her sensible, orthotic-filled shoes and stomps across the deck.

'Gran, wait,' Jason calls. He shoots us a *what the hell?* look, before following. Dorothy shakes off his attempt to coax her back to the table then walks away.

'What was that all about?' I ask.

'I can only guess it's because she's making the wedding cake and has a dog?' Jason's voice goes up in question at the end.

Rory clears his throat. 'Sorry if I upset anyone.'

'Nah, mate,' Jason says quickly. 'It's not your fault. Maybe we should have just bought a cake.'

I touch Jason's arm. 'You were so set on having Dorothy make it.'

He shrugs. 'When she offered, I thought it would be a nice touch.'

'Worst case scenario, someone can bring us a supermarket mudcake,' I say.

His screwed-up nose tells me what he thinks of such a cheap solution and I'm reminded of how many times my celebratory events have been catered in such a way.

He exhales heavily. 'I'm afraid she's getting worse. This isn't the only odd behaviour. There were her glasses in the freezer and then the chair thing. It doesn't go with any of the redecoration. I looked it up and it could be a French Louis-the-something original. And do you know what she said?'

I share a puzzled glance with Rory, but look away just as fast. I'm second-guessing every look, every thought. 'I don't know.'

Jason adopts her authoritarian manner. 'It's the hall chair, Jason. End of discussion.'

I fight a smile. 'It *is* her shack. To her, it's just an old chair, an uncomfortable, bulky one at that. Remember, we hid behind it as kids?' My voice fades. Because, of course, that was me and Ollie.

Jason doesn't seem to notice. 'She won't even show me the cake.'

'Maybe she wants it to be a surprise,' Katja suggests.

'Or maybe she knows it's a disaster,' Jason replies. 'I don't want to embarrass her but I don't want to go to cut the cake and there be none.'

This seems to really be bugging him. 'Do you want me to talk to her?' I offer.

Jason lifts his head. 'Would you?'

'Sure.' It comes out light and breezy but the truth is, I'm faintly terrified at the prospect.

14

MELANIE – THE MOTHER

THURSDAY MORNING – TWO DAYS BEFORE THE WEDDING

'It's not going to make a difference.'
The voice from behind me echoes the nagging thoughts in my head, but I take my time attaching the piece of paper demanding the removal of the old jetty to the fence before turning.

My neighbour, Giovanni, has added a stained, striped shirt to his usual outfit of far-too-tight swimming trunks and his hairy belly bulges at the buttons. Much of his face is hidden beneath an old fishing cap and although his whiskers are long and bristly, his smile is sympathetic. 'The council are not going to change their minds.'

My hands tighten on the last few posters. 'I've already been told as much earlier this morning by our delightful mayor.' I can't help the hint of accusation in my voice since he's a voting ratepayer.

'The woman won in a landslide; you can't blame me. Besides, she was the best candidate.'

'She's a menace.'

He doesn't argue. 'Coffee?' he asks instead, nodding to the kiosk up beyond the foreshore.

'That would be great, thank you.'

I'd prefer something stronger, but I appreciate the gesture. It's his way of apologising for the scene last night. He can't help it. Unlike the saws and the sanding machines in his workshop, the people noises get in his head.

It's not like I can judge anyone for how they handle their demons.

We fall into step, crossing the sand towards the stairs up past the jetty in an easy silence. He's not one for small talk, but his familiar scent of sawdust and hot metal comforts me. It's properly light now and as we get close to the stairs I notice a pile of what looks like old clothes dumped underneath the jetty where the shadows are their deepest. The sight of the recently dumped rubbish reminds me of what Mayor Fiona said about littering and I'm about to tell Giovanni about her threat when he nudges my elbow.

I follow his gaze up the stairs to see Terry standing at the kiosk counter. Dressed in white shorts and matching polo, dark sunglasses hiding his eyes, he appears incomplete without Tammy curled possessively against his side. I can't help the shudder at the sight of his fake tan and fake, toothy smile and the way he leans in to flirt with the server. The poor girl has to be younger than his daughter.

Terry's much-too-loud laugh carries to where we've both slowed, neither of us willing to get close enough to have to exchange pleasantries.

'I'm sure I can keep up with any of those young lads.'

Terry's voice deepens suggestively. 'And of course, I have the benefit of experience, if you know what I mean.'

The girl's face pales but she keeps her customer service smile fixed in place.

Giovanni's hand on my shoulder stops me as I realise I've taken a stride in their direction. 'I know this girl, she's got it under control,' he murmurs.

Instead of handing Terry his coffee order she waits a beat, then asks, 'What do you mean?'

Terry frowns.

She holds on to his cup. 'You said that you have the benefit of experience. Please explain it to me.'

Now, we're not the only ones following the exchange. The other early morning patrons look on with interest as Terry shifts his weight uncomfortably.

'Explain it to you?' Terry repeats.

'Yes,' she nods. 'Describe what you meant by referring to your experience and keeping up with younger lads.' Her voice is pleasant but there's steel in her gaze.

Terry huffs. 'I'd like my coffee, thanks.'

She smiles politely. 'And I'd like not to be sexually harassed in my workplace.'

Not even Terry's tan can hide the red staining his cheeks. He glares for a moment then stalks away from the counter.

'But what about your coffee?' she calls after him.

I bite back a cheer.

I'm sure Terry sees us as he storms past but there's no acknowledgement. I should be glad not to have to make small talk but my stomach tightens. He won't have liked that. Not at all.

Soon after getting our coffees, Giovanni and I part ways. Him to his usual fishing spot on the jetty and me back to number fifty-seven. I make my way back down onto the sand, the coffee cup hot against my skin and the aroma of freshly made brew overwhelming the usual salt and seaweed. The bundle of clothes I noticed earlier catches my eye. It's definitely moved. Maybe someone's tried to clean up.

I walk on.

Suddenly, the clothes move in such a way that I realise it's actually a person, with an old army jacket draped like a blanket over dark khaki clothes. They're wearing a cap and mostly in shadow. More movement and I can make out the dark pool of their eyes. Staring at me.

My blood chills.

Despite the distance of at least a hundred feet between us, our gazes meet and a jolt of recognition goes through me. Is that someone I know?

I lean forward, trying to see better. I make out cheekbones jutting out and lips so pale they blur into chapped and blotchy skin.

No. I don't know anyone like that.

But they're still looking at me.

'Do you need help?'

The person is far enough away that maybe my voice doesn't carry. Or they ignore it. A relief, really; it's not like I have anything to give them. Still, I've done my duty and offered aid. I can leave with a clear conscience.

But as I walk back towards the shack I can't stop thinking about those dark eyes. I look back over my shoulder and the person hasn't moved.

And then, just as I'm almost out of sight, when the distance makes the person under the jetty nothing more than a darker patch in the shadows, there's movement.

Someone is with them.

I should feel relief, but instead I walk even faster.

15

SOPHIE – WEDNESDAY JANUARY 19TH

TWELVE YEARS AGO

Sophie knew Ollie would only come back to get her to make Mum happy, but this was her chance. Maybe Pip would be there, in the moonlight, and he'd realise he was falling in love with her.

Sophie stood on the edge of the bath and tried to angle her body so she could see her outfit in the small, warped mirror. If Sophie never again heard the lecture on how many kids would love a beach shack, it would be too soon. But surely a decent mirror wasn't a luxury?

She turned this way and that. She'd have to face the fact that with her mousy hair, flat chest and braces she'd never look like one of the cool beach girls. She'd never look like Adele or Kirsty.

She jumped down and stared her reflection right in the eye. 'I don't want to be pretty and vacuous anyway. I am interesting and talented and I'm going to be a star.'

Vacuous had a good ring to it. Someone like Adele probably didn't even know that word. A stab of guilt at the bitchy thought took the smile from her face. It wasn't Adele's fault she was gorgeous and Sophie wasn't.

Giving up on any last-minute fixes, Sophie headed out to the porch to wait for Ollie, glad Mum and Dad had gone for drinks at one of the neighbouring shacks. At least she could avoid more lectures.

A minute later Ollie gestured from the sand for her to join him.

As they approached the jetty, somehow different and cooler in the glow of the evening light with no families around and few fishermen, Sophie tugged at the seam of the dress she'd thought looked so mature back at the shack. She trailed her brother up to the group where someone had music blasting next to a bonfire, and she tried to look like she belonged. But she felt all eyes go to her and none of them looked friendly.

'Didn't know we were running a baby-sitting service,' Daniel mocked. For once Kirsty was missing and it seemed to make him even nastier than usual.

Jason laughed so hard at Daniel's joke Sophie thought he'd pop something.

'It's fine, guys,' Ollie said. 'She's all good.'

'Sophie's okay,' Adele agreed so fast it was like they'd planned it.

Daniel did not look convinced, and Sophie thought for sure he'd tell her to get lost, but he just shrugged. 'Whatever, man, but she better not kill the vibe.'

Ollie grinned. 'She won't.'

Sophie tried to look the most un-killer like that she could manage but realised she probably looked constipated.

As the others returned to their conversation and someone

turned the music louder, Ollie shepherded Sophie a little away. 'Look, just try not to,' he waved, 'draw attention to yourself.'

Her heart leapt. She'd been sure he'd change his mind. 'So, no impromptu musical theatre numbers then?'

Ollie shuddered. 'No. And don't worry about Daniel. He's a good guy once you get to know him.' He looked behind him. 'And whatever you think you see out here, you don't. Get me?'

Sophie couldn't help looking at the kids in the shadows. An older girl she didn't recognise was taking something from Daniel. A fifty dollar note fluttered from her hand, caught before it hit the sand. Sophie looked back at her brother, nearly asking him about it before catching herself. 'Yeah.'

'We're good?' Ollie said.

'We're good.'

Palms sweaty, Sophie found a spot on the outer edge of the fire. She tried her best to nod in time when the girls near her talked about people and things she knew nothing about, while watching Ollie in case he left without her.

Sophie didn't see how it started. Someone, maybe Daniel, giving Jason a friendly push. He stumbled into another of the boys, one whose name she didn't know, with a mullet that would have been untrendy even when they were in. Mullet Boy's drink slipped from his hand. It spilled, instantly soaked into the thirsty sand.

'You little—'

The retaliatory shove sent Jason sprawling. Face first. He came up spitting sand. His eyes wild in the bonfire light and pale fists swinging. The boys came together then tumbled to the ground. A blur of arms and legs and curses, trying to wrestle for dominance while the others laughed around them.

Until the bigger boy squealed. The high-pitched sound froze Jason as he was about to swing.

'Get off me.'

The panic in Mullet Boy's demand slid through Sophie's gut. Instantly quelled the laughter.

Jason clambered off and to his feet.

Something dark was spreading under the thigh of the other boy. Blood? Whimpering, Mullet Boy shifted, revealing a gash, deep and oozing, and a razor fish shell, black and dripping blood, sticking up from the sand where he'd landed.

Jason skulked back as one of the girls hurried over with a towel. 'Teach you to mess with me,' he mumbled.

But only Sophie heard.

It was after ten and dark by the time Ollie gestured at her from across the bonfire to leave. Mum would probably still be drinking and playing cards with the neighbours but without Pip there, Sophie was more than ready to go.

Adele came too, and they were barely away from the others when Sophie began to wish she'd walked home by herself. Ollie had drunk enough of whatever was in the bottle he'd shared with Daniel and Jason by the rocks that he couldn't keep his hands off his girlfriend.

'Have I told you you're pretty, baby girl?' he asked Adele with a slur, pulling her close and kissing her loudly.

'Hello, you guys are not alone,' Sophie said.

'Don't care,' Ollie replied and kissed Adele again.

Sophie made a gagging sound. 'Yuck.'

Ollie kept his arms around Adele. 'What's yuck about it?'

'The "baby girl" thing for starters. She has a name. Talk

about objectifying women.' Sophie looked to Adele pleadingly. 'You can't like that surely?'

Ollie kissed Adele again before she could reply. 'It's a term of affection,' he said when he came up for air.

'Surely,' Sophie continued, her focus on Adele, 'you can't actually—'

'Leave me out of this,' Adele said, cutting Sophie's feminist rant short. 'I have enough sibling fights at home and I don't want any part of yours.'

Sophie tried one more time 'But—'

Adele smirked. '*But* the truth is I could listen to him call me that all day.'

16

ADELE – THE BRIDE

THURSDAY MORNING – TWO DAYS BEFORE THE WEDDING

When I said I'd talk to Jason's grandmother about the cake I didn't expect him to hustle me over straight after breakfast. But there's no answer to my knock, not even any yapping.

'Dorothy?' I call. 'Is this a good time? It's me, uh, Adele.'

When there's still no answer, I push the door open. This woman is going to practically be my grandmother and she's never been anything but friendly to me; there's no reason to be this nervous.

'We had to vote to remove her from the board at work. Her erratic behaviour had begun to frighten customers.'

Jason's explanation of taking over the company back when we first started dating suddenly rings in my brain. What exactly did he mean by 'erratic'? I wipe the images of random attacks on staff and enter the living area. 'Hello?'

It's largely unchanged since we used to play in here as children. In contrast to Jason's shack, this is more intimate, with a timeless, coastal getaway feel. White painted wood paired with colourful soft furnishings. There's nothing cheap here, but the wealth is understated.

'Adele! What are you doing here?'

I'm not proud of how high I jump, but seriously the woman just appeared on the other side of the expansive timber kitchen bench, her dog under her arm.

She chuckles. 'The kettle just boiled. How about a cup of tea? It's about time we got to know each other. You'll hold Laila?'

'Yes. And that sounds lovely,' I say, as she bundles the tiny dog into my arms.

Laila lifts her face, tongue out, and attempts to lavish me with doggy kisses as Dorothy fills a pot with loose leaf tea and adds boiling water.

'I have a new blend from a little business that works with charity partners to provide mental health support for teens.' She smiles. 'Good cause and good tea, what more could you want?'

My lips part in surprise and Laila uses the opportunity to give me a lick that flicks my teeth. Surreptitiously, I wipe my mouth. This is not the confused woman that Jason has been so worried about.

I sink into the plush cushions of the couch, and Laila abandons me to curl up next to her owner. I'm wishing Jason had never sent me here when Dorothy speaks.

'I have made excellent progress on the cake,' she announces.

'That's great to hear.'

'You're sure about this wedding, dear?' she asks, her gaze razor sharp.

'Yes,' I say quickly, trying to hide my surprise she'd asked.

Too quickly? I don't know. It's not like I'm not getting practice at answering exactly this.

'I understand from what Jason has said that you're involved in the business?'

'Not exactly,' I say, while mentally trying to work out how to explain what I do to an octogenarian. She might have run Ellingsworth Hotels for a while but that doesn't mean she's likely to know much about social media. 'I, uh, consult on how a company might appear—'

'I'm old, not stupid,' she snaps. 'Do not talk down to me, young lady. I probably changed your nappies.'

Okay then.

I take a breath. 'Although my degree was in business, my job is focused on optimising our client's social media presence by creating innovative solutions to best target the right audience, at the right time.'

She nods. 'We've noticed a difference in interest and follow through since you took us on, however I'd wager it's still no replacement for doing a damn good job.'

I blink. She must still have access to the company figures. I wonder if Jason knows.

'You're right,' I agree. 'Any marketing plan is only as good as the product.'

Her lips purse. 'And what is your opinion on the product?'

I hesitate. Why is she asking? Has Jason set this up? I doubt it; he speaks about her like she's an ancient crone, not the sharp-witted woman in front of me.

'Spit it out, girl,' she says. 'No one likes a dillydallier.'

'I'd prefer a few more numbers and other details to make any finite calls,' I begin as she passes me a teacup. Seeing her about to tell me off again, I add, 'However, it seems the business is drifting from its core values. The recent ventures to larger developments like the one at the other end of Refuge Bay might be coming at a cost to the brand.'

She sips her tea thoughtfully. 'Without the numbers, I'd think the same thing, but the developments are profitable. Surprisingly so. However, you're right on the rest of it. Ellingsworth Hotels is more than a business. It's a family. No amount of money is more important than that.' She's staring out the window now and I get the feeling she's talking to herself as much as to me. 'It takes a certain skillset to see the big picture.'

'Jason's doing a great job.'

'Hmmm.' She sniffs. 'For the privileged man, the world works in his favour. You've done well in your career so far off your own steam.' Her gaze is intense, and I'm reminded of that 'bug pinned to the spot' feeling of a job interview.

'I am proud of all I've achieved.' But as I say it, I'm thinking about the other comments – about business and pleasure and commitment – that have appeared on the hotel socials I manage since I noticed the first.

'You should be.' Dorothy rests her cup on its saucer. 'Jason is known for his business acumen. Sometimes, in the rush of counting dollar signs, I think he's forgotten he inherited that from somewhere.'

Clearly, she's talking about herself, but with her attention again on the window and on stroking Laila's soft fur it doesn't seem like I'm expected to answer.

When she turns back from the view, she frowns. 'What were we talking about?' Her face crumples. 'Who are you?'

Laila seems to pick up on her owner's distress and growls.

'Don't be upset. It's me. It's Adele.' Careful not to get too close to Laila, I take Dorothy's hands. They're warm, dry and papery, and she clings to me like a lifeline.

'Adele?' she says softly, distress becoming recognition.

I smile my relief. 'Yes. That's right.'

'It's so lovely that you're here. Things are hard sometimes,' she says. 'You understand that, don't you?'

There's something layered there but she's lost me. I nod.

She squeezes my hands. 'Thank you, dear. I'm glad we had this chat.'

Jason's appearance at the glass door saves me from having to think of a way to extricate myself. 'There you both are,' he says brightly. As though he didn't send me here. 'Anyone want a cool drink?'

'That would be lovely, dear,' Dorothy says. 'There's water on the bench.'

Jason heads that way and stops short. 'What's this?' He's gesturing to a sign taped to the refrigerator door.

Dorothy smiles. 'Wouldn't want anyone getting a sneak peek.'

'Do. Not. Open,' Jason reads aloud. 'Secret wedding business.' He touches a padlock on the handle and his frown deepens. 'It's locked.'

He doesn't need to look at me this time. Talk about strange behaviour.

'And the cake's in there?' Jason sounds like he's been dropped into a comedy sketch, playing the dumbfounded grandson.

'What else could it be?' Dorothy yawns loudly. 'I need a rest. See yourselves out.'

'Of course,' I say, getting to my feet and encouraging Jason outside.

'Thanks for talking to her,' he says when the door closes behind us. 'I appreciate it.'

He kisses me and I try not to think about how, from Saturday, I'm agreeing to kiss no one else 'til death do us part.

We head back to Jason's place. Since our hands are clasped, I can't miss the buzz on his wrist indicating he's received a message. When he glances down, I look too, registering the first word, '*Don't*,' before he angles his wrist away.

'You hiding something?' I tease.

'No.'

His curt tone doesn't invite further questions and I can't help thinking of what Katja said about having secrets.

'Hey.' I catch his other hand. 'We're getting married, you can talk to me.'

'What if it's a romantic surprise?' he asks.

'You wouldn't be looking like a pet died. If something's wrong then I want to support you. Misery loves company and all that.'

He sighs. 'I didn't want to upset you.'

'Why would a message upset me?'

His eyes close briefly. 'It's a warning not to marry you.'

'Me?'

His lips curve. 'You're the one I'm marrying.'

But my brain is reeling. He's being warned about me? I think back to the headless bride I found, the message on the flowers and the odd comments on the work socials. 'Show me.'

He brings up the message from an unknown number:

Don't go through with it.

'It's a stranger.' I grasp the small amount of relief this prospect allows. 'If it was someone we knew, they'd be in your contacts, wouldn't they?'

'Not necessarily. There are dozens of ways to send anonymous texts.'

'You're an expert, are you?'

This time, he smiles properly. 'I can google with the best of them.'

It takes a heartbeat and then I realise. 'Wait, if you've investigated already then that means it's not the first message you've received.'

He doesn't deny it.

'How many?' I ask. But my brain is stuck on *who* has done this. Who is so against me marrying Jason that they have gone to this much effort? The difference in him lately that I'd put down to wedding stress must be from these messages.

'Maybe four,' he says, when it becomes clear I'm not going to let it go.

'Maybe? How can you not know? If someone was sending me bloody warning messages I'd have been keeping track.'

But Jason remains calm. 'I thought it was a prank. I still feel that way.'

I study his face, but he seems sincere. 'It's not a very nice prank.'

'Hey,' he says, 'it's no big deal. Relax and think about your afternoon of girl time.'

He's planned it specially so I force a shaky smile. 'I'm looking forward to it.'

Jason's arm comes around my shoulders, and he pulls me against his side. He's strong, solid. This was what I wanted, someone I can – quite literally – lean on.

'Why would anyone do this?' I ask. 'Is it too much to want to be happy?'

'Don't worry,' he says kissing my forehead, 'I'm not going to listen to them.'

17

ADELE - THE BRIDE

THURSDAY AFTERNOON – TWO DAYS BEFORE THE WEDDING

Katja is sitting cross-legged on the other end of my bed a little after lunchtime when Mum appears, clearing her throat to interrupt our conversation.

We'd been talking about the Ellingsworth Hotels account, after my conversation with Dorothy got me thinking about their brand, and a couple of hours have vanished while we brainstormed ideas. A welcome distraction.

'The car is here,' Mum says. She's grinning like the proverbial cat with cream. 'It's so impressive.'

I'm excited, but since finding out about Jason's messages it's like I can't breathe properly. I want to be happy but these worries have me feeling like 'eager bride' is a role I'm playing. Smile on command. Look the part. Act the part.

'Til death do you part.

Mum bounces ahead of us down the stairs. 'You girls are so lucky. Back when I married Terry, I thought I was fortunate getting my nails done by a girlfriend. Nothing like this. Half the neighbours are out having a look.'

The edge in her voice makes me unsure if she's excited or jealous.

'Are you sure you don't want to come?' I ask.

'Come on, Tammy, join us,' Katja echoes. 'You know you want to.'

Mum waves us away. 'No, this is for you young girls. I'll expect updates on the platforms.'

I try not to roll my eyes. Mum's never quite gelled with social media. She's too keen or not enough, posts the wrong things at the wrong times, and her lighting is invariably awful. As a professional it grates on my nerves, but she won't take my advice. I'm thankful she's refused; I do not want her particular brand of sideshow taking over.

'What are the chances Sophie turns up?' Katja mutters.

'She'll be here,' I say.

Given the buzz around the place, she could hardly miss the car's arrival, but there's no sign of her. I text her to make sure she has no excuse.

The white stretch Hummer is as stunning on the dusty road as it is out of place. With the door open I can see the black leather inside with room for at least ten people.

'This is the most exciting thing to happen around here for weeks,' Mum says happily.

She's right, if the heads poking out all along the road, having a look like it's a parade, are anything to go by. I scan the crowd, realising with a pang that most of the faces are strangers. Not all of them. Melanie stands alone, her expression neutral.

I smile at her and she smiles back, and I feel a bit better about the show of it.

There's no sign of Jason, but in case he's watching from

somewhere, and to make up for any sign I wasn't ecstatic at the gesture, I make sure to act extra enthusiastic as I approach the small red carpet the driver has unfurled. It's the least he deserves.

'Nice of you to join us,' Katja says when Sophie slouches into view.

I shoot my friend a glare. It's not like I wasn't thinking something similar, but we have to spend the next few hours together. With her arms crossed, Sophie gives off recalcitrant student in trouble with the headmaster vibes. I expect a snarled comeback but she simply shrugs.

We each accept the glass of French champagne offered by the chauffeur and climb inside the vehicle. It's as luxurious as I imagined. The driver closes the door and I feel some of the tension in my shoulders seep out. I sip the drink. I've always been happy enough with Australian sparkling wines, but there's something to be said for the real thing.

'I could get used to this,' Katja says.

Even Sophie appears relaxed, and her drink is more than half-finished.

'Maybe marriage wouldn't be so bad,' Katja muses as the vehicle purrs along the country roads. 'If I could find someone who wouldn't bore me within five minutes.'

'Or drive you to distraction because they breathe more through one nostril than the other,' I tease, reminding Katja of one of her break-up reasons.

'Then there's their family,' Katja adds.

I mock shudder. 'Poor Jason! Have you met my mother?'

'I don't know,' Katja replies. 'That Dorothy is a handful.'

I chuckle.

'My Laila doesn't like men.' Sophie's high-pitched

impression of Dorothy is disturbingly accurate. 'She'd nip all of them in the balls if she could only jump that high.'

I find myself laughing.

After a second, Sophie grins back.

'Wow, you smiled and your face didn't crack,' Katja observes, raising her glass.

Sophie giggles and, if I close my eyes, in that moment, she could be the happy teenager who followed Ollie around so adoringly.

'Dorothy is a tough old thing,' I say, thinking of the odd mix of bewildered and shrewd in our conversation earlier. 'I hope I have half her spirit when I'm that age.'

'I'll drink to that.' Katja drains her glass.

A few minutes later the vehicle glides to a spot outside the lush surrounds of the Oasis Wellness Retreat. We're led along a stone path, through deep green ferns that would be at home in the tropics and into our private hideaway. Inside, by the welcome pool that fills the air with a fresh, clean scent, we're introduced to Mariel. Dressed in a simple white shift dress that emphasises her gorgeous brown skin and long dark hair, Mariel explains in a calming tone that she will be our host for our afternoon of pampering. With a warm smile, she directs us to change into the robes and slippers provided for us, then leaves.

'Oh, thank heavens,' Sophie says at the sight of the slides. 'My feet are killing me.'

I'd noticed her Doc Martens and how easily she pulls off moody, art type. 'I thought they'd be comfortable.'

'They will be, but I picked them up at an op shop last week and they're not broken in yet.' She wrenches them off her feet. 'They were a bargain though.'

'That's awesome,' I say.

Awesome? Inwardly I wince. Hopefully Katja didn't notice. Op shop finds just seem so authentic compared to buying the latest fashion.

I turn my back on the others and change into the provided robe.

I don't know where this need to impress Sophie Rhodes has come from. I genuinely hadn't given her a thought for years. Years when I lived and worked and partied and loved as though Oliver Rhodes and his whole family never existed. Is it because she knows what it was like to watch the paramedics trying so hard to save him? To understand he wasn't coming back. Is it because she, like Jason, was there when he left the railing, that I've become so desperate?

I exhale and make a promise to myself to try to enjoy the afternoon. Mostly it works. The massage is expert and with the three of us being treated by three different women it makes conversation virtually impossible.

A couple of hours later, with Sophie's massage finishing, Katja and I are directed ahead to the nail room, invited to relax on the plush recliners and left alone.

'What's going on with you?' Katja asks.

It's my opening to tell her about the messages but I don't take it. Like I brushed over her noticing the social comments earlier. There's a shame that comes with knowing someone is so passionately against me. 'Just wedding stress,' I say.

'If that's your story, you stick to it,' Katja replies. Her tone is light but she's watching me carefully, like she's afraid I'm about to turn bridezilla on her.

'Not fair,' I say. 'I have been perfectly reasonable through this whole process. In fact, most of the decisions about this wedding have been made by Jason. I have been really bloody accommodating.'

Her lips twitch and I hear the echo of my screeching tone.

I close my eyes and try for a calming breath. 'That doesn't count.'

She laughs.

And after a second, I do, too.

Then Sophie comes in, and the chance to share my fears is lost in a debate about whether the hint of tart, green apple in the cleansing drink is enough to outweigh the other ingredients that might be good for us but taste dreadful.

Not talking about the messages is one thing, but not thinking about them isn't quite so easy.

18

MELANIE - THE MOTHER

THURSDAY AFTERNOON – TWO DAYS BEFORE THE WEDDING

I thought I'd have to convince Sophie to go on the day spa excursion, but she'd been ready to go – dressed completely inappropriately of course with those ridiculous boots – when I returned from putting up the flyers. She'd taken one look at the heading 'Killer Jetty Must Go', rolled her eyes and disappeared into her room, not emerging until it was time to leave.

I admit I added a splash of something to my takeaway coffee to mute the sting from Sophie's lack of support, although goodness knows I should be used to it by now.

I'm sure I caught a look of bemusement on Adele's face at the sight of the ostentatious limousine waiting to collect them. I'm certain she has more taste than that.

I'm still shaking my head at the display as the dust settles. With a few hours ahead to myself, I head back towards the shack, thinking about a nice long nap when something lurches at me from the shadows behind the old boat shed.

'I saw you.'

I flinch at the venom in the words, but turn slowly,

attempting to get my suddenly pounding heart rate under control. I do not want Terry Pippen to see that he frightened me.

'Afternoon,' I say. 'To what do I owe this…' I pause, discard *pleasure* and settle on, 'Visit?'

He crosses his arms. 'You were following me at the jetty. You and that bum, Valente.'

I snort a laugh. 'Giovanni and I were getting coffee. The fact that you were there making a fool of yourself has nothing to do with either of us.'

'I don't believe in coincidences,' he growls.

'And I don't have time for whatever this is,' I lie. 'Please leave.'

'It's been twelve years,' he says. 'You need to get over it.'

He has his child. He can't imagine what every day – every second – of that time has been like for me. My hands go to my hips. 'Why are you here?'

'My girl is getting married, and I do not want you to spoil that for her.'

This is not a man anyone would have on a shortlist for father-of-the-year and a sudden interest in Adele's wellbeing doesn't quite ring true. I consider his clothes, the tan, the face modifications. Like his wife, Terry's had a hell of a lot of work done to battle the effects of time and I'm guessing none of it came cheap. Then there's the constant home renovations and redecorations and their excessively long retirement.

'I get it now. Jason's your meal ticket.'

His gaze darts away, confirming my guess. Part of me wants to say I thought he was better than this, but it would be a lie. Even twelve years ago, I didn't really think much of him despite what we did. Probably makes it worse.

He exhales hard. 'None of this is about you.'

For all his bluster, it doesn't make sense that he'd seek me out. He, more than anyone, has nothing to gain by stirring up the past. But maybe that's it. 'You scared?'

He takes a step closer, so I have to breathe in his cloying aftershave. 'You do not want to make an enemy of me.'

I'd laugh, except standing this close it's impossible to miss the fact that he's much bigger than me and there's a dangerous edge to his voice. Things must be worse next door than I thought.

He must see the flash of fear in my face because he smiles again. He looks down at me… looks down on me. 'You've really let yourself go.'

I refuse to even try to see myself as he must. I've changed, I know it, but I don't waste energy thinking about the shaving-her-legs, regular-hair-appointments, alcohol-free woman who was determined to change the goddamned world. She died with Ollie.

'I'm not interested in impressing anyone,' I say.

His hand cups my cheek and I can't help recoiling at his damp touch. 'You didn't used to complain. Used to beg for it.'

I jerk away, unsure if the wave of repulsion through me is for him or myself. 'We were all different back then.'

He smirks. 'Take care, Melanie.'

It sounds a hell of a lot like a warning. But I can't help myself. As he's striding away, I call out after him. 'She shouldn't be marrying that man.'

Terry doesn't look back. Then he's gone.

Slamming the door closed after entering the shack doesn't help expel my frustration. And the gulps of whiskey burning down my throat only help a little.

Now Terry-goddamn-Pippen thinks he has me intimidated.

I take another sip, breathing in the spicy, caramel aromas from the spirit and feeling the underlying sting of the alcohol. A balm to my ragged nerves.

Whiling the hours away watching the updates of Adele and her bridesmaids at the day spa, *hashtag blessed*, and Jason and his best man on some chartered spear fishing expedition begins to grate. It's all happy smiling faces – even Sophie's. If Adele could simply realise she's about to make the biggest mistake of her life, then this could all be over without anyone getting hurt.

My brain keeps replaying the conversation with Terry. He'd been unusually argumentative. Something that makes me get up and check I locked the doors before curling up on Ollie's bed. I drift off, but when I wake sometime later, I feel anything but rested. Inside my head there's a constant throbbing, reminding me of when Sophie did those awful years of tap dancing, and my mouth is gritty like the beach after a storm.

I drag myself to my feet and go to splash water from the kitchen tap onto my face. Who does Terry think he is?

He doesn't know me. None of them know what I'm capable of.

The silver flask with its soothing contents beckons but I leave it alone for now. I know when I've had enough, and I need my senses sharp for the function tonight. I head outside, hoping a brisk walk will help.

Turning away from the jetty, I let the wind tug at my hair and tiny grains of sand sting my face. Out here, some of the debris of the day seeps away into the salty air. Out here, I can breathe.

*

An hour later I'm almost back to the shack. The beach is deserted, the afternoon beginning to cool and any day trippers have likely long since begun their drive back to Adelaide. The sun sinks towards the horizon and I turn my face to it, soaking up the lingering warmth. The wheel of the gulls overhead warns of someone approaching. The high-pitched squeal of a child has my heart galloping in my chest.

I swing around.

A chubby-cheeked boy toddles towards me on the sand. A hat covers his head and a long-sleeved rash-vest moulds to his top half, while his little, rounded legs are bare and sandy.

'Look out for the waves,' cries a young woman who runs down the beach behind him.

Her call drives the boy on in shrieking excitement. His eyes are aglow as his legs propel him towards the water.

I blink and it could be Ollie, it could be my baby playing on this beach as he did so often in those magic years.

He's heading straight for the ocean. Where boys drown.

'No!' I cry. I run, stumbling, and I grab him, managing to wrench him to safety before his feet can touch the water.

The boy squeals again, in pure terror. And those big eyes are wide and staring up at me. His mouth begins to quiver.

I drop his wrist. Flinch, as I take in the red marks left on his skin.

Upon reaching us, the woman falls to her knees and gathers the boy into her arms. She murmurs something comforting as he clings to her. Her hands pat over him, checking for damage.

Then, she looks up at me. 'What the hell do you think you're doing?'

I flush. 'I'm sorry. The water. I thought...'

Ignoring my stumbling attempts to apologise, she again clutches him close. His shoulders are shaking. Is he crying?

'I'm sorry,' I repeat.

I mentally replay the scene, realise that I've interrupted a game.

I look down and see the marks on the little boy's wrist. Marks I made. Nausea climbs up my throat. There are real tears streaking the boy's cheeks and the woman can't even stand to look at me as she backs away.

'I'm really sorry.'

And then I'm stumbling across the sand. I need to get away from what I've done.

19

SOPHIE – THURSDAY JANUARY 20ᵀᴴ

TWELVE YEARS AGO

Sophie returned to the beach shack before dinnertime the next day as she'd promised Mum, but her head was still with Pip. They'd spent the afternoon watching *High School Musical*, giggling as they compared Zac Efron to Daniel. It had been fun – except when his mum screamed at his dad about some expensive lawnmower he'd bought – but Pip hadn't held her hand even when she'd rested it purposefully next to him.

She was so wrapped up in analysing what that could mean that she nearly collided with Adele going the other way. Sophie mustered a smile as the older girl ducked past her but Adele didn't smile back.

And as Sophie stepped inside, it wasn't hard to tell why. Ollie stood there staring Mum down, his arms folded and jaw set.

'It's one night,' Mum said. 'It's not going to kill you to spend time with the family. Catching up with these people is important to me.'

'It's dumb that I need to come,' Ollie insisted. 'I had plans with Adele and the others.'

Mum didn't soften. 'You're barely seventeen. You and Adele don't need to live in each other's pockets.'

'Says the person who probably married the first guy who'd date them,' Ollie sneered, with a look at Dad.

Mum reeled back like he'd slapped her. 'This isn't up for debate.' She turned away to grab her handbag.

Ollie took the opportunity to roll his eyes. 'Nothing ever is,' he muttered.

'Once you're paying the bills we'll have a vote,' Dad said, trying to break the tension.

It didn't work.

Ollie glowered through the whole drive to Tuckersfield Hotel and the meal, barely eating his favourite fish and chips. He gave the couple they were having dinner with, some friend of Mum's from university and her husband, one-word answers to their questions about school and what he wanted to study.

He stayed sullen even when Mum offered to splurge on sundaes.

It didn't matter that Sophie was perfectly polite and made the woman smile with her tale about backstage disasters, Mum spent most of the evening speaking through gritted teeth and telling her friend to be grateful she didn't have children.

Despite Ollie's sulky refusal of dessert at the restaurant, and his grumpy display that was borderline rude, Dad kept trying to snap him out of it the whole way back to Refuge Bay.

Where Mum was all 'why couldn't you behave for one night' and 'don't you care how you're making everyone feel?'

Dad was jokes and teasing, and by the time they were back to the bay, he'd managed to make Ollie crack a smile.

Sophie watched her parents' performance of their version of a good cop, bad cop routine. All for Ollie. All to make Ollie feel better. Even though it was Ollie who'd caused all of this with his tantrum.

Dad stopped the car at the kiosk at the end of the shacks, only open so late because of the summer hours.

'Ice-creams?' he asked.

This time Ollie didn't shake his head. He was the first out of the car and walked ahead with Dad, making jokes. Mum trailed them, her happy gaze fixed on her angel son.

Sophie followed last of all, forgotten in the need to get Ollie onside. But with everyone happy now, she couldn't be mad. Could she?

She tried not to think too hard about the answer and hurried to catch up as Dad put his arm around Ollie's shoulder. He had to reach up to do so, because this summer Ollie had overtaken him in height. Dad made a big show of stretching and they all laughed, even Sophie.

But as she did, she felt a trickle of unease, like a drop of icy sea water dripping down her spine. She turned, scanned the dunes, the young palm trees and the murky, bruise-purple light without seeing anyone. She blinked and then was almost going to step into the small kiosk when she saw him.

Jason, stood near the jetty, in the shadows.

Sophie went to lift her hand and call out, but he ducked his head and hurried away. She wanted to believe that he hadn't seen her or her family. Wanted to believe that the twisted snarl of envy on his face wasn't meant to be directed their way.

But she was sure he'd been staring right at them.

20

ADELE – THE BRIDE

THURSDAY AFTERNOON – TWO DAYS BEFORE THE WEDDING

Sophie, Katja and I are seated, glasses in hand, in the same stretch Hummer that collected us and we're almost back to the bay. I'm so relaxed that I'm wishing for a nap rather than the pre-wedding party Jason has planned for tonight, when Katja suddenly straightens.

'What's that?' she asks, peering out of the tinted window to where there's a large vehicle ahead of us on the road. 'Another surprise from Jason?'

I peer at the truck that appears to be squatting across my parents' driveway. 'Maybe.'

I press the small button to speak to the driver. 'You can leave us here,' I say, aware he'll otherwise get stuck.

'Thank you, miss,' he replies.

The Hummer purrs to a stop and we wait for the door to be opened.

'Is it a removalist?' Sophie asks, handing her empty glass to the driver.

As she speaks I make out the faint yellow writing on the

side. 'Okely Bros. Removals.' And the pleasant glow from the champagne vanishes.

'Why is it here?' Katja asks.

'Mum's always redecorating something,' I say lightly. But I thought Mum had completed everything for the weekend.

Katja shrugs. 'Maybe it is something from Jason.'

'Probably,' I agree quickly. This idea eases the faint tightening in my chest, the strain of the pressure of Mum's constant need to keep up with the latest trends, spending more and more.

There's a burly man with a clipboard next to the truck's open back and I wave the girls on without me. 'He seems a bit lost,' I say, hoping they can't hear the forced joviality. 'I'll see what's happening.'

I slow my steps so Katja and Sophie will be out of range by the time I reach the man with his thinning dark hair and compensatory handlebar moustache. I don't know what this is but instinct tells me it's not good. Maybe it's the way the guy is frowning or the fact that Jason is unlikely to use a company that's so clearly shoddy.

'Can I help you?' I ask. 'That's my parents' shack.'

He looks up, frowns. 'Unlikely, love. Unless you have a wad of cash in that little purse of yours. Your da and my friend are having a little chat round the back while your ma sorts it out.'

The unease in my stomach becomes nausea.

Of course they've done this.

They couldn't just be happy with their nice shack; they've gone and bought stuff on some payment plan without having a plan to pay for it. I head towards the back of the truck.

Thud.

A deep moan follows. I fling myself around the corner to see Dad stagger into the side of the truck, his hand rising to cup his face. The man standing over him has at least a foot and sixty kilos on me. He's wearing a singlet and tight shorts, his tattooed skin shining under the sun like he's been dipped in butter.

Dad raises his hand telling me to stop as I realise I've stepped forward to intervene, though what I'm going to do against man-mountain I don't know.

'It's fine,' he says.

Man-mountain's gaze slides all over me. 'She's a pretty one.'

Dad steps in front of me. 'This is between us. We'll get you the money, it's just taking a little longer than we thought.'

I close my eyes. 'What the actual f—'

'Darling.' Mum, who's appeared from wherever she went to sort this out, cuts me off. 'Be nice.' There's disapproval in her tone.

'Swearing's a problem?' I sputter. 'Not the huge guy who smashed Dad's face in.'

'You're being dramatic,' Mum says but she darts a nervous glance at Dad. 'I've sorted it.' Then to the man. 'You'll have your money in a moment.'

Man-mountain gives me another look that makes me feel like I'm the dessert he'll get if he just eats all his greens and then wanders around towards his partner.

'What's going on?' I ask.

They share a look, Dad rubbing at his jaw. 'We were going to wait until after the wedding,' Mum begins.

'Tell me.' Somehow I choke out the command.

'This isn't a big deal,' she says.

'How can you do this? Mum, this is my wedding weekend.'

Her mouth twists. 'And it always has to be about you, doesn't it? Never a thought for your poor old mum and dad and all they've done for you.'

My protests die in my throat. She won't listen, she never has. When I force myself to look at her I'm not surprised to see her complete lack of concern. I've wondered so often how she doesn't have that stomach-curling shame when things like this happen, although I guess if she did, they wouldn't keep happening. If only Pip was here. He'd understand. He's stood with Mum in the grocery line while her card was declined in the same week she bought another big TV. He had the pitying looks from dance teachers when we were late with the fees.

But he's not here.

First things first. I need to get this sorted out.

'Ask them to wait a bit longer.' I'm already bringing up my bank app on my phone. 'It will just take me a few minutes to sort out my accounts.'

'You don't need to rearrange anything.' Mum has a smug look that does nothing to calm my threadbare nerves.

'What have you done?'

Mum's phone buzzes. 'Right on cue,' she says after glancing at the screen.

I see the name and my knees threaten to give way. 'Please tell me you haven't.'

As usual she ignores me, answering the call that's from my fiancé.

'Tell Jason it was a mistake,' I whisper urgently.

She shakes her head and mouths, 'Too late.' Then she's greeting him and it's clear whatever message she left him included every awful detail of this.

My skin feels at once too hot and too tight.

She half-heartedly covers the phone. 'Darling, stop making that face. It doesn't become you. Jason says he'll handle it.'

I nod, a wooden movement that hurts my neck, the muscles there are so tight.

As Mum gushes her thanks, I struggle not to scream. Any possibility of walking away from this wedding – not that I want to – disappears. I have to marry Jason. My desperate play to maintain some semblance of independence has been swept away by my parents. I see a future where this happens again and again and again, and I want to be sick.

I don't though. I keep my head high, take the phone from Mum and thank my fiancé as the truck rumbles to life and drives away. And Jason says all the right things about it being no problem. I should have known Mum and Dad would turn this into a nightmare.

21

ADELE - THE BRIDE

THURSDAY EVENING – TWO DAYS BEFORE THE WEDDING

Just before we're about to head to Jason's for the party, Katja looks at her reflection in the floor-to-ceiling mirror and decides she's not feeling her outfit.

'I'll wait,' I say, although I know Jason won't be impressed, and that's on top of whatever it is my parents conned out of him.

Katja shakes her head. 'I'm fine. I won't get lost.'

At least now I can face the awkward meetup after Jason paid off my parents' debt – without a witness.

Downstairs, Mum and Dad are waiting for me. 'We should be there early to help get ready,' Mum explains. 'It's the least we can do.'

I can hardly bring myself to talk to her, so arguing isn't an option. Dad has a red mark on his jaw from the punch and the sight of it has my own hands curling to fists. How could they?

As per Jason's request, I arrive about fifteen minutes before the guests are due. He had the cleaners and caterers in this afternoon, and with nothing practical to help with, I would have only gotten in the way earlier. Hosting with Jason mostly involves agreeing with his decisions.

Whoever he's paid for tonight has done a brilliant job. The already gorgeous outdoor area has been improved by the addition of stylish fairy lights and lanterns that give a magical glow to the space. There's more greenery than there was this morning, with trailing vines spilling from white pots that match the white bowls and linen.

'You like?' Jason asks.

'It's gorgeous.'

He holds me at arm's length, taking in my candy pink strapless dress, white heels and the natural waves I spent an age curling into my hair. 'As are you,' he says before brushing my lips with a kiss light enough not to disturb my makeup.

I can't remember if I told him what I was wearing but his shirt has a faint pink stripe and he's suave in his black chinos. 'You look nice, too,' I say.

Mum sashays towards us like she owns the place. 'Jason, darling.' She embraces him and her cheek kiss leaves a lipstick mark that Jason tries to unobtrusively wipe off.

Dad's greeting is no less effusive. 'Everything looks brilliant.' He claps Jason on the shoulder. 'Thanks for everything earlier, son. You helped us out of a pickle.'

Son? I want to gag but that wouldn't help my efforts to keep my smile in place. Nor would it aid in getting this mortifying interaction over with as quickly as possible.

'No problem,' Jason says.

He puts an arm around Mum but his gaze is on me. 'I will always look after my family; you should know that about me.'

'I'll drink to that,' Dad says. 'If you want to direct me to the beers?'

Jason smiles and points at the bar fridge. 'I'll join you. And would you ladies like a champagne?' he asks.

I force my smile wider. 'That would be wonderful, thank you.'

Mum titters her agreement, too, and, as Jason pours the bubbly, Dad hands out beer like he bought it.

Then he has the gall to say to Jason, 'You really should have let us help out with tonight, mate. Let us show how thrilled we are that you're joining the family.'

'Terry's right,' Mum adds.

Jason waves them away. 'It's my pleasure. Although they are running a bit late with the hot food I ordered.'

It's like they've all made some silent pact to ignore the fact that if Mum and Dad have violent debt collectors visiting, they're in no position to cater a party.

Jason pulls me aside and lowers his voice. 'This thing with your parents this afternoon.'

'Thank you for helping,' I say again.

He waves that away. 'You need to know. They're *really* not good people.'

Somehow his tone and expression make the simple words chill my blood. 'Are my parents in danger?'

A nod. Simple. Finite. And then, 'But I'll meet the guy next week and come up with a way to sort it out permanently. Hopefully, what I paid them today will hold them off until then.'

Next week, once we're married. 'Thank you.'

'There's something else.'

I want to tell him to keep whatever it is to himself but instead I ask, 'What is it?'

'I called the caterers, and there's no hot food coming.'

I try to hide my relief that it's nothing to do with my parents. 'How?'

'Apparently I cancelled the order this morning. Except I didn't.'

'I don't understand.'

He crosses his arms. 'Someone claimed to be me and cancelled the order.'

My relief vanishes. 'Who would do such a thing?' But then I answer myself. 'Whoever sent the messages.' I scramble to think, aching in my chest that someone's done such a thing to try to spoil our night. 'This isn't so bad.' His face looks like he's about to argue and I get that he wants everything to be perfect but we can deal with this. 'I promise.'

I tug gently at his arms until he lets me pull him close. 'We have all the cold things, and the drinks – people would really notice if they were missing. We can order pizza from Tuckersfield.' I name the nearest town. 'Surely someone will deliver if we give them a big enough tip.'

He nods, still frowning but his hands are now wrapped around mine. 'Good idea, I'll sort it out.'

'Of course you will.' I kiss him for good measure and he's almost smiling.

'You're amazing, you know that?' he murmurs.

The arrival of Jason's family breaks up the conversation, and the way my parents greet them like hosts has me wanting to bare my teeth like Laila, who allows me to pat her.

'You are so good with her, dear,' Dorothy says approvingly.

'It's not hard when she's such a cutie.' I scan Dorothy's face but there's no sign of her earlier confusion. 'I love how you two are matching tonight.'

Dorothy appears pleased I noticed that Laila's little hot pink collar is the same hue as the bright flowers in her owner's floral dress. 'Wait 'til you see what we've got planned for Saturday.'

As I smile, I make a mental note to warn Jason that Laila is apparently on the guest list for the wedding. He's disappeared inside and I hope the pizza place has some gourmet options to make him happy.

More guests arrive and I find myself so busy greeting everyone there isn't time to dwell on my parents. I have to trust that Jason knows what he's talking about and we can bail them out once we're married.

I don't realise that Katja hadn't arrived until I see her crossing the beach towards the party. Tall, broad and stunning in a sleek, black, strappy dress, her tanned long legs showing through the lacy lower half. But it's who she's with that makes me lose the thread of my conversation with the mayor. Fiona Lewis appears a little nonplussed as I trail into silence but since I don't even know why she's here among family and friends when she's neither, I can't bring myself to care.

'Excuse me,' I say. 'There's someone I must speak to.' I don't wait for her response before approaching my friend. My friend, who seems to have collected Sophie Rhodes in her travels.

I send Katja a silent look asking, *'How did this happen?'*.

'I had a fashion crisis and called her,' Sophie says, interpreting my look. 'I hope I haven't made us late.'

Her admission is almost as unexpected as the striking combination of the light caramel corset she's paired with a black tulle skirt and her trademark boots. Boots I now know are really uncomfortable. And it's that insight she shared earlier that lets me smile, despite wondering when exactly they exchanged numbers.

'I'm just glad you're here now,' I say.

'What do you need us to do?' Katja asks. 'Mingle? Make sure no bachelors are lonely? Make nice with the future in-laws? Serve food?'

I chuckle. 'All of that. Except serve, Jason has hired waitstaff for the evening.'

'Did someone say my name?' Jason asks.

I let him pull me close. 'I was telling them you have the catering under control.'

'I do.' His emphasis tells me he managed to order the pizza. At a lift of his hand, one of the waitstaff appears with a tray of champagne.

The girls follow my lead and take one. We clink the glasses together.

'How was the spa session?' Jason asks.

'It was marvellous,' I say quickly. 'Thank you.' I turn to remind the others. 'It was Jason's gift to the three of us.'

'Thank you,' Katja and Sophie say in chorus.

Jason smiles. 'I'm just glad I could spoil the three of you. In the meantime, Rory and I had a great afternoon spear fishing, returning with quite the impressive catch.'

I look away and catch Sophie curling her lip. I gasp and the champagne goes down the wrong way. When I've assured everyone I'm fine, Sophie's face holds only concern and I'm left wondering if I saw anything at all.

The moment is quickly forgotten as I make the rounds, ensuring everyone's having a good time. Although the staff are excellent, I sneak into the kitchen a few times under the pretext of checking on things for a brief reprieve. It lets me escape conversations I don't want to have, like when I see Rory making his way towards me. If he has a question about the wedding, he can ask Jason.

It's fully dark and the party is well underway when my phone buzzes. I pause in the relative privacy of the kitchen to check the message, hoping it's Pip telling me he's in the country, afraid it's not.

It's spam. News of some mega-sale or other. I slide my phone away before I can be caught doing something so crass.

I know that someone's simply messing with Jason and I but I can't let it go. From the quick look I had on the internet, Jason was right and disguising your number isn't difficult, but they keep messaging. And there's the party food, the flowers and the headless bride. As well as the feeling I've had a few times walking between the shacks that I'm being watched.

None of this is helping my – what I'm sure are perfectly normal – pre-wedding jitters.

Earlier, I found myself scrolling through Jason's social media looking for an ex-girlfriend who might not have let go. I'm studying family and friends closely and I even looked up a couple of my ex-boyfriends to make sure they've all moved on.

If someone wants to screw with my head, then they've succeeded.

A sharp hot slab of fury climbs in my chest. This is supposed to be my special weekend and I'm in here on my own, second-guessing everything.

No more.

Whoever it is can hide behind their screen like the gutless wonder they are, and watch as the wedding goes ahead.

I'm about to go back to the party, my smile in place, when I see it. Outside, in the dark gap between Jason's and his grandmother's shack. There's a face. And it's looking right at me.

Heart thudding, I stare at the spot, trying to make sense of what I'm seeing through the reflections from inside. It could be a trick of the light, but my chest is squeezing and there's an insistent tingle on the back of my neck. I edge closer. Somewhere, someone laughs. I can't help but blink and by the time I get to the window there's only a faint smudge like someone's cloud of breath against the glass. And then that fades too, and I can't be sure there was ever anyone there.

22

MELANIE – THE MOTHER

THURSDAY EVENING – TWO DAYS BEFORE THE WEDDING

I'm a little late to the party over at Jason's shack. After the incident on the beach with the child, I required a stiff drink and a hot shower to regain my equilibrium. Not only because of how upset I made him, but I'd had a strange feeling of eyes on me from my neighbours.

After greeting Adele – she's simply stunning tonight in her pink strapless dress and hair that belongs in a shampoo commercial – I grab a drink from one of the waitstaff and take stock. Fairy lights have been strung above the deck like the final rays of sunshine have been caught and suspended above our heads. Their glow gives everything a hint of gold, like the whole world has been given one of those filters young people like so much on their pictures.

It's impossible to miss the movement of the happy couple through the crowd. People turn to follow them like flowers facing the sun. There are enough people here that I'm able to easily avoid having to speak to Jason. Safe in the shadows, with dozens of people between us, I let myself take in this grown-up version of the boy I couldn't stand.

Clean shaven, neat hair. A smile and body made handsome enough thanks to orthodontics, expensive lotions and personal trainers. Helped by tailored, expensive clothes. All in all, a well-put-together package. Which makes him, on the surface, alongside his wealth and background, a reasonable match to Adele. And he's attentive to her, I'll give him that.

The crowd shifts then. It parts and, despite the distance and the fact I would have sworn he didn't even know I'd arrived, his gaze meets mine.

I flinch.

There's no question in that look. He knows exactly who I am. I lift my chin and refuse to look away. He might have fancied himself up and convinced all these people to come tonight, but I know he's the same snake he's always been.

I know what he's done.

A little later, as I eat some rosemary crackers and brie cheese to soak up the alcohol I've already consumed, I'm wondering if I should have confronted him.

'You should try the beetroot and mint,' says a woman standing next to me. 'It's divine.'

'Maybe next time.'

'How's Jim?'

I blink at the question. Not because I've forgotten the existence of my ex-husband, more because the idea of someone thinking I'd have a clue is faintly shocking. It jars me to admit, 'I don't know.'

I walk away before I have to explain further and grab another drink. The end of us was nothing special. For a while after Ollie died we simply survived in the same space. He pulled himself from the pit of grief first, and didn't offer me a hand out. Or, maybe he did, but I wasn't ready to take it.

Getting himself together meant exercise and that meant making new friends at the gym. New friends became a new special friend, and then it was over. I don't blame him. In fact, I'm grateful. Jim was there for me when no one else was, and he told me all that I'd missed in those last weeks of Oliver's life.

If not for him, I wouldn't know Jason is to blame.

As the evening wears on, I manage to avoid Jason and more party conversation by staying on the move. A few times I pass by Sophie, who appears more comfortable here than I would have guessed. The other bridesmaid, whose name I should know, seems to have taken her under her wing and they make quite a contrast. Sophie's slender darkness and the bubbly personality of the other girl.

With the excuse of needing the bathroom, I make my way inside. The house is as expensive and personality-free as I would have guessed.

It's when I'm snooping on the top floor, about to enter the closed double doors of what I'm guessing is Jason's bedroom, that I hear it.

'You need to stop her.'

I freeze, recognising the unmistakable command of the mayor's voice. But who is she talking to?

A raucous laugh from the party makes me miss the reply.

But then Mayor Fiona speaks again. 'Don't forget that I can make things very difficult for you. It might have taken time for me to work out the finer details but I know enough.'

'You have no proof.'

My breath catches in my throat. That's Jason speaking.

'How willing are you to ride the scandal out?' she asks. 'You'd want to be confident that no one will back up my version of events.'

'Someone in your role has a duty of care.'

'Not to you.'

There's a long silence and I think maybe that's it, but then he speaks again. 'This isn't the time or the place. For fuck's sake, she's just downstairs. Anyway, she won't back you up.'

'I don't need her to.' Mayor Fiona sounds so certain.

'We had an agreement,' Jason snarls.

'I'm not sure that means what you think it means. Don't—' Her voice cuts off.

Is that the sound of a scuffle? I move closer, desperate to know what's happening.

'Don't what?' he asks, suddenly closer to the door than he was before.

I stumble away, hoping the sound will be lost in the noise from below.

'Don't step forward?' he asks. 'They say "don't poke the bear" and I'm pretty sure it's even more dangerous mere hours from the bear's impending nuptials.'

'I'm not frightened of you,' she says.

'Then you're nowhere near as clever as I thought you were.'

'Do what you said you'd do,' she snaps, 'and I wouldn't have to speak to you at all.'

'I'm going back to my party,' Jason growls. 'Feel free to get the hell off my property at your earliest convenience.'

I don't wait to see the door open. I've never made it down a flight of stairs so quickly.

I'm outside again when I see Jason emerge. There's nothing in his face to suggest he was recently arguing in his bedroom with Fiona Lewis. Although I look out for her to follow, there's no sign of her having been there.

Could I have misheard?

I try to think back but the details have already faded on an alcohol mist. The sense of antagonism remains like a dark shadow. She was there. I heard her.

When there's no sign of her minutes later, I have to admit it's possible she's not here at all. So when she suddenly speaks from right next to me, 'Melanie Rhodes. Of course, you're here,' I gasp.

'Mayor Fiona. I would say it's a pleasure to see you,' I pause. 'But I wouldn't be telling the truth.'

Her eyebrows lift. 'Equally.'

'First the jetty and now here. Almost like you're following me to my celebration with old friends.' I throw it out there, wanting her to deny it and say she's here for Jason.

'Friends, hmm?' she says instead.

'Yes.' The lie doesn't bother me.

'You might want to watch your back,' she says. 'Speaking of friends.'

I want to tell her to run along home to her cat, and that if she was less ambitious, one of the parade of men through her social media might stick around and turn into a husband. But then she'd know I've been stalking her online.

'Thanks for the warning,' I say. 'Speaking of warnings, why fight me so hard on the old jetty?'

Her lips part.

Is she going to tell me the real reason she's so involved, or what she has to do with Jason? I hold my breath.

But then her expression hardens, and eyes shutter as a nasty smile curves her lips. 'Perhaps it's that I'm sick of people like you meddling in council business. Or perhaps,' she leans so close I can smell her jasmine scent, 'I just don't like you very much.'

23

MELANIE – THE MOTHER

THURSDAY EVENING – TWO DAYS BEFORE THE WEDDING

After Fiona leaves, the conversation around me smooths into a blur. The feel-good factor of an imminent wedding makes for a decidedly celebratory atmosphere. The waitstaff circling with trays of drinks doesn't hurt.

Then someone turns down the music and it's time for speeches. The mother of the bride is the first to pick up the microphone.

'Don't worry,' Tammy says to her daughter. 'I'm not going to embarrass you.'

Adele's smile looks a bit tight and I don't blame her. Tammy's known for oversharing.

'I'll save that for Saturday,' Tammy adds to a wave of laughter.

Adele's cheeks turn pink.

Tammy waits for the laughter to die down. 'I'm so glad we're here together to celebrate this marvellous occasion. No one can deny that having known each other since childhood, these two are clearly meant to be.'

I try not to cringe as some of the guests throw furtive looks my way. I force my mouth into a smile and try not to feel sickened at what I've become. Playing nice will be worth it.

I keep the smile in place as Tammy shares the story of Jason asking for their permission to propose and how thrilled they were. Maintain it when she shares some anecdote about catching Adele trying on her jewellery as a toddler and insisting she was practising to be a bride. And am still smiling when, at last, Tammy lifts her glass.

'Please, join me in a toast.' She pauses to allow us guests to refill our glasses, and then lifts hers even higher. 'To my precious Adele, and her lovely Jason.'

'To Adele and Jason.'

Pushing aside my distaste, I follow the rest of the crowd in raising my glass to the happy couple.

Adele takes over then, and thanks everyone for coming. I tune out her words, knowing she'll be saying all the right things and try to see deeper, to gauge how she's really feeling. As much as I want to see doubt, there is none.

Then it's Jason's turn. He reiterates the thanks and then looks to his bride to be. 'In agreeing to be my wife, Adele has made me the happiest man alive.'

I recoil at his choice of wording but no one else seems to notice.

He pulls her closer. 'Adele knows there's nothing I wouldn't do for her.' He lifts his gaze to take in Tammy and Terry. 'Nor by extension her family, and I will be forever indebted to them for how they've welcomed me.'

'No,' Terry says gruffly. 'There are no debts between family, mate.'

Everyone is smiling and looking suitably touched, but for big spenders like Tammy and Terry there's a lot of mentions of debt and gratitude. I think suddenly of the removals van out on the street by Tammy's place.

Jason's still talking, looking into Adele's eyes. 'I look forward to sharing our vows in front of the people who matter most to us, but most of all...' He takes a breath like the emotion is overwhelming him. 'I can't wait for us to spend the rest of our lives together.'

When the crowd returns to their groups I find myself stuck with those who've had shacks here for half a lifetime. Jason and Adele are arm-in-arm under sparkling lights, looking like they stepped from some aspirational lifestyle magazine.

'They're so gorgeous together,' Tammy says. She makes a show of dabbing at her eyes.

I fight not to roll mine, as Laura nods her polite agreement. Dorothy, however, harrumphs. I'm so distracted wondering what that might mean that my first clue that Jason and Adele have joined us is when Jason speaks.

'Wonderful speech, Tammy.'

His smooth, polished voice reminds me of the time I scraped my fingers across the sharp metal teeth of a grater with lemon in my hand. The sting sharp but almost predictable.

They're talking around me and I'm nodding but it's hard to focus on Tammy's too-loud reiteration of how excited she is for the big day. Dorothy mutters that Laila – I think that's the dog – hates long speeches.

Any moment now, they'll look to me.

It's like teetering over the edge of a high-rise, knowing I could lose my footing any second, but being unable to step away from the drop. Seconds become minutes and I grip my empty glass and long for a refill, or to flee, but that would only draw more attention. So instead, I wait. But then Adele and Jason are called away by the tall bridesmaid and I'm exhaling a happy sigh of escape.

It's louder than I intend and the gazes of those nearby swing towards me. Jason stops. Whirls around. And like that, I'm over the edge and in freefall.

'What is your problem with me?' He seems hurt, unless you know what to look for.

I know, but I don't want to get myself uninvited from this wedding.

'I don't have a problem with you.'

Adele touches his shoulder but he shakes her off.

'It burns you seeing us happy,' he says. 'You seem to take our joy as an affront to you personally. I'm sorry that Ollie's not here.' He chokes up. 'Goddamn it, he was my best friend. I'm grieving, too.'

He's grieving too.

The ridiculous sentiment bounces around in my brain, getting louder and louder until…

'Rubbish,' I blurt.

What have I done? Too late, I wish the word back. *Stupid fool.*

'By all means,' he says. 'Tell me what you really think.'

Now I've started this there's nowhere to go but the truth. It all comes down to one simple fact. 'You waited.'

His brows lift. 'I don't understand.'

'You saw him go in, you knew he was in trouble and you just watched. Doing nothing is as good as making a decision. First you encouraged his reckless behaviour, gave him your drugs and then you let him drown. You might as well have held him under.'

'Mum!' The cry comes from Sophie – there's no one else alive to call me such.

He shakes his head. 'Anyone who knows me knows that I'm a huge supporter of youth charities that deal with kids and drugs. I do this in memory of Ollie and because I wish I'd known what kind of trouble he was in back then. You weren't there that day. We were having fun; we always had such a good time together. Ollie seemed fine at first, maybe showing off a bit and then…' He drags his hand across his eyes in a parody of grief. 'And then it was too late. There was nothing anyone could do.' He turns to Adele. 'You were there, tell her, honey.'

Sympathy for me shines from her gorgeous face. 'Oh, Melanie, it was too fast. Jason's right, we couldn't do anything.'

Somehow he's fooled Adele. My eyes sting but I will not cry in front of these people.

'We miss him too,' Jason says gently. He closes the distance between us and takes my hands. They're warm and dry when I expected cold and slimy. 'I'm glad we've talked this out.'

Around me it's like they all hold their breath, waiting for my reaction.

'I should probably go,' I say.

Adele's hand rests kindly against my shoulder. 'Do you need company?'

She's such a thoughtful girl. It makes the fact that she's tying herself to Jason for the rest of her life so much worse. 'I'll be okay,' I say. 'Thanks.'

The sand is cool where my sandals sink into it, but the air is fresh, rather than cold. The further I get from the party, the easier it is to breathe. The sight of a small orange glow near the edge of my porch slows my steps.

'Who goes there?' I demand.

The little light – the end of a cigarette, I see now – is extinguished. 'It's just me. Rory. I'm the best man.'

I hadn't paid much attention to the man deemed Jason's closest friend other than to mentally disapprove on principle, but there's something about him basically hiding out here that makes me reassess. It's not that he's like Ollie. More that he seems so very, very different to Jason.

'Everything okay?' I ask.

His laugh is at once self-deprecating and forced. 'I'm all good. Honest.' He shoves his hands in his pockets. 'You have a good night.'

As I head into the sanctuary of my shack, past the table with the puzzle whose piece is even now in my pocket, I've already pushed Rory to the back of my mind and I'm back thinking about the confrontation with Jason. Why didn't he rescind my invite there and then?

I don't know, but he's made a huge mistake. He doesn't know what I have planned.

24

ADELE - THE BRIDE

THURSDAY NIGHT – TWO DAYS BEFORE THE WEDDING

I'm back at Mum's before midnight with everyone mindful of us needing to 'get our rest before the big day'. As I sit on the end of my bed, having changed into old grey trackies and a comfortable hoodie, I know there's no way I'm going to sleep any time soon.

I creep out of my room. Any thought of talking to Katja is halted by the loud snores coming from her bedroom. Making my way down the stairs I automatically breathe a little louder but my childhood defence against raised voices doesn't stop them carrying.

Loving? Fighting? With Mum and Dad there's never been much difference. And always about money.

And then I'm outside and closing the door and the only sound is the waves on the shore. A glance back towards Jason's shows it's dark there and I hope at least he's getting a decent night's sleep.

Hands in pockets, I hunch my shoulders against the breeze, trying not to think of the threats and the face and the flowers. My bare feet sink into the sand as I hurry past Giovanni's place. He always gave me the creeps with his weird sculptures and sad eyes. There were rumours about him; that he'd had a family and they died. He had a family and he killed them all. That he wasn't allowed to have a family because of the terms of his parole.

As an adult I know none of it's true, but I can't help my feet.

I'm out of sight of our shack when the crunch of sand has me whirling to look behind me. 'Who's there?'

Rory emerges from the darkness. 'It's me.'

'What are you doing? Did you follow me?' My heart is racing.

'I was out getting some fresh air, trying to clear my head, and saw you go by.'

'Then you followed me.'

His lopsided smile is adorable. 'You just seemed so deep in thought that I didn't know whether to bother you. I can go, if you want.'

I glance back towards Jason's, thinking about where he's supposed to be staying and why.

He must read my mind because he says, 'Everyone's asleep.'

The man is impossible to stay mad with. 'The beach is public.'

We walk on in silence and the swirling thoughts in my head drain away to simply breathing in and out. He doesn't speak and that in itself helps me relax. He does, however, walk closer and closer until our arms bump into each other and I can smell that hint of smoke. Jason would definitely not approve. My fiancé is very particular about what he puts into his body.

Maybe it's the late hour or being so close to where Ollie

died or the impending wedding but when I turn to Rory at the jetties it's to ask him for a smoke.

He's already staring at me. Since the party he's pulled on a battered old leather jacket and a black beanie and a few of his curls have escaped. He's unshaven and his eyes are dark, infinite pools, getting darker as our gazes clash.

What I was going to say dies on my lips as his hand lifts to cup my cheek.

'We can't,' I whisper, but what I really want to say is, *please*.

And he seems to read it in my face. Probably not a difficult task if I look anywhere as desperate as he does. Desperate to be closer, to touch, to do something about this ache inside me. Being around him but not being able to act on this thing between us has required a will that I'm struggling to maintain. And it's clear he wants me as much as I want him.

I've done this to myself.

Jason and I were casual to start with – nothing serious or exclusive – and the Rory thing was a bit of fun and I didn't know they were close, but then suddenly Jason was proposing and Rory doesn't want to let go.

'Tell me to kiss you,' he growls, stirring heat low in my belly. 'Tell me you need my mouth on yours because you're as goddamned hot for me as I am for you. Beg me, Addie. You know you want to.'

The thrum of my body makes words impossible.

Then he's kissing me, and I should stop him and I want to but it's everything I've needed since he walked across Jason's deck yesterday and I had to act like he was almost a stranger.

Am I having an affair with Rory?

I've tried not to think about it too hard. Easy enough when his mouth is on mine like it is now. Even easier when his hands are snaking under my hoodie and my belly is contracting at his touch. Mostly, well, I do my very best not to think about Rory at all.

My lips part at his expert tease and my fingertips find the curls at the back of his neck. I've risen to my toes, pressing closer. Kissing and kissing and losing myself and all my worries in the smoky, minty taste of him.

A sudden change in the hitherto constant sound of the wind and the waves slams me back into reality. I'm getting married in two days and I'm practically grinding on the beach with the best man.

I pull away. 'I heard something.'

'No,' Rory says, kissing me again. 'No, you didn't.'

Fear of what, or more like who, could be out there overwhelms my want for him and propels me back until I collide with a jetty pylon. I bite off a curse and scan the darkness.

'No more. This was a mistake.'

'You said that last time, but here we are.' There's a hint of petulance in his voice.

I spin away from him and stride over the sand. What am I doing? I'm supposed to be getting married to Jason, and it's not like I could be in love with Rory. We don't talk, we screw.

Everything is in place for this wedding and I've made a commitment to Jason that I can't break. One I don't want to break. In my head I see the seriousness in Jason's eyes when he talked about the loan shark people. I see our perfect Sundays with coffee on the balcony of his apartment when I know I'm exactly where I'm supposed to be.

Rory's hand on my shoulder stops me. 'I'm sorry,' he says,

pushing his hair out of his eyes. 'You make me lose my head and I can't think straight around you.'

I ignore the thrill of illicit power. 'I'll do the thinking for both of us. We need to act as though this never happened.'

'What if I can't?'

'I'm sorry, but you don't get a choice.'

He grasps both my hands. 'Don't marry him.'

Despite the conviction in his words, he seems as surprised by what he's said as I am.

Although just minutes ago he had his fingertips sliding under my waistband and his lips tasting the pulse in my throat, I can't help the feeling that this has come out of nowhere.

'We were just fooling around,' I say. 'It never meant anything.'

'Didn't it?'

I tug myself free. 'You don't want to do this.'

'Don't tell me what I want,' he says. 'I know how I feel when we're together, and it's like nothing else.'

This is a bad idea, lingering here with Rory in the dark where we could be seen. It's always a bad idea. But even as I think this, even as guilt and shame settle over me, rank and pungent like when the seaweed rots in the sun, I don't move.

'Why now?' I ask. 'It's not like this wedding is a surprise. You're his best man.'

'I've wanted to say something a million times.'

'Right, just not enough to actually speak. You know what something like this could do to Jason, given everything.'

Rory exhales through gritted teeth. 'I get he's milking you for sympathy.'

'How could you say something like that?'

Some of Rory's bravado deflates. 'He's not who you think he is.'

'You're wrong. I know Jason. I've known him for longer than you have.'

'It's not a competition,' he snaps back. 'Anyway, it's not like you've been close. You have this place in common but back then it was never him.'

'We all grow up,' I say.

'So, you live all this life apart, then you meet again through work. When you get a chance to pitch for the Ellingsworth Hotels account.'

I nod. 'We reconnect, and the rest is history.'

His lips press together like he's holding something in. Then, 'Jason engineered that whole thing.'

This big reveal doesn't shock me. I guess I knew on some level it wasn't fate bringing us together. 'He pursued me?' I say. 'That's a compliment.'

'Is it?' Before I can answer he continues. 'What if you'd refused that first invitation? Would he have taken no for an answer?'

'I said yes.' But I know I haven't answered the question.

And from the slight shake of his head, I think Rory knows too.

'There have been complaints,' he says.

'Like?'

'I can't say any more.' Now he's not meeting my gaze.

'This is ridiculous.' Jason pursues what and who he wants and I like that about him. 'What kind of complaints?' I repeat.

Rory shuffles backwards, hands finding his pockets. 'It's not my place to share.'

Head down, I turn and walk away without looking back. My future – the future I want – is with Jason and I need to get some sleep. After all, I wouldn't want to look tired for the wedding.

25

SOPHIE – FRIDAY JANUARY 21ST
TWELVE YEARS AGO

The next afternoon, Ollie tramped in through the door and let it slam behind him.

Sophie had been reading on the couch and jumped at the unexpected crash.

Mum lifted her head from her traditional holiday jigsaw but didn't reprimand him. Of course not, it wouldn't do to have the favoured son offside. Sophie knew if she'd thrown a tantrum like he did at the restaurant Mum would be mad for days.

He leaned over Mum's shoulder studying the jigsaw. 'Is this just random flowers?'

She held up the box to show him the front. 'It's designer.'

He made a 'yuck' face but in the exaggerated way that made her smile. 'Yeah, um, great.' He seemed to think and then blurt, 'What about a family movie tonight to make up for me being a jerk?'

Mum's cheeks coloured with pleasure. 'That would be lovely. You can choose. I'm sure your dad won't mind staying in tonight.'

'What won't I mind?' Dad called out from where he was

filleting the fish he'd caught that morning. He came to the door, the sharp knife in his hand bloody and gross.

'A family movie tonight,' Mum said.

They shared a look.

'No romantic crap,' Dad said.

Sophie watched them, wondering why nobody thought to ask her what she might want. Sometimes she got so sick of the way Mum favoured Ollie and Dad just went along with it. She reckoned Pip was the only person in the world who liked her more than her brother.

She was still annoyed about it when she passed Ollie's room half an hour later. He was playing one of Gramps' old records, the scratchy sounds of the player nearly as loud as the saxophone solo.

Sophie winced. 'Do you really like this stuff?'

'You mean as opposed to Taylor whining about some guy breaking her heart or a musical theatre snorefest?' He shrugged. 'It makes Mum happy.'

'Firstly, she writes more than break-up songs, and, second, you're such a suck up.'

He grinned. 'Watch and learn, little sister. Keep her onside and she doesn't ask any questions.'

'I could tell her a thing or two.'

'But you won't.'

He was right. Telling Mum anything would probably end up with her in more trouble than Ollie and she'd never be allowed out with her brother again.

She was about to leave the doorway when Ollie sat up.

'What do you think of Kirsty?' Ollie asked.

Sophie remembered the way the girl's hand always curled around Ollie's arm. 'She's old,' Sophie said. 'And not in a cool way.' There was something about that girl that jarred. Made her think she was hiding something.

Ollie shook his head. 'Man, I do not understand girls.'

It was well after midnight and hours after their family movie had ended when Sophie got up to go to the bathroom, stopping by Ollie's room. There had been something about his smirk when she wished him goodnight that had stuck with her.

Empty. Now his sucking up all evening made sense.

She'd spring him when he got back and convince him to take her next time. She yawned, stretched and settled onto Ollie's bed.

His rough shake of her shoulder woke her up. She must have drifted off. 'What are you doing in my bed?' he whispered.

'What are you doing not in yours?'

'None of your business.'

Sophie sniffed. 'Have you been drinking?'

'What, are you? The fun police?'

'Mum would kill you if she—'

'Well, she won't because no one is going to tell her. Anyway, it's pretty hypocritical of them to lecture us when they're getting pissed every night.'

Sophie sat up. 'Yeah, but they're adults, they know what they're doing.'

He shook his head.

'What?' she asked.

'You know that life isn't one of those musicals you perform in, don't you? Shitty things happen.' He should have sounded scathing but there was reluctant admiration in his voice. 'Anyway, you won't tell on me.'

'I might.'

His head tilted, consideration on his face. 'No, you won't, because you'll come with me next time.'

Her heart leapt.

'And,' he continued, 'if you even think about breathing a word or a hint or whatever to the parents,' he paused, grinned. 'Then I'll tell Mum you've been screwing Pip.'

The offer and the threat.

He would do it, too. And Mum would believe him. Because he was Ollie, and Mum reckoned he'd dropped to her arms from the freaking stars. Her miracle baby, when doctors had told her she'd never conceive naturally. It didn't seem to matter that the doctor's doomsday prognosis should have made Sophie's conception even more of a marvel.

She nodded. 'Fine, but you'd better not go without me.'

'Deal.'

As she tiptoed back to her room, she couldn't help the bounce in her feet. Girls at school talked about their brothers breaking their stuff and giving them scars. *Her* brother had invited her to sneak out with him. It had only taken a little sisterly blackmail.

But she hadn't gotten details. She took a few quiet steps back along the corridor and was about to open Ollie's door when she heard something.

'I'm sure she's gone.' Ollie's voice, but with a strange husky tone.

Then the reply, 'I was sure she'd see me.'

Adele.

In Ollie's room! In the middle of the night! There was the rustle of Ollie's blanket and the softest sigh of the old bed springs.

Sophie's cheeks grew hot. *Go,* she told herself. But she stayed.

'This is for always?' Adele asked.

Despite the door between them, Sophie couldn't miss the need in that question.

'Always,' Ollie replied.

'Tell me,' Adele demanded.

'I love you now and I'll love you tomorrow,' Ollie murmured. 'We'll get through school and we'll get a place and no one will be able to tell us when we can be together.'

'Wait,' Adele said. 'Will we get married?'

'Of course,' Ollie replied. 'Whatever you want.'

'By the water, near sunrise, with bare feet, and flower crowns.' Adele sounded wistful. 'Maybe on a boat?'

'Whatever you want, baby girl. But there has to be cake.'

Creak.

Sophie spun towards the end of the hallway. Was Mum or Dad awake? There came the thud of a foot hitting the ground. Their door moved, revealing a glimpse of burgundy velvet. Mum's dressing gown.

Sophie stumbled forward, no longer trying to be quiet. Each step a loud thwack on the floor, impossible to miss, even if you were lovers caught up in each other's arms. Then, as Mum's frowning face appeared, Sophie added a loud groan.

'Sophie?' Mum asked blearily. 'Are you okay?'

More moaning, a clutch of her arms across her belly. 'I think I'm going to be sick.'

Mum hustled Sophie towards the tiny bathroom. 'What are you standing out here for then? Do you need a bucket?'

'Maybe,' she managed.

'I'll get you some water.'

'Thanks.' As Sophie sank to her knees in front of the rust-marked toilet bowl, she crossed her fingers she'd given Ollie and Adele enough time.

She made a few gagging noises, not difficult given the overpowering lavender scented cleaner Mum used, then flushed the toilet before Mum returned.

'Think maybe it was something I ate,' she said. Mentally she congratulated herself, talk about Tony Award winning performance.

Mum turned away from her as Ollie came down the hall rubbing his eyes as though he'd just awoken.

'Are you okay?' Mum asked him. 'Do you feel sick?'

'I'm good,' he said. 'Just wondered what all the noise was about.'

'Nothing for you to worry about,' Mum said. 'Go back to bed.'

He nodded, catching Sophie's gaze and giving her a tiny wink.

'I feel better already,' Sophie said brightly, heading for her room.

Mum frowned. 'Night then.'

When the door closed behind her, Sophie crossed to the window. She pressed against the cool glass looking for any sign of Adele. That had to be her slipping away around the corner of the shack next door. Sophie was about to head back to bed when something else moved. A figure scurrying away in the shadows by the shed.

Her belly twisted. Someone was out there spying on Adele and Ollie.

26

ADELE – THE BRIDE

FRIDAY, VERY EARLY – ONE DAY BEFORE THE WEDDING

My phone screen flashes, lighting up the small bedroom. I'm awake, but not really. Enough to register the glow on the screen that means I've received a message. It's a little past four a.m. and I'm too groggy to catch the contents of the text on the screen before it disappears. I snuggle deeper into the bed.

If it's important, they'll call, I think, before sinking back into a restless slumber.

It's after five when I surface again and the sky is beginning to lighten.

I remember the message, and unlock my phone to read it. What I see has me muffling a sob, my hand over my mouth. My eyes fill with hot tears. I blink them away, and read it again, and then again, hoping that this is some kind of nightmare.

But the words are still there.

I love you, but I can't do this.

I'm sorry.

Jason.

27

MELANIE – THE MOTHER

FRIDAY MORNING EARLY – ONE DAY BEFORE THE WEDDING

I bolt awake. My body is primed, and already in survival mode before my bleary brain can catch up. Then I make sense of what I'm hearing.

Somewhere nearby, someone is crying.

The crier's anguish snakes into the shack through door and window gaps, carried on ocean breezes. It's definitely coming from outside, but I can't tell any more than that. Is it from Tammy's place? Giovanni's?

I sit up, clutching Ollie's blanket across me while straining to hear, but the crying has stopped. Now, there's only the usual dawn quiet of the bay.

It's light enough that, looking around me, I can see the familiar outlines that make up Ollie's room. The crooked edge of the cupboard door, the chest of drawers squatting right up against the foot of the bed, and the roughly square frame of the old window.

I cross to it and peer out into the semi-darkness but there's no sign of anyone at all. There's a white ute over by the worksite for the new build across the road. It seems early for anyone to be out there but other than that it's deserted.

Maybe it was a nightmare. I touch my face, almost surprised to find my cheeks dry. I woke crying, more often than not, in those early months after Ollie died.

Losing Ollie literally took the joy from my world.

Parents love their children, but the bond between Ollie and me was different. His little face would look up at me like I could defeat every one of the superheroes in his comics. We shared endless cuddles over books or scraped knees. He was my world. And I was his, too.

Before the likes of Jason Ellingsworth got into his head.

Logically, teenagers are supposed to pull away from their parents but this was more. It was like that boy flipped a switch and completely changed Ollie's personality. He'd kept secrets, taken risks and ultimately followed Jason's example, and in doing so on that jetty, he'd paid the price.

It's time for Jason to pay, too.

I catch a glimpse of my lined and haggard face in the dusty window and flinch. What would Ollie think of my plans? I'm not sure he'd even recognise the bitter shell I've become.

I look away as a sudden slice of memory from that last summer catches me unawares. It's nothing extraordinary. In it, I'm simply walking back along the sand towards the shack from the jetty with Jim at my side. Sophie's earnestly twirling ahead of us to some musical number only she can hear, and Ollie lopes along a little behind. It's so vivid, I feel the warmth of the sunshine, taste the scent of someone cooking a barbecue dinner. I remember, I glanced back and caught Ollie's eye.

'Too cool to walk with your folks, are you?' I'd teased.

He'd smiled, jogged a few steps to catch up and slipped one lanky arm over my shoulder. The weight of it a gift I was only too willing to carry.
'Never.'

28

SOPHIE – SATURDAY JANUARY 22ND
TWELVE YEARS AGO

The next afternoon, Sophie sat a little away from the others on the jetty. Mum had taken some convincing to let her out of the house since she'd been so 'sick' but finally she'd relented.

'Here.'

A bottle of Coke appeared in front of Sophie. Tiny condensation droplets shining on the outside and bubbles fizzing up inside. Jason was holding it.

'I don't have any money,' she said.

He shrugged. 'My treat.'

The sun blazing overhead made refusal impossible. 'Thanks,' she said as he sat next to her.

As she opened the lid it hissed and the bubbles stung her nose, but the liquid inside was so cold and refreshing it was all she could do not to moan in pleasure.

Side by side, leaning back against the railing, they each drank in silence. Jason didn't look at his phone and he didn't scan the group further along the jetty for others to talk to.

She began to relax. So, this was what it was like to be accepted.

But before long the silence began getting to her. He'd bought her a drink; it was up to her to make conversation. Right then, a little distance away, Daniel stepped out onto the part of the jetty that jutted over the dark water between the two jetties, clambered onto the top of the railing and when everyone around him cheered, he launched himself into the water. When he climbed the ladder back up he was surrounded by slaps on the back and compliments from everyone, including Ollie.

'Have you been friends with Daniel long?' Sophie asked, then immediately wished the mum-sounding question back.

'A while.' Jason sipped more of his drink. 'He's okay when you get to know him. Like Ollie.'

'What do you mean?' Sophie frowned. 'That guy is nothing like my brother.'

'Ollie's definitely more golden-boy, I'll give him that. I mean, Adele probably thinks he's different. And Kirsty.'

There was something in Jason's voice that cramped her belly. 'What about her?'

'Adele? Well, she's—'

'No, not Adele.' She waited until he met her gaze. 'Kirsty. What about her?'

There was in odd gleam in Jason's eyes. Pleasure? Triumph? The reflection of the endless ocean? 'You should ask your brother.'

Sophie chewed on her lip, wishing she'd never accepted his stupid drink.

'Hey,' he said. 'I didn't mean to upset you.'

'I'm not upset.'

But she was glad when Daniel called him away and he left her with an apologetic smile. Thanks to Jason, she found herself watching how Kirsty seemed to touch Ollie nearly as often as Daniel, and each time Adele looked miserable.

Sophie was still musing about what it could mean, if anything, when hands covered her eyes from behind. The long, fine shape of his fingers as well as the choc mint scent of his favourite sweets told her who it was before Pip spoke. 'Guess who?'

'The local murderer Mum must know personally, the way she keeps warning me about them?' she guessed.

He laughed and she revelled in the vibrations from his chest. Maybe he'd seen Jason talking to her and come over because he was jealous. It would be so easy for him to wrap his arms around her and she could lean back into him and…

'I just wanted to tell you we're leaving,' he said, stepping away. 'Mum wants us home for some fancy afternoon tea for someone from Dad's work.'

'Sounds awful,' she said

No wonder Adele had seemed sad, she probably didn't want to be away from Ollie all afternoon. Surely that meant that Ollie and she would sneak out tonight.

She called out after Pip, 'If Adele invites you anywhere please just say yes.'

His head tilted in question. 'Yes?'

'Yes.'

When Sophie trailed Ollie into the shack at dinnertime, Dad lay on the couch, mouth open and snoring and Mum was banging plates by the sink. 'You're late,' she said without looking up.

'It's not even—' Ollie began.

'I told you we'd eat at six,' Mum continued, cutting him off.

A glance at the clock told Sophie it was only a few minutes after but clearly Mum wasn't in the mood to hear it.

'I reckon the cold ham and salad will be fine,' Ollie said.

Mum spun around, swaying a little as she came to a halt. 'I do not need that attitude from you.' Some of her words slurred.

Ollie's eyes flashed. 'You don't need another drink either, but I doubt that will stop you.'

Sophie smothered a gasp.

Mum was too intent on Ollie to notice. Her eyes narrowed. 'Congratulations. Consider yourself grounded.'

Ollie opened his mouth to argue, but instead he stormed into to his room and slammed the door.

29

ADELE – THE BRIDE

FRIDAY MORNING – ONE DAY BEFORE THE WEDDING

My fingers tremble as I hit the button on my keyring that will let me into the car park beneath Jason's building right in the centre of Adelaide. With the central market so close, the faint noises of vendors setting up for the day mingle with the sounds of the early commuters on nearby streets.

The gate to the complex slides open, whisper quiet, and I drive in and park in the empty space next to Jason's car. He's here, as I guessed. And he hasn't prevented my entry.

Mum, who promised to keep any questions at bay while I was gone, assured me – while practically shoving me out the door – he wouldn't have messaged if he didn't want me to follow. Him ignoring my calls on the drive doesn't fill me with confidence, but I have to believe she's right, because I can't stomach the alternative.

The lift is waiting, and a moment later I've punched in the code for the penthouse and I'm rising towards the top floor.

He wants to marry me.

I repeat the mantra I've had on replay in my head for the last two hours. This is simply a blip or a test or…

Or he saw you making out with his best friend and changed his mind.

At the thought of Rory, I touch my fingertips to guilty lips. No one saw us. Certainly not Jason. If he had, there'd have been bloodshed.

It doesn't take long for the lift to climb the twenty-seven storeys to the penthouse apartment but I use the few seconds to check my reflection in the dark glass wall. Knowing Jason's preferences, I chose my dusky pink dress with its hand-crafted detailing, knee length and tie waist. The curls from last night only needed a light brush and I masked the black circles under my eyes with concealer and a gulped energy drink on the way here.

The reflected woman smiles and if I didn't know better I'd think she was happy. Hopefully, he'll see the well-put-together wife he wanted and change his mind. Then the lift doors are opening and I'm approaching the light oak door at the end of the small hallway.

It opens before I can decide whether to knock and Jason's standing there.

Shit.

I'm not surprised by his neat navy polo short and pressed linen shorts, his smoothly shaven jaw nor his freshly showered scent, but I was hoping for something less measured.

I'd pictured this on the way here, letting myself drift into fantasy where he instantly realised he'd made a mistake and I fell into his arms. I should have known better; that isn't us. This needs to be played entirely differently.

'I came,' I say simply.

He opens the door wider. 'Then I guess you'd better come in.' And there it is, vibrating beneath his usual polished tones, a tremor of uncertainty. In that instant I realise he wasn't certain I'd come after him.

I swallow past a nervous lump in my throat and let him lead me inside as though I haven't been in the luxurious space before, haven't admired the view across the city from the curved balcony, cooked in the stunning marble and oak kitchen, nor had sex in front of the spectacular fireplace on the plush white rug.

He's opened the stacker doors so the inside blends to the balcony and he leads me to the outside lounge drenched in early morning sunshine, where there's a jug of iced water on a tray with a single, clean glass.

'Would you like a drink?' he asks.

'I didn't come here for refreshments.' It comes out snappier than I intend, and I take a deep breath. 'No, thank you.'

I sit at his direction and Jason sits on the adjacent chair, close enough that he could reach out and place a hand on my knee. He doesn't. His phone is lying on the glass coffee table, its screen dark. Suddenly everything clicks.

'You got another message,' I say. 'Didn't you?'

His throat works like he's trying to decide what to say. 'There have been more.'

I hold his gaze, my blood pounding in my ears. 'Show me.'

But he doesn't move to his phone, instead crossing to where his laptop is open on the marble kitchen bench. As he returns to his seat, a press of his finger on the button unlocks the device. There, cascaded on the screen are windows open to his different social media accounts. And in every one there is a private message.

Do us all a favour and call it off.

End this joke.

Don't marry that bitch.

My fingers tremble and I press my hands together so I don't reach out and stab at the delete key. Who would do this? Why?

'They're not why I left,' he says.

'Just a happy coincidence?'

'God, Adele, don't make this something it's not.'

I lift my head. 'Tell me, then. You got me here, I'm listening. Tell me what's going on and why you decided to call off the wedding.'

'Because I don't think we should get married.'

For a moment, I picture myself standing, sighing a pretty sigh, like the old fifties movie stars were so good at doing, then walking out the door. But there's too much between us.

'Why?'

'Because of you.'

My stomach is knotted. There's so much that he could mean by those few words. Because of me and Rory? Because of me and Ollie? Because, when it comes down to it, I'm too much like my mother to snare someone successful?

'You'll need to give me more.'

His jaw tightens. 'Because you have doubts.'

There it is, spoken aloud despite all he doesn't know. Conversations with Katja. Inability to sleep. Fooling around with the best man. None of it screams certainty. And that's without being unable to imagine that come Saturday night I'll be Mrs Jason Ellingsworth.

He's waiting for me to respond. A pulse now beating in his throat, veins standing out in his neck.

Fuck, I just missed my cue for instant reassurance.

The longer it goes without me saying anything, the more important my next words become.

'If you know me at all, you know I don't make decisions lightly,' I say carefully. I take a deep breath and look him right in the eye. 'And I don't have doubts about this wedding.'

His head falls into his hands on a gulped sob.

And that's when I understand just how much he wanted to hear me say that. When he lifts his head, his eyes shine with unshed tears. 'I want to believe you.'

I blink back my own emotion, finding it impossible not to be touched that a man who's usually so in control is letting me see into his soul. 'Then believe me.'

'If I come back then, that's it, we're doing this.'

'Yes.'

He moves to kneel in front of me, cupping my face in both hands. 'I want this.' He kisses me reverently. 'Adele, I want this desperately. I cannot picture a future without you by my side. You alone know how I've spent so long too terrified to picture a future at all.'

Our foreheads touch. 'I do.'

Because he shared his secret with me.

He kept the diagnosis and treatment private from most of his friends and family, deciding, with some overblown desire not to cause pain, to fight the battle on his own. He wouldn't have even told me if I hadn't found out accidentally when a treatment made him so ill he had to cancel a date, and I came around to deliver a care package.

It's part of the reason our wedding has happened so fast. The reason we went from casual to serious so quickly. Jason's brush with his own mortality has made him determined not to waste a day.

'Lying alone there in that hospital bed after my first surgery, I feared I wouldn't get well enough to marry. I didn't think I'd have anyone in my life to stay alive for.' He pauses and I brush away a single tear from his cheek. 'And then, I reconnected with you. Everything changed, and I started to believe in tomorrow and all the tomorrows after that. But I need you to be all in.'

'I am,' I say, this time without delay.

'I want you by my side tomorrow. I want you there in six months when my check-up is good news. I want that slim hope that I'll be able to have children to prove correct, and us to make a family. I want you there in five years when they tell me I'm still all clear.'

I entwine my fingers around his neck and pull him close. 'Everything will be okay.'

He relaxes into me. I hold him like that until the unspoken clamour of all the people waiting on us back at Refuge Bay becomes too loud to ignore. When I ease back he takes the hint and stands. He holds out a hand and I let him pull me to my feet.

'Shall we?' he asks.

I nod and he makes short work of gathering up his things. I try not to notice that he didn't bring much with him besides his laptop. Likely he left in a rush.

Or I've been played, and he never intended to stay away.

I ignore the nagging voice in my head. Barely fifteen minutes here and I've gotten what I came for. He's coming back to get married and as long as Mum has done her job, it will be like none of this has happened.

But somehow, as we take the lift down and walk side by side across the car park towards our cars, I grasp that this victory is completely his. Part of why I want this wedding is to be partners, and the balance is off.

'I'm all in,' I say.

He nods.

'You should know, however, I'm not the kind of woman to be messed with.'

'I know.'

Hopefully, he understands the warning.

It's only when I'm getting back into my car that I see the small lump of plastic on the dashboard. I pick it up, but slowly, the way I'd approach something that could bite.

And in a sense it does.

It's one of those plastic cake toppers found in cheap wedding stores. Correction, it's half of one. The bride is alone; the place where her hand would have joined the groom has been precisely cut free. Her separateness is oddly unsettling, as though part of her is missing. However, it's the bride herself that has dread setting like concrete in my stomach. Where her face should be is melted, the plastic deformed and warped.

Someone has left this here. I scan the surrounds but of course there's no one there. Maybe I missed it earlier. My hand closes around the misshapen figure like I can squeeze the truth from it.

Who is behind this?

30

MELANIE – THE MOTHER

FRIDAY MORNING – ONE DAY BEFORE THE WEDDING

Friday morning, I shower then wrap myself in my dressing gown and shuffle out to the kitchen in desperate need of coffee and something to soothe the jitters from another bad night's sleep. Did I hear someone crying or was it another nightmare? There's nothing on the wedding party's socials and I can't ask Sophie if she knows anything since as usual she's not here when I need her, having apparently gone for a walk.

Strange, because she's never been one for exercise. I bet she wouldn't be missing in action so often if Pip was here. Or maybe she would. For all their friendship, she must be jealous that Adele's brother is living her childhood dream.

I'm gulping down coffee, scalding my throat when a message flashes on the wedding party group chat.

> Morning tea cancelled. Bride and groom required elsewhere this morning.

The message is from Tammy, and when Dorothy replies questioning what could be so important, the mother of the bride refuses to answer. However, her addition of the camera and newspaper emojis and three smiling faces aren't exactly subtle. I'm not surprised given Jason's money and Adele's looks that their wedding would make the social pages. I bet Tammy's beside herself with glee.

It leaves me with an aching head and time on my hands.

A couple of painkillers washed down with whiskey does little to help the thudding from last night's drinks, but it dulls the pain enough that I can think straight again.

That overheard conversation between Mayor Fiona and Jason at the party nags at me. I was so busy making myself scarce when I thought they would catch me listening that the details have vanished, but there was an agreement and maybe a threat. But who was the one making it?

I was sure for a second out there on the deck that Fiona was about to reveal something important. Could there be more than council disagreement behind her antagonism towards me? Something from the past?

There's a brief biography and her vision for the area on Fiona Lewis's mayoral page on the council website. These I can practically recite, and I've had more than a passing look at her social media. Nothing on either suggests a reason for her to dislike me.

However, I haven't tried exploring her work history. I pull up the search engine on my phone and have to squint to read the letters as I type them in.

Seconds later the local hospital website loads. Although limited, it's surprisingly up to date. It tells me the facility services the town of Tuckersfield and the surrounding area, including Refuge Bay. It includes visiting hours, car parking, disabled access and emergency services. However, it does not list employee information. I'm guessing whoever is in charge doesn't want patients looking up details on who to sue.

Desperate now, I type her name straight into the search function. The first few options are those I've already discarded – work and personal – but the next one has me putting the phone face down so I don't have to see the words.

But I've seen enough to know I was right. The link is to an article about Ollie's death.

Bracing myself, I begin to read. I skim the article for the mayor's name, even as I try to avoid taking in anything not related to her. But no matter how hard I try, phrases jump out at me.

'Spike in drug-related youth deaths.'

'City visitors creating a burden of harm in regional area.'

'I spoke to him and he told me everything. I have sources.'

All of them are well-timed jabs at my chest and stomach. One punch, two. Each word part of a rain of blows that land in my most sensitive places.

I force myself to read on. Past the journalist's quotes from unnamed sources about Ollie mixing with dangerous people, looking across every line for her name. Despite trying to focus on finding mentions of Fiona, I can't help the familiar spiral of rage at the implications made in the papers at the time. The journalist used my boy as the poster boy example of holiday culture gone wrong.

The edge of the phone bites into my hand and I have to force myself to relax. They were fired, it's over. But I know it never really will be, not when this kind of thing stays on the internet for anyone to read.

I don't care what the toxicology reports said. Just because there might have been something in his bloodstream, it doesn't mean he took anything. We see all the time in the media where girls are warned about predators spiking drinks, but never boys. Or given the more rudimentary technology back then it could have been some kind of false positive. Or a lab tech error.

I know… I *knew* Ollie.

He would not have taken the cocktail of drugs the coroner says they found in his system. I'm no fool, I know he was led astray that summer and I have to live with having allowed that to happen. If anything, it was Jason. Jason who had the undesirable friends. Jason who tried to lead my boy off course. Jason who succeeded.

The text on my phone screen swims in front of my stinging eyes but I drag in deep, steadying breaths.

And there it is, right near the end. *Dr Fiona Lewis*. Although the article doesn't say specifically whether she was involved at the scene or the hospital, she was asked for comment about the cause of death.

> 'Although he appears to have drowned, we can't rule out that there may have been contributing factors.'

My mouth twists in a snarl. *Contributing factors*. It's not hard to read between the lines. The journalist with their axe to grind certainly did, linking what happened to Ollie with their exposé on what they termed 'the hidden drug culture' of the area.

Apparently they'd spent months undercover collecting information.

That journalist made my son's death the footnote in their campaign against the whole region. Made it seem like it was inevitable that there would be casualties. That my boy was nothing more than the end result of whatever their investigation had suggested was seething underneath the surface of Refuge Bay and the surrounding regional towns. This article was one in a larger series railing against the bad influence of city holiday makers and the vices they brought to the vulnerable in the area.

And in every article, Ollie's death was mentioned.

At first raising the possibility, then implying, then eventually outright questioning whether, basically, Ollie Rhodes got what he deserved when he jumped off the jetty that day.

'He was a good boy,' I whisper, my throat tight.

Now I know she was there; I need to know about her and Jason. It won't change my plans, but I don't like surprises.

I settle down on the couch and bring up Jason's social media pages and business site, along with council decisions on development in the area. I shouldn't be surprised at how many projects he has in the pipeline, considering that garish place he's built next to his grandmother's and the way money practically radiates from the man. His family are well off but he has wealth on a different level.

Is he simply a very good businessman or is there something else behind his meteoric rise? And what does it have to do with our lovely mayor?

There is a connection between Fiona and Jason, and I'm going to find it.

31

SOPHIE – SUNDAY JANUARY 23RD

TWELVE YEARS AGO

Following Ollie's lead, Sophie stepped up onto the edge of the chest of drawers and hitched her leg over the windowsill, then dropped to the ground. She waited, hardly daring to breathe while he propped the window back in place, then followed him out to the dirt road. Every scrape of her foot had her listening for Mum or Dad but soon they were several shacks away.

'What are we doing?' she whispered. 'Are we meeting the others? Aren't you grounded?'

He stopped. 'Lose the billion questions or I send you back. I don't care what you tell Mum.'

She shut her mouth and continued to walk next to him in silence, sometimes needing to skip to keep up with his longer legs. They cut through one of the empty blocks to the sand. She wanted to ask more questions but instead tried to take in her surroundings. The moon shone out over the sea and most of the shacks were in complete darkness. Her blood thrummed through her veins and she tried not to imagine Mum right now checking one of their rooms.

No, with the amount of wine she and Dad had shared over the dinner Ollie refused to eat, she'd be bound to sleep through.

About ten minutes later, they climbed the steps up from the sand to find the path deserted. Ollie stopped beneath one of the small, flickering lights to check his phone. Before Sophie could summon the nerve to ask why, Adele's willowy figure solidified from the shadows along the road, and next to her was Pip.

He'd come.

Sophie's insides did a little dance at the sight, but she tried to project casual. The wind making her eyes water made that difficult.

'Are you crying?' Pip asked when he was close enough.

Not the 'you look stunning' reaction she'd hoped for, a realisation highlighted by Ollie and Adele's greeting kiss.

'No,' she snapped. 'It's windy.'

'No need to bite my head off,' he replied.

At least Ollie and Adele had finished their smooching and she didn't have to answer.

'Hurry up, you two,' Ollie said, already heading towards the jetty.

Usually, Sophie would have had a comeback but the whole sneaking out with Pip – even if technically he'd come with his sibling – had her not quite thinking straight.

'Far out,' Daniel muttered as they approached where he stood with some of the others. 'This a fucking crèche or something?'

Sophie ignored him. Who cared what he said, when Pip had snuck out to be with her?

'So, what are we doing?' Adele asked.

'There's a party,' Jason said. He shifted his weight from one foot to the other. 'It's an underground thing at the yacht club. You need to know the password to get in and—'

A punch in the arm from Daniel cut the smaller boy off.

Daniel scowled and waved at Sophie and Pip. 'It's not for babies.'

Ollie clapped him on the back. 'They're fine, I promise. And Sophie's cashed up to make the buy to make sure we all have a good night.'

'I am?' she said, then seeing Ollie's glare she quickly corrected herself. 'I am.'

She could practically feel Pip's dismay but didn't let herself look at him. Ollie knew what he was doing.

Daniel stared Ollie down and Sophie got the feeling this antagonism between them was about more than just her and Pip being there.

'She's buying then?' Daniel said eventually. 'Wouldn't want this to be your way of wimping out.'

Ollie ignored the chicken sounds coming from some of the boys. 'I'm good.'

As they set off for the party, Pip seemed to hang back.

'Don't bail,' Sophie said. 'I can't do this alone.'

'None of this is really my scene.' He must have seen the hurt in her face. 'Except you,' he added.

'Then come, but only talk to me,' she said. 'And Adele is here.'

They both knew the older boys wouldn't be seen to tease him too badly for fear of getting on his big sister's bad side.

He sighed. 'When you're famous, I expect front row seats on opening night.'

'Forget being in the audience, you'll be there on stage with me.' She linked her fingers with his, trying not to show the thrills the casual contact sent through her. Pip liked her; she knew it. If he could just see her as more than a friend they'd be perfect together.

This time of night the yacht club appeared deserted but as they drew close Sophie could feel, somewhere deep in her chest, the throb of the music coming from inside. They repeated the password that Ollie had whispered to them to some scary-looking bearded guy and were allowed through to where everyone seemed older and cooler. The pale pink of Sophie's dress suddenly felt childish but she kept her head high walking up the stairs then through to the back of the place. Wearing black was for sheep without imagination.

Standing with her out on the balcony, away from the crowded, smoky dancefloor throbbing with pierced bodies, Pip rubbed at his jaw. 'Seriously, Sophie, we don't belong here.'

Part of her agreed, but maybe the yacht club wasn't the problem. Maybe they were. She had an idea. 'Let's not be us, then.'

'I don't understand.'

She nudged him, loving the excuse for contact and took a breath, her brain working to catch up with her mouth as her spark of an idea crystallised. 'Allow me to introduce myself, I am Duchess Sophia.' She held out her hand as though she were wearing a long white glove and being introduced to a nobleman.

Pip hesitated, then grinned. 'Delighted to meet you, I'm sure. And I am Prince Ky.' He took her hand and kissed the air above it with a bow.

She hoped the darkness meant he couldn't tell that the air

kiss had spread goosebumps along her arm. As long as she ignored dread lurking in her belly about whatever Daniel was expecting her to buy, the shouts from the throng of sweaty people and the occasional sounds of glass smashing, they had the perfect romantic spot.

Maybe tonight was the night Pip would realise they were in love.

32

MELANIE – THE MOTHER

FRIDAY, EARLY AFTERNOON – ONE DAY BEFORE THE WEDDING

A noise from out the other side of the shack draws me from the porch, through the living area to the screen door where Sophie just went out. It wasn't a wail, because Sophie wouldn't be so dramatic these days, but as she stares down at her trendy little hatchback car, she gets awfully close.

'What's wrong?' I ask, stepping outside. And then, registering the time, I add, 'Aren't you supposed to be at the wedding venue?'

Although the family morning tea was cancelled, whatever occupied the bride and groom hasn't changed the plans for the rest of the day and a guided tour of the wedding venue is in the schedule for the afternoon. This one is a bridal party only affair, alas.

Sophie's jaw juts out in that insolent way she's always had about her. 'My car isn't going anywhere.'

'What's wrong with it? Is it the battery because I could try to—'

'No.' Her dark eyebrows scrunch up disdainfully. 'Flat tyre. Two in fact. Some idiots vandalising the place, probably.

I have a spare but no one will get out here in time to get another. Adele is going to be pissed.'

'Can't you get a ride with them?'

She shakes her head. 'They left already. Ugh, this is a nightmare. She's going to think I'm deliberately bailing on her.'

Somehow I manage to keep myself from pointing out Sophie has brought this on herself. If I was Adele, I'd have cut her from the bridal party months ago.

'I could take you,' I offer.

Sophie straightens. 'You're not busy?'

'I can spare a few hours.' I try not to sound too enthusiastic in case Sophie refuses just to spite me. 'Unless you have a better idea?'

Sophie checks the time and then does a slow circuit of her car as though to make sure she hasn't imagined the damage. 'I could borrow your car?'

'Sorry. If something happened with you driving, my insurance wouldn't cover it.'

'It's fortunate you're here then.'

I can't miss the sarcasm in her voice, but I ignore it. 'Yes. Unless you want to try and get an Uber. Or a taxi. You might get lucky.'

'But we're a long way out,' she finishes drily. 'And it probably won't get me there in time.'

I nod.

Her next sigh sounds a lot like defeat and it's followed by a simple, 'Okay.'

Something has changed. Yesterday, before the spa session, she wouldn't have given a second thought to letting the bride down.

Today, it isn't an option.

Then there's the outfit. Her loose white shirt tied over a short black dress is positively sunshiny compared to her usual attire.

I almost ask what's caused the difference but I don't want her to change her mind.

'Shall we get going then?' I say instead.

Sophie grunts something that I take as agreement. I grab my handbag from the bench, but it's the automatic touch of the puzzle piece in my pocket that has me risking Sophie's wrath and taking a few extra seconds to take a quick detour and lock up properly.

By the time my phone tells me to turn at the huge gates signalling Creekwood Estate, Sophie's only a few minutes late. We follow a sweeping driveway through the working vineyards, past a picturesque, heart-shaped dam that I saw in the featured photos on the website and up to the venue proper that turns out to be several buildings huddled together at the top of a hill.

We park and Sophie doesn't argue when I get out of the car. She's long past needing me to walk her inside but this is my reward for being a good Samaritan and driving her. I need a sneak peek at the venue.

We follow signs to reception. I veer along the cobblestone path to our right, earning myself a grimace from Sophie, but allowing me to have a look in through the open chapel doors and take in its white walls, the light streaming through the stained glass and the rustic wooden pews. I know from the website that those hiring the wedding venue can choose between the chapel or the romantic lawn setting for the service. I'm guessing from the size of the chapel it was guest numbers that made Adele and Jason choose the outdoor option.

The discreet desk is empty, but there are voices coming from the Barn Room, and the demanding, strident pitch clearly belongs to Tammy. Sophie is already heading that way, not waiting to see if I trail her, which of course I do.

As we push open and step through the huge double rustic barn doors I have to muffle a gasp. The website does not do this room justice. From the rough exposed redbrick walls to the wooden ceiling arching above the enormous beams that cross high overhead, to the deck decorated with string lights and taking in a stunning view of rolling green and distant blue, it's the stuff magazine photoshoots are made from.

Adele, Tammy and the other bridesmaid are standing by the huge windows that line one wall on what appears to be a dancefloor. There's no sign of Jason. The three women turn as one when the door clunks closed behind us.

I brace for my reception, but if the just sucked a lemon sourness of Tammy's mouth is any hint, then I should probably have waited in the car.

33

ADELE – THE BRIDE

FRIDAY AFTERNOON – ONE DAY BEFORE THE WEDDING

'What are you doing here?'

My question is directed at Melanie, but it's Sophie who leads the two of them across the room, her boots loud on the polished concrete floor.

'It was in my schedule,' Sophie says defensively. 'Should I leave?'

My teeth come together and I exhale carefully; she doesn't know what I've already been through today. 'No, please don't, I want you here to run through the service.'

'I think she means me,' Melanie says.

'Brilliant deduction,' Mum mutters from behind me.

I turn and touch her arm. 'Could you make sure Jason doesn't need me?' I nod towards the kitchens, willing her not to make this harder.

'My pleasure.' She hurries off with a final glare at Melanie, and I know she'll make sure he doesn't return before our unexpected guest is gone.

I can't guess how Jason might react to Melanie's presence, and after what happened this morning, the last thing I need is Ollie's mother to create a scene. I know she's hurting but I can't have her ruining my wedding.

'Don't mind me,' Melanie says cheerfully. 'I was simply making sure Sophie got in okay, and taking the chance to have a bit of a sticky beak.' Her smile is warm, neighbourly, completely unlike the mess she was last night.

'You could have come with us,' I say to Sophie. 'Saved your mum the trouble.'

Her cheeks flush. 'I had an unavoidable work call that I thought wouldn't be a problem but then had a flat tyre last minute.'

'Two, actually,' Melanie is quick to inform me. 'Probably teenagers, or she's really unlucky.'

My belly constricts. It could be kids at a loose end, or it could be another example of trying to mess with the wedding. Although, why damage Sophie's car and not mine or Jason's?

Why do this at all?

Melanie is still speaking, and I have to force myself to concentrate.

'I'll wait in the car,' she says to Sophie. 'Come out when you're done.'

'No,' I say quickly. 'Sophie can come back to the bay with us; it will save you waiting.'

Melanie slumps a little. 'That's so kind of you, Adele. Do you think anyone would mind if I use the bathroom first?'

'That shouldn't be a problem.'

'See you back at the shack,' she says to Sophie. Then she heads back out towards reception with a final wave of farewell to me.

With Melanie gone, I breathe easier. Although I felt sorry for her last night standing there with all those pitying faces, her accusations were way out of line. Although Jason seems fine now, more of the same is a stress we don't need.

Mum returns, cheerful when she sees Melanie's gone, and corners Sophie to show her the menu. It means only Katja follows me when I slip outside onto the deck under the guise of checking out the view.

I stand by the very edge, overlooking the lush green of the grounds, trying to picture myself here tomorrow getting married. For the ceremony, we chose the outdoor spot, which is a little below here. Green, leafy trees provide a natural canopy for the guests, augmented with subtle extra shading. Lines of chairs draw the eye to a hand-crafted oak pavilion, giving a framed postcard view to the vines. White silken folds sweeping down from the highest point shelter where Jason and I will stand, raised so we can be seen by our guests. Some of the flowers are already in place between the chairs, along with small wooden barrels for bottles of water in case it's warm.

It's stunning, and exactly the kind of place I might have chosen, although it was Jason who found it and Jason who put everything in place.

I can't appreciate it though, stuck as I am on what happened to delay Sophie. What if someone meant to vandalise my car but damaged hers by mistake?

At least with Jason out of sight, I can stop flinching every time he looks at his phone, wondering what new message he's receiving. But I can still imagine.

> Get out while you can. It's not too late to walk away. She's not who you think she is.

Katja's hand on my shoulder jerks me from my spiralling thoughts.

'Are you okay?' she asks.

'I'm fine.' I keep my gaze firmly on the view but I can still feel her shaking her head.

'This is more than just nerves.'

So far I've managed to avoid being alone with her and thus answering questions about this morning. The plans that felt too solid to budge are now more like a tower of cards. One wrong move and it will fall apart.

'Where were you?' she asks. 'And don't give me the media emergency crap.'

I sneak a glance sideways, making sure we're alone out here. 'It's complicated.'

She folds her arms.

It's not like I tell Katja everything. I know the best relationships require a certain filtering of the truth, but she's pissed off now and she has a way of getting answers a private detective would envy.

I sigh. 'I drove to Adelaide.'

'Because?'

'Because…' I exhale carefully and turn to look her right in the eye. 'Because that's where I figured Jason would have gone when I got the message that he'd called off the wedding.'

Her blue eyes widen such that I fear for their continued attachment to her head and she whistles softly between her teeth. 'That, I did not expect.'

'Me neither.' I try to keep my tone light but some of my hurt must shine through.

Sympathy creases her features. 'What happened?'

I shrug. 'Well, I talked him out of cancelling so everything's great, I guess.'

'It doesn't sound great.' She hesitates, glances back towards the windows. 'Did you stop to think that maybe this was your opportunity to...'

'No.' The lie I come back at her with is as vehement as I can make it.

'But Adele—'

'But nothing. There's too much at stake with this wedding.'

'This is the rest of your life we're talking about. You should make sure this is what you really want. That Jason is *who* you really want.'

'What's that supposed to mean?'

Another glance and she lowers her voice further. 'I know about Rory.'

There it is.

Hearing it said aloud by my bridesmaid isn't the shock it should be. She's observant and maybe I've been pushing things, guilt making me want to get caught.

But now the moment is here, I want it gone. 'What about him?'

She shakes her head. 'Don't make me say it aloud.'

I drop my gaze and try not to cry. I feel her arm come around my shoulder. It's nice to have someone care about me. Not like Mum, worrying I'll ruin her chance at paying off her debts. 'It's all in the past,' I say, ignoring what happened on the beach. 'If I'd known things with Jason would get serious I wouldn't have... we weren't...' I hear the words coming out my mouth and hate myself a little.

'You have to do what's best for you. If you want someone else then surely that's telling you something.'

'You don't understand.'

'Then tell me.'

'I can't leave Jason,' I whisper.

'Why? He'll be hurt, sure, but he'll get over it. As gorgeous as that little setup down there is, you don't have to be standing there tomorrow.' She rubs my back. And I can almost feel her brain whirring, practically hear her thinking. 'There's more, isn't there? Is he threatening you?'

I want to laugh at how quick she is to assume I have some excuse for what I've done. I do not deserve her. We've just accepted without further discussion that I am screwing the best man and she wants to get mad at Jason.

'I can't leave Jason because I couldn't live with myself if I did.'

'What is it he has over you?'

She's so close to asking the right question, but there are limits to what I will share. Not about the past, not about my foolish parents. It's time to end this discussion and move forward to what should be the happiest goddamn day of my life.

I swallow, and then I tell her what I promised Jason I wouldn't tell anyone.

'Jason has cancer.'

34

MELANIE – THE MOTHER

FRIDAY AFTERNOON – ONE DAY BEFORE THE WEDDING

In my search for a bathroom facility I don't need, I manage to explore most of the inside of the venue except the kitchen, since that's where Jason must be. I glimpsed the miniature 'message in a bottle' wedding favours, and admired the hand-crafted place cards.

I linger in the elegant restroom with its stylish and invitingly lit mirrors, marble sinks and a rest area complete with seating and a fireplace. There are freshly laundered white towels and several different hand soaps and lotions. I try each of them, and am just settling on the basil and mandarin as my favourite when the door opens. Adele freezes in the doorway, her lips parting in a silent 'oh' of dismay.

'I was just leaving,' I say quickly.

She says nothing, but the clench of her jaw suggests a woman who came in here looking for escape. Not the actions of a woman keen to get married tomorrow.

'You look like you need a bit of a breather,' I say gently. 'I can recommend the couch, it's even more comfortable that it looks.'

She perches on the edge of the white chaise longue and

although she's upright, I get the feeling it's all she can do not to collapse with her head in her hands.

'Do you want to talk about it?' I ask.

'I'm fine.'

It's clear she's anything but. I sit beside her. 'You can talk to me.'

She sighs. 'I should get back out there. They'll be waiting on me to make decisions.'

'About?'

'Cake service. Drinks. Exit music.' Another sigh, this one shaky. She stands, and swallows. 'Honestly, it's fine. I just thought we'd decided all of these details already.'

I stand too, blocking her path. 'You don't have to do this,' I say, not trying to hide my urgency. 'You don't have to go through with this wedding.'

She bites her lip. 'I didn't say I—'

The door bursts open and Tammy enters in a cloud of cloying perfume. 'What's going on here?'

'Nothing,' Adele says quickly, but she sniffs a little.

'We're just talking,' I add.

Tammy's arms cross in front of her low-cut top. 'What are you telling her?'

'I'm not telling her anything, I'm listening,' I retort. 'You should try it.'

'None of this is about you,' Tammy says, stepping closer so she's right in front of me and I can see her eyelashes are clumped together by her mascara.

'Well, she's clearly upset.' I wave at the poor girl. 'Adele is making a serious commitment and she should be sure.'

Tammy's lip curls. 'Because you know so much about marriage? You can't even keep your own husband.'

I laugh. 'I'm no expert, obviously, but I'm not sure turning a blind eye to years of screwing around and accepting whatever bad hand you're dealt makes for a perfect marriage either.'

'Enough,' Adele says.

We both turn to look at her.

'Now is not the time for any of this,' she says.

'No.' I insist. 'That's where you're wrong. Now is perfect if it means you make the right decision. It's not too late.' My heart is thrumming with excitement. It couldn't possibly be this easy, could it? 'Any arrangements can be unarranged.'

'No,' Tammy snarls. 'They can't. And before you say it, this isn't just about the money. There are people involved, feelings involved.'

Adele holds her hand up to halt Tammy's tirade. 'Stop it. I'm not going to back out. So you can relax.'

'I am relaxed,' Tammy snaps.

'Or at least your priorities are,' I say.

'How dare you?' Her hands reach out and somehow she's closed the distance between us. Her hand is raised and red-tipped nails are coming for my eyes.

I just stand there. Too stunned to move. Too shocked to even make a sound.

Only Adele's hand on Tammy's chest stops those nails dragging down my face. 'Mum, enough.' And then to me, 'Please, leave.' Then she places her arm around her mother's shoulders and leads her to the door without looking back.

I take a moment to gather myself. A sip from the bottle in my handbag helps to settle me and by the time I've popped in a mint I can almost laugh about Tammy losing her temper.

Almost.

There was a second there when I didn't recognise one of

my oldest friends. If not for Adele, I think she would have hurt me. I'll need to remember that.

I head straight for the car park before they call security to escort me from the premises. Head down, I'm not really paying attention to my surrounds. I'm at the end of the cobblestone path, in touching distance of my car bonnet, when a faint crunch of gravel makes me look behind.

'What the hell?' I cry, my hand going to my chest.

Jason is standing close enough that I can smell the smooth, musky scent of his aftershave and see where his navy polo shirt has a few tiny white spots at the collar, like he's just taken a bite of some sugar-dusted dessert.

'Were you going to leave without saying goodbye?' he asks. His polite question doesn't take away from the fact that he seems to be towering over me.

I offer a sarcastic wave. 'Goodbye.'

His hand comes out and he grips my elbow before I can move to the car, the contact unlikely to be seen by anyone looking from the venue, but the imprint of his fingers vice-like.

'What the fuck were you doing in my house last night?'

I blink. Try to match his words with his pleasant expression.

I want to snatch my arm away and flee but making another scene so hot on the heels of what happened in the bathroom would probably stretch even Adele's patience. 'I was invited. It was a party.'

'Not in my bedroom, it wasn't. You need to stay away from my private spaces or you'll be sorry.'

'I didn't go in your bedroom.'

He leans so close his breath warms my cheek. 'I'm not a fucking child, Melanie. I know you were listening.'

I think back to my hasty escape. I was sure I got out of

sight before I could be seen by anyone coming out of that bedroom. Of course, he must have cameras.

'You invited people into your home,' I say. 'It's not a crime to go looking for a bathroom.'

'You were sneaking around.'

'My bladder isn't what it used to be.'

'What did you hear?' The question is ground out from between clenched teeth, and his grip tightens to painful.

I'm debating how to answer when he stares at me so hard I fear he sees right into my frantic brain.

The tension in him lessens and he drops his hand. 'You heard nothing. Or you wouldn't be here alone with me now.'

I don't point out that he's the one who cornered me. 'I don't understand.'

'You don't need to. This whole thing is your fault, really.'

I reel back at the truth of it. I know that. God, how I know that. But he couldn't, could he?

He shakes his head. 'That's right, your precious Ollie didn't get to grow up because of you. Spare me the sob story. I didn't want to say it in front of the others, but he talked.'

'What do you mean?'

'I think you know what I mean.'

He's guessing, he must be. I'm not going to fall for it. If Jason knew anything he'd use it without hesitation, but there's a rushing in my ears and it feels like the whole world is closing in around me.

'Leave me alone,' I say, although he's already let go.

I manage to get in the car on trembling legs and start the engine but I keep my gaze fixed on the glaring figure in the mirror until it disappears from view. Then I can think properly again.

THE WEDDING PARTY

Jason was worried about what I might have overheard. What was he talking about with the mayor that would make me afraid to be alone with him?

35

ADELE – THE BRIDE

FRIDAY AFTERNOON – ONE DAY BEFORE THE WEDDING

Having hid in the bathroom after I was sure Melanie had left, I can confirm the plush white chaise longue is as comfortable as she said. However, knowing if I don't return to the others soon, someone will come looking for me, I stand and check my reflection. Hoping the exhaustion of the morning isn't showing on my face. I curve my lips and the woman in the mirror smiles obediently, the glassy tiredness in her eyes easily mistaken for anticipation.

The excited bride.

Guilt sits heavy on my chest that I need to force the smile at all. Jason deserves better. He'll get better. I straighten my spine, lift my head and –

Beep. Beep. Beep.

I cover my ears against the painful shriek, looking for the source of the beeping splitting the air. Part of me registers heavy steps running outside the door.

A smoke alarm?

I inhale but catch nothing but the perfumes of the soaps and diffusers filling the bathroom. I approach the door, the thud of my heart a counterpoint to the high-pitched warning coming from overhead. Everything I've seen on 'in case of emergency' ads on TV tells me to be wary in case of flames on the other side.

But then it bursts open and Katja is there, eyes wild. 'There you are. There's a fire on the grounds.' Then, over her shoulder to someone I can't see, 'You go, I found Adele.'

'What's happening?' I ask.

'We have to evacuate. The building isn't under threat at this stage but they want us out as soon as possible. Your Mum is looking for Sophie now and hopefully Jason and Rory are together.'

I allow her to hustle me out of the bathroom where there are venue staff who direct us towards the car park. At the doors to the reception room, I look back out the huge windows opening to the deck.

'No,' I cry.

Katja turns that way slowly, her face showing no surprise at the scene that's made me hold the wall just to keep upright.

Now, as I watch flames lick along the white swathes of material over the vows pavilion and turn the gorgeous oak to smouldering black, I can smell it. The sweet chemical of satin melting and shrivelling, globs of it dripping onto leaves while smoke billows. The scent is acrid on the back of my throat.

'We have to leave,' Katja insists.

But I can't look away from the flames and the smoke, increasing even as sprinkler systems outside try to put the fire out.

'My vows.' It comes out on a sob that turns into a cough as more smoke filters through from outside. I bend over, gagging, tears stinging along with the smoke. 'How could this…?' is all I manage as I gag again. The heaving of my stomach as the realisation of it all keeps me hunched and shaking.

A hand touches my shoulder.

I glance up. It's Jason, his usually composed features grey with panic. 'I'm here.'

He opens his arms and I fall against him. With him supporting me, almost carrying me, we make our way out to the emergency area as I register the wail of fire engines over the incessant beeping.

Outside, the venue's event planner meets us, her face grave. 'We are very sorry and this is highly unfortunate, but I believe all your party are safely accounted for.' She gestures to where Mum and Sophie are with Rory, being given water by more staff. They all appear unhurt.

The fire trucks are out of sight, presumably trying to get the blaze under control.

'What the hell happened?' Jason asks the question to which we all want the answer.

The woman swallows. 'We can't be sure right now.' Her gaze darts in the direction of the building as the beeping stops. 'Sounds like they've ascertained it won't get to the building and hopefully the vines are safe.'

Jason pulls me a little closer. 'What does that mean for us? For the wedding?'

'Was it deliberately lit?' I blurt before she can answer. 'Or was it some kind of electrical fault? How did it start? Do you know how the fire started?'

The woman blinks and I can feel everyone looking at me as my voice rises higher and higher.

All that matters is Jason. I look up at him. 'This is more sabotage, isn't it? Someone's done this.'

He cups my face with his hands. 'We don't know that.' And then to the woman. 'Do we?'

She audibly gulps. 'We won't know anything until it's investigated by the proper authorities but I can't see how it could happen accidentally. The speed it took hold of the greenery… the way it spread…' She can't look at me as she speaks. 'The grounds are large and, during the day, open and accessible. It's not like we can keep anyone out.'

The thread of control I had on my emotions snaps.

I bury my head in Jason's shoulder, not caring about the rest of them, and let him hold me. Even as I take his comfort, he's murmuring to the woman, arranging for us to leave and sharing details with some fire officer in case they need to speak to any of us.

'Although no one saw anything suspicious?' he says. It's a question and I lift my head to see that the others have moved closer.

They all shake their head. Except for Mum. 'Melanie was here. I wouldn't put it past her to try to do something like this.'

'Mum left ages ago,' Sophie counters. Her eyes wide and I can't tell if she's defensive or worried.

But as the fire officer asks each of us about what we saw – all nothing – I realise that we were all split up when the fire began.

And suddenly, I don't know who to trust at all.

36

MELANIE – THE MOTHER

FRIDAY AFTERNOON – ONE DAY BEFORE THE WEDDING

A bit later that afternoon, Sophie still hasn't returned to the shack when a firm knock on the porch door startles me into the present.

Thanks to the sun, it's impossible to make out who it is. My heart rate jumps at the thought of Jason finishing our car park chat but I ignore it. I refuse to be scared of that little upstart.

Before unlatching the lock, I drag a hand over my face to give it some colour, smooth my hair back and quickly check the time. It's later than I thought. I've lost time again. I can't afford to keep doing that.

I open the door and find myself looking down at the top of Dorothy Ellingsworth's grey head. She seems to be murmuring something, reminding me of the dementia rumours.

'Can I help you?' I say carefully.

She lifts her head, allowing me to see the small dog cradled in her arms. 'Sorry, dear, Laila was fussing. I thought we could have a cup of tea.' Her immediate move to sit at the outdoor table doesn't give me a choice in the matter.

'What do you have in your tea?' I ask.

This earns me an approving nod. 'Green tea if you have it. And I much prefer a pot to tea bags, but I don't really mind.'

I hope the sinking feeling in my stomach doesn't show on my face. 'I can't remember what I have in the cupboard but I'll have a look.'

A few minutes later I present two cups with supermarket-brand black tea bags in them and pour boiling water from the kettle.

She dunks her teabag, then adds some milk from the carton. 'Lovely.'

'Would you like a biscuit?' I ask. The chocolate wafers were scrounged from the back of the cupboard and placed on a tray to disguise the fact that they're a knockoff of a fancier brand. At least they are in date.

Dorothy shakes her head. 'Not for me, dear.'

Her dog is straining to get to the treats so I move the chocolate out of reach.

'Thank you,' she says.

'She's gorgeous. Have you had her long?' It's not the question I want to ask, but her manner makes it impossible to demand what the hell she wants.

'Laila has been with me for a few years now. She's a wonderful and loyal companion. And doesn't give me any bullshit.'

I suck in air when Dorothy swears, leaving me coughing and spluttering.

'Are you okay, dear?' she asks.

I wipe my watering eyes. 'I'm fine, thanks.'

She looks around, making me acutely aware of the unswept porch and the dirty windows. 'It's nice how you've kept the older feel of this place. It gives it character, which is missing from so many of the monstrosities around the bay.'

I can't be sure but I think she looks towards Jason's place. 'I like it.'

Dorothy nods. She places her mostly-full cup back in the saucer and pats her dog some more while looking out at the sea as though she's never seen it before. I'm beginning to think she's going to stay like that until I physically force her to leave so I can get ready for the pre-wedding dinner tonight, when she turns back to me and speaks.

'As lovely as it has been to catch up, I must admit I did have an ulterior motive.'

'You did?'

'It's time, Melanie. You need to let what happened on the jetty go.'

I stare at her, trying to make sense of the abrupt subject shift. It's like I was happily standing in the shallows and a big wave has knocked me over. 'Let it go? My son is dead.'

She nods slowly. 'A tragedy, but you can't keep on looking for someone to blame.'

Jason. She's here about Jason.

'He's lucky to have someone looking out for him,' I say.

Not that it will help.

Dorothy chuckles in a way that has me wondering if I somehow said my thought aloud. 'Oh, dear,' she says. 'You've got me all wrong. It's not him I came here for.'

'I don't understand.'

'And I don't expect you to.' She scratches the top of Laila's head. 'Holding on to this will only cause you more pain.'

'What the hell do you know about how I feel?'

'When you outlive both your husband and your son, you

learn a few things. You're hurting yourself more than anyone. There's more than just you to consider.'

I bristle.

She pats my hand. 'Yes, he was yours, but he was loved such that his absence changes us all. He was your boy, but he was a friend, a boyfriend, a brother.'

'You want me to pity them?'

'No,' she says quickly. 'I want you to find a way to live instead of whatever it is you're doing.'

'Thanks, but I'm fine.'

'You say you're fine, but you're down here all the time and we both know it's not for the beach. You have some silly jetty vendetta and then there's that bottle you carry in your handbag. The one you're dependent on to get through the day.'

I feel my skin get hot. How long has she known? Who else has noticed?

I cross my arms. 'I don't know what you're talking about.'

'We both know you do.' She sighs. 'I want to help.'

'No one can help me.'

'You're right. Only you can help yourself, and what you're doing now, well it isn't it. Melanie, you need to know that you've done enough.'

Her sincerity pricks at the hard exterior I've built around my heart. 'I'm confused.'

'This is why I came over here. In case no one has told you, in case you haven't realised it – you have done enough. You can rest. You have fought for him.'

'No.'

She sighs. 'Please, promise an old lady you'll try a bit harder to be kind to yourself.'

It's been so long since anyone looked at me and saw how much I was hurting that I discover I'm quite unable to say anything at all.

She stands and shuffles across the porch, and then down onto the sand.

When Sophie walks in a few minutes later with news of a fire at the wedding venue, it's easy to push Dorothy's visit from my mind. She tells me they'll squeeze into the chapel after all or try to set up somewhere else on the grounds for the vows.

'It's not what Adele wanted though,' I say.

She's looking at me strangely. 'Mum... You didn't have anything to do with it, did you?'

'Of course not,' I say quickly.

It doesn't take away the suspicion in her dark eyes. I can't meet the gaze that's so like my Ollie's that it hurts.

Needing to get ready for the dinner in nearby Tuckersfield means she doesn't linger to question me more.

A few minutes later, I'm standing in the ancient bathroom in my underwear, trying to apply mascara for the third time. A task made more difficult by not particularly wanting to look at my reflection and the persistent trembling in my hand.

What I need is something to steady myself.

I step across the narrow hallway into Ollie's room and cross to my small suitcase in the corner. My urgency turns my fingers into thumbs. I don't usually unpack much when I'm here, not wanting my things draped around this room. My hand slips, driving the metal edge of the clasp into my palm. Tears sting but I distract myself by picturing Ollie loping through the door.

But I go too far. In my head, I'm back to that day, arguing with Ollie. Seeing his beautiful face twisted in anger, hearing the last words he ever said to me.

'Don't you worry about me.'

I squeeze my eyes shut but can't escape the memory of the stiff set of his shoulders as he stalked out of the shack. Leaving me standing there, furious he'd dared argue, convinced he was heading for trouble.

And I was right. So goddamn right.

But there's no solace in knowing it. I should have held him tight and never let go. Instead, I just bloody watched him leave.

The pulsing pain in my hand brings me back to the present. The case opens but my relief is short-lived. My clothes, shoes and accessories are all neatly where I left them but the bottles are gone.

Rocking back on my heels, I try to think. Could I have drunk them all already? I search my memory, but the last few days blur. A sip here, a sip there. *Remember how you passed out the other night? And don't forget the black spots.* No, I'm certain I haven't drunk that much.

I stumble out to the kitchen, go through the cupboards, throw open door after door but there's nothing. I'm on my knees on the cracked lino when there's a voice from the hallway.

'Ready, Mum?' It's Sophie, and her tone is bright and breezy.

I manage to haul myself to my feet.

'What are you doing?' Sophie asks, scorn in her voice.

My neck burns hot with shame and I know she can see my legs trembling. And the pasty, veined skin of my bare thighs, and the stretch marks wrinkling across my stomach.

More importantly, I need something to drink before this dinner.

'I have an urgent errand,' I say. 'I'll meet you at the restaurant.'

She doesn't bother to respond, walking out into the evening sunshine without waiting for any more excuses.

37

SOPHIE – SUNDAY JANUARY 23ᴿᴰ

TWELVE YEARS AGO

Sophie had lost track of the time when she left Pip in their spot hidden out on the balcony to use the bathroom. On her way back upstairs, she saw Pip with Ollie and they were clearly coming to find her.

Her stomach dropped.

'It's time,' Ollie said.

She'd tried to block out Ollie's promise to Daniel about her making a purchase, but the seriousness in his face brought it back to her. As people pushed past them, Ollie tugged her back down the stairs and passed her three crisp notes.

She stared down at the money then clutched it out of sight. 'Where did you get this?'

'Never mind,' he said. 'Look, you have to do this or there will be trouble for us both. Daniel already doesn't want you around.'

Suddenly Sophie could feel eyes on her and looked across the dark, crowded space. She could see Daniel standing there, drink in one hand and the other wrapped around Kirsty's waist. Kirsty seemed to be staring at Sophie and Ollie. From his position by Daniel's other side, Jason gave her a thumbs up and the sight of it made her feel a little better.

'Can't you do it?' she begged.

Ollie shook his head. 'He's set on you.'

The thud of her heart drowned the heavy bass. She'd been trying to ignore this side of Ollie's new friends but breathing in the scent of beer and something earthy she didn't recognise, she couldn't any longer. 'Okay,' she said. 'I'll do it.'

Ollie pointed at a dark corner where there was a hulking figure seated at a small table, wearing a black T-shirt and with a peroxide crew-cut that flashed neon in the lights from the DJ. 'Tell Tank you want—'

'Tank?'

He nodded.

'Original.'

Ollie's face changed, becoming harder than she'd ever seen before. 'Please, it's not a game.'

'Are you in some kind of trouble? Is this for you?'

He held up his hand. 'Not the time.'

Suddenly the sweeping laser lights made her queasy. 'How much do I ask for?'

'She'll know,' he said, his relief obvious.

'And do I expect change?'

'God, Soph, this isn't a supermarket.'

'Well, I don't know any of this, okay?'

'Yea, I know,' he said, sounding a little less frustrated. 'Just ask for the stuff, give her the money. Then, take what she gives you to Daniel.'

I'm a hardened criminal, Sophie thought to herself as she approached the small table. She loosened her limbs and added a bit of a strut to her walk, doing her best to get into the role. *I'm not afraid of no bitch called Tank.*

One look from Tank shattered Sophie's attempt to be anything but a terrified teenager. She did as Ollie had told her, voice shaking nearly as much as her hands. Tank seemed amused, growling at Sophie so she jumped. Then actually laughing at the reaction. In mere seconds it was over and Sophie scurried over to where Daniel was waiting.

'Here.' She shoved the stuff that looked like a big pouch of what she'd seen him selling to other kids into his hand and didn't wait for his acknowledgement. She thought she heard more laughter as she stumbled away.

'You survived,' Pip said when she reached him.

'Barely.' She tried for a smile. 'What do you think it was?'

'I don't...' His voice trailed off and eyes widened. It would have been funny if he didn't appear so terrified.

'What are you looking at?'

Sophie flinched and spun around. The snarled question had come from one of the guys who'd been loitering around Tank, those she'd mentally registered as the dealer's security team.

'N-nothing,' she stammered.

The guy leaned right in close, his orange, greasy hair falling forward. 'I wasn't talking to you, bitch.' He pushed past her to Pip. 'You were looking at me, weren't you?' Greasy punctuated each word with a jab at Pip's chest.

'No,' Pip said, stumbling over the word.

'You were,' Greasy replied. 'I'm not fucking interested, you freak.'

Sophie looked around for Ollie, or Adele or any of the others. Where had they gone?

This was bad. She knew it on an instinctive level. But she didn't know what she should do. Leave Pip to get help? But what if she couldn't find Ollie? What if she found him and he didn't come?

Besides, maybe she had this all wrong.

'I wasn't doing anything, honest.' Pip held up his hands to show he wasn't a threat. 'I swear.'

'Don't believe you.' More jabs from Greasy pushed Pip back until he stood against the wall with nowhere to go. 'What matters is that I don't want no fag checking me out.'

Pip's face drained of colour. 'I wasn't—'

The first blow happened in slow motion. Sophie could almost feel it in her own stomach. She bent double as Pip sagged. The second hit his cheek. And he hit the ground. Sophie imagined she heard a crack with the next but her eyes were streaming tears and she couldn't be sure with the lights and the music and the punches. And Pip was not fighting back.

'Leave him alone,' she cried. Screaming, she grabbed at Greasy, pulling him back. He tried to shake her off but she clung on. 'Please,' she begged, 'leave him alone.'

Greasy managed to push her off. She landed so hard she felt the shock through her bones. She crawled towards Pip, knees scraping the concrete floor. Greasy spat once, then disappeared into the throbbing darkness.

Sophie stayed. 'Are you okay? Where does it hurt? The guy's gone.'

Tears streaked Pip's beautiful face. 'He's gone?'

Suddenly, they weren't alone. Ollie and Adele were there and Sophie could see her own anguish mirrored on the other girl's face. 'Is he okay?' Adele asked.

'I don't know,' Sophie said.

'Get up,' Ollie said. 'You're fine.'

Sophie blinked up at the brother she thought she knew. Ollie was supposed to be one of the good guys, but good guys did not act like he had tonight. 'He's hurt.' Ignoring Ollie's directive, she brushed some of the sand from Pip's arm. 'Do you think something's broken?'

Pip moaned from deep in his chest but didn't say anything.

Sophie leaned so close she could feel the shakes through Pip's body. 'Do you need the hospital?'

'We can't go there,' Adele said. 'Ollie's right, we have to get out of here. If Mum and Dad find out about this, we'll be in so much trouble.'

Someone came towards them in the darkness and Sophie wasn't proud of the instinct that had her wanting to run. But when they stepped into the light it was only Jason, his hands shoved in his pockets.

'What's going on?' he asked.

Adele glared at him. 'One of Daniel's friends beat the crap out of my little brother.'

Jason stopped so the toe of his sneaker was nearly touching Pip's leg. He looked down as Pip gulped back another sob, and the revulsion was clear on his face. 'He must have done something to provoke him.'

'He didn't,' Sophie managed, but her voice was small.

Jason ignored Sophie, holding out his hand to the boy on the ground. 'Get up.'

Pip did as he was told, lumbering to his feet, but he didn't take Jason's help. And he didn't say a single word all the way back to the other end of the bay.

38

ADELE – THE BRIDE

FRIDAY EVENING – ONE DAY BEFORE THE WEDDING

As his parents and mine get into separate sleek, black cars that are waiting on the road outside the shacks to take us to dinner, Jason squeezes my hand.

'The chapel will be perfect for the vows,' he murmurs. 'Don't stress.'

Rather than point out all the reasons we didn't choose it initially, I nod. 'But what if one of us had been down there? Someone could have been hurt.'

'No one was.'

He seems so sure it was an accident but I can't help connecting it with everything else. It seems like someone is serious about stopping this wedding.

Before I can give voice to my worries again, he winces. 'I just need to grab something; I won't be long.'

The first of the cars are pulling away, heading for dinner.

Katja checks that Dorothy is settled in one of the waiting vehicles and then walks towards me. 'Should I go and see what's delaying Sophie?'

'I'll come.'

Near the old shed out the back of the shack, a gust of wind sends a windchime ringing oddly. 'Do you see that?' I stride over and grab at the piece of wire tangled among the strings. The cause of the discordant note is moulded into a disturbingly feminine shape. Her triangle body makes a dress, and there's a distorted head on top with twisted hair flowing from it.

Katja shrugs. 'It must have been blown into the windchime.'

I grit my teeth. 'This is a figure of a bride. It's obvious. And someone has left it here for me to find, so they can mess with my head.'

She squints. 'I know you're upset about the fire but it's just an old bit of wire. Or maybe, wait, doesn't that neighbour of yours have a workshop? Maybe it's from there.' Her face brightens. 'I looked him up. Did you know his sculptures go for thousands?'

'Giovanni?'

'Yep.'

I didn't know but neither do I care. 'How could it have got here?'

But I'm not expecting her to answer. I look down at the figure again. Could I be imagining things? There's some psychosis where the sufferer sees human shapes in inanimate objects; I read an article about it once.

Before I can say anything further, my other bridesmaid appears from her yard alone. 'Mum will meet us there,' Sophie announces as I slide the wire into my bag. She doesn't wait for any questions.

Jason has returned and sees me looking towards the Rhodes' shack. 'I'm sure Melanie's fine.'

'You're right.' I let him lead me towards the open door

of the rear vehicle where Katja has joined Dorothy inside. 'I don't want us to be late.'

He smiles and I know I've made the correct choice.

Settling into the leather seat of the chauffeured vehicle, I accept the glass Jason is holding out and don't look back as my door is closed. As we drive the scenic route, the only sound is the music playing through the discreet speakers. And the snuffles of Laila as she snuggles into Dorothy's lap.

Jason had tried to prevent his grandmother bringing the little dog, citing the health and safety rules of the establishment. Dorothy in response called the restaurant on loudspeaker and made him listen to their assurances that they adore her emotional support dog and are looking forward to her visit.

'Emotional support dog?' he'd queried.

'Large donation to their last renovation fund,' she'd replied.

And he could hardly argue at her using the tactics he'd usually employ to get his way. It hasn't stopped him grimacing whenever he looks at the two of them.

'Aren't you hot?' Jason asks.

I follow Jason's gaze to Dorothy's legs and the thick sensible tights encasing them. He's not usually so interested in women's fashion so I suspect his question is more about the warm little body on her lap.

'A lady isn't dressed without stockings,' she says.

He doesn't appear convinced. 'Shall I ask the driver to turn up the fan?'

'Oh, Jason,' she tuts. 'Stop fussing. I'm quite capable of asking him if I want. I haven't lost my mind yet, dear. You can trust I know what I'm doing. Like with the cake for tomorrow. You wanted fairy floss, is that right?' she asks, her eyes twinkling.

'Very funny,' he says.

I clear my throat to cover a giggle.

'You understand that you can't—' With what appears great effort he clamps down on his obvious irritation.

Too late though, as Dorothy can hardly have missed it. She lifts her chin. 'If you have something to say, you say it.'

He shakes his head. 'I don't.'

Her smile is somewhat victorious. 'Good.'

It doesn't take long and we're off the dirt road and heading to where Jason has booked out part of the best restaurant in Tuckersfield. The main hotel has been there for as long as I can remember, but as the shack prices at the bay have skyrocketed, it's transformed accordingly. The Catch boasts a menu that would rival many in the city, showcasing the best local ingredients.

Not for the first time since our heart-to-heart at the wedding venue, I catch Katja sneaking looks over at Jason, a furrow in her brow. I already wish I hadn't told her about the cancer. Subtlety is not her strong point. It's not like he's going to drop dead tonight.

What I didn't tell Katja, what I can't ever tell her, is what happened a few weeks after my birthday. Jason had gone all out with a magical weekend escape, and it should have been wonderful. But I spent the whole night wishing I was at the pub with my girlfriends.

Not that I wasn't having a nice time. I just felt this sudden, desperate need for my old life. For a relaxed night with the girls. I'd suggested we have a break.

And Jason had been lovely. He'd said all the right things about wanting to give me space and understanding and us growing together with time apart.

Then I heard from Rory, of all people, in passing, that Jason was in hospital.

In hospital.

Of course, I rushed to his side. And when I saw him on that bed with all those wires attached and his skin deathly pale I'd asked him why he'd not called me.

He said he'd been giving me space.

It was exactly what I'd wanted, but it felt like I'd let him down. I stayed at his side. Stayed at his place when he was released. Helped him recover. And somehow, we were closer than ever.

We're going to be married.

And we'll stay that way. Unless... something unthinkable happens. My mind drifts back to the warnings and the fire but I force myself not to dwell on it.

At least Rory went in the other car. Hopefully, he'll stop pouting whenever he looks my way. I can't even imagine the mood at Jason's place when they're alone or what it had been like on their spearfishing trip. If Pip was here there would at least be another male. Thinking of my absent brother has me checking my phone for any messages, which inevitably leads me back to wondering if Jason's received any more warnings.

Jason touches my knee. 'Everything okay? You've barely touched your drink.'

His question draws both Dorothy and Katja's attention.

'Of course,' I say quickly, taking a big sip of the sparkling wine. 'Pip is cutting it fine, that's all.'

'He'll make it,' Katja says.

'How do you know?' I ask. 'It's been days since I've heard from him.'

She smiles. 'Because he wouldn't miss your big day.'

I hope she's right, but she doesn't know that Jason and Pip haven't always got along. Back when we all spent our summers here, Pip wasn't the star of the stage he is now, and not everyone was so accepting of boys who didn't fit the stereotypical masculine package.

'Don't worry about it,' Dorothy says, but the brief offer of comfort turns quickly to pragmatism. 'There's nothing you can do.'

I drain the rest of my drink. The woman has a point.

As a convoy we take the scenic route to the restaurant, arriving about half an hour later, the other cars parking just in front.

Dorothy clutches my arm. 'Adele, dear, you don't mind accompanying an old woman, do you?'

'Of course not,' I say as everyone else heads inside.

'Our chat was so lovely the other day and I'm so pleased you're joining our family.'

'Lovely,' I echo.

'Yes, it seems you're quite the businesswoman,' Dorothy is saying. 'You know Ellingsworth Hotels was under my stewardship for some time after Jason's father passed.'

'Yes, you still have quite the formidable reputation around the office.'

'Oh, that's kind of you. I was just muddling along.' Her words sound like an elderly lady but the sparkle in her eyes suggests the notoriety was well earned. 'I did wonder something else on the business front.'

Spit it out, I think. 'Whatever you want to know,' I say aloud.

'Where do you see yourself in the future? In five years?'

It's a question I've been asked often before, in job interviews and the like, so the answer flows without much thought because it's been my dream since I first understood what the red on the envelopes in our letterbox meant.

'I'm a leader,' I say. 'A boss of some sort, running my own business so I can fulfill the vision I have without bending to others. Personally, I'll be independent, in control and already investing in my future.'

Her eyes narrow. 'And Jason?'

'He'll be by my side,' I say quickly.

Her drawn-on eyebrows lift. 'I never knew my grandson was so supportive.'

There's a beat where I should agree with her but I miss it and the moment's gone.

39

MELANIE – THE MOTHER

FRIDAY EVENING – ONE DAY BEFORE THE WEDDING

I listen for the purr of the cars to fade before making certain the sliding door to the beach is locked and leaving out the back. It's unsettling to be so security conscious here where I've always felt so safe but I can't forget the mayor's warning and the feelings I've had of being watched.

I check the time on my phone. There's none to spare. Maybe I don't need to go all the way to the bottle shop. There's been drinks galore flowing at Jason's place. I find myself on the deck at Jason's before I've had a chance to think. My tread is silent on the smooth, warm wood and the fairy lights strung across the space are already on and twinkling, but it seems deserted. Presumably this evening's staff aren't here yet.

As I suspected, the outside fridges are full. My hand is on the door to one when I remember Jason confronting me about trespassing. Heart thudding, I scan the space, looking for cameras. I'm not exactly up with the latest security technology. Maybe there are none out here, or maybe he's watching on his phone right now.

Bang.

I duck. That sounded like a small explosion. It's then I notice all the lights have gone dark. I've lived alone for long enough that I recognise a blown fuse.

Hopefully, the loss of power will take out the security system and Jason will never know I was here. Either way, I'm here now. The whiskey I grab is some fancy Japanese type, but I'm not complaining. I'm turning to leave when movement inside the house catches my eye. I strain to discern anything beyond the reflection of the water behind me. But then I see it. The familiar swish of a blonde ponytail attached to someone quickly climbing the inside stairs. A heartbeat later, it's gone, but I would know that hair anywhere.

Mayor Fiona is inside Jason's shack.

That fuse blowing is awfully well timed. If someone wanted to have a look inside the shack, now would be perfect. Having found what appears to be a high number of council approvals on Jason's applications, it would make sense they were somehow working together. And from what I overheard, it seems their partnership is no longer cordial. He's threatening her, and she's the type to want to hit back, which means she needs ammunition. Fiona Lewis would have reason to want to find something to use against Jason, or at least try to mitigate what he has on her.

But how could she have got inside? Even with her motivation, I just can't picture her as a breaking and entering type. Maybe with all the people going in and out she found an unlocked door.

The buzz of a message from Sophie breaks me from my thoughts.

'You'd better be on your way.'

It's the reminder I need to get moving and I head for the

car, already undoing the bottle for that much-needed salve. Besides, if Fiona's desperate enough to sneak into Jason's shack, what might she do if she's caught?

At the restaurant, I walk past the fancy cars and touch a shiny bonnet. It's still warm. Confident I'm not too late, I stop in the doorway and take a moment to catch my breath. The whiskey I stole has done its work, and I feel almost in control.

'Can I help you?' A waiter stands in front of me.

I look past him, scanning for the wedding group. This place is nicer than I remember. White tablecloths cover light oak tables and the pendant lights overhead give a touch of mood and intimacy to each grouping. Instead of carpet soaked with lingering odours of fried food and tap beer, the dark floors gleam with a fresh polish and glassware glitters alongside silver cutlery.

But the windows beyond sit deep like they did before. The wood edges frame the sun setting over rolling wheat fields, and the view hasn't changed at all. I remember the night Ollie sat here through dinner, sullen and withdrawn. I should have known then that things weren't right with him. I should have banned him from spending time with Jason Ellingsworth.

As embarrassed and mad as I was with Ollie that night, I would give anything to be able to have that time again. I'd smile at his tantrum. Buy him a treat that he didn't deserve. Hug his unyielding frame to me, until he rested his head on my shoulder.

'I'm sorry, ma'am, but we're all booked this evening,' the waiter says loudly.

I blink at him, still lost in the past.

'Do you have a booking?' he asks. Now he's overpronouncing each word like I'm senile or hard of hearing. It's par for the course. A place like this is all about looking down on people.

'I'm with the Ellingsworth party,' I say, hating that name in my mouth, hating having to use it for currency.

The waiter's face changes, becomes helpful. 'They are in the Stanley Room. Please come this way, ma'am.'

I trail him towards a set of double doors and through to a separate space where I can see everyone around the table, some seated and others pulling out their chosen chairs while deep in conversation.

I nod my thanks, and he takes it as his cue to leave.

Thanks to another of the waitstaff taking drinks orders and Dorothy's little dog yapping, no one looks my way. Although I'm sure from the tightening around Sophie's mouth she's seen me.

The seat next to my daughter is empty and I'm about to sit in it – thankfully down the opposite end of the table from Jason – when the groom himself looks my way.

'Here at last,' he says.

'I hope Sophie explained that I would make my own way here,' I say to Adele, rather than answering Jason.

'Not a problem,' she says, about to taste some wine offered by the waiter.

I swear Tammy is vibrating with her need to say something about my tardiness. Terry doesn't look my way but the twist of his lip suggests he's about as pleased as his wife.

It's hard to be popular.

I'm perusing the menu, when Tammy's words to Jason drift down the table. 'You're right, I think you two are destiny.'

I freeze. It feels like the world stops spinning. It wasn't said to me but Tammy must know her words would have carried. Destiny that means my son was fated not to be here.

'I think destiny is a load of codswallop,' Dorothy says loudly. 'Which means bullshit for you young folk.'

Adele gasps, coughing as her sip of wine goes down the wrong way. Her bridesmaid pats her on the back, earning a glare for her attempt to help.

Conversation resumes along the table, with the waiter offering her water and Jason hurrying to play the concerned fiancé. Someone asks the waiter about the vintage of the red wine, and I settle back in my seat.

Instinctively, I know that it's only a momentary reprieve.

40

ADELE – THE BRIDE

FRIDAY EVENING – ONE DAY BEFORE THE WEDDING

As I dab carefully beneath my watering eyes so as not to smear my makeup, I have never been more thankful for nearly choking to death on a sip of sauvignon blanc.

Seriously, what was Mum thinking? What she was saying didn't sink in until I saw Melanie about to cry. Her wearing her grief like a crown of gloom is hardly adding to the vibe of the weekend but Jason's the one who invited her.

'Was the pummelling really necessary?' I whisper to Katja.

'I was trying to create a diversion,' she replies with a smirk. 'I wanted it to look realistic.'

After that, conversation flows around us. I keep my smile in place, try not to think I can still smell smoke lingering from the fire. I can't help wondering if all brides get to the point where the longing for the wedding to be over outweighs everything else.

When Jason informs the waitstaff that we'll be ready to order soon, it prompts me to have a look at the menu, and it's when I'm looking down that I see a message on Jason's watch. I pull his hand into my lap in a gesture I hope passes as affectionate, allowing me to read the screen.

DO NOT MARRY HER.

Instinctively, I scan the room, but a familiar figure in the doorway has me forgetting the message, and leaping from my chair.

'I'm here,' Pip declares, spreading his arms wide. With his fair hair slicked back, and wearing a blue and white paisley shirt and light blue trousers, it's like he's brought summer with him. 'Let the celebrations begin.'

I close the distance between us and Pip lifts me up off the ground, twirling in a circle. He was so undersized for so long; my brain still struggles with him having the strength to lift and carry his stage partners, let alone me. Yet here in his embrace is where I feel safest.

When he puts me down I mock hit him on the shoulder. 'About time.'

He winks. 'Have to make an entrance.'

I can feel everyone waiting for us to join them. I let Pip embrace me again and before he lets go I murmur, 'We need to talk properly. Mum and Dad have been a nightmare.'

'Later,' he promises.

Soon, he's swarmed by others. Mum manages to namedrop his latest show at least three times in case anyone forgets he's a star. Dad hovers, as always awkward with Pip's obvious confidence after a lifetime of making him feel small. And, of course, there's Sophie. His best friend.

He responds to greetings from those still seated, taking a

moment to charm Dorothy who's clearly pleased with him gushing over how adorable Laila is. He meets Rory and it's strange to hear him called by his given name, Kyle.

'I'm just Pip here with family,' he corrects.

Then, finally, he's in front of Jason. Again, I'm surprised by how big Pip is. It's odd to see him towering over my fiancé by a couple of inches.

'We've been waiting for you, brother.' Jason holds out his hand.

And just for a moment Pip hesitates.

My brain lurches back in time to twelve years ago, only days before Ollie died. That awful boy with his rage and his fists. Afterwards, Pip lying there, small on the ground, broken. Jason holding out his hand, disgust on his features. 'Get up,' he'd growled.

And I know Pip well enough to know he's remembering it too.

I want to shout, *he's changed*. But I don't. Mostly because abruptly, sickeningly, I'm not entirely sure that it isn't me who's different now.

Then Pip is grasping Jason's hand and I'm breathing again. 'Happy to be here,' Pip says. 'Congratulations.'

It's after the appetisers have been served and the bubbly that Pip requested is being poured freely by the waitstaff that a loud thump cuts off conversation at our end of the table, the silence rippling along the length of it until everyone is quiet.

Dorothy's standing. 'I must have bumped it, sorry.'

'Do you need me to take you to the bathroom?' Jason asks.

Her mouth flattens. 'Don't forget I taught you how to go potty.'

Jason sinks back into his seat. 'Of course.'

Dorothy's gaze takes us both in. 'What are your baby plans?' Her question draws everyone's attention.

My cheeks get hot. 'Oh, well, really I haven't really...'

'She's only young,' Melanie interjects in my defence.

Dorothy considers. 'Maybe so, but I lost three little ones before I had Jason's dad. So, youth or not, these things cannot be taken for granted. As I'm sure you know as well as anyone.' Dorothy's eyes become glassy and the silence that follows is so loaded no one dares breathe. 'You know, Stephan was very nearly not born at all. I think that perhaps nature was trying to give me a message.'

I was so fixed on Dorothy that I didn't notice Jason move, but he's suddenly at her side. He wraps an arm over her shoulder as he leans down to pick up the handkerchief on the edge of the table that she must have dropped in her agitation. 'I'm sure whenever we're blessed, if we are, it will be a joyous occasion,' he says. 'You don't need to worry.'

She lets him settle her back in her chair but I don't miss her mutter to Laura, 'You had trouble with Jason, too. It's nature, you know.'

I'm scrambling to understand what Dorothy meant by the whole 'nature's message' line. And her bringing up Stephan Ellingsworth at all is strangely shocking. Jason's dad died when he was a kid and they act almost like he never existed. There are no photographs nor family stories. I'd directly asked Jason about his dad once, back in that 'getting to know each other' phase. We'd been staying at some ski resort and it was after a day out on the slopes while enjoying mulled wine.

Jason's eyes had darkened. 'He was weak.'

'What do you mean?' I'd asked.

But Jason wouldn't say any more, and every time I've tried

to raise the subject since, he's shut me down. It's not like *I* don't have things I'd rather not talk about.

As soon as I can, I excuse myself and head towards the bathroom, hoping for a moment to compose myself. I'm so flustered that I don't realise I'm not the only one away from the table until I round the corner and almost walk into Pip and Sophie.

I freeze. They haven't seen me.

Sophie's shaking off Pip's hand. 'It's not like I could have refused to come. Of course I don't want this. Do you? Maybe someone should do something about it.'

I jerk back around the corner, trying to understand what I've heard.

Pulling myself together, I manage to find a different way to the bathroom. It doesn't surprise me that Sophie's got in there before me, but it's her friendly smile that stops me.

'Don't pretend.' I try to keep the waver from my voice. 'I heard you with Pip.'

Her smile falters.

'Am I supposed to mourn my childhood sweetheart forever?' I ask.

'I just never thought you'd marry *him*.'

I can't miss the emphasis. 'Why?'

But then the door behind me is opening and she's shaking her head. 'What do you want, Mum?' she asks.

Melanie smiles. 'Can't a woman seek out the bathroom?'

She's coming towards me and Sophie tries to stop her. 'Leave it, Mum.'

Melanie glares. 'I know what I'm doing.' She turns to me and I wish I'd taken the chance to flee. 'It's just that Jason's so different to Ollie.'

'Is he?' Sophie asks, saving me from having to answer. 'How? They were friends. Jason didn't lead Ollie astray.'

'He did,' Melanie insists.

I take my chance and I'm at the door and close to freedom before Melanie realises.

'Adele, wait.' Her words slur and the smell of whiskey seems to radiate from her. 'Just one more thing. It's important.'

Lingering guilt over all the mistakes in the past keeps me there. 'Go ahead.'

'He was happy, wasn't he? That last day. You have to tell me honestly; did Ollie die happy?' Her eyes implore me to give her comfort.

'Yes,' I lie.

But the truth is loud in my head and my memories. That argument we had. The terrible things we said to each other. I leave, but not before seeing Sophie's face and something on it worse than judgement. It's understanding. Just how much does she know?

Sophie was right that Ollie wasn't a saint. That boy could be as frustrating and sulky and damned argumentative as the worst of them, but Melanie isn't completely wrong either. Ollie was different to Jason, different to me. Better than both of us. And that's something I have to live with.

Somehow, I pull myself together by the time I reach the table. A couple more glasses of wine help through the rest of a delicious dinner. My spirits lift as the dessert dishes are cleared. Another step in the journey is almost over.

Jason had mentioned having organised payment so I'm surprised when one of the waitstaff approaches Pip. 'Your receipt, Mr Pippen.'

'Consider it a wedding eve gift,' Pip says.

'He can afford it these days,' Mum says loudly. 'He's very successful, you know.'

'Thanks,' I say quickly. 'You shouldn't have.'

Next to me, Jason's features are neutral but I can feel the annoyance as eventually he adds his gratitude to mine. He likes to be the one making generous gestures.

Is this the start of some kind of macho pissing contest between them, both trying to show who's richest? Or was it simply my brother being generous? I don't know, but maybe Pip being absent until now has been a good thing. I'll just have to do my best to keep them apart until it's over.

41

SOPHIE – WEDNESDAY JANUARY 26ᵀᴴ

TWELVE YEARS AGO

Sophie lay on her bed, door closed, her headphones on. With Mum and Dad at some dinner party at the other end of the bay, she'd hoped Pip and Adele might have come over. She'd imagined the romance of watching the Australia Day fireworks. She'd even painted her nails with the national colours and worn a pretty halter neck top with her cut-off shorts. An outfit she'd decided was cute but not trying too hard.

It had been a few days since the awful night at the yacht club party. Pip hadn't talked about what happened but he'd developed a black eye and moved gingerly. And, of course, Mum had forgotten completely that Ollie was grounded.

When Sophie asked Ollie if he was seeing Adele, he'd said she and Pip were out with their parents, and about fifteen minutes later it was Jason who'd come by to hang out.

Jason, who'd come in carrying a tennis ball he'd found on the sand.

Thud.

There it was again. The noise coming from Ollie's room, of

something hitting the wall right next to her head. A sound so penetrating that even turning up the volume of Taylor singing about some boy not being sorry couldn't defeat it.

'You're not sorry,' Sophie muttered towards the boys next door. 'But you will be.'

Leaving her headphones on the bed, she crept to her door. She'd catch them in the act and take the ball and throw it into the sea, even if it made Ollie mad. She'd yelled three times for them to stop and they'd completely ignored her the first time, then laughed the other two.

Her door opened without its usual squeak and she listened for any change in the next room. The hum of conversation punctuated by raucous laughter and the bouncing ball continued. She stopped at Ollie's door.

'Would you do Kirsty?' The question came from Jason.

'In a heartbeat,' Ollie replied. 'Like, if not for Adele, obviously.'

Sophie pushed open the door.

Ollie jumped at the sight of her and shoved something in his pocket before she could see what it was. Jason too was shifting something out of sight, but then Ollie blocked her view. He was up on his feet and closing the distance between them, big and angry with the glassy eyes of a stranger. 'What the fuck do you want?'

Sophie flinched at the venom in his voice, unable to miss his phone open with pictures he'd uploaded of the group from the beach, the girls in bikinis. Had they been comparing them? Gross.

She folded her arms, hoping he hadn't noticed her reaction. It wasn't like they'd never fought before, but lately he could be mean.

'Nothing,' she said.

'You came in here,' Ollie snarled. 'What the fuck do you want?'

She swallowed hard. If it wasn't for Jason looking on she might have cried. As it was, she could feel the tears building. 'Just stop the ball thing. Please.'

Ollie stared at her, his hands were clenched into fists and his shoulders were all hunched up around his ears and she found herself edging backwards. She flashed back to the yacht club and the boy punching Pip, expression almost the same.

Unconsciously, she braced herself.

He wouldn't hit her, would he? She held her breath, hating the fear freezing her in place.

Then, Ollie's shoulders slumped.

He turned and grabbed the ball, before looping it gently in the air towards her. 'Sorry. You take it.'

Incredibly, considering her usual lack of coordination, she caught it.

'Nice one,' Jason said.

But it was Ollie she was looking at. 'Huh?' she said.

That seething anger fizzing beneath his skin had gone, and he was Ollie again, but the darker version seemed to be appearing more and more lately. She'd thought about mentioning the change in Ollie to Mum and asking if she'd noticed anything but Mum wouldn't understand. Likely she'd subject him to an inquisition and just piss him off even more.

Ollie grinned. 'Then I can't be tempted to throw it.'

She gripped the soft little ball like a lifeline. 'Thanks.' Then she backed out of the room before she could make him mad again.

What if next time she pushed him too far?

42

MELANIE – THE MOTHER

FRIDAY NIGHT – ONE DAY BEFORE THE WEDDING

About two hours into the increasingly raucous after-dinner party on Jason's deck, I go looking for fortification from the bar. Having left my reading glasses in my bag I don't bother trying to decipher the label, opening the damn thing is complicated enough.

Victory! I breathe in the smoky, grainy scent and attempt to pour a nip. Most of it ends up in the glass and I drop a serviette over the puddle I left behind. Turning to make my escape, I nearly collide with my daughter.

'Mum!' It's a plea and a rebuke at once. 'Haven't you had enough?'

'Embarrassing you, am I?'

'Yes. And you're embarrassing Ollie too,' she adds in a low voice. 'He wouldn't want you to act like this. He'd hate the attention and the way you're spoiling the party. You could head home now and sleep it off and it would be a relief for everyone.'

'Who are you to speak for Ollie?'

She shakes her head. 'His sister? His friend? You're the

one who didn't know him. You've built up a picture of some angel.' She takes a breath. 'Admitting Ollie had flaws doesn't make him any less, doesn't make you any less.'

'Enough,' I beg, heart thundering.

'No, it's not,' she says. 'Not until you stop walking around like some avenging ghost.'

A hand comes down on Sophie's shoulder, ending her horrible rant. 'Leave Melanie be,' Dorothy says.

Sophie stares at the older woman, as if Dorothy's betrayed her, and then she shrugs free. 'I don't want to do this anyway.'

Dorothy looks like she's about to say something else when the background music cuts off with a screech. When I compose myself enough to look over, Fiona Lewis is standing there, holding the end of a cord. Wearing an off the shoulder pink top, black skirt and with her hair in her trademark high ponytail tied with a pink and black glittering scrunchie, her attire says party, but her eyes are narrowed.

'I'd like to make a toast,' she announces.

Everyone is looking at her, including Jason and Adele who have been lured out by the commotion. They share a surprised look between them.

'You don't even have a drink,' someone calls.

Fiona grabs a full glass and raises it high. 'To our host, Jason Ellingsworth.'

There's a murmur in response but I don't join in. Neither does Dorothy, who moves closer to the action, her dog under her arm and her eyes wide with interest.

Fiona raises her hand for quiet. 'You people all think you know Jason, but you don't.'

An expectant hush descends. Red is blooming in Adele's cheeks but Jason appears unbothered. Given the way the

Fiona and Jason were arguing last night, his indifference is borderline pathological. Everyone on the deck waits for her to continue.

'He's not the man you think he is,' Fiona declares. 'And I have the proof.'

There's a choked gasp behind me. When I turn, Sophie's pale, her hands over her mouth.

'What's wrong?' I murmur, only half of my attention on her, not wanting to miss anything Fiona has to say.

Sophie doesn't answer but stumbles away into the darkness. Pip follows her so I don't even try. She'd rather his help than mine anyway.

While I was distracted, Jason crossed to Fiona. He places an arm around her shoulders and says something I can't hear. However, I remember the grip of his fingers from the car park; I know how convincing he can be.

'Everything's fine, folks,' Jason says loudly. 'She didn't realise the punch was alcoholic.'

Someone, probably Tammy, giggles. Jason smiles too. There's a heartbeat where I think Fiona's going to argue, but then her shoulders slump. She nods.

Jason leads Fiona inside, appearing like he's comforting her but I know that's unlikely. Chatter starts up again, louder than before as though everyone is determined to be extra merry. Adele is staring after them but she doesn't follow.

I watch through the huge windows as Jason and Fiona head through the shack and towards the hallway that leads out the front. He must want to hustle her off the property. I hurry across the deck and down onto the path along the side of the house. It's deserted. The loud click of my heels on the concrete has me slipping off my shoes for quiet as I carefully unlatch the side gate. Ducking through, I stick close to the wall.

At first the yard by the road appears empty of life. I keep low, moving between the parked cars until I'm almost out to the street. Plush lawn gives way to gravel and I'm regretting discarding my shoes with every step, until I hear voices. I strain to listen.

That's them, behind me, I'm sure of it.

I peek out and see Jason standing over Fiona, fists clenched, mouth twisted. 'You know she could destroy everything.' His voice is low but I can just make out his words.

'You don't need to tell me.'

'Then do something about it. Do something about *her*. Or I will.'

'Are you threatening me? Because I'm not afraid of you.' But Fiona's insistence sounds like fake bravado. 'I could have told them everything. Don't forget what brought us together in the first place.'

The answering pause is so long I am scanning for cover.

But then Jason speaks again. 'As if you'll ever let me forget.'

'Wait,' Fiona says. 'We haven't finished our conversation.'

Jason's heading for his front door. 'That's where you're wrong,' he says. 'We're done.'

He keeps walking, and she just stands there as he shuts the door firmly behind him. She watches after him but then she heads towards the road, coming right at me.

I hesitate. The hysteria of the scene on the deck and the anger when she argued with Jason have been replaced in her face by a hollow pain I recognise. Hopelessness.

I step into her path.

Her eyes widen. 'What do you want?'

'Tell me what all that was about.'

'None of your business.'

'I heard you two arguing. Whatever alliance you had is no longer working.' I try to soften my tone. 'Why are we not on the same side here?'

For just a second the veneer of civility cracks and the venom on display beneath it has me stepping backwards. My head might be foggy, but clearly this woman hates me in a deeply personal way. But why?

He told her to do something about the loose cannon in their plan and I realise, suddenly, that could be me. 'What are you planning? Why do you need to shut me up?'

'Get over yourself.'

'I heard everything. I know Jason ordered you to get rid of me.' Even as I say it aloud, the idea of her turning physical is preposterous except for that look I saw on her face.

'It must sting,' she says eventually.

I just blink at her. She'll have to narrow it down.

'That of all the people in the world, she's marrying his best friend,' Fiona clarifies.

I shrug. 'Everyone loves a wedding. Besides, Adele is no one's possession.'

'Your kid is still dead.' She shakes her head. 'You think this is all about a wedding and a jetty but your little obsession is nothing. Do you hear me? It's nothing.'

'Tell me then,' I say. 'Explain what's going on to a foolish middle-aged lady. You're working together, I know that much. And I did my research on his company dealings.'

Her arms cross. 'Really? Computer whiz are you?'

I was sure they were working together – against me – but maybe this is bigger. 'The usually slow-moving council has been positively lightning fast with approving deals on land tracts for a hotel development around the jetty.'

'Is that all you've got?' She shrugs. 'You'll find I didn't vote on at least half of those approvals. Anything else?'

'Blackmail.' It's a stab in the dark, literally given the shadows out here, but my eyes have adjusted enough that I see her flinch. 'I've hit a nerve. But who is threatening who?'

She's shaking her head but she's still listening.

'Maybe you know something he wouldn't want shared with his wife to be,' I say. 'Or has he got something on you? Medical negligence?'

'I'm damn good at my job,' she spits.

'Really?' I swallow hard. 'You couldn't save my son. I found an article, know it was you who was with him at the end. Did he tell you something about Jason?'

'Your son has nothing to do with this. You're obsessed. Oliver was high and irresponsible and he put those who tried to help him that day at risk. The poor boy said nothing about Jason because he never regained consciousness.'

I reach out but stop short of touching her. 'Tell me, then, please. Was he in pain?'

There's the briefest softening of her face. 'No.'

I should press her about Jason, but my cheeks are wet with tears because Ollie didn't have pain. I didn't realise how much I feared he suffered.

'Why do you hate me so much?'

She hesitates. 'You are so wrapped up in yourself you don't think about the fallout from your vendetta. Other people hurt, and those people have families who hurt for them.'

'I don't understand.'

'Go back to the party, Melanie, and forget you were ever

here. Or better yet, go home. Stay out of Jason's way or I promise you'll regret it. You can't help any of us now.' With that, she strides away.

I stare after her until my eyes hurt and she's little more than a shadow among the gums and the construction site on the far side of the dirt road. And it's then, just as I'm about to do as she suggested, that I see another figure join her. Friend or foe?

Her final words echo in my head, heavy with despair. *You can't help any of us now.*

'Fiona?' I call. But I've lost sight of her. I stumble out onto the road, past my place and then Giovanni's. 'Fiona?'

But there's no sign of her. There's no sign of anyone at all.

43

ADELE – THE BRIDE

FRIDAY NIGHT – ONE DAY BEFORE THE WEDDING

Later in the night, I'm wondering what happened to our intimate gathering. The vibe is different to last night, louder and with more faces I don't recognise. Stuck as not-quite-host but part of the main attraction, I've been trying to circulate. Sometimes at Jason's side, our hands entwined and sharing congratulations, and sometimes alone. At least I've been too busy to think about the fire and there have been no further incidents.

Mum corners me and frowns. 'You're looking a bit peaky.'

Knowing argument is futile, I nod. 'I'll find a bathroom and put some colour on my cheeks.'

'Don't dawdle,' she says, before turning to talk to someone else.

I make a face at her back, only realising Dorothy's in view when she mutters, 'You go, girl.'

Upstairs in Jason's private suite, I skip the makeup and head for the balcony. From here I can see mostly water, the black expanse of the sea stretching out to the horizon. At the shore, a woman I don't recognise lifts her floral dress and wades out up to her knees, squealing as she runs back to the sand. Looking down, there's a sliver of the deck below. The hum of conversation makes individual voices impossible to recognise, until Pip breaks into a line from one of his shows and his rumbly baritone stands out.

I find myself smiling with a flush of pride. Some days I still can't believe the famous Kyle Pippen is my little brother. I'm thinking of one of his first performances as a little kid – where he fell mid-number and managed to incorporate it into the routine – when I realise that the man out on the edge of the deck below is Jason. He's laughing at something Katja's saying and despite me studying his features, he shows no hint of artifice. It appears he finds her interesting and entertaining.

It should be a good thing. After all, I want him to get along with my best friend. But I can't help remembering when, before he knew how close Katja and I are, he referred to her with distaste as 'that awful, overbearing Viking chick.'

You wouldn't know he'd made such racist judgements about her looking at him now.

Maybe he's simply grown to appreciate her good qualities. Or maybe he's faking and I just can't read him at all. I try to examine why it's making me so annoyed, a task made difficult by the number of wines and those espresso martinis that Pip made for everyone.

The door opens and someone steps out next to me onto the balcony. It's Sophie. Her arms are wrapped around her waist. It could be against the cool breeze off the water but it's more the cradling of someone wounded.

'Were you looking for me?' I ask.

Sophie shakes her head. 'Just taking a breather from the crowd.'

I don't buy it, considering she could have gone back to her mum's shack. Does she want to finish whatever she started to say in the bathroom at the restaurant?

Her gaze is on me, those eyes so like Ollie's. I wonder what she sees, and if she's still unsure of me. I wonder how much she saw that day.

I banish the thought. It's not my place to convince her of anything. She's just a bridesmaid. And soon she'll simply be someone that I used to know.

'You're right,' she blurts. 'There is something. Something I need to tell you before tomorrow. I don't know why he asked me here – and yes I know it wasn't you who wanted me.' She takes a ragged breath. 'But Jason isn't who you think he is.'

'This again.' I've had a few drinks and it comes out a lot nastier than I intend, but I'm sick of this. Sick of it all. 'No offence, but the mayor already tried that one and hers was far more dramatic.' I stare her down. 'Have you ever thought I know him a hell of a lot better than you do?'

'But—'

'No. I'm getting married tomorrow and you either turn up or don't. I've tried with you but to be honest, I'm way past caring.'

She sighs like I've disappointed her. And I hate that it matters to me.

'I hope you'll be happy,' she says and strides back inside.

I watch her go. Stupid tears pricking my eyes. And that sudden rush of anger vanishes. 'Me too,' I whisper, trying not to cry.

With Sophie gone, I fall back to my old habits and send an SOS. Given the crowd downstairs I'm not sure he'll even see it but I wait in the dark, hoping, and within minutes the door opens again.

Pip's come to my aid as requested, despite being the centre of attention down there. At least I can still count on him.

'You needed me?' he asks.

The tears threaten again. 'Always.'

He crosses to my side. 'I'm here now. Has something happened?'

'You promised we'd talk about where you've been.' That's not exactly why I called him up here but it feels less pathetic than simply needing company.

'Okay, then,' he says. 'Talk.'

Nerves freeze my tongue. I like to think I'm good at my job, but he's world famous at his. And he's bigger than me these days, different. Jacked up muscles, fake tan and white, shiny teeth make him a caricature of the man he always wanted to be. There's no manual on how to find the brother in the stranger.

'You're late,' I say.

His bravado drops and he pulls me to him in a hug. I take a deep breath, smelling mint and chocolate. 'White Knight?' I ask, recalling his favourite chocolate bar. 'Aren't they discontinued?'

'Gift from Sophie,' he says.

It's thoughtful of her and it makes me feel even worse about snapping at her.

'Anyway,' he says. 'I'm sorry. Really, I am.'

'Not good enough. You were supposed to be here. You promised that you had scheduled weeks off between shows. I needed you here this week.' I don't try to hide my hurt and I'm kind of glad when guilt clouds his features.

'I didn't plan to be late; I swear. It was more of a snowball thing.'

I study his face, trying to match up the man in front of me with the partner-in-crime for teenage sneak outs, and my soldier-in-arms surviving world-war Mum and Dad.

'It's been crazy, Pip,' I say eventually. 'I can't believe I'm getting married.'

'Me neither.'

'But I'm supposed to grow up sometime and Jason will make a good husband.'

He doesn't answer. And he doesn't meet my gaze.

That unease I felt in that moment of them meeting at the restaurant returns full force. 'He's not the boy he was. You of all people should know that people grow up and change. You said you approved of him; you said that weekend he flew over to talk to you in New York cleared the air. Please tell me you meant that.'

Pip takes my hand and squeezes it between his. 'As long as you're happy, then I am.' He takes a breath. 'You are happy, aren't you?'

'Of course,' I say quickly. I want so much to be, which is almost the same thing.

Pip's gaze sweeps my face and I think for a second he's going to say more. About security not being as important as I think, about how it's not too late to change my mind, about Jason. But he says nothing of the sort.

Instead, he smiles.

And I don't know whether I'm relieved or angry that he's let this go so easily. I squeeze his hand. 'We should probably get back to the party.'

44

ADELE - THE BRIDE

FRIDAY NIGHT — ONE DAY BEFORE THE WEDDING

When Pip and I return to the party I catch Jason's eye and it's obvious he's been wondering where I've been. I hurry to his side and he presses a quick kiss to my mouth, much to the delight of everyone in the vicinity.

Jason returns to the conversation that appears to be about a new construction at the other end of the bay and thankfully I'm not required to do anything but nod occasionally. It allows me to scan the crowd for Sophie, but both she and her mother seem to have left. There's no sign of the mayor either. At least there won't be any further scenes.

Mum taps me on the shoulder. 'You didn't fix your makeup, did you?' she murmurs. 'Your cheeks are washed out and your lipstick gone. You don't want to give Jason reason for second thoughts.' She scurries back to Dad's side.

I should ignore her but now I can't stop thinking about how I must look. 'Excuse me,' I say to Jason. 'I shouldn't be long.'

I collect my small clutch bag and head for the second, smaller downstairs bathroom. Hopefully, I can make the repairs without interruption by anyone else needing to use it. I'm far enough away from the party that when I round the corner it's almost silent. And that's when I see Rory, leaning against the wall. He straightens as I go to pass.

'You can't pretend there's nothing between us,' he says.

I shake my head. 'I'm not sure you have a full grasp on just how good at ignoring things I really am.'

He fills the hallway with his messy good looks and sexy scent. There's that hint of smoke again and I wonder if maybe I've sprung him coming in from having a sneaky cigarette.

'I've been thinking,' he says, eyes intense. 'What if Jason didn't exist?'

'But he does.'

'If he wasn't around you'd be with me.'

He sounds so damn sure. 'You think?'

His voice lowers, gains an edge. 'He's sick after all, maybe he won't be a problem for much longer. Although, how sick is he really?'

'I don't understand.'

His eyes are dark, and for the first time he feels dangerous. And then he's close. So close. And his hands find my waist with an urgency that has my whole body on alert. Instinctively, I press as close as I can to him. And I know in that instant I am going to kiss the best man from my imminent wedding, with my fiancé close enough to hear us breathing, and there doesn't seem to be a thing I can do to stop this insanity.

Somewhere in the shack a door slams. I jerk backwards, my heart hammering. God, what was I thinking?

The other night out on the beach was stupid enough but here, in Jason's house… What kind of woman does that make me?

I don't look at Rory, walking away from the temptation that could destroy my life. On shaking legs, I find the bathroom and then I'm inside and I've locked the door. I sink against the wall, trying to get my racing heart under control. It would be so easy to blame the alcohol for what almost happened with Rory, but I'm afraid it goes back to the whole whirlwind of this relationship and, of course, to Ollie and all that happened that summer.

What was I thinking?

No answer comes. I splash my cheeks with water and fix my makeup. I close my eyes for a moment and breathe deeply. Then I open the door. I can't hide in here forever.

With the kitchen empty, I take the chance to return my bag to its out-of-the-way spot under the bench.

When I straighten, Jason is standing close enough to touch. 'I've been looking for you.'

I try not to think what might have happened if he'd found me with Rory. I lean back against the cold marble of the kitchen bench and turn to face him properly. I try to smile. 'I needed a makeup fix; then thought I'd tidy a little.'

'I didn't realise I was marrying such a domestic goddess,' he teases.

But I can't laugh. I can't stop thinking about Rory. Could someone have seen us? Would Jason believe me if I said his friend made a pass at me? Maybe. I can be convincing.

'Are you listening?' Jason asks, an edge to his tone.

Don't make him angry or he'll leave, a little voice that sounds a lot like Mum whispers in my head. *No man likes a shrew.*

'Sorry, I was thinking.'

'About?'

Rory's comment questioning Jason's illness triggered a memory from when I went to his penthouse to beg him not to call off the wedding. 'You said you wanted me with you at your next visit, in six months, but by my calculations it should be only four, shouldn't it?'

His jaw tightens. 'I wasn't trying to be precise.'

'It's a fair difference.' I can't help pushing after what Rory said. Was he suggesting Jason has exaggerated his illness?

'What's that supposed to mean?'

'Nothing. I'm sorry.' I go to leave, squeezing past him, but he grabs my wrist. Not enough to hurt but enough that I feel his strength. Feel the muscles built with the help of a personal trainer at an expensive gym. No casual sport for Jason, no chance of losing to anyone else, only the dedicated sculpting of what he wants his body to be. His focus on fitness and health impressed me at first. It matches his work drive and even the way he sets himself one book of note to read a month to broaden his mind.

But I'm beginning to wonder if that same careful assessment was made of me. When he whispers he loves me, is it genuine emotion talking, or part of some calculated move?

Why am I even thinking like this?

He steps back. 'You promised there would be no more doubts.'

'It's those messages and the fire. Then there were flowers with a strange note and this horrible wire shape.' I can see he's confused and I don't blame him. I'm babbling in my effort to explain. 'There was a picture too. Of me, except it didn't have a head. Wait, I'll show you.' I cross to where I left my bag, open it and pull out my small makeup compact. Only, there's nothing there. The ripped picture of the bride is missing.

'What am I supposed to be looking at?'

'There was a picture in here, now it's missing.'

Someone must have taken it. Who? It's not like there hasn't been opportunity with it being left unattended most of the night. *Here*. With those who are our nearest and dearest.

'It was here,' I say. 'I swear.'

'Now is not the time for games.'

Every instinct tells me I should back down, at least back off, but instead I open my mouth. 'Is it you who's having doubts?'

One side of his mouth twists. 'I'm the one who proposed.'

'And I accepted.'

'Fine.' He strides out into the crowd, smiling as though we haven't just – I don't even know what this was – in the kitchen.

I breathe out hard and shake free of the negative thoughts. I can handle this, and I can certainly handle Jason.

I remember one night, maybe three months after Ollie died, I lay awake in the darkness sobbing. Mum came in, perched on the end of my bed and told me Ollie's accident had given me a chance to avoid making the mistakes she'd made. She told me, then, that love doesn't pay the bills.

She was right. Successful men take handling, but the benefits of being with them outweigh the costs. I knew what kind of man Jason was and I made the choice to be with him.

You get the treatment you allow and he needs to know he's pushed too far.

Another memory hits me, this one from my early teens. Mum on her knees begging Dad not to leave her for some tart he'd been screwing on the side. The snot on her lip, the desperation in her eyes as she'd begged.

I'm not going to be that woman.

I'm going to go into a partnership knowing exactly what I'm doing with a clear head and heart. Jason's the man for me and I will make this work.

The guests have thinned by the time I walk back out onto the deck. I adopt a happy bride-to-be smile and make myself walk towards him. When I reach the spot at his side, everyone in the group acknowledges me, including Jason. His arm comes around my waist and he smiles, although there's no kiss this time. He continues his conversation and his arm falls away from my waist for him to gesture and make a point. When he's done, he doesn't return his arm to my waist.

And even though I'm right at his side, Jason doesn't look at me. It's nothing overt, but I understand he's giving me the cold shoulder. I'm not the only one bruised by our conversation in the kitchen.

I'm stupidly grateful when someone hands me a drink because it gives me something to do with my hands. It's only as I'm sipping the cool liquid and feeling the bubbles against my lips that I remember Jason mentioning his security cameras.

A hot flush of heat rises in my throat.

It's all I can do not to run back inside and search for the devices. I'm trying to appear pleasant for the benefit of those around me, even as my brain is scrambling. Surely he won't be checking footage between now and the wedding. Before the excitement of the wedding is over, I'll find the recording and I'll make sure it's destroyed.

But what if I can't?

I sway a little, try to catch my breath with my chest suddenly too tight.

'Adele, honey? Are you okay?' Jason's arm comes around me and his face is a picture of concern.

I should be glad he's speaking to me again but all I can think is that I've screwed up worse than I imagined. A fleeting moment in a hallway could ruin everything.

I force a smile. 'It's been a long day. Maybe we should wrap things up. After all, tomorrow is a special day.'

He pulls me closer to his side. It seems I'm forgiven. 'Everyone,' he calls, loud enough to be heard over the chatter around us, 'time to go home. I have to get to bed so I can marry this woman tomorrow.'

There's a cheer in response from those around us, but I think I'm going to be sick.

45

SOPHIE – THURSDAY JANUARY 27TH
TWELVE YEARS AGO

The next afternoon, thanks to the gorgeous sunshine and lack of breeze, there were more kids than usual out at the jetty and it meant there was even more of a crowd for the boys to show off to. They'd been doing more and more dangerous tricks. Jumping off the new jetty into the open sea had progressed to the more exciting gap between the two structures.

'Go on, Ollie, I did it.' Daniel said. He gave Ollie a long look up and down and then smirked. 'Unless you're chicken.'

'What did you call me?' Ollie squared up to the older boy.

Daniel shoved him hard in the chest. 'You heard me, chicken. Don't try to change the subject, just make the jump if you dare.'

Ollie hesitated and Sophie could guess he was hearing Mum's lectures on not doing anything stupid. Mum would kill him if she found out he did something so unsafe. She didn't even know he'd been jumping off the railing. Flipping from the other side backwards – as Daniel was suggesting – was even more dangerous.

The show-offs loved the extension near the end best where it jutted out between the two structures over the dark water. There, it was only a couple of boards wide, narrowing past a gated section so small only two or three people could fit on it at any one time. And when they did, it groaned in protest.

But it made everyone else waiting behind a natural audience, added risk and any trembling knees from the jumper were too far away to show.

Daniel leaned past Kirsty, who as usual was watching and judging everyone, so he could only be heard by Jason, and whispered something.

Jason snorted with loud laughter. 'Nah, man,' he replied. 'Ollie's not like that. He's not soft. Or at least I didn't think he was.'

Her brother might be bigger than Jason, better looking, and broader. But the longer the word 'soft' hung in the air, the more Ollie seemed to shrink.

'You don't have to prove anything,' Adele said, her hand on Ollie's arm.

Bright pink splashed across Ollie's cheeks as he shook her off. She'd just made everything that much worse.

Sophie wanted to step forward and tell Ollie not to do anything stupid and that taunting from idiots didn't mean anything, but she knew it would shame him more.

'I wouldn't do it,' Pip muttered.

'Of course you wouldn't,' Ollie snarled.

He dropped his towel, edged through the gap in the gate, walked to the rail and climbed over it like a man on a mission. He paused just long enough to stare Daniel and Jason down, gave them a sarcastic salute, and then leapt back out over the water, somersaulting once before entering the water so cleanly it would make an Olympian proud.

Sophie couldn't help cheering along with everyone else when he surfaced, a wide grin on his face, fist pumping in the air. She turned to see what Pip thought but he was over talking to Adele.

'Not bad of Ollie there.'

Sophie looked the other way to discover Jason leaning against the rail beside her. 'It was okay,' she said.

'Everyone's saying he's so good at everything, it would be great if just once he did a belly flop or something.'

She shrugged, wondering if he realised how sulky he sounded.

'What did you think of my jump before?' he asked.

The truth – that it wasn't as good as the other boys', thanks to his flailing arms – wouldn't go down well, she was smart enough to know that. 'Pretty cool.'

He nudged her shoulder, the touch warm, skin against skin. 'You know, you're not so bad.'

He seemed to be waiting for her to speak, maybe thank him for the compliment, but her brain was clean out of brilliance. 'Um yeah,' she said.

'Yeah,' he said back, with a grin.

It wasn't all that funny, but she knew enough about the way girls at the jetty acted to laugh like he was the world's greatest comedian.

He looked pleased. 'We should maybe hang out sometime.' He lowered his voice, touched her arm. 'Just the two of us.'

Sophie hesitated because it was Jason and she'd known him kind of half her life, which meant she knew that although he could be funny and charming, he sometimes had a temper.

He'd sulked when the others left him out, thrown tantrums when things didn't go his way, and run off at the slightest aggravation. Worse, he'd shown flashes of cruel delight when telling smaller kids they couldn't join in.

But that was kid stuff and he was Ollie's friend. He was older and rich and not bad looking. Maybe if Pip saw someone else showing an interest, he'd realise she was more than just someone he could be friends with.

'Sounds good,' she said.

'Great.'

Later, as she and Ollie were walking back towards their shack for dinner, Sophie couldn't stop thinking about the altercation with Daniel. 'What's going on with you?'

'Nothing,' he said.

'You're doing silly things, like that dare on the jetty. A backwards flip? Just because some loser taunted you? You could have been killed.'

'Silly? What are you, a nana?' His arms folded. 'You going to run and tell Mum?'

That had been Sophie's thought, but only briefly. Mum would worry that he'd land badly and get caught in the dark water with its unstable currents. 'No, but that old guy who was fishing might tell someone.'

'Giovanni? Nah he's barely on the planet. Too caught up in whatever's made him…' Ollie made a 'crazy' gesture.

'What about the drugs stuff?' she continued. She thought she'd seen Daniel pass Ollie something while she'd been talking to Jason.

'I don't do drugs,' he said, his jaw tight.

She knew she should let it go, quit before he refused to let her come out with him anymore. One word from Ollie and she wouldn't be allowed to hang out with the older kids. Daniel would love to see the back of her.

But some things were more important than being part of the cool crowd. 'You buy them. And Daniel takes them, and I saw him give you something today after you jumped.'

He shook his head. 'You don't understand.'

As he stormed off ahead, kicking sand out of his way, she decided that if understanding meant doing dumb stuff, then maybe she didn't want to.

46

MELANIE – THE MOTHER

SATURDAY, EARLY HOURS – THE DAY OF THE WEDDING

Creak.

My eyes fly open and I stare into the darkness. I know that sound, it's the floorboard in the hallway. Sophie getting up for the bathroom or someone in the shack?

I don't move, faking sleep, hope the rapid-fire thud of my heart won't betray me and try to keep my breathing steady. All the while, I listen.

There's nothing more. It must have been Sophie.

I roll over, pulling the scratchy material of Ollie's blanket closer around me. I can't have been asleep for long. After the run-in with Fiona Lewis, I finished my whiskey bottle and passed out as soon as I lay down. But it's after midnight which means it's…

The wedding day.

I close my eyes, willing sleep to take over so I have the energy to face the morning. Another drink is tempting but my head is already foggy and I'll need to have my wits about me if I'm to follow through with my plan.

Before the sound woke me, I was dreaming of Ollie alive

and well. The long days spent here in the sunshine, carefree and happy.

Eyes squeezed closed, I try to return to the blissful oblivion. But now I'm properly awake and my brain insists on replaying my final moments with Ollie. Him lying on that metal table in that darkened room. So cold. So still.

My chest cramps at the memory so every defiant beat of my insistently living heart hurts, and my bones are sand. And in my memory I'm slipping, falling to the linoleum. Back in that room filled with too bright lights and a sickly, tropical scent that couldn't cover blood and bleach and pain.

I try harder to forget. But my brain, ever traitorous, instead flips memories and replays over and over again the words shouted across the beach that awful day as I ran towards the jetty.

'He's dead.'

The moment when I knew, as only a mother can, that the horrified cry was meant for me.

I pull myself out of bed, keeping the old blanket wrapped around my shoulders. Careful to be quiet, I make my way outside onto the porch. The neighbouring shacks along the bay are dark and silent. It seems like I'm the only one awake in the world.

I would have thought, if there were any justice, that the moment the clock ticked past midnight it would have turned grey and stormy, with thick black clouds and a bitter wind. But, no. Instead, the clear, moonlit sky promises one of those magical autumn days ahead.

Like so many times before, my bare feet make their way across the sand towards the water. I dip my toes, feeling the chill that suggests cooler weather will soon follow this late burst of summer, just not in time to spoil the wedding.

The injustice of it is sour on my tongue. A wedding is another milestone that Ollie will never have. Like graduating, his eighteenth birthday party, his twenty-first. And all those events that lie in the future for these young people. A career, a child, a family of their own. Thinking of each of them sends a pain stabbing against my ribs and I don't know whether it's more for what I've lost, or for what he has.

I scrunch my toes and the tiny pricks from broken shells keep me in the present. There's too much at stake now for me to indulge myself in thinking of all the might-have-beens that Ollie's missed.

As I head back up to the shack, I see a silhouette through the gap out to the road. A human shape framed by the faint glow of the moon. It reminds me of the figure I saw confront Fiona on the road earlier tonight, after her argument with Jason. The prickle of awareness on my scalp and the person's complete stillness suggests they're not someone out for a night walk. They're watching me. I remember the noise that woke me. Perhaps they're responsible.

I take a few steps towards the shack, sneak another glance down the side. They're still watching me, probably sure they're safe in the deep shadows.

Who could it be?

I can't make out much from here, my eyes are too old and too tired to absorb that kind of detail in the night-time darkness. My stomach tight, trying to appear unconcerned, I make my way across the sand. Although, it's not like they're trying to hide. Past caring or sure they can't be seen? Each step takes me closer.

Still, they don't move.

My path is taking me straight for the sliding doors back into the shack but at the last second when the building itself takes me out of sight I change direction, bursting out into the narrow gap between the two shacks.

There's no one there.

I close my eyes and lean against the side of the porch. Am I seeing things?

Opening my eyes again doesn't make the figure appear, but there was someone here, I'm sure of it. Leaving Ollie's blanket on the nearby table, I push on into the darkness. I scan the ground, study dirt, sand and rocks for evidence that I didn't imagine the person.

I find nothing.

I reach the back. The sheds and dilapidated fence are as they should be and there's no sign of anyone. That leaves the construction site across the road and the open bushland beyond. A place with plenty of places to hide.

Before I can think too hard about the malevolence I felt in that stare, I cross the road. As I scurry from one tree to another, part of me wants to laugh at how I would look from behind. A glance back shows all the shacks with blinds drawn, lights out and doors closed. Unsurprising given that it's the middle of the night.

There's a noise from ahead but I can't be sure what it is. The scraping is much louder than a footstep, rather like something being dragged, but then it's gone and I can't be sure I heard anything at all.

Heart thudding, I push through the gap between the temporary fencing of the construction site. The 'No Entry' sign seems to catch the moonlight, flashing bright white in the darkness but I ignore it. I focus on the frames and the plasterboard and the pallets of bricks. Whoever I saw must be here somewhere.

'I'll find you.'

My growled promise into the night doesn't provoke any response. The echoing emptiness a reminder that no one knows where I am and if something happened to me here, no one would notice until morning. I move more slowly. My next, careful step finds softness rather than the hard concrete I expect.

I muffle a cry, instinctively jerking my foot back. My brain conjures all kind of horror – fingers, a foot, hair, but it's none of those. Just a scrap of material.

Wait. I pick it up and the glitter on the fabric catches the moonlight, scattering like tiny pinpricks of light. Pink and black. I pull and it stretches out in my hands. A scrunchie, identical to the one Fiona Lewis was wearing and still with a hint of her jasmine scent. I think of her threatening Jason. His tightly leashed anger, so much more terrifying than an explosion of rage.

But how did it get here?

It's too much of a coincidence to imagine some female tradie dropping an identical hair accessory here while she worked. And I doubt it could have been snagged on a gum branch and blown here accidently.

I try to think, but the earlier whiskey is making my brain fuzzy. Thoughts twist and jumble in my head. A sick image appears of Fiona lying in the dark nearby, needing help and me unseeing and unknowing, just walking away. I search the area more carefully, looking behind bags of cement and propped up window panes. If only I'd brought my phone with me, I'd have better light.

But the moon shows enough that within minutes I can be sure Fiona's not here.

I pass the scrunchie from hand to hand, stretching the elastic. Maybe Fiona dropped it herself as she cut through here for some reason. It makes no sense, but none of it does. What's certain is that whoever or whatever I saw from the beach isn't here now.

Could I have imagined the whole thing?

47

ADELE – THE BRIDE

SATURDAY, EARLY HOURS – THE DAY OF THE WEDDING

It's late or maybe it's early. Either way my eyes are heavy and my brain mushy from the long day and night of pre-wedding socialising. Combined with the champagne, I figured I'd fall asleep straight away.

Yeah, so much for that. Warmth from the afternoon sun lingers in the small, boxy room and I swear the mattress is suddenly filled with rubble. I keep my eyes closed, try to remain motionless. Do my best to ignore the discomfort and the faint hum of a mosquito who hasn't got the 'summer is over' memo. Focusing on my breathing, I try to relax every muscle.

I need to sleep.

But the determination not to move doesn't last. After throwing back the sheet, I stand and tiptoe to the window. I push back the curtain and lean my forehead against the pane, allowing the cool of the glass to soak through me. The faint throb of my head is harder to ignore with no distraction.

I seek out the dark mass of the water, hoping the gentle movement of the waves lit by the moonlight will soothe my mind. My eyes are heavy, I yawn. Then I see something that shouldn't be there.

A woman by the shoreline.

She's close to the edge like she's fighting the urge to go in. It's Melanie, I realise with a jolt, and she's wrapped in Ollie's old blanket, the one I lay on when he…

I stop myself thinking any further. Tonight is not the night to think about Ollie and certainly not while watching his mother. Maybe she can't sleep either.

I'm tempted to go down, but then she turns towards me. I shift back as she lifts her gaze to scan the shacks, but I continue to watch her, knowing she won't be able to see into the unlit room. She strides away and is soon out of sight.

I yawn. I'm never going to fall asleep standing here. With a sigh, I return to the bed and the cheap mattress that seems to have gotten worse since I left it. Slowly, I drift away, sinking into the black.

Then I'm at the altar. But it's not our wedding venue. It's a church.

Recognition jolts through me. I've been here before. It was the church where we farewelled Ollie. And that's when I notice everyone is dressed in black. Instead of the guests Jason and I have invited, there are rows and rows of funeral attendees. Young people I don't know. Old relatives with grey heads bowed in mourning.

I look down and I'm wearing black, too, and the thin, silver band on my finger is the ring Ollie gave me when he asked me to be his girlfriend. When I look up there's his casket surrounded by peony flowers and flickering candles, and if I walk closer I can lean over and—

I wake with a gasp.

It was just a dream.

My damp hair sticks in clumps to the back of my neck. The line between dreams and reality wavers. It's just a random collection of synapses firing. But reminding myself of the science doesn't bring relief.

Trying to ground myself, I stare around the room for familiarity, but there have been too many remodels since I tacked a poster of Nina Simone to the wall in an attempt to impress jazz-loving Ollie.

I didn't take into account what being in Refuge Bay would be like, the ghosts it would raise. So much history and so many lies.

At least Jason really knows me. Knows the very worst of me and my biggest mistake, made on a rush of hurt and anger. And he wants me anyway.

I check the time again and groan. It's late, too late the night before my wedding to be awake. My eyes feel like I've washed them in sand, but my brain is still buzzing. There's no way I'll be sleeping at all without help.

After throwing back the covers, I pad across to the small bathroom where my makeup and toiletries have been left in an ever-expanding mess on the clean white surfaces of the benchtop. In the bottom of my makeup bag is a sleep relaxant. It won't knock me out, but it should help give me a few hours' rest without leaving me too groggy.

An image flashes in my head of me arriving at the wedding with my eyes all puffed shut, mouth open and drool running down my chin. I break the tablet in half. Natural or not, I want to be careful. It dissolves on my tongue as I flip the light switch off and head back to bed. I pull at the blanket at the foot of the bed, and something small and hairy flops out onto the sheet.

I bite back on a cry. What the hell is that?

I drop the blanket and stumble away, snatching my phone off the bedside for the torch app. Blood rushes in my ears. I blink, trying to make sense of what I'm seeing. Furry and small, but not moving. Not an animal but a soft toy and… Is it dressed in wedding attire?

Heart rate slowing, I approach the bed again.

Now that I'm thinking straight and with the light from my phone, I can see that the thing on the bed is a little bear wearing a wedding dress, with a veil stuck over its little furry ears. Mum must have left it in here for me as a good luck charm for tomorrow.

I grab at the bear's arm, intending to place it on the bedside table but it's heavier than it should be and, as I lift it, the tiny happy head tilts back at the neck and something tumbles out from its throat like gore from an open wound.

I drop it, but I'm too late. Handfuls of shells and sand pour out from the toy onto my crisp white sheet. Its head tips back at a horrifying angle, the little face still smiling up at me.

Acid climbs in my throat. I take two more steps back as though the thing is going to come at me, but of course it doesn't. Tears sting my eyes.

Who is doing all of this? Why?

I stand there for long seconds, and I imagine walking down the stairs, out the door and not stopping until I'm far, far away.

And then I think about whoever's doing this, with their gutless little presents and their cowardly hiding in the shadows and I think about them winning. Because that's what I'll be doing if I give in to the fear. I'll be letting them win.

And I've never been a good loser.

I exhale hard and square my shoulders like all those times I had to smile through the neighbours watching a visit from the debt collectors. Then I dump the sheet and its contents off the bed. Blocking this out of my head is purely an exercise of self-control. I place my phone on the side table, climb onto the mattress, pull the thin blanket over me and close my eyes, willing the sleep aid to do its thing.

I will sleep. And in a few hours, I will wake up and get ready to marry Jason.

No mutilated teddy bear is going to stop me.

48

ADELE – THE BRIDE

SATURDAY, NINETY MINUTES BEFORE SUNRISE – THE DAY OF THE WEDDING

Dark, grey water – the kind spewed up from the ocean's depths after a storm – swirls at my feet. It's my wedding day and my feet are bare, and I wonder what happened to the satin heels I bought to match my dress. The splash of rose on my toenails is hidden in the churning depths. Around and around go the white-flecked waves, pulling at me, dragging me down.

I'm sinking.

This is another bad dream. It must be. But telling myself that doesn't snap me out of it. The water is deeper now, icy and surrounding my knees, my hips, my chest. Soon it will fill my mouth and my nose with icy liquid and I'm not going to—

'Adele?'

Jason's voice slams me out of the dreamscape and into the bed at Mum's beach shack. But wait, what is he doing here? Isn't it our wedding day? Then I remember there's some maimed teddy bear bundled up somewhere on the floor.

'Adele?'

I force open gritty eyes to see Jason leaning over me, his smoothly shaven face concerned where it's lit up by the lamplight.

'Wake up, sleepyhead.'

'It's like really early,' I manage. I'm desperate to wake up properly, but it's hard to surface from the nightmares and that moment of instinctive terror when I woke to find him sitting on my bed. A quick look down towards the ground near the bed shows the wrapped-up bear out of the way and unlikely to be noticed. That's one thing less to worry about, but, 'What are you doing here? We're not supposed to see each other until later.'

'You know that's superstitious nonsense, and it is pretty early, but…' He takes a deep breath. 'If we want to get married this morning then we need to get out of here pretty soon.'

'I'm lost. Don't we have the day planned? The ceremony is at four.'

'Well, about that. I know you weren't happy with the chapel for the vows, so I've sourced an alternative.'

'An alternative?' I know I sound inane but I'm still so bleary.

He grins. 'How does exchanging our vows in an intimate ceremony over the water sound to you?'

'Not at the jetty,' I say quickly.

He shakes his head. 'I'm not that stupid.'

'Where then?'

'A friend has a yacht that's available this morning. I've been assured the setup will be just as gorgeous as what we had planned. I was hoping to have more notice, but if you can be ready and at the jetty in an hour, we should be heading out on the water as the sun is rising.'

I scramble to do the maths. He's right, with more than an hour until sunrise, if I can get ready in time we'll have the stunning morning light. He's thought of exactly what I'd want, obviously been working on it behind the scenes. 'It sounds incredible.'

His mouth curves. 'This way it will be just those of us in the wedding party and a few of our family. Privacy now, and a party later. We'll get the best of both worlds. This might be a good thing in the end. It takes all the pressure off, doesn't it?'

He's like a puppy who doesn't know if he's done something good or bad.

I'm trying to put a name to the tightness in my chest. It's thoughtful and romantic and means he's listened when I've bemoaned the need for a big wedding. But...

His smile slips. 'You don't want to do this?'

'I was thinking logistics,' I lie. 'Hair and makeup, etc.'

'You look amazing right now.' He smiles at the cute summer pyjamas Katja bought me, with 'bride' in gold lettering on white satin.

'You're definitely biased.'

The change of plans is sinking in and there's a kind of lightness that comes with it. The wedding will be done in a few hours, and I can relax. The lurking fear from the messages and the fire and the dread that there's something even bigger ahead will be over.

Almost no one will know about the change in plans.

With the official photographer missing, I can do my hair and makeup like usual, leaving the formal arrangement I'd planned for the professionals to help me with to later, before the main photos and the media presence.

I flash back to that time with Ollie, lying in bed, planning our dream wedding together. What Jason's described sounds like what we'd planned back then, but there's no way Jason could know about that. It's a coincidence.

Like the honeymoon?

I push the thought aside. Jason couldn't have anticipated that there would be a fire.

'I'll be ready.' I lift my hands to his solid chest and push gently. 'But only if you get out of here.'

'I'll let everyone know, and I'll see you at the boat.' He takes my hand. 'I can't wait for you to be my wife, and I'm kind of glad it's going to happen sooner.'

There's a possessiveness under the warmth. He's studying me more closely than I'd like, given I'm still not properly awake. A sudden panicked thought hits me. Has he seen the security footage of Rory and me? No. He couldn't have.

But his gaze holds more than love.

I know all your secrets.

I mentally shake myself. Jason has wanted me most of his life. That isn't something that switches off. But I must not underestimate him.

'I'll be at the jetty,' I promise.

49

SOPHIE – FRIDAY JANUARY 28TH
TWELVE YEARS AGO

'Where's your brother?' someone asked.

It was early, the day after Ollie's stupid dare and Sophie was sitting on the rock wall by the kiosk where she'd promised to meet Pip.

'Don't know,' she said, watching for Pip to appear rather than looking around.

Suddenly, there was something in her hair and the guy's breath on her skin. *Yank.* He pulled at her hair so hard she fell back into his chest. A firework of pain exploded in her scalp. Bright sparks of it radiated through her neck and into her spine. She bit back a cry.

'I said, where the fuck is your brother?'

She twisted but the movement hurt and she couldn't see his face. She thought she saw a glimpse of orange. Was it the guy who punched Pip? One of Daniel's friends?

'Don't move,' he growled.

She didn't have much of a choice. The only thing stopping her from falling was the guy's hand in her hair and his body behind her. Strands of her hair came out. She felt them tearing free, each one the sting of loss of so much more than just hair.

He was hurting her, but she wouldn't cry. Stuff letting him see her pain. She told herself that this was just a scene in a movie and her character wouldn't bow from this attack. She tried to swallow but the angle of her neck made it impossible.

'Let me go,' she managed.

In response, he pulled harder and she stifled a yelp.

'If I let go, you'll splat your pretty little head on the concrete. Still want me to?' he snickered. 'Thought not. Now tell me where I can find your brother.'

'What do you want him for?'

His voice lowered. 'Seems someone's been talking out of turn. Telling stories about things they shouldn't be talking about.' He reached out and knocked her iPod so it fell with a crack. 'Posting pictures, maybe. Maybe it was you.'

'I haven't.'

'Reckon your brother has some explaining to do.'

'I don't know where he is. Maybe with Ad—Jason.' Instinct made her change the name halfway. Not so much wanting Jason beaten up but from an innate urge to protect another girl.

'There, that wasn't so hard.'

The guy loosened his hold, but slowly enough that she didn't over balance. Once he let go enough she pulled free and jumped down, turning to face him, her body trembling on high alert, ready to flee.

It was the guy from the yacht club.

'Leave my brother alone,' she said, glad the tremble in her knees wasn't evident in her voice.

He smirked. 'You have no idea what he's really like, do you?

He knows what he's involved with, knows the consequences of tattling.'

He shook his head and sauntered away like nothing had happened.

She waited to be sure the guy had left before she went looking for Ollie, finding him as expected with Adele on the beach outside her place.

'Can I talk to you?' she said.

He must have seen something in her face. When they were far away enough that Adele couldn't hear, she told him what had happened with the scary guy.

A range of emotions played across Ollie's face as she talked. Confusion, then understanding, then pure terror before he blinked and smiled like there was nothing amiss. 'He's just a friend of a friend.'

'If you're in danger—'

'It's fine,' he snapped. 'Nothing to worry about.'

But Sophie had seen his reaction. Ollie was in trouble.

50

MELANIE – THE MOTHER

SATURDAY, AN HOUR BEFORE SUNRISE – THE DAY OF THE WEDDING

'Mum? Wake up.'
I surface to a hand on my shoulder and Sophie's voice, clipped with irritation.

'What's wrong?' I ask as her face swims in and out of focus.

'You need to get ready for the wedding.'

I look to the window where it's still dark outside. 'It's not for hours.'

'There's been a change of plan.' She hesitates. 'We have to be at the jetty by seven.'

Last night's whiskey heaves in my stomach. 'They're not—'

'No,' she says quickly. 'Not there. On a boat. The ceremony is this morning with just the bridal party and family. You can come, but they won't wait.'

I notice then her fresh, clean scent and the rosy shine of her cheeks. 'You've already showered.' She doesn't deny it. The delay suggests she thought about leaving me here in my hungover stupor, but for whatever reason she's decided to give me this chance to attend.

'Thank you.' I try to put every drop of gratitude I feel into those two words, wanting her to know, afraid of making her uncomfortable. 'I'll be ready.'

She simply nods, but I think there's softening in her face.

A quick shower, the minimal makeup and twisting my hair back into a burgundy clip I bought to match my dress, means I'm wedding prepared in under ten minutes and there's still more than half an hour until I need to be at the boat. I make sure everything I need is in my handbag and head outside. Just before the door shuts behind me, I call to Sophie over my shoulder so she knows where I am.

Now that I'm properly awake, I can't stop thinking about last night. The details of following the figure from the beach to the deserted construction site have blurred, but the scrunchie still on my wrist this morning brought back the dread that something has happened to Fiona Lewis. Maybe there's some rational explanation for how she could have been parted from it without a struggle, but I can't think of one.

Her social media hasn't been updated since yesterday. However, it's not even dawn yet, so that might not mean anything. Phone in hand, I debate sending her a direct message, but she probably won't respond.

I'm standing in the dark looking across at the building site when I sense a presence behind me. I relax, recognising Giovanni. Most people around here don't understand Giovanni. They've never bothered to get to know him. Maybe they just haven't had a reason to look past the cantankerous exterior of the reclusive artist. But of all my neighbours here at the shacks, he's the one I'd trust with my life. For nothing else but the simple fact that he tried so desperately to save my son's.

When he speaks, his voice is gruff as always, strained from

battling the noises that haunt his brain. 'There's been someone over there.'

'Do you think their intent is...' I trail off, then settle on, 'nefarious?'

His chuckle is low and rusty. 'I don't know about them fancy words, but I think you should be careful.'

'Last night I thought I saw someone and followed them over there. I have a bad feeling about it.' I don't begin to explain everything with the mayor and Jason and how drunk I was. Nor, if not for the scrunchie, how I'd fear it was all in my head.

'We could have a quick look now?' he offers.

I hesitate, aware of the time ticking towards the wedding, but it will only take seconds to walk across. 'Thank you.'

When I look his way, his mouth relaxes. Not a smile, those are rare, but I know him well enough to feel the warmth. As we reach the building's skeleton and duck through the fencing, Giovanni pulls a torch from his pocket.

'Are you always this prepared?' I ask.

He shrugs. 'Don't have one of them posh phones.'

The torch's beam is far brighter than any app, and he makes short work of sweeping the light across the space. There's nothing unexpected, but with my worries, every brick could be a weapon, every scuff mark the sign of a struggle. On the far side of the concrete slab, there are two lines in the dirt, roughly parallel. When I approach the spot, Giovanni follows.

'Last night, I thought I heard something... someone being dragged,' I say and point at the lines, my hand unsteady.

'You think that's some folk's heels?'

'I don't know.'

He moves closer and crouches, his hand rubbing at the bristle on his chin. 'It's dark, you're already imagining the worst, and a noise from this way catches your attention. Could it have been one of them nefarious types dragging a body out of the way? I don't know.' He turns to look beyond where the marks disappear off the edge of the slab. There's only the dark bushland beyond. 'Or it's from something like that old wheelbarrow over there that doesn't have its tyres properly pumped up.'

'More likely,' I agree.

Giovanni nods towards the shacks. 'I'm thinking you have somewhere to be all dressed up like that.'

'Thank you,' I say. I try to put in those two words how grateful I am for everything these last years. If everything today goes as I hope, I might not get another chance.

'None needed. Get going.'

And I do. Except as I head back across the road in the semi-darkness, I can see from the empty driveway at Jason's that those staying there have left, however there are still lights on over at Tammy and Terry's. I'm not surprised. The bride will take longer to get ready.

A check of the time tells me I have twenty minutes until seven. And there was a door unlocked at Jason's yesterday.

Don't forget the cameras.

I haven't, I tell the warning in my head. But if the wedding goes ahead, then nothing I do now will matter. If something terrible happened to Fiona for her to lose that scrunchie, then Jason must be involved, and he'll never be more distracted than now.

Less than a minute later, I let myself in to Jason's shack through a laundry entrance. I don't try to keep quiet. I know from his social media that Jason is already at the boat and he's the only one who scares me.

I move through the lower floor, from the bedrooms to the open plan living at the beach side of the shack, gradually gaining confidence from the stillness and silence that I'm alone. I'm tempted to smile for the cameras but instead keep my head ducked as though that could possibly hide me.

Remembering where I spotted Fiona yesterday, I take the stairs. The upper floor is clearly Jason's private domain. From spare rooms and bathrooms to his office and the massive bedroom, there's nothing obvious. Cupboards and desks that might contain incriminating documents are all locked.

My phone buzzes with a message from Sophie.

> I'm leaving in five minutes. If you're not here I'll ride with Adele.

'On my way,' I reply.

Jason's bedroom is minimalistic, but when I allow myself to skim a hand across the neatly made bed – seriously, how did he have time for that this morning? – the material is soft and luxurious.

There's only the ensuite bathroom left to investigate, and I cross to it quickly, aware that Sophie will happily leave without me. The expansive space is bigger than our shack's living area. Huge marble tiles line the walls, and the freestanding bath might as well be a swimming pool. I pull open the vanity drawers one by one, finding nothing. I don't know what I expected to find. It's not like Jason is going to have left a smoking gun lying around with the place crawling with visitors.

The whole place is neat, fastidiously so. I glance into the small toilet cubicle as I pass it. Even the toilet rolls on the holder on the ledge of the window above the cistern are neatly aligned.

I'm not going to find anything here.

On a rush of pettiness, I reach out and move the nearest toilet roll a little to the right.

That's when I see it.

A smudge of red, dried to a rusty brown. Blood. Easily missed even for a man as careful as Jason. I picture him stumbling in after whatever he did with Fiona, leaning on that ledge while he emptied his bladder. It's possible.

I snap a photo, unsure how I'll use it and then hurry down to meet Sophie with my steps lightened.

Maybe careful Jason hasn't been careful enough.

51

ADELE - THE BRIDE

SATURDAY, AN HOUR BEFORE SUNRISE – THE DAY OF THE WEDDING

Having tasked an excited Mum – 'oh darling, it's going to be magical' – with making sure Dad is ready and the car good to go, I focus on preparing for the ceremony with Katja's help. I'm thankful for the removable outer skirt that streamlines my classic, sleeveless design even further, meaning it will fit the more casual venue of the boat. I'll wear the gorgeous flowing skirt and associated petticoats for the formal photos later.

The dress will be last thing I put on before I'm out the door. Until then, I stay in my wedding underwear that holds everything in place and compliments those endless gym sessions since we set the date.

Katja and I get ready side by side in the tiny upstairs bathroom. The hair straightener is cooling on the floor. I used it to add a few beachy waves to my hair that's otherwise loose on my shoulders. Our makeup is spread out around us, and when Katja finds a playlist with all the biggest songs from when we were teenagers, it feels more like we're about to go out for a night on the town rather than prepare for my wedding.

Although such an occasion would usually include Pip if he was in town. So many nights with him perched on the end of my bed, singing harmonies, glass of bubbles in hand. When I asked about him, Mum said he'd grabbed his suit and headed to Jason's place. I ignore that it feels a little like he's abandoned me. He'll be on the boat, and that's what matters.

I keep having to remind myself that this is really happening.

I'm applying shimmering eyeshadow in an array of tones to match the bridesmaids when Katja catches my gaze in the mirror. 'Did you know about this?'

I hesitate, while choosing the perfect shade from my eyeshadow palate. 'No, of course not. We were planning separate breakfasts, but he knew I wasn't happy about the chapel.' As I say it, I try not to think about why it was moved there in the first place.

'You're not worried about the fact that you've seen each other before you walk down the aisle?'

'That's just a silly superstition.'

'Whatever you reckon.'

'It comes from the time of arranged marriages, all so the groom couldn't see the goods and decide he didn't want to follow through at the last minute. Jason assures me it won't be a problem.' It's hard not to think of his calling off the wedding as I say this, hard not to fear something else will go wrong.

Katja doesn't seem placated.

Maybe it's the lack of sleep or the nerves, but I'm not as in control as I'd like to be. It's this place. Here, I flirt with being the Adele I've fought so damn hard not to be. Romantic and wild and living without thought or deliberation.

Consumed by guilt.

There are pictures of me from back then, and when I compare them to now, I swear you can see shadows of what happened in my eyes.

Katja frowns. 'You okay?'

I know what she sees in my face. The lines deepening across my forehead. The slight purse of my lips as my teeth grind together. 'Yes.'

She turns to face me properly, with mascara only on her left eye. The lack of heavy definition gives her right eye a tired, ghostly gleam. 'I'm not just talking about the early ceremony.' She makes a show of looking left and right, like some TV spy making sure we can't be overheard. 'Any more doubts?'

Her stage whisper makes me laugh as intended, but I know she wants an answer.

'I'm good. I can't deny there was a moment where I imagined walking away – thanks, Melanie Rhodes – but that was nerves. I've thought about this. I've made my decision.'

'I could keep her off the boat,' Katja offers.

It's tempting, but the time for not inviting her was weeks ago, not when she's next door probably getting ready in front of some shrine she's built to her dead son. 'I wouldn't want to push her over the edge.'

Katja frowns. 'She's unstable?'

The impulse that had led me to share the gossip has already become regret. 'It's fine,' I said quickly. 'I can handle her.'

'And what about Rory?'

Images leap to my brain. Sex in the office, his hand on my

knee underneath the table, the way his eyes darken when I lick my lips. I shake them away.

'If he really didn't want me to marry Jason, he'd have done something about it.'

'You don't usually rush into things,' she says carefully. Too carefully.

'What's that supposed to mean?'

'I've been thinking about what you told me yesterday at the winery. That's a lot to deal with. No wonder you've been stressed. Obviously, he's well now?'

'Yes. He's in remission.' The language feels strange in my mouth. 'The prognosis is excellent.'

'Is there anything else you've been keeping to yourself?'

I think about telling her about the warnings but then I think of her scepticism over the twisted wire bride we found. 'Why? Are you going to suggest dumping a cancer patient?'

'Better than marrying one and you both ending up miserable.'

'This is what we both want.'

'You're sure about that? He did walk out. Maybe that wasn't a test,' she says.

It's insane that the possibility Katja's suggesting should come as such a shock, but it does. More because of the thoughts that follow. If Jason wants out, could he be behind all the messages and the trinkets and even the fire?

'He loves me.'

Before Katja can reply, Mum bustles in on a cloud of expensive perfume I know she can't afford, and I'm reminded that there's even more at stake because of my parents.

'What are you doing still in your underwear?' she cries. 'It's time to go.'

I finish my makeup without letting myself meet Katja's gaze.

I have a wedding to get to.

52

MELANIE – THE MOTHER

SATURDAY, JUST BEFORE SUNRISE – THE DAY OF THE WEDDING

The stunning yacht at the end of the jetty, with its white hull gleaming as the sun begins to rise, is almost enough to distract me from the memories that come from being in the place where Ollie died. Sophie strides ahead of me and I wonder if she's thinking of her brother or if she's more interested in catching up with the bride's group. They must have arrived a couple of minutes ahead of us and are visible further along the jetty. They're nearly at the boarding gate. This new addition thankfully well away from where Ollie jumped.

I feel suddenly that this might be my last chance to speak to Adele. I'm nearly caught up to the bride when Tammy appears in front of me.

'Whatever you're about to do...' she says, 'don't.' I open my mouth, but Tammy's finger touches my lips, her eyes cold and determined. 'No.'

Maybe this is the resolve that's kept her with Terry, despite everything he's done.

'Don't, Mum,' Adele says, having noticed us stop.

But Tammy steps closer still, her hand now covering my mouth. 'Keep your advice to yourself. No one wants to listen to the ramblings of a drunk.'

'Mum, enough.' Adele's voice holds warning and her hand grips Tammy's elbow, pulling her away.

And it's suddenly obvious they've talked about this before now.

I slow to a stop, flushing, only partly aware of Tammy going with Adele.

Yes, I like a drink or two, but only when it's needed. No more, no less. And perhaps a glass or two in the evening when I know I have nowhere else to go. Maybe being here has made me indulge more than usual, but that's understandable, isn't it?

Sophie sighs heavily as she passes me.

I follow. As the sky glows orange, my name is checked off a list by a young man at the gate, dressed in dark trousers and a neatly pressed white shirt. Then I'm walking along the jetty the last ten metres or so to the small gangplank onto the boat. I take off my shoes as requested when I get on board, but I don't go into the body of the vessel, as luxurious as it looks, wanting to stay out of everyone's way.

Here, I can imagine the soft sounds of the waves on the hull are whispers from Ollie.

'Mum, you're doing the right thing.'

My hopes of avoiding Jason are dashed when he appears in the distance on the jetty, emerging in his black suit in the golden light. Surely, he was already on board? He's carrying a piece of paper that he slides into his pocket. His vows? My chest tightens and I can't help looking for an escape, but where I'm standing I'll be exposed by the lights if I move.

I'm trying to press back out of his way, but short of going over the edge there's no way to not be seen. He's approaching and my heart rate is going up and I'm going to have to speak and I don't know if I have it in me to perform the role of excited wedding guest.

He's nearly to the gangplank, and any moment he'll—

'Mr Ellingsworth?'

Jason turns back towards the young man at the jetty gate. 'What is it?'

'This woman is requesting that we let her on board but she's not on the list.' He gestures to someone behind him. Her hands are gripped around the small gate like she's about to force it open or, failing that, vault over the top. She has dark hair, but her face is in the light and there's something familiar about it. Maybe she's a local I've seen before.

Jason's mouth tightens. 'Then she doesn't board.'

'She is quite insistent, Mr Ellingsworth. Could you please come and speak with her?' There's a strangled note in the young man's voice like it's taking quite a bit of effort to prevent the woman opening the gate. 'You need to calm down, ma'am.'

Jason hesitates and glances towards the boat. I'm sure he will see me, but a man I assume to be the captain – from his grey moustache, authoritative hat and pompous stride – steps out onto the back of the boat.

'Everything okay out here?' he asks.

'One moment,' Jason says. He closes the distance to the gate, his stride furious.

'Where is she?' the woman cries. 'Tell me what you've done with her.'

'I don't know what you think is happening here, but it's got nothing to do with me,' Jason says. He begins the walk back up the gangplank.

'Please,' she cries. 'You have to listen to me.'

'No, I don't.' He doesn't look back.

The woman pulls at the young man's arm. 'Please, let me through. He's done something to my sister.'

Jason ignores her, so busy staring straight ahead he's unlikely to spot me.

'I'll go to the police,' she calls after him, scrabbling at the young man blocking her way. 'I know what you did. She told me everything about your little deal, shared her evidence. I have sources.'

Jason begins to untie the rope holding the boat alongside the ramp. 'Let's go.'

The captain looks past him towards the young man. 'We can't leave yet. We need Mitchell to—'

Jason's hand lifts for silence. 'I think Mitch can have the day off, don't you?'

The captain considers. Nods.

As he passes me, Jason's face is blank and cold.

I try to fade into the background.

The captain looks apologetically to Mitch. 'You'd think they'd be better prepared,' he mutters. 'They booked this months ago.'

My head spins. Months ago? This is supposed to be a last-minute change of plans. No wonder Jason has seemed so relaxed with getting here. He planned this. Does that mean he was involved with the fire at the winery?

I hurry to catch up with him inside, trying to make sense of it all. Movement of the vessel suggests we've set off, leaving the distraught woman behind. There was something familiar about her, but I can't place the face.

Who is she? Who is her sister?

I slow to take a glass of amber liquid from several on a tray at a small bar. Then, glass in hand, I catch up to Jason at the point where the plush leather and real wood of the inside of the boat opens out to a deck with a makeshift altar at the far end. I'm in time to see him kiss the cheek of his mother – who's there with Ruth – smile charmingly at Terry and Tammy and then watch his lip curl at the sight of the little dog in his grandmother Dorothy's arms.

As I step out into the open space behind him, my stomach lurches despite barely feeling the sea below. The sun is glowing on the horizon and the lighting on the boat's polished deck highlights the edges of a plush black carpet marking the aisle. At the end there's a simple yet stunning altar, the arch of deep green foliage sprinkled with tiny pale pink blooms. I press my palm hard against my chest trying to keep the ache inside. It should be my boy standing with Adele up there.

I'm so distracted I almost walk right into the groom. He might be smiling, but there's a tightness around his eyes that suggests he's upset about the confrontation on the jetty.

Perfect.

I don't need to fake a wide smile. Now is not the time to mention I know he planned all this. 'Nerves?' I ask kindly, holding out the drink. 'You look like you need this.'

He hesitates, but only for long enough to look past me to where he must see the waiter with his tray of drinks, because he takes the glass from my hand and drains the contents before whirling away towards the captain of the boat.

And so, it begins.

53

SOPHIE – FRIDAY JANUARY 28ᵀᴴ

TWELVE YEARS AGO

Later that day, after she'd pretended to Pip she'd missed meeting him by the kiosk because she had a headache, rather than letting him know the guy who'd bashed him had hurt her too, she stood on her own by the edge of the water, letting the waves break over her bare feet and the water suck the sand from beneath her toes.

There was the unmistakable sound of huffing behind her as someone approached across the soft sand but she didn't turn around. If someone wanted to creep up on her for murderous purposes they were doing a rubbish job of it, and at this point it didn't feel like her life could get much worse anyway.

She kept her gaze fixed on the horizon. *Do your best, murderer.*

'Everything okay?'

She recognised that gravelly voice. The potential murderer who'd stopped next to her in the shallows was her dad. And if Sophie kind of stared at him open-mouthed when she realised as much, it was fair enough. He didn't usually seek her out for conversation.

He must have guessed her thoughts because he shrugged. 'I know. Probably the wrong question. Or the wrong wording. Maybe I should have tried, "What's up, dawg?" instead.'

She shuddered. 'No, you should never try that.'

'Yeah, well. I'm no good at this stuff.'

'What stuff?'

He kicked out, sending a spray of water into the air. 'Talking to teenage girls.'

Sophie considered pointing out he didn't do a lot of talking to Ollie either, but didn't want to scare him off. 'Maybe you could just think of me as a person?' she suggested.

'A person, huh?' He seemed to consider. 'Okay, *person*, is everything okay?'

It was stupid but the simple sincerity of his question made her throat ache.

Mostly because nothing was okay. At all. In fact, everything was completely and utterly awful, but there was no way she could begin to explain. No way he'd ever understand. And with that realisation came a stab of annoyance. One question couldn't fix her problems. It was too late to start caring now.

'Does it matter?' she snapped.

'It matters to me,' he said. 'Even if I'm terrible at showing it.'

She kicked at the water, more viciously than he had, so her toes caught sand and the spray drenched them both, leaving her tasting salt water.

But Dad didn't move.

Didn't take it as an excuse to tell her off and walk away.

She couldn't tell him her worries about Ollie taking risks and going too far and not being himself, without explaining why she was so concerned. And that involved too many secrets. Secrets that weren't hers to share and would get more than just her in trouble.

It's not like Dad could do anything about it, anyway. Except tell Mum and then Ollie would hate her and she'd be even worse off than she was now.

'I'm fine,' she said.

She strode forward, shucking off her shorts, her bikini, bought to impress Pip – not that he'd noticed – as always underneath. Breathing in, she caught a whiff of seaweed rotting somewhere nearby. A few steps and she dove into where the waves broke. The crash filling every sense. The grit of sand in her mouth, salt stinging her eyes, the pounding of it, until she surfaced in the cool of the other side. Coming up to relieve starving lungs, her hair dripping in clumps down her back.

Dad hadn't moved.

She strode out of the water, grabbed her clothes and headed up towards the shack, not even looking at him as he fell into step beside her.

Ollie was the only one there when they entered the shack.

'Where's your mother?' Dad asked.

'Dunno,' Ollie said without looking up. 'Shops.'

'Good.' There was something in Dad's voice that stopped Sophie before she left the living space. 'Because I wanted to talk to you alone.'

Ollie lifted his head, the spacey look in his eyes so often lately was missing and he seemed to recognise their usually jovial dad was serious.

Dad held out a little bag like the bigger one Sophie had bought for Daniel. 'I found this in your room. Is it yours?'

Ollie jumped to his feet. 'What the fuck were you doing in my room?'

'Not sure that's the right answer, son.'

Sophie watched them, her stomach in her throat.

Ollie hesitated. Then his whole body collapsed in on itself. 'Please don't tell Mum. It's not mine. I swear. Seriously, it's not. You know me, Dad, you know I'm not into that kind of thing.' The last was choked out as he wiped a tear from his cheek.

Dad's expression softened. 'Whose is it?'

'Jason's,' Ollie admitted. He shot Sophie a warning glance. 'But not how you think. He's getting rid of it for someone and he's just trying to help them out. He must have dropped it. I promise I'm telling the truth.'

Sophie could see Dad wavering. 'If you kids are in trouble…'

'We're not. You always told me to look out for others.' Ollie sniffed. 'I just want to make you proud.'

Dad nodded. 'Then you won't mind if I bin it.'

He hesitated but only for a heartbeat. 'Go ahead. And you won't tell Mum? She'd never understand.'

Dad was clearly pleased with Ollie's implication that he was just that much cooler. 'She probably doesn't have to know.'

'Thanks, Dad.' Ollie underlined the sentiment with a hug.

Sophie watched on, heard the lies in Ollie's voice, and wondered why she'd ever thought she was the best actor in the family.

54

MELANIE – THE MOTHER

SATURDAY MORNING, SUNRISE – THE DAY OF THE WEDDING

'More champagne, ma'am?' A waiter holds a distinctive bottle at an enquiring angle towards me.

Before I can answer, there's the soft touch of a hand on my arm. 'Maybe you should pace yourself.'

I shrug Sophie off but, undeterred, she places herself between me and the waiter. 'Mum, please?'

There's a vulnerability about her that I simply do not associate with Sophie. The pleading in her eyes slips like a soft sea breeze through the cracks in the walls I've been so careful to maintain all these years.

I keep my head high and pray the hot slice of shame in my stomach doesn't show on my face. I wave the waiter away. 'Maybe next time.'

Sophie smiles. And for a change it's not cutting or sarcastic, simply relieved. 'I have to go and help Adele.'

'I might see if they can get me a water.'

She leans close and brushes a kiss on my cheek.

Something inside me cracks, and I watch her walk away, my vision blurred by unexpected tears.

It's only when the waiter hurries to get me a sparkling water – I know if I don't have something in my hand, I'll find myself sipping champagne – that I realise it's only me and the parents of the bride left on deck. The others must have gone inside. I've taken pains to avoid situations like this over the last twelve years, but clearly Tammy's feeling no such qualms. High on her role as mother of the bride, buzzed on champagne, she's red-cheeked and heading right for me. I should have known our conversation wasn't over when Adele drew her away on the jetty. Hell, I should have known it wasn't over twelve years ago.

I could make myself scarce, find the groom alone and get what I came to do over with, but my feet don't move. I take the waiter's proffered glass of water and wait. Typical that her long, low-cut dress is borderline bridal, the cream and silver sequins catching the deck lights and shining over her svelte figure. Anything to steal some of the spotlight.

She sneers at the glass in my hand. 'Planning to make a fool of yourself?'

I take a sip, not bothering to tell her that it's water. 'What is it you're so worried about?'

'Only my daughter's happiness. You must understand by now I don't see you as a threat. I've already won.' Her husband reaches her side, and she curls her hand on his arm.

It's all I can do not to laugh. 'I don't want him.'

She blinks. Her lashes – extensions I'm sure – fluttering up and down like little hyped-up caterpillars. 'You'll excuse me if I don't believe the word of a husband-stealing drunk.'

'Husband-stealing?'

'You tried and failed, and that's why you're all alone.'

'I'm alone because my son died, not because of what

happened with Terry. I have no interest in a philanderer who tries to screw anything in a skirt. I'm wondering, though, just what it is that makes you so goddamned attached because I know it's not his prowess in bed.'

Her eyes practically pop out her skull. 'Why you little—'

She's spluttering as Terry grabs her wrist and pulls her back from launching at me.

I take the chance to hurry away. They are not why I'm here.

Alone on a smaller deck away from the others, despite being sure I don't care what Tammy thinks, I lift my glass to my mouth with trembling hands.

'This is embarrassing.'

Part of me registers the low hiss of disgust in Terry's voice, but I don't really pay attention. He's never been important in any of this, not even back then. Something he doesn't seem to understand.

But his hand grips my wrist, jerks me around.

'I'm talking to you.' Terry's eyes are narrowed, and faint red lines have bloomed in his cheeks.

Even as I realise he's angry, really angry, part of me is thinking about just how much laser treatment he'll need to get rid of those broken capillaries.

'I heard you.' I shake my hand free and try to ignore the pain where his fingers dug into my skin. 'I just don't care.'

'You can't fool me.' He moves closer, his bulk forcing me backwards.

I concede ground, unwilling to begin a wrestle with the father of the bride, but then I feel the rail behind me. The gentle slap of water on hull comes from beneath us and the deck lights shine in the spray. There's no one in sight.

'I'm not trying to fool you,' I say. 'I'm not trying to interact with you at all.' I can't help my teacher voice coming out. My god, as if I haven't spent enough of my life dealing with angry little boys having temper tantrums.

'You need,' he snarls, spit flying, 'to leave me the hell alone.'

'Okay.'

'Don't play dumb with me.' He wipes a hand across his mouth. 'This whole performance, the way you've followed me around, panting like a dog on heat. Well, there's only so much a man can take.'

I blink.

His tone is deadly serious but it's taking every ounce of my control not to laugh in his face.

'I am not here to seduce you.' I don't manage to keep the amusement from my voice.

And he might be full of himself, but the man isn't completely stupid. His whole face darkens and his lips draw back to show those oddly perfect teeth. His hand comes out and grips the area just below my throat. 'It would be so easy,' he says, pressing lightly, 'to give you a little push.'

A larger wave smacks against the side of the boat. Fine saltwater droplets spray my back as I grip the rail with both hands. He couldn't dislodge me, could he?

He wouldn't.

Besides, someone would hear and come to my rescue. But would they come fast enough? Would they get out here before the waves dragged me under? And what if I hit my head? I could sink below the surface without a trace.

My heart rate jumps, and he must feel it beneath his palm because his heavily botoxed face actually crinkles in pleasure. His hand slides lower, finds the saggy skin where my breasts once jutted pert and full. His lips twist into a sneer.

A hot rush of rage pushes aside the fear that kept me paralysed. My knee lifts hard and fast, finding its soft target.
Oof.
The air escapes his body as he crumples at the waist and staggers backwards.

I don't wait around to see if he manages to stumble right off the boat but head inside and down into the depths of the luxury vessel. I came here with a purpose and it's about time I followed through.

55

ADELE – THE BRIDE

SATURDAY MORNING – THE DAY OF THE WEDDING

Despite having seen Jason already this morning, I asked Mum to tell him that I'll wait below deck alone until the ceremony. It gives me breathing space from his family and, even more importantly, from Mum. Although Katja wanted to stay with me, she promised she'd run interference instead. A photographer Jason sourced from the crew took a few 'getting ready' style pictures of me with an impressive-looking camera then left me alone, sighing about the romance of it all as they left.

The benefits of being given the main cabin on a luxury boat like this is the access to a small private balcony. When I'm sure I'm alone, I slide open the door and step outside.

I stare out over the railing. The hint of a chill prickles across my bare arms. It's the first sign that the false summer we've been enjoying won't last. Despite the clear sky earlier, a few clouds are gathering overhead, coming together in wisps and clumps then drifting apart like they can't quite make up their mind whether to storm. It's going to rain, it's just a matter of time.

For now, it's still streaked with the warm glow of sunrise. And surely we'll soon be out of phone reception, meaning there won't be any last-minute warnings for Jason. Unless, of course, the sender is on board.

I turn to see Sophie standing a few feet behind me, her shape lit up by the lamplight spilling from the suite. I gasp. My hand goes to my chest where my heart is pounding. How did I not hear her come in? How long has she been standing there?

And as she takes another step towards me, there's something in her face that chills my blood. The pure revulsion is there and gone in an instant, replaced by a warm smile. But I saw it.

The way I was leaning over the rail she could have easily gotten close enough to give me a shove. I would have hit the water, my dress becoming a deadweight as it soaked through. Dragging me down beneath the surface. I would have disappeared into the deep before anyone even knew I was gone.

I shake myself and banish the ridiculous thought. She's not here to hurt me. But with her eyes on me, Ollie's eyes, I'm flung into my memories. Suddenly, I hear his voice. *You're desperate.* My hands clench on a surge of remembered anger. He'd said more, spat stuff about me wanting attention, being possessive and jealous. Said I was just like my mother.

Not now.

I push the past away, drag in a breath, relax my hands.

Deliberately, I make myself walk towards Sophie. 'It fits,' I say with a gesture at her dress.

THE WEDDING PARTY

Sophie looks down as though she hadn't really thought about it. 'It does.'

I give her a smile, hoping to break any tension between us. 'And it looks good, the colour suits you.'

Her eyes seem to light up at the compliment and I wonder, not for the first time, why she wears so much black.

'Hey,' I say. 'Thanks for being here, even though… Anyway, I appreciate it. I was afraid you might not come at all.' I wish it didn't sound so needy.

'Ollie wouldn't want me to let you down.'

My throat aches. 'I miss him every day.'

'Do you? Because that day…' She swallows hard. 'I thought, that day that he died. I thought I saw…' Her voice falters.

My whole body stops. Every part of me still. What did she see? Is this the moment I've waited for? My reckoning?

But then she's shaking her head. 'It doesn't matter. It was a long time ago and I was just a kid. Just be happy, okay? Ollie would want that for you.'

I exhale, it's all okay and she's given me the permission I've needed. 'I think I will be.'

'Can I get you anything?' she asks. 'Your mum said I should ask or she'd come looking for you. I know you asked to be left alone until the ceremony, but I figured…'

I mock shudder. 'You saved me.'

She shrugs. 'Mums can be hard work.'

I think of hers and everything, and I should let it go, but I have never been good at doing what I should do. 'Jason wanted you to be in this wedding,' I admit. 'Not me. You were his choice.'

Her eyes widen. 'Did he tell you why?'

I think back to those early conversations, trying to sort out all the details. By the time we'd talked about it I couldn't imagine having anyone else but Sophie. 'Because of your brother.'

'Ollie,' she muses. 'It was always about him for Jason. Him and you.'

Of course, she has no trouble with his name. 'You think there's something more?'

She takes a shaky breath. 'Do you really want to know?'

In the last few days, she's had all the opportunity in the world to share her secrets but hasn't taken it. 'Do you really want to tell me?'

She catches her lip between her teeth and there's a sudden shine to her eyes.

Knock, knock.

We turn as one towards the cabin door. It swings open to reveal Pip. He leans his head in. 'Not interrupting anything, am I?'

And without another look at me, Sophie crosses to him. She's saying something I can't hear past the rushing in my ears, a sound that distinctly reminds me of that feeling you get when a truck or train passes way too close and your heart races with the realisation that you could have so easily been hit.

Then Sophie is gone and it's just me and the brother I adore, only he's not looking at me with pride shining from his eyes but rather there's concern. I hate that the sight of it makes tears sting.

'I thought you were with Jason,' I say.

He shrugs. 'He seemed like he wanted a word with his best

man so I thought I'd leave them to it. Never let it be said that I can't take a hint.'

I blink hard to keep the tears at bay. It's an emotional day but this is ridiculous and I do not need panda eyes for the photos.

'Hey,' he says, his voice gentling. 'You're upset.'

'I'm fine.'

'No, there's something wrong.' He crosses his arms. 'I can tell.'

'I'm just a bit tired. All the excitement.' I allow myself a small yawn for effect. I don't need to fake it.

'Of course you're tired. I can see it in your face.' He holds up a hand before I can take offence. 'Despite the expert coverup. And no wonder you're exhausted with all the late nights out on the beach.'

It takes a moment for what he's said to sink in. 'How did you know about the late nights? You weren't here.'

'The group chats,' he says quickly.

'Right, although you can't tell from them how late the evenings went or where.'

His jaw works and he won't meet my gaze. 'I can tell from your face.' Red splotches appear on his neck. The lifelong giveaway that he's stressed or lying.

'No.'

'What do you mean, "no"?'

'I mean…' I step closer and stand right in front of him so he'd have to actually move away to avoid my gaze. 'You have been here, haven't you? It's the only logical explanation. You've been here at the bay and you've been watching me.' I think of the prickles on my neck and the sense I wasn't alone.

I think of how he's always hated Jason. 'You're behind the warnings not to get married, aren't you?'

He doesn't answer, but hangs his head in that naughty-puppy way he has. Which is answer enough.

I should be mad at him. And I am. But I'm also relieved. Because Pip being the culprit is better than what I've imagined.

'You scared me.' I push hard at his chest. 'Did you think about that? I was scared.' I push him again. Then I'm beating against him with all the fear I've been trying to keep at bay.

He doesn't fight back, just takes blow after blow until I don't have anything left.

Then he catches my hands and holds them to him. 'I'm really sorry.'

'I needed you on my side. Was it all you, all the papers and the bear and the messages? And the fire?'

'I'm no arsonist,' he says with distaste but then he nods. 'The other stuff. I had to do something. He's not a good guy.'

'We're not little kids anymore. People change. Jason's changed.' My voice rises. 'You scared me, Pip. I've been thinking I have some kind of stalker out to get me.'

He runs a hand through his hair, mussing up his usually neat perfection. 'I think you're making a mistake.'

'I'm not. You have to believe I know what I'm doing.'

'You're right, I'm sorry. It's done, okay. I swear.'

I stare at him, study the features of someone I thought I knew so well. Do I know him? Does he mean it this time or is there more to come? How far would he go to derail this wedding?

'I'm here to support you,' he's saying. 'But if you don't want me in the wedding I understand.'

Him not be at my side? It's unimaginable. Despite everything he's done and the faint doubts about whether his interfering is really over, I need him there. It annoys me to have to say it and I feel the risk in doing so. 'I'm not going to kick you out.'

'I just want you to be happy.'

'I will be. Now leave, before I change my mind.'

56

MELANIE – THE MOTHER

SATURDAY MORNING – THE DAY OF THE WEDDING

I push and the door to the small room deep in the bowels of the boat opens soundlessly. I enter and it closes behind me, silencing the noises from above. Good, no sound should carry.

Jason is inside the bathroom, right where I thought he'd be, no small thanks to the laxative I gave him in the whiskey. With his mother feeling seasick and having seen both his groomsmen stalking from the suite, I knew he'd be alone.

He's at the basin with his back to me. I could do it now and it would be over. The weight I've carried these last twelve years would finally be lifted. My son could finally rest in peace.

But I don't move.

He turns to face me. Not seeming at all surprised. Not at all afraid. I hate that the most.

'Not going to stab me in the back?' he asks,

I swallow hard.

'What do you want?' he asks, leaning back against the

small basin, the only hint as to any internal discomfort a slight stiffness. 'What do you really want?'

The answer is as simple as it is terrible and even now the words get stuck. Because good, decent people don't think like I do. Admitting that I want him dead would be losing the last of my pretence at being civilised.

Yet, it's what I came here to do.

When I realised I couldn't talk Adele out of marrying him, I knew there was only one alternative. I hid one of the old filleting knives Jim left behind at the shack in my hand bag. I gave him the laxative to get him alone in the bathroom, and I followed him without anyone seeing me. But now it's time, and I'm standing here, and my hands are shaking and I am not doing what I came here to do. My breath hitches on the hard pain in my chest. This is worse than all the years of waiting and grieving and missing my beloved son. This is failure.

His eyes narrow. 'What do you want?'

'It's just the two of us here now, you can drop the act. Stop pretending you ever cared. We both know you only ever saw Oliver as competition. You gave him drugs, encouraged him to jump and refused to help him. You might as well have held him under.'

'Oh, Melanie.' He sighs. 'I actually feel sorry for you.'

'No.'

'Yes.' He straightens, suddenly appearing much bigger in the cramped space. 'I pity you and your delusions. All these years in mourning. And for what? A son who complained about you every chance he got, who railed at your rules and who grimaced at your touch.'

Pain jolts through me. I want to scream or cry, but I'm frozen, eyes closed against the sight of him

'He knew about you fucking Terry,' Jason continues. 'He knew, and he thought you were the worst kind of cheating trash.' He chuckles. 'Finding out your mum is a whore really messes a boy up. Might even make him take risks he shouldn't.'

I'm trying not to listen, but the words get through, and he's right. I know he is. That's what I've been fighting so hard all these years. I knew he'd seen me with Terry.

It was my fault.

I'm still reeling, my eyes closed and the room around me fuzzy when there's a sound behind me. My eyes open as my mistake hits me like a blow. He's blocking my way out.

Backing as far away from him as I can in the small space, I hold my phone aloft. 'I'll call for help.'

'You can try,' he says. 'Reception out here's a bitch though.'

I see he's right. 'The SOS function might work.'

'It might,' he agrees.

I press at my phone, but nothing happens. And Jason, damn him, is amused. Then, in a movement so fast I feel the grip before I register him reaching towards me, he grabs at my wrist, squeezing until I let go of the phone and it drops easily into his other hand.

'What are you going to do?' I tug but can't get free of him. 'Hurt me? How the hell are you going to explain this?'

His fingers on my wrist tighten. 'I won't have to explain anything, because you will.' He drags me over towards the sink. 'You'll write a note in lipstick on the mirror saying farewell.'

'No.'

Smack.

My ear rings and the world wobbles. Pain spreads in a hot flood and tears well in my eyes, but it's the shock almost more than the pain. He slapped me. He actually slapped me.

He snatches my bag from over my shoulder and opens it. 'Quite the stash you have in here. Tape, a bottle for the courage you clearly needed, and a knife, of course. I'll take that.' He pushes the bag minus the weapon hard into my belly. 'Write.'

'What are you going to do with me?'

He raises a hand, smiling when I flinch. 'Write your farewell.'

I think about refusing but he's so much stronger than me, and my head's ringing. Playing for time, I fumble and drop my bag, scattering the contents, and then slowly pick up the lipstick – a neutral matte ironically named, 'Just What I Need'. I hesitate, trying to think of something clever that will tell them what really happened here.

'Now,' he snaps. 'It's not rocket science. Maybe something like "It's all too much".'

My blood chills and I sway on the spot. How could he know? I don't say it aloud, but he reads the shock in my face.

'I know,' he says. 'We *all* know.'

These are the words I left my family with when I decided after Ollie died that I simply couldn't do it anymore.

'Yes,' he continues. 'We all know that you tried to do something about your miserable existence, but typically you failed, and poor Jim found you. Was that the final straw that ended the marriage? Really, you're like a walking information manual of what not to do.' He smirks. 'I'll make sure to learn from your mistakes.'

I stand frozen with the lipstick next to the mirror, but

inside my world is shifting. I thought all these years that no one knew of that time. Of Jim finding me in the bath. The ambulance. The months of treatment. The lies to explain my absence to friends and family. To Sophie.

Jason holds up his fingers and counts off my failings. 'Don't screw around with the neighbour. No letting your kid die. No pathetic suicide attempts. Oh, and don't become a decrepit old drunk. Does that cover it?'

It hits me then, the difference between us. I can plan and wish for him to be gone, but he's just going to do it. I'm going to die here.

'What are you smiling at then?' He's annoyed.

'You wouldn't understand,' I say, beyond caring if I piss him off.

Because killing me gives me my son back. I will be with my Ollie again. And maybe, deep down, *that* is what this has all been about. I knew Jason was a monster. Why else would I push him so far?

I'm resigned to my fate.

Then the door handle moves.

57

ADELE - THE BRIDE

SATURDAY MORNING – THE DAY OF THE WEDDING

When the door to the suite opens again only moments after Pip leaves, I assume that it's him returning.

'Forget something?' I ask without looking around. I'm standing in front of the well-lit mirror in the small ensuite bathroom checking my makeup.

The door clicks closed and heavy steps approach without a word.

I spin around. Rory stands a few feet away, stopped next to the expanse of the king-sized bed. His suit is impeccable but his eyes are dark and wild and his hair is dishevelled like he's just surfaced from bed or hopped off a motorcycle or kneeled crying his love's name on the moors, and I can't help but melt at the sight. He really is every woman's dream bad boy incarnate.

He draws in a shuddering breath. 'God, you are stunning.' It comes out as almost a growl.

Goosebumps rise on my skin in response, but I manage to keep my face impassive. 'I bet you say that to all the brides.'

He shakes his head. 'Just you. It's only you, damn it, but you know that.'

Oh, tortured really does look good on him.

I find myself standing only an arm's reach away. I don't remember walking out of the bathroom, I didn't mean to move towards him, didn't notice myself doing it, but he's like every single thing I've ever been told not to touch that draws me closer.

'You shouldn't be in here,' I say, hoping he can't hear the waver in my voice. 'Jason will be looking for you.'

He shakes his head. 'I doubt it. He thinks I'm talking to the boat's captain.'

'Is there something wrong?'

Rory moves so close I can feel the heat from his body. 'Only that he's asked me to perform the fucking ceremony.'

'But how?'

'I got my licence for my sister's wedding, remember?'

'Of course,' I say, although his family obligations aren't high on my list of things to keep front of mind, if I'm honest.

He paces a few feet away and then spins to face me once more. 'How can you sound so blasé about this?'

'I'm not.'

'It's one thing for me to stand there at his side, and I dreaded that, but asking me to be the one to bind you two together? Make you husband and wife? I can't do it.'

A new fear wipes everything else aside. 'Did you tell him that?'

Rory hesitates, rakes his hand through his hair again. 'I said I'd speak to the captain to check whether it is even possible, but assuming he has all the relevant paperwork I can do it, and Jason knows as much. He was smiling when I walked out. I don't think he even realised that he'd just dropped a bomb on my heart.' He reaches me in two determined strides and his hands grip my shoulders, somehow gently and urgently all at once. 'You can't go through with this wedding. We belong together, baby.'

'Don't call me baby.'

He drops his hands to his sides where they curl into frustrated fists. 'So, you want me to stand there, perform the service and be the one to marry the two of you.' He shakes his head. 'You're asking too much of me.'

I hesitate, try to read whether he's really in love with me or just caught up in the drama of the situation. 'I'm not asking anything of you, simply because I do not need your permission.' I try to be gentle. 'I'm marrying Jason today and I will be his wife by the time we get off this boat whether you conduct the ceremony or not.'

'You're talking like you have no choice.'

'Nothing is simple Rory, you of all people have to know that.'

His head bows. 'You do not belong with him. You can't be stuck with him for the rest of your life. You deserve to dance beneath the moonlight and sing karaoke in the rain.'

Mentally, I roll my eyes. Okay, it's definitely the situation he's in love with. Clearly my own fault for messing around with such a romantic. 'I can't call off the wedding.'

'There are other options,' he says, darkness in his eyes.

'Like?'

He tugs my hand to the door where he picks up a gym bag he must have brought with him. There's something poking out the end, something long and pointed. He tugs open the zip, revealing a long metal device, a piece of rubber, sharp points.

It clicks. It's the speargun from their boys' afternoon while we were at the spa.

'What the hell?'

He pulls the bag closed. 'Say the word and I'll handle it.'

His question from last night plays again between us.

But then sense takes over and I back away from this gorgeous man, unsure whether the sudden clammy fear on my palms is from what Rory might do or the dark turn of my own thoughts. 'You need to get out of here and take that thing with you.' I turn from his imploring gaze, ignoring the sensation of something ripping in my chest. 'Please, Rory, if I mean anything to you at all, leave now.'

58

SOPHIE – SATURDAY JANUARY 29ᵀᴴ

TWELVE YEARS AGO

A big party at a neighbour's shack on Saturday night meant Mum barely registered when Sophie and Ollie headed out for a gathering at the jetty. She'd simply called for them to take marshmallows for the bonfire.

Since turning up with marshmallows would be reputation-ruining, Sophie and Ollie devoured them on the walk to the jetty. Sophie was sure Dad would stop them going out but it seemed he'd believed Ollie's story.

Ollie had refused to discuss the drugs Dad had found with Sophie, threatening to ban her from ever going anywhere with him again when she tried.

As usual, Ollie was soon sitting with Adele, while Sophie and Pip tried to keep off everyone's radar. They stood back from the flames as darkness fell, Sophie sipping a Coke that Jason had thrown her a few minutes earlier when he'd arrived with a cooler full of drinks.

'You shouldn't hang out with Jason so much,' Pip said out of nowhere.

'Why?' Sophie couldn't help the flicker of hope that it was

because Pip wanted her for himself. 'You jealous?' She tried to sound teasing but she instantly saw on his face that she'd missed the mark. She'd given away far too much. 'I'm joking,' she said quickly.

'I don't…' He took a breath, the red splotches on his neck giving away his nerves. 'I'm sorry, Sophie, but you need to know, I don't like you like that.'

She stared at him for a long moment, her brain trying to process the words, to make sense of the pain in his eyes and the sadness in his face. The drink slipped from her fingers, spilling into the sand.

'You're a great girl,' he continued. 'And you're my best friend in the whole world. I just don't have romantic feelings for you. I'm so sorry.'

He was sorry? He felt *sorry* for her.

The agony shooting through her chest as her heart splintered, pushed her backwards. She stumbled but didn't fall. She had to get away from this boy and his pity. She'd never ever be able to look him in the eye again.

'Sophie?'

She couldn't bear to be near him, couldn't let herself stay there because breaking into tiny pieces in front of the boy who'd destroyed her wasn't an option. But at the same time, she couldn't make herself move, terrified if she did she might fall apart completely.

'I don't want to hurt you but I'm serious about Jason, he's not a good guy. You don't really like him, and he probably doesn't like you. Not really. He's using you.'

Sophie's heart thudded hard. In her own way she'd been using Jason but she could hardly tell Pip that. Instead, she focused on the anger building inside her. 'Why couldn't he like me? Huh? Is it that hard to imagine someone could be interested in me just cos you're not?'

'That's not what I meant.'

'I don't know what you mean these days and, seriously, I'm not sure I care.' She managed a shaky breath, drawing smoke-filled air into starving lungs. 'Scratch that, I know I don't care a bit.'

His gaze met hers and she forced herself to match it, putting every bit of fury into her glare. She thought they were friends, but all he wanted to do was tell her how unattractive she was. Well, too bad, she was done listening.

'Are we done here?' she asked.

He bit on his lip, and then sighed. 'Just be careful, okay?'

'I always am,' Sophie snapped back. 'And look where that's gotten me.'

She didn't watch as Pip walked away but she felt the distance growing between them like an ache. When he was far enough away, she let the sob out of her chest and let her shoulders fall. Why couldn't he have just liked her back? Why did he have to say that stuff?

Once she might have talked to Ollie but even now he was showing off, eyes wild, obviously drunk at least.

'What's wrong?'

Sophie looked up sharply; she'd thought she was alone. 'Nothing. I'm fine.'

It was the older girl, Kirsty. Away from the others, she didn't make Sophie's skin crawl like she did in the group. She seemed more chill, with her messy hair and her eyeliner thick and smudged at the edges giving her a bruised look. She seemed genuine instead of fake. Sophie imagined Kirsty might be someone who'd smile if she served you at the supermarket checkout and actually mean it.

Kirsty lowered her voice. 'You don't have to lie. You can just say everything's crap.'

'Everything's crap.' Somehow she managed not to cry. Pip knew she liked him and she'd gone and stuffed up their friendship. How could she have been so foolish? 'Worse than crap. It's complete shit.'

'Fair.' Kirsty hesitated. 'Not all older crowds are like this.'

Sophie thought there was some kind of warning in her words but couldn't make sense of it, not with the pain beating in her chest.

And then just because Kirsty was there and she was older and she was listening, Sophie couldn't help blurting, 'Do you ever feel like something really bad is going to happen?'

Instead of sneering, Kirsty nodded. 'I feel that way most of the time.'

59

MELANIE – THE MOTHER

SATURDAY MORNING – THE DAY OF THE WEDDING

'Mum? Are you in there?'

It's Sophie. In my head I hear her name in Ollie's voice. *Sophie*. God, but he loved his little sister.

I force myself to move, needing to get past Jason to the door. He grabs at me but I push him hard. He stumbles. *Crack*. The back of his head hits the mirror. It shatters. The rain of glass like an explosion in the small space, scattering shards across the floor.

I fumble with the door handle.

'Mum?' she asks.

The stupid thing is locked. He must have done it while we were talking and now the old-fashioned key refuses to budge beneath my trembling, sweating fingers.

A hand comes down on my shoulder. And like I'm no more anchored than a buoy floating adrift on the open sea, he shoves me so I land on the closed toilet. There's nothing to show for my effort to warn Sophie except a slightly darker spot – blood? – on the back of his head that disappears when he smooths his hair down.

'You'll regret that, bitch,' he mutters and unlocks the door.

'Sorry,' Sophie says when it opens. 'I was looking for Mum, it's probably crazy but…' Her voice trails off as she sees me.

'Don't—' I begin but it's too late.

She's already inside.

Jason closes the door behind her. 'That was almost too easy.'

My daughter looks between us. 'What's going on?'

Jason is, as ever, implacable. 'Your mother had some crazy plan. Of course, she couldn't follow through and you interrupted her as she was about to take her own life in regret.'

'I wasn't,' I manage. I try to stand but my legs are not working properly. 'I might have come here to… never mind why I came. He's trapped me and he was going to kill me.'

'Melanie pretty much has got it in one,' Jason says before Sophie can speak. He holds the filleting knife with an easy assurance that discourages any approach. 'I kind of thought she could hold it in both hands and fall. Quite dramatic.'

'Kill us then,' Sophie says, moving so she's between me and him. Strong and defiant. 'Go on, get it over and done with. I fucking dare you.'

He shakes his head. 'You two are both insane. Clearly the apple doesn't fall far from the tree. But even I know I can't explain multiple bodies. Not yet, anyway,' he adds, with clear threat.

'We'll tell them what you've done,' Sophie says.

He shrugs. 'You can try, but…' He makes a sign for 'crazy'.

Desperate, I'm scanning the small space when I see it amongst the things fallen from my handbag lying right at my feet. The black scrunchie I found that looks so much like Fiona's.

It hits me. The woman on the jetty, familiar and screaming about Jason doing something with her sister. I didn't think of the mayor because of her darker hair, but how many people are going missing around here overnight?

Last night the mayor sneered at me about people's families getting hurt. All I've done is got a journalist fired… Could it be connected?

'What about the mayor?' I guess.

His eyes flash; I've hit a nerve. 'What about her?'

I pick up the black scrap of material, wave it at him. 'I found her scrunchie. I know you did something. Where is she, Jason? Her sister was insistent at the jetty. They're very good with forensic evidence these days, and bodies have a way of being found. Did she fight back? I know her, she would have. Can you be sure you left no DNA behind? There was a mark of blood in your bathroom; I've sent pictures to the police.'

His jaw tightens.

'What's this about the mayor?' Sophie asks.

'Dr Fiona Lewis,' I explain. 'Jason's done something to her.'

'You don't know what you're talking about. Either of you. Both as weak and pathetic as everyone else on board.' He's still waving the knife but he's rubbing at his stomach that must be really cramping by now thanks to the laxative. 'You'll stay alive. Wouldn't want you to miss celebrating the wedding of the year. Just have to keep you out the way until it's over.'

'You can't do this,' I cry.

'But you see, I can.' He pulls tape from the roll that I brought with me and then uses the knife to slice off a piece. He places it roughly over Sophie's mouth, easily avoiding her attempt to kick out.

'He was cold by the time I held him,' I blurt. 'Ollie was. So cold.'

I feel Sophie flinch and I'm sorry for that, but I need Jason to hear it.

Jason doesn't react. Having known him for a long time, I think that is telling enough. He'd dismiss me if he could.

'Not from the water temperature,' I continue. 'Like when I'd pick him up as a toddler and wrap him in a towel and he'd be blue and shivering. This was different.'

'Shut up.'

'He was gone and I knew that nothing would ever bring him back.'

He comes at me, tape in hand, the rip of it a sound that tears away the last of my hope as he binds my hands and then he's about to cover my mouth with it.

'Fuck you,' I manage.

He smirks. 'How completely unoriginal.'

Then the tape is forced roughly over my lips.

He moves to the door, shakes himself and steps out into the empty hallway. My faint hope that someone might be out there and see us vanishes. In the last moment before the door closes, his gaze sweeps over us. 'There are winners and losers in life,' he says. 'Guess which you two are?' The door closes and there's a click as the key turns in the lock. He must lean right up to the edge of the door as he speaks because his voice carries clearly from the other side. 'Just like your precious Ollie.'

I stare at the door, wishing I'd done everything differently. My throat tightens. Jason's right. I'm a foolish old woman.

I've failed.

And I've managed to drag Sophie down with me.

60

ADELE – THE BRIDE

SATURDAY MORNING – THE DAY OF THE WEDDING

Hands wrap around my waist, and I bite back on a scream as I catch a glimpse of Jason's reflection. 'Oh, it's you.'

'Were you expecting someone else?'

'I was expecting to be alone, and for you to be waiting up on deck beneath the canopy. What are you doing in here?' It's impossible not to imagine him walking in on Rory. 'They'll all be waiting,' I add weakly.

He holds me close. 'They can wait a minute. They can wait five.'

'Is something wrong?' I study his face. He seems a bit off, almost rumpled. The black suit is not perfectly buttoned, the nap of the velvet detailing on the collar and lapel not brushed smooth.

'The opposite. I just…' He lowers his gaze to the floor, clearly embarrassed. 'You'll think it's silly'

'Go ahead.'

'I wanted one more kiss before you were a married woman.'

I can't help the chuckle escaping. Of all the possible reasons for him to be in here, this I wouldn't have guessed. He's so damn sweet to me. 'Kiss me then.'

He does, gently and seemingly mindful of not smudging my lipstick. For a moment, everything but us disappears and the nagging fears in my head are quietened. But then the kiss is over, and the clamouring thoughts begin their chorus in my brain.

'Have you heard any update about the fire?'

He shakes his head. 'It might simply be bad luck.'

'Or they might go further next time,' I counter, unwilling to tell him about Pip and the messages.

'Then we'd better hurry up and get this done.' His fingertip touches my cheek in a soft caress. 'Meet me upstairs?'

'Maybe,' I tease. And then, before he can leave, knowing that the next time I see him it will be too late, I swallow and add, 'Jason?'

He pauses at the door and smiles at me, his eyes loving. 'What?'

There are so many questions swirling in my head and it's become impossible to tell which should be asked. 'Did you...' I falter. 'Did you engineer our meeting that day?'

He meets my gaze without flinching. 'I did.'

'Tell me.'

He takes a breath, glances towards the door that leads to the rest of the boat, but it's not like they're going to start this thing without us. 'You need to understand that when you get the news that you have cancer it changes everything. I'd seen you months before, I can't remember where. But you took my breath away.'

'When?'

'The details don't matter. Just that I was too afraid of

rejection to approach you. But then I found myself being wheeled into surgery and I understood what fear really was.'

A lump of emotion forms in my throat. 'You were so brave.'

'I didn't have a lot of choice. As they put me under and I feared I'd never wake up, I ached with missing that chance.'

Tears prick my eyes. 'Oh, Jason.'

'I vowed if I made it through that surgery and the treatment afterwards I'd find you. That goal kept me going.'

'I'm glad you did.'

'Me too.'

'Now get out of here,' I say with a quiver of emotion still clouding my voice. 'I have a wedding to go to.'

I'm not alone for long. The next tap on the door is the one I've been waiting for, and it's immediately followed by Katja's voice. 'We're ready for you upstairs.' She follows up with an off-key humming of, 'Here comes the bride'.

I take one last look in the mirror, my gaze taking in the pretty flush of my cheeks, the loose curls, the look of the bohemian wedding I'd once fantasised about with Ollie. My heart cramps and I let myself picture his goofy grin, imagine him tugging my hand towards the altar, impatient to start our life together. Then, I mentally let him go.

'I'm coming.'

Katja is waiting outside, her support radiating in that way of a friend who will walk right at your side into a fire even if she knows you're going to get burned.

'Your mum said to tell you not to tarry past fashionably late,' she says.

'Of course, she did. Now it's tempting to wait longer.'

'But you won't,' Katja counters.

I nod, knowing that any retreat now would be giving in to nerves, and I refuse to do such a thing.

Katja walks ahead.

Halfway up the stairs to the deck I glance back to where there are corridors leading to the rest of the boat. I thought I heard a thud, but everyone should be up on deck waiting for the ceremony. It was probably the creak of the boat.

I hadn't noticed on my way down how narrow and steep these stairs are. It would be so easy to slip and if I slipped... I look down at the hard, timber floors below, picturing the impact. Well, it wouldn't be pretty that's for sure.

Although I wouldn't need to worry about stumbling over my vows.

My legs shake more than I thought they would as I make my way towards the huge glass doors that will take me out to the ceremony. It's one thing to plan a wedding, quite another to find myself about to be standing at the end of the aisle.

The boat engine stills, the sudden quiet amplifying the splash of the anchor and then the gentle waves on the hull. Conversation hushes.

'The bride approaches, my friends. It is time.' The captain's announcement sends a fizz through the small crowd, reminiscent of the sound a firework makes just before it goes off.

As I step outside, I scan those gathered to witness the wedding.

My brother stands with my fiancé, a hint of the petulant in his features lingering from earlier, his acting not quite a cover for the guilt of having to admit what he's done. Rory's at the end of the aisle, barely masking a scowl. My parents are not far away, eager to give me away. Jason's mother and Ruth are together, their hands linked, their smiles welcoming. Dorothy is seated over there with her little dog, the creature apparently asleep on her lap.

It hits me that there are two people missing. 'What about Sophie?'

'Melanie's gone and fallen apart, hasn't she?' Jason explains. 'Sophie's comforting her.' His tone holds just the right amount of concern and frustration. 'I don't want to delay. The others are all here and at least she won't do anything to interrupt us now.' He pauses. 'Unless you want to wait?'

There's something about his words or his face. Something that makes my belly swish in time with the gently moving boat. But it's far too late for second thoughts. With Rory officiating and Sophie caught up with her mother, it leaves us balanced. Katja will stand with me. And Pip with Jason.

I nod. 'They'll be there at the party.' Besides, it's not like I ever really wanted Ollie's family as witness.

'Come on then.' The encouraging voice comes not from Mum, desperate to get Jason and his wealth officially into the family, but Dorothy. 'Some of us aren't getting any younger,' she explains with a smile.

My brother is trying to catch my eye, but it's too late. I decide in a rush that whatever message he's trying to give me will have to wait. Jason and I are connected in a way that no one here can really understand. That day twelve years ago we stood together while Ollie Rhodes took his last breath and we're united by those seconds in a way impossible to explain.

The question asked of me so many times: *Am I sure I want to marry Jason?*

Mostly, yes. I can handle getting married. But the closer

I get to the moment, the more the idea of *being* married, to him, forever, squeezes every drop of colour from the future.

It turns out everyone is asking the wrong question.

I can stand here at the makeshift altar and get through this ceremony, and I'll do it in goddamn style with a smile on my face. But as someone, somewhere, hits play for the entrance music to begin I realise that beyond that is where the problem lies. Because I'm pretty fucking sure here and now no security is enough; I cannot be married to Jason for the rest of my life.

I cannot.

My parents walk at my side along the short aisle. At the end they practically fall over themselves to hand me to Jason, a reminder that there are those who want this very much. Who need it for their own reasons.

'Okay?' Jason asks softly as he takes my hand.

My lips curve obediently despite the realisation and the spark of something like a plan. Not letting myself meet Rory's glowering gaze helps too. Thinking of Rory reminds me of the question he keeps coming back to.

'*What if Jason didn't exist?*' he'd asked. What did he mean?

Jason looks at his friend then, and he smiles widely. Surely, *surely*, he can see that Rory isn't happy. Jason can't be that oblivious.

It hits me like the waves outside have become a tsunami, almost taking my legs from under me where I stand.

Jason *can't* be that oblivious.

He knows. And he's decided to go ahead with the wedding, but he wants to make sure Rory suffers, thus asking him rather than the captain to do the honours. My breath shudders in my chest and I hope the spinning feeling in my head isn't obvious for everyone to see. I need to think, need to make sense of this and I'm right out of time. Could anyone be so cruel?

That I dated Ollie first burned Jason, he's never been able to hide his jealousy, disguising it as shared grief and relentlessly quizzing me about our relationship. I've played along as much as I can. That's why I didn't argue about Sophie and Melanie coming to the wedding and being involved. I figured he deserved to know I wasn't hiding my choice of husband. I thought I could give him that.

I breathe again.

No, the pressure and stress has got to me. Jason can't know I've been screwing his best man behind his back. He's just happy to have Rory here and to be marrying me.

Rory clears his throat and gives me one last pained look as the sun breaks over the horizon. 'Welcome, family and friends.' He pauses, swallows hard, and takes a breath before continuing. 'We are gathered here this morning to witness the union of Adele and Jason.'

61

MELANIE – THE MOTHER

SATURDAY MORNING – THE WEDDING

'Earth to Mum? Are you there?' Sophie asks. 'As if this whole weekend wasn't bad enough. Of course, it ends up as a complete shitshow, with that psychopath locking me in here with you.'

I don't know how long I've been staring at the locked door, thinking of everything I should have done, before Sophie's words penetrate the fog.

Somehow she's managed to get her hands free and remove the tape from her mouth while I've been mentally railing at the injustice of the whole situation. My head is still pounding from when Jason struck me and it's like everything is just a fraction out of focus.

She uses a piece of the smashed mirror to cut the tape binding me and then lets me take off the portion covering my mouth. *Ouch*.

'I'm sorry I'm not good enough company for you,' I say when I can speak.

'Good enough?' She laughs on a sigh. 'I'm not setting a

high bar here, Mum. Occasionally being present would be nice.'

'I am present.'

'Really? Or are you wrapped up in memories of Ollie?'

My cheeks get hot. 'I'm not going to forget him. You don't understand.'

She sighs. 'I know that you feel responsible.'

My fault, my fault, my fault.

The litany rings in my brain like it has so many times in the last twelve years. A constant refrain that hurts all the more because it's true. 'I should have kept track of who he was with and what he was doing.' I've said it a million times but it doesn't make it any less true.

Sophie hesitates, pity shadowing her eyes. 'It's not just that, is it? He saw you with Terry.'

Something in me ruptures and the memory I've done all I can to erase rears up in my head. I'd hoped Jason was lying but Sophie knows too. I'm the reason Ollie was so bloody angry that day. The reason, ultimately, that he died.

Me fucking Terry Pippen in the sand dunes.

'How did you know that he...?' I can't say it aloud, not when she's looking at me with such pity. It's worse than the anger.

'I worked it out. There was stuff with Jason happening.' She raises a hand to cut off anything I might think of saying. 'And Adele. Most of which he'd brought on himself. Don't say it.' Again, she lifts a hand to silence me. 'But I knew there was something else. Over the years, none of you have played it quite as cool as you think you have.'

I think of Terry and Tammy, of Jim's hurt and how we forget what kids might understand.

'So, he saw us?' I know she's already said it, but I need to hear it again.

'Yes.'

I bow my head. No wonder he was so reckless that day. He'd just seen his mother with his girlfriend's dad. It would have been confronting and embarrassing and disgusting.

'It was my fault.'

'It was an accident,' she replies.

So many wanting me to move on. 'I can't just switch off my guilt and get over my son's death.'

Her eyes close. 'I'm not asking you to.'

'Then what are you asking? Assuming Jason doesn't come back here, flash his ring to show he got married, and kill us both?'

She exhales hard. 'Well, if we're talking fantasies… You need to do better, or you'll end up alone.'

I study her face for a threat. A threat I can get mad at, but there's only resignation.

'It's not that simple,' I say eventually.

'Isn't it? What about when I have kids?'

I swear the whole boat tips in that moment. It's not something I've dared let myself imagine.

'Are you pregnant?' My gaze slides to her stomach but it's impossible to tell. 'Is there a father? Are you seeing someone?'

She grins. 'You don't need a husband to have a child these days.'

Her smile that I'd thought so different from Ollie's easy

grin is suddenly the same. The sight of it hurts, more painful than anything Jason tried, but it's a pain I welcome. Ollie living on in his sister. What then, a grandson? A new child to love, free of all my fuckups.

I think of her making her own success, of when she stood between Jason and me and dared him to kill us. 'You don't need anyone,' I say.

Her face softens. 'When I have a child, *if* I do, I want you in our lives.'

She's offering me the carrot to pull myself out of the hole I've fallen into but all I feel is regret that she needs to. Because I already have a baby to love. One who's prickly and stubborn and strong-willed and beautiful and is right now, right in front of me.

I blink back tears.

'I'll try to do better.' I give her a promise I think I can keep. 'I'll get help.'

'That's a great start.'

We stay in silence for a while, but now the usual tension between us has been replaced by something kind of like companionship. Sitting in this designer bathroom, feeling the gentle rocking of the boat, I discover that I don't care as much about what's happening above as I would have thought.

Jason and Adele are getting married and I didn't stop it. When it came down to it, I couldn't stop him. I don't know if Ollie would be ashamed or proud that I couldn't go through with it, but I'm at peace knowing I tried.

Sophie and I chat in a way that I'm not sure we ever have. I talk about a baby – not pressuring, but definitely encouraging. Time passes as if our surroundings were normal, and then suddenly Sophie jumps to her feet. She pulls something from within her big, chunky black boot. Whatever it is, it glints in the light as she turns towards the locked door.

'What's that?' I ask

'Pocket knife,' she says without looking around.

62

ADELE – THE BRIDE

SATURDAY MORNING – THE WEDDING

'I present to you the newlyweds, Mr and Mrs Ellingsworth.' Rory's voice rings out over the small crowd and one of the boat's staff hits play on the sound system. Immediately, Nina Simone croons about a new dawn and a new day, and I'm feeling anything but good hearing the husky notes of a voice I associate so closely with Ollie.

'You had her poster on your wall,' Jason whispers, obviously pleased with himself.

I nod, keeping the smile pasted on my face and let Jason lift my wedding-ring adorned hand in his like a victory salute.

Mrs Ellingsworth.

That's who I am now. One short ceremony and everything I've always been is lost in favour of being someone's wife.

I'm still here.

I want to cry it as my parents embrace us both. I want to scream it as Laura and Ruth approach us and they, too, congratulate Mr and Mrs Ellingsworth. Pip and Katja are next, and I dare not meet either of their gazes lest my inner turmoil is shining from my eyes, regret reflected in the blue of the gorgeous morning sky.

I cannot be married to Jason.

Neither of them linger with the congratulations. Pip disappears. I guess he's looking for Sophie who I still can't believe didn't bother showing up. I thought we'd connected.

Then it's Dorothy embracing me in a squeeze that makes Laila squirm between us and give a muffled yelp. 'My darling girl, welcome to the family.' Jason's grandmother's grin is so wide it shows false teeth and a lot of gum. Her obvious delight at the whole situation is infectious and I feel my own smile relaxing from the rigor mortis pose of a minute ago.

This is fine.

I'm aware of the photographer taking snaps around us, although she's careful not to intrude. I'm also aware of Rory, his usual attraction somehow magnified by the broodiness he's not trying to hide. The moment of clarity where I'm sure Jason knew about me and his best man seems ridiculous now. To know and marry me anyway would be pathological.

Then, at Jason's suggestion, we're posing, just the two of us, in front of the altar, and the endless blues of sky and sea are reflected in the camera's lens.

The photographer looks at the shot she's taken, puts her hand to her chest and then wipes a tear. 'It's beautiful.'

'We'll save the family shots for later,' Jason says, tone abrupt and without even looking at the young woman.

'Thank you,' I add with a smile. 'But there are others we need to include who haven't made it this morning.'

'Of course,' the photographer agrees, beginning to back away.

'No,' Dorothy says, bustling over. 'Take one with me. At my age you don't put off anything. Me and Laila with the newlyweds.'

Jason's jaw tightens. He hates being overruled but Dorothy's already directing the photographer on her best angle as she steps between us.

'And make sure you get Laila looking at the camera.'

I can feel the tension in Jason's arm where we touch. 'Make it quick,' he says. 'We have celebrating to do.'

The young woman takes a few shots, working with significantly less confidence than before and then shows the product to Dorothy.

She squints at the screen and tuts. 'Just a couple more if no one minds. Laila's not even looking. It's important not to miss moments like these. You appreciate that when you get on in years.' Dorothy returns her attention to the photographer. 'Could you click your fingers to get Laila's attention just before you take the picture?'

Jason exhales hard but he doesn't argue. The photographer obeys Dorothy's order and takes a few more photos. I can feel my face getting numb from trying to maintain my smile.

'Enough,' Jason announces as 'It Had to Be You', begins playing and Dorothy begins to dance. He steps around his grandmother, dropping a kiss in the vicinity of her head.

She mutters something and his brows lower briefly before he reclaims my hand. 'Shall we have a celebratory drink, Mrs Ellingsworth?'

I'm ashamed to say that I do have a moment where I think he's speaking to his mother or grandmother before my new title hits me afresh. I meet Rory's gaze then and for the first time since I saw him from the top of the aisle he appears happier. Did he see my reaction?

I look away.

63

SOPHIE – SATURDAY JANUARY 29ᵀᴴ
TWELVE YEARS AGO

As much as Sophie wanted to get away from Pip after he broke her heart, pride made her stay at the bonfire, and some good acting let her smile and laugh until she almost believed herself that she was okay.

It was after midnight when she found herself sitting a little way from the blaze in the dark shadows of the old jetty. There had been a group of them gathered but now it was only her and Jason.

'The others are leaving,' she said pointing to where the group was spreading out, calling farewells.

He offered her a crooked smile. 'Am I keeping you up?'

She was still looking at the others. Ollie and Adele had snuck off ages ago and it wasn't like her brother was going to come back for her.

Just at that moment, one of the figures on the sand by the still flickering flames separated from the others, paused, and seemed to look back their way. She couldn't be sure from this far but her gut said it was Pip.

'I can stay a while,' she said quickly dragging her gaze back to Jason.

He leaned over and brushed her hair back from her face. 'Don't worry, I'll make sure you get home safely.'

When, a few seconds later, she dared look at where Pip had been, there was no one.

There was the sound of rustling next to her and then Jason pulled a vodka cruiser out from his bag. 'You want some?' He asked. 'I snagged it specially for you, because I know girls like these.'

She barely hesitated before taking the bottle from him. 'Thanks.'

The outside was wet with condensation but the cool of it felt good against her skin. With him watching her, she lifted the bottle to her mouth and took a long sip of the painfully sweet drink. The rush of sugar hit the back of her throat and she had to make an effort not to gag. Her first real alcoholic drink should have been with Pip, but instead she was here, alone with Jason Ellingsworth. She gulped a bit more.

'Steady on,' Jason said. 'It's more potent than it tastes. I wouldn't want you doing anything you might regret.'

'Really? Like what?' she said, her voice sounding like one of the cool girls in the movies. She heard the words coming out of her mouth like she was playing a part on the stage.

Jason edged closer. 'I have a few ideas.'

She took another sip as he moved closer and his arm slipped over her shoulder and when she lowered the bottle again, the liquid inside was nearly gone. How had that happened so fast?

She drained the last of the bottle and when Jason leaned

over to kiss her, she let him. His mouth was warm and she could taste beer on him. It didn't make her heart beat faster but it wasn't awful. When his tongue tried to make its way between her lips she pulled back.

Irritation flashed across his face. 'You're such a tease.'

'I'm not,' she insisted, but she didn't even sound convincing to her own ears. The tears threatening earlier were suddenly spilling from her eyes.

His arm snaked around her waist. 'Don't cry.'

She sniffed. 'It's just the smoke off the fire or something, I swear.' She waved her hand in front of her face as though to clear the smoke away.

He shifted so he had a leg either side of her and pulled her against him. 'I'll protect you.'

She kind of liked the sound of that. It would be nice to have someone looking out for her. This time when he tried, she let him open her mouth and tried to find the whole thing enjoyable.

'Trust me,' he murmured between kisses that were no more exciting than when she'd practised on her pillow, just a bit wetter. 'I won't hurt you.'

But the impact of his mouth on hers became harder and unforgiving, and when he tried to work his hand beneath her top, his fingers pinched at her skin.

She didn't pull away because she'd been around the older kids enough to know that this was what happened, and she didn't want to hurt his feelings.

He seemed so happy to be here with her and that was nice. When he gave her another drink, it went down even faster than the first and things began to get a little blurry.

When he kissed her again, she was able to imagine it was

Pip. This allowed her to kiss him back with more enthusiasm and he seemed to like it.

'That's it, baby.'

His voice made her draw back, breaking the spell of her imagination but then he gave her another drink. She was past thinking now. She just wanted the escape of the alcohol, the way it stopped all her worries playing on repeat in her brain.

And when she smiled, he seemed even more pleased.

'You like this, don't you?'

A laugh bubbled in her chest. Did he really think this had anything to do with him?

'What are you laughing at?' he snarled.

'Nothing,' she managed, but the giggles wouldn't stop, even though something in his expression was making her heart beat faster and her want to shift away from him in the sand.

His hand on her waist stopped her moving. 'You don't want to do that.'

'I have to go,' she blurted. Not sober, but panicked, afraid and knowing that this wasn't where she wanted to be. She scanned around but they were completely alone in the darkness, the hour late and the jetty making deep shadows that meant no one would see them unless they were really close.

'No, you don't,' Jason said. 'You can't.'

'Please,' she said. 'I don't want to do this.' But somehow he was on top of her and her skirt that she'd picked out to impress Pip was riding up. 'I really should—'

His lips silenced anything she might have said and they stayed there while his hands pawed at her body. She couldn't move with the weight of him and the certainty of him and the sense that she'd let this happen so it wasn't fair to say anything now.

When finally – finally – it was over he stood in front of her and held out a hand. She could see it despite resting her head on her knees that she'd pulled up to her chest after straightening her clothes. She wrapped her arms around her legs, holding tight, holding the shakes she couldn't seem to stop.

His hand hovered there for long heartbeats.

When she didn't take it, the fingers curled briefly into a fist. She didn't flinch. Didn't brace. Didn't try to move out the way. So what if he hit her? It didn't matter now. Nothing did. But he didn't. Instead, his hand dropped to his side and he kicked at the sand.

'You can't tell anyone about this. Everyone saw you stay here with me. No one will think you didn't want this. Because we both know you did.'

Her denial died in her throat as she replayed the knowing looks, the smiles, the fact that up until she didn't want what was happening, she had. She'd kind of liked kissing him, she'd not really tried to stop him.

Had she wanted it? And if she had, why did she feel so bad?

She waited until he'd disappeared into the night before slowly making her way along the sand then up to the road towards number fifty-seven.

A chill on her back brought her out of the trance she'd been in since Jason left her. She quickened her footsteps, trying to listen for anyone following. Her breath became loud in her ears. It was silly to be suddenly scared; there was no one around and it was Refuge Bay not the city. But she broke into a run along the pot-holed road, wanting to get far away from Jason and the thing she'd decided not to think about.

The wind had picked up. Sand and dust flew into her skin with each gust, stinging like tiny pricks. When she ran out of breath, she slowed again, shivering although it wasn't really cold. As she peered into the darkness, old straggly trees in the empty scrub on the other side of the road became figures and then trees again like a nightmare come to life.

The sight of her shack had her mentally shaking her head at letting her imagination get the better of her. Movement in the trees ahead slowed her steps.

It was Ollie and Adele, lit up by the moonlight and the occasional back porch light of the otherwise darkened shacks. They were standing close together near an old shed. If they looked this way, they'd see Sophie and ask where she'd been. Maybe they'd see something was wrong. She realised there was wetness on her legs that she might not be able to hide. *Please let there be no blood*, she thought.

'I can't believe this.' Adele's voice carried to where Sophie lurked.

Ollie dragged a hand down his face, a mix of anger and confusion in the deep frown grooving his forehead. 'I didn't even do anything.'

'That's not what I've heard,' Adele replied.

'I wouldn't.'

'So, you want to tell me you don't think she's hot?' Adele wiped her cheeks where tears shone. 'I don't believe you.'

'You're being ridiculous.'

'I knew it,' she cried. 'You're breaking up with me.' She'd caught hold of his T-shirt and her nails dug into the fabric, catching on a loose thread and tearing a tiny hole.

He stared down at her. 'Let me go.'

She gripped tighter and the fabric ripped. 'I saw you watching her.'

'You're desperate,' he said. 'Constantly looking for me to fuck up so you can complain about it. You're just like your mum. Poor and desperate. You know what? Fuck this,' Ollie growled. 'You don't fucking own me.'

Sophie stumbled back, away from the anger and the fighting and the shattering of something she'd thought so strong. But even with her head bowed and hands over her ears, Sophie caught Adele's final, strangled, 'I hate you,' before the other girl fled into the darkness leaving Ollie to slam his hand over and over against the nearest shed wall.

64

MELANIE – THE MOTHER

SATURDAY MORNING – THE WEDDING

Sophie bends over and considers the small lock on the door and then selects one of the attachments on the pocket knife. She jiggles something. There's a soft *pop*, and a screw falls into her palm. Then another. And then the rest of the lock mechanism.

I think my jaw actually hangs open. 'How did you know to bring that?'

'I didn't,' she says. 'Not specifically. I carry it with me. As a location manager, it comes in handy more often than you might think.' She spins the compact device in her hand then extends a small blade. 'This does, too. I once made myself a promise I'd never be at anyone's mercy ever again.'

'Why didn't you do something when he was here?'

She doesn't answer.

Clearly, she expects me to work it out myself. 'Because he's bigger and stronger and he had a huge knife and everything about him suggests he'd kill. That he might have already done so.'

'Got it in one.' She runs her finger lightly along the edge of the blade. 'Not that I didn't want to. Also, I don't think it's up to us to stop that wedding. We're better leaving these people to their miserable lives together.'

'But Adele—'

'Knows exactly what she's doing.'

With freedom imminent I can't help but ask, 'What are we going to do when we get out there? We need him to pay for what he's done.'

I don't have to point out that it will be our word against his, and we're not in friendly territory.

'What can we do?' she asks, resigned. 'We can tell them, but we don't have any evidence.'

My idea that the woman at the jetty is Fiona's sister has solidified. I try to think back. It's been years since I read about the journalist who was fired thanks to my complaints. Complaints I exaggerated in my need to make someone pay for my son's memory being tarnished. Her being the mayor's sister would explain a lot.

I fumble with my phone.

'There's no signal,' Sophie points out.

'I know.' I resist snapping that I established that when Jason was going to kill me.

I'm not looking for anything new, only the articles I've read a million times and saved for reference. I scroll down the first, muffling a curse when it has no by-line, but there are more. The next has me exhaling in a kind of whistle through my teeth. Kirsty Lewis.

I try to picture the bedraggled person on the dock as an award-winning journalist, and for the first time I appreciate what my complaint must have set in motion. And, at the heart of her distress today, Jason and the missing mayor.

'Those articles about Ollie were written by someone undercover. Was there an older girl, someone new to the group? A Kirsty?'

Sophie's expression answers before she does, 'Yes.'

'Before we left the jetty, there was a woman claiming he'd done something with her sister. I saw him with Fiona after their altercation last night on the deck.'

'You were drinking.'

I ignore her pointed implication that anything I think I saw can't be trusted. 'But what does she have on him? The dealings for all the construction for the holiday apartments near the jetty are the end result of whatever's between them, not the cause.'

'I might know.' Sophie's voice is small.

'How?'

She doesn't answer and I think of the easy way that she pulled the small knife from her boot and her confidence in handling it.

'There's more, isn't there? More to having that knife?'

For a second I'm not sure she heard me as colour leaches from her face. 'Do you really want to do this now?' she asks.

'If there's something you need to tell me…'

She shrugs. The laugh that follows is a pained sound that unexpectedly hurts me deep in my chest where I thought there was only missing Ollie.

'You couldn't have noticed, maybe, I don't know, about twelve years ago?' she asks.

'Noticed what?'

Her eyes flash. Anger. Hurt. Pain.

'Jason Ellingsworth assaulted me.' Her voice is wooden, like she's reciting a shopping list. 'I was fifteen and stupid and

I put myself in a situation where he could take advantage of me but that's no excuse for what he did.'

I'm close to her before I can think about it and I wrap my daughter in my arms. Hold her close while the shame of all I've missed burns inside. 'I'm sorry,' I say finally when I can speak again. 'I'm so sorry. Oh, my girl.'

I hear her throat work and then she carefully pulls away. Her face is dry but the emotion in her eyes leaves me in no doubt what it cost her to tell me.

'I have spent so long working towards the point where I can even say that he did something wrong. I knew it was bad, I don't know if I more than mumbled "no", but there was no consent. I didn't ask for what happened, no matter what he told me at the time.' She sighs. 'I saw the local GP for emergency contraceptive. I saw Fiona Lewis.'

'He needs to pay for what he's done.'

Her eyes close briefly. 'I'm not going to give him the chance to humiliate me in front of those people.'

Her strength is so much more than I ever imagined or gave her credit for. 'How are you even managing to be here?'

One side of her mouth lifts. 'A lot of therapy. Pip's support. The need to show Jason that I'm not someone he can leave cowering.'

Pride flares inside me.

'Also,' she says. 'I wanted to be there for Adele and, to be honest, I didn't really trust you not to make this a disaster.' Her gaze flicks around the space, at the mirror and the pieces of tape and the broken lock.

'You misjudge me,' I say. I pull her close again. 'We can stay in here until we hit land and then skip all the wedding shenanigans.'

'Really?'

I jerk back at her tone. 'What?'

'You'd miss all of that? You'd miss knowing exactly what's going on?'

When I follow her gesture to above, I imagine I hear some cries of celebration. Despite everything, it pulls on my focus like a story I've been following for so long that the desire to find out how it ends is practically ingrained.

And she must see it in my face.

'Yes,' I say quickly, but it's too late.

She shakes her head. 'I'm not going to hide from him now. Let's go and congratulate the happy couple. And,' she adds. 'I reckon Jason will shit himself when we appear.'

'He might give himself away,' I say hopefully.

'Maybe, but I doubt it. He'll get his comeuppance, just maybe not today.'

I trail her slowly out into the hallway towards the narrow stairs leading to the upper deck. The movement suggests we're already on our way back towards port. Which means...

'They're married.' I whisper it, then roll it around in my head waiting for the pain, but it doesn't come. It hurts less than I ever guessed it would. I still hate that psychotic son of a bastard for what he did to my children but him marrying Adele doesn't mean anything except she's grown up to have shitty taste in men.

'Mum?'

I manage a smile at my brave daughter who's already at the stairs. If she can face him then I can walk up there with my head held high. Although...

'Hold on a second,' I say, turning away. I'll duck back and grab a shard of mirror. Damned if I'll let Tammy sneer at my rumpled state. She'll think I'm trying to get attention. God knows what Jason has told them about why we missed the wedding.

But Sophie hasn't heard me. By the time I've patted down my hair and checked my face to see the red mark from his slap is almost gone, she has disappeared.

And I'm alone in the bowels of the boat.

65

ADELE – THE BRIDE

SATURDAY MORNING – AFTER THE WEDDING

A crew member approaches us with a tray of drinks. Given the occasion, I follow Jason's lead and take a glass of champagne. We clink glasses and he kisses me lightly before I can take a sip. As I lift the glass to my mouth, the bubbles tickle my nose and only supreme self-control prevents me draining the glass.

The others already have drinks in hand.

'Careful,' Dorothy says, but she's not looking at me gulping courage. Instead, she's talking to Jason. 'You've had that medication.'

Jason glares. 'It's nothing.'

'Seasickness tablets,' Dorothy whispers.

Jason takes another large sip of his drink as if to spite her.

'Good drop, son,' Dad says to Jason, waving the glass like he's an expert. Dad follows up his compliment by embracing him. 'So glad to have you in the family.'

I feel, rather than see, Pip wince. This is the man who still struggles to accept his own son, yet he's practically slobbering over the new member of the family. Mum isn't far behind, gushing over everything from the boat to the sunshine, like Jason has organised that, too.

Somehow Mum and Dad crowd Jason so much that when I turn to listen to Katja, I become separated from my new husband. Rory approaches me with intent and I pretend to spot Dorothy gesturing to me and hurry over to her side. Now is not the time for a one-on-one chat with a man who begged me not to get married less than half an hour ago.

Dorothy is seated on the edge of a lounger with the little dog on her lap and I'm absurdly pleased when Laila leans in to my pat of the top of her head.

'She really likes you, dear,' Dorothy says.

'She's very sweet,' I reply but I'm watching Jason speak to my parents and now his mother and Ruth as well.

He's saying all the right things, even making a joke or two with the boat captain, but I know from the tilt of his head, the ever so slight clipping of his tone that he's seriously pissed off.

Keeping my excited, happy bride demeanour in place, I watch as Jason seems to become more annoyed, not less. Is Dad putting his foot in it somehow? Maybe I should go over there.

'I think it's me, dear,' Dorothy says suddenly.

I do my best approximation of a charming smile. 'What's you?' Even as I ask, I study her face for signs she's having one of her episodes, but her eyes are clear.

She nods at Jason. 'The tantrum my grandson is rather failing to suppress.'

At this perfect description I have to fight a giggle.

'Or,' she continues, 'it could be my insistence that Laila was as important as any other guest and the quip that I might leave everything to her was the last straw. Or it could be the earlier incident at the dock. Do you know what that was about?'

I feel Jason's gaze on me like he's aware we're talking about him. 'No idea,' I say truthfully. 'He said it wasn't important.'

Dorothy appears sceptical. 'Hopefully, whatever's bothering him, he cheers up before this afternoon's big party.'

'Hopefully,' I agree.

But studying Jason, I'm not so sure. The vein at his temple protrudes in a way that underlines just how much effort it's taking for him to remain pleasant. There's also what seems to be a light sheen of sweat and a greenish pallor to his skin. Maybe the seasickness tablets aren't working. Jason looks up then. It's too late to pretend I wasn't watching him, and besides, Dorothy waves.

'Just talking about you,' she calls.

'And what did you come up with?' he asks.

'I was telling Adele you're almost as lucky as she is.'

'Wise words,' he says. He winks at his grandmother and flashes me a smile that seems so genuinely happy I have to wonder if I was reading too much into his expression.

A hand wraps around my wrist. Dorothy. The skin on her fingers drooping over bare bones but the grip strong.

Her pink stained lips curve into a smile and her words are so low they're for my ears only. 'Don't fuck this up.'

Then she gives me a slight push, and, reeling from the

vehemence of her words and puzzling whether she means the wedding or the marriage or life in general, I find myself moving away from her as directed towards my husband, where everyone is drinking and talking and laughing, getting merrier with every drink top up.

The captain approaches and stops next to Jason. 'We'll increase the speed now if you're ready. I know you have lots planned.'

Jason nods and the man scurries away.

A minute later there's a slight bump and the purr of the engines get a little louder.

I'm half-listening to Mum recounting a story I've heard a million times, about her own wedding and the interruption when the priest asked if there was anyone who objected – Pip mouthing the familiar punchline behind her: 'Uncle Ed stood up and told a joke that made the reverend blush.' But at the same time, I'm also wondering just what else Jason has planned.

There's a brush on my arm. Jason. *My husband*. I'm sure there will be a point when that's not a surreal thought but I'm not there yet.

'I'll be back in a moment,' he murmurs.

He kisses me, brief but possessive. *She's mine*, he's saying.

As Mum starts another story, I'm aware of him going inside, and glimpse him heading up a short flight of stairs to the top deck. What could be up there that's drawing him away now? Could he have gone to find Sophie and Melanie? Or is it a reaction to the way he's been nursing his stomach? Do I really care?

I cannot be married to this man.

'Adele?' Mum's annoyed.

I force a smile. 'Excuse me, I'll be back in a moment.'

Without giving her a chance to argue, and ignoring Katja's questioning glance, I follow Jason inside. Now is not the time for us to be apart.

66

MELANIE – THE MOTHER

SATURDAY MORNING – AFTER THE WEDDING

I mean to catch up with Sophie, wanting to be by her side to face the others, but I find myself in an unfamiliar part of the boat. Maybe the blow from Jason affected me more than I thought. I press on. It's a big boat but I'll find the wedding party eventually.

My steps are soundless on the plush carpet, a feature I don't remember noticing before. I stop at a door I don't recognise and strain to listen for the others but there's only the rushing of the boat cutting through the water.

I push, and the door swings open. I'm hit by the bright blue of the sun shining off the water across a private balcony area that must run half the length of the boat. A burst of white sea spray appears above the balcony rail in an arc. Rapid blinking allows my eyesight to adjust. That's when I realise I'm not alone.

I open my mouth to speak, but they haven't seen me.

He's close to the rail, a guard that's only knee height to allow for a diving platform out over the edge. He wipes at his mouth like he's been vomiting, one arm held protectively across his stomach. As I watch, frozen, Sophie, the daughter I feel like I've only just found, closes the distance to him. Her strength and rage is a palpable thing.

He doesn't seem to be able to help himself, the smirk on his face vanishes. He steps backwards still clutching his waist, even closer to the rail.

I can't hear her words but it doesn't matter; she's spitting truth and fire and he's shrinking before her. Pride flares up but as she lifts her hand towards him, there's a flash of sun striking metal. The pocket knife. I almost cry out, not for his sake but hers...

'No.'

Not from me, but someone else out there calls to her and stops her before he can react, the command of it loud enough for me to hear inside. They turn as one, like clowns at the sideshow, mouths open.

Dorothy appears on the balcony, dog under her arm, and he seems relieved to see her. She says something and the tension across Sophie's shoulders vanishes. At a flick of Dorothy's wrist, the imperious gesture of someone with decades of being obeyed despite her diminutive stature, Sophie's head bows and she leaves, staggering inside to see me standing there.

Her cheeks are wet. The knife I'm sure I saw somehow secreted away.

'I wasn't going to—'

'Look.' I cut her off and point back outside to where grandmother and grandson stand together. Laila bares her teeth and something white flutters from Dorothy's hand. Dorothy says something that's drowned in the sounds of the water and the engine. In response, he bends down. The movement slow and pained.

'She said to me she'd handle it,' Sophie whispers, her voice shaking. 'Said I should go. That she had it under control.'

Dorothy moves towards him. The action playing out in front of us like a silent movie.

My brain registers something amiss before I even realise what I'm seeing. The fine hairs on the back of my neck stand on end. My words catch in my throat and become a scream locked in place, because what I'm seeing makes no sense.

Why on this earth would she...?

What surprises me most is the lack of fight from him. He's still bent over as she plants two hands on the side of his chest and pushes. It's like he's so certain that this can't be happening to him that he doesn't think to call out. I imagine I feel the shove from where we stand in the shadows of the open door.

I don't move. Can't move. Can't even breathe.

Splash.

67

ADELE – THE BRIDE

SATURDAY MORNING – AFTER THE WEDDING

Mum accosts me at the door as I return to the main deck, fussing at me like I'm some recalcitrant toddler. 'You can't disappear at your own wedding,' she says in a kind of stage whisper. 'I've been trying to cover for you but people have been asking questions. And where's Jason?'

She says 'people' like she's been holding off a crowd. I scan the space, realising that my missing bridesmaid and her mother have decided to show their faces at last. The two of them are standing together, and there's something unusually optimistic about Melanie that I can't read. Could she have decided to simply be happy for us?

Before I can ponder it, Mum is at me again. 'Where have you been?'

'With my husband.' I emphasise the title, knowing she can't argue with me prioritising Jason. 'And then I detoured to check the salt-drenched spray from the boat hadn't messed up my hair and makeup.'

She brightens at this. 'You can have some photographs on the jetty when we dock.'

I don't tell her there's no chance in hell of that happening. Not with Melanie and Sophie right here. I try to move past her. 'I should speak to my guests.'

'Oh, yes,' she agrees. 'You should. That young man, Rory is it? He was looking a bit miserable earlier. You should make sure he's doing okay. After all, Jason's best friend should be your friend, too.'

It's almost funny just how oblivious to every social nuance my mother is. I could walk over there and make out with Rory and she wouldn't notice.

Thinking about kissing Rory is a mistake. My head fills with memories and I can feel heat spreading through me. He's no psychic but he must have seen my thoughts in my face because he smiles and comes towards me.

Melanie is still watching me with that odd expression. Maybe I should speak to her instead and make sure that whatever kept her and Sophie below deck is resolved.

Thud.

I turn towards the bang of wood on wood. Feel the others around me do the same. It's Dorothy. She's standing at the altar with Laila tucked under one arm and her walking stick in her hand. I could have sworn she wasn't out here a minute ago.

Thud.

Another strike of the stick against the deck ensures she has everyone's attention. 'I have something to say,' she slurs. She sounds drunk and even from here her eyes have that distance, suggesting she's not quite with it.

A prickle of unease slips down my spine. Jason would not like this. Where the hell is he anyway?

'Come closer,' Dorothy orders. 'I'm too old to shout.'

I do as I'm told and feel the others gather around me, clumped just below Dorothy in front of the place where only minutes ago Jason and I exchanged vows. My parents, Pip and Katja stand on one side of me, Jason's mum Laura, and Ruth are on the other. Melanie and Sophie hang back and I can feel the warmth of Rory behind me. Is that his breath on my skin or just an ocean breeze?

Laura takes an extra step up towards her mother-in-law, about to reach out to maybe guide her to a seat or something, but when Laila growls she falls back.

Dorothy looks at each of us in turn. 'There are moments,' she says, 'moments when as a parent or grandparent you observe a child's behaviour and you have to decide. Is it simply boyish cheek? Is it teenage selfishness?' She pauses. 'Is it normal? Whatever the hell that is.'

This time Ruth goes to speak but Dorothy cuts her off with a glare.

I shiver, suddenly cold. My arms wrap around my waist. Where is Jason?

'And if it's not,' Dorothy continues, 'and we all know on an instinctive level when it's not, then it's decision time. Do I do something about it? At what point do we cease being responsible for our children's behaviour?' Her gaze sweeps across us, the pale eyes probing in a way that makes me squirm. 'What about when we're talking psychopaths?' She takes a breath. 'Well, I say never.'

'I don't understand,' I whisper giving voice to what we're all thinking. I find myself bracing although I don't know what blow she could execute that would explain the dread sticking my feet to the deck.

'I'd rather have my own kind's blood on my hands than, ultimately, an innocent's.'

The chill that began in my stomach spreads through my limbs. 'What are you saying?'

She shakes her head as if we're all a bit slow. 'I'm telling you that you won't find Jason below deck, in the cabin, or anywhere else on board this boat.'

Someone gasps. I don't see who but my throat feels raw. Could it have been me?

'I'm sorry, but I still don't understand.' Even as I say it though, I feel the lie, because I think I'm beginning to see where she's going with this. I just can't believe it.

Dorothy's lip quivers and she lifts her hand to her throat. 'Jason fell overboard.'

'What? When?' My exclamation is lost in similar cries from those around me.

As one we turn towards the water. The wind has picked up, making tiny white caps on tiny waves, but there's no sign of anyone.

Dorothy doesn't even bother to look. 'A few minutes ago.'

'That's impossible, he was just here,' I whisper, a sob catching and strangling the words. 'Impossible,' I repeat.

I'm aware of the crew moving into action, shouts of 'Man overboard', but it's like it's happening somewhere else. The engine judders. My knees try to respond to the change in the boat's movement but it's too much.

There's a rush in my ears. The sky above me slips sideways. I'm falling.

'Hey.' Hands at my waist steady me. Strong, familiar hands.

Rory helps me to a chair and for a change I'm numb to his touch.

I can't take my eyes off the seemingly endless blue expanse. My husband is somewhere in that water.

68

MELANIE – THE MOTHER

SATURDAY MORNING – AFTER THE WEDDING

I don't make a move to comfort Adele after Dorothy's announcement. I don't offer platitudes, nor recriminations. Instead, with Sophie at my side, we sit and watch the flurry of activity as the crew bring the boat around and I assume someone inside makes the mayday call back to the mainland for assistance.

My head is still reeling, trying to process what I saw on that private balcony. I would do anything for a drink, but I'm not going to risk wrath from Sophie by asking someone for one.

I want to be happy. Or at least satisfied.

Jason is gone. She's done what I couldn't and removed him from the world. But I just can't believe it. I scan the water, looking for signs of him. Trying to match the seemingly endless deep blue sea stretching from the hull of the boat to the horizon with the exact spot we were in when I saw him go overboard.

My heart rate is yet to settle and I'm half expecting him to appear from some hiding place announcing that it was some test to screw with our heads.

'They'll find him,' Sophie whispers. Impossible to tell from her wide eyes and shaking voice whether it's fear or hope.

'I don't think so,' I say quietly, and we return to scanning the water for signs of Jason.

My head replays the moments after he went in, when Dorothy stared down into the water – I'm guessing making sure he stayed under – before making her way back inside the far door.

As the engines go quiet, I leave Sophie and cross to the rail, noticing Laura do the same thing near the front of the boat, scanning the water for any sign of her son. I stand looking over the edge of the boat, my weight moving with the gentle rise and fall of the deck beneath my feet. The water around us is a deep dark blue, but it's not the murky black of the space between the jetties.

Going under here would not be the same as it would have been for Ollie.

The result, however, will be.

As a mother I should feel something in response to the agony on Laura's face, but I have hurt too much for my own son to have anything left for hers.

Adele, the gorgeous widow-bride, moves between Laura and the spot where Dorothy has taken a seat inside. Her bridesmaid is by her side but the best man is missing. Terry took Tammy to one of the cabins to rest when she announced it was all too awful to bear.

The captain approaches Adele and Laura, who's now being quite literally held up by a stony-faced Ruth, with his gaze firmly on a spot over their shoulders, his lips pressed together.

'The expert divers will take over and we'll be returning to dock,' he says.

The women bow their heads, accepting. There's no grieving wail, no insistence we remain out here, and because of this I breathe easier.

Jason is not coming back.

The return journey is quite the sombre affair with all of the guests retreating to different areas of the boat. By unconscious agreement we all make our way to the back of the boat as we get closer, wanting to get off this cursed vessel as soon as we can. There's no conversation, and mostly dry eyes. It seems shock overwhelms any other emotion.

As the boat motors into the bay and I see the old jetty ahead, the engineer's report from what seems a lifetime ago rings in my brain. *It's simply not derelict enough to require demolition.*

We're getting closer, the engines yet to slow, going fast enough in the captain's desire to get this trip finished, that I could almost imagine we might crash.

A crash...

I jump to my feet and weave through the stunned wedding party. Maybe Sophie says my name but I don't stop. She's the future, but first I need to finally, properly deal with the past.

We're closer. The familiar stretch of sand and the shacks I once believed really were a refuge from the hustle and bustle of city life are in sight. And ahead, the twin jetties.

I didn't get to see Ollie in those last seconds. It didn't matter that I ran when I heard his name. I've never been athletic, but that day I sprinted hard. Legs pumping. Lungs bursting. But even as I ran, even with the panic clawing at me, I thought there would a future. That the day at the jetty would be a terrible story we'd all remember. I never imagined he'd be in an ambulance by the time I got there. Already pronounced dead.

The knot of grief in my chest twists and hardens.

There are people waiting at the end of the new jetty. The authorities, I presume. In a minute, we'll dock, and the questions about what happened out on the water will begin.

This is my last chance.

As I climb the stairs to the captain's bridge, I'm hit by a sudden memory. The funeral and the wake and me gulping whiskey like Ollie would drain a can of soft drink if allowed a treat. As it burned my throat I laughed at how pointless all those mothering attempts at veggies and being healthy ended up. I laughed until the tears streamed down my cheeks, all the while feeling the disapproval from the others at the bar. They'd all seemed so far away and insignificant, like ants crawling beneath frosted glass. I fought Jim's arm as he'd tried to lead me away.

I'm so sick of being told when and how and where to react to the single worst moment of my life.

The captain isn't on the bridge, likely gone to meet the authorities as we dock. Instead, a young woman's at the wheel. Someone a little more my size.

I imagine it takes a lot of training and practice to successfully dock such an expensive craft and this woman appears in control as she works a silver lever that I'm guessing is a throttle. When she touches it, the engines hum in response. A large wheel lets her steer, and there is an array of small screens, knobs and buttons that I'm sure mean something to her but are beyond my understanding.

A glance through the window shows we're closer now,

engines still whirring to give us the momentum to get us around the old jetty, after which I guess we'll slow to a stop.

She's concentrating and hasn't noticed me. It seems impossible that she can't hear the drumming of my racing heart, that she isn't startled by each ragged breath.

We're alongside the old jetty, its timbers dark lines against the bright blue water. My hands shake. I picture Ollie, wide grin, as he stands on the edge of the world, about to jump.

Now.

I leap forward, knock the young woman aside, push hard on the throttle and yank the wheel. A shout of glee escapes my chest as I feel the body of the vessel move beneath me. Then any sound is lost in the scraping, shuddering impact of hull on wood.

The wheel is wrenched from my grasp and I'm knocked aside, bouncing off the wall onto the floor. Blood drips from a scrape on my arm as the young woman fights to regain control. But she's too late. The old jetty has splintered before the weight of the boat, pieces of it flying through the air and then sinking beneath the waves.

I've done it. I grin at the blood on my arm and the bruises already forming on my knees. I feel no pain.

69

ADELE – THE BRIDE

SATURDAY MORNING – AFTER THE WEDDING

Thanks to Melanie crashing the boat, we need to be ferried from where it's wedged against the old jetty, over to the dock by a police vessel. Fortunately, no one was hurt and I could sense the captain's relief that he wouldn't have any further injuries to explain. The police boat leaves us to go and assist in the search for Jason... for Jason's body. My brain still can't imagine that he won't be found safe somehow, and I can't seem to stop the shaking in my legs.

No one seems to notice I'm shivering despite the sunshine.

Before the authorities can finish introducing themselves, Dorothy steps forward. Laila is snoozing under one arm. She holds out her other arm, a silent command for assistance; her gaze, bright and intent, is square on me.

It takes a heartbeat to sink in. I'm family now.

I cross slowly to her side, aware of them all watching. I make the mistake of looking at Mum. Not for help, God I've long since stopped expecting that from her, but what I see has me looking away fast. I can see the calculation of what all this – Jason's death – might mean. There might as well be dollar signs in her eyes.

I swallow bile. At least let there be a body before she's spending his money.

Dorothy waits until I'm at her side and her hand is on my arm, such that she's the picture of a broken, little old lady, before she speaks.

'Let's not waste any time pretending you young folk are likely to work out what happened here. Jason went over the edge out there and I, alone, am responsible.'

My gasp is lost in Laura's cry. Ruth is holding her up from collapse.

Dorothy shoots her daughter-in-law a decidedly derisive look. 'Pull yourself together,' she snaps, before returning her attention to the authorities. 'It was an accident, of course, although unfortunately the captain has said there are no cameras out on that deck.' Her hand goes to her chest. 'In fact, he tried to attack me.'

'Why?' Laura sobs. 'My beautiful boy.'

Dorothy rolls her eyes. 'Your boy was like a rotten beam and they have to be cut out before they bring everything around them down. He came at me, his grandmother, because I threatened to reveal what he did.'

Sophie stiffens. Before I can wonder at her reaction, Dorothy is continuing.

'He hurt that girl,' she says.

Another glance at my missing-in-action bridesmaid shows that she's lost all colour in her cheeks. Did Jason do something to her? Is that what all this is about?

But Dorothy isn't looking at Sophie. 'You'll find the body of

Fiona Lewis in scrubland behind the shed at the very back of his property near the dunes.' Her head bows. 'You understand that I didn't want to believe it myself, but I couldn't let him get away with murder. I wanted him to do the right thing and confess. I confronted him and begged him to do so.' When she lifts her head there's a proud line to her neck. 'I wanted him to take responsibility.'

The authorities share a look, clearly confused. I'm sure they're not the only ones.

'How did it happen?' the woman asks.

'We were near the edge of the boat and when he came at me...' Her voice breaks. 'I had to...' She sniffs. 'It was an accident. A terrible accident.' One tear falls from her pale, red-rimmed eyes then another. 'But he admitted before he fell that he killed that mayor woman.'

No one moves for a moment. The only sound is the lap of the waves against the pylons and the squeal of a seagull wheeling overhead. Then Dorothy presses Laila into my arms and holds out her wrists like they're already in handcuffs. 'Arrest me and take me away.'

70

SOPHIE – SUNDAY JANUARY 30ᵀᴴ

TWELVE YEARS AGO

The next morning Sophie got up and dressed on auto-pilot. Her eyes ached from crying but Mum was too busy arguing with Dad – he'd apparently suggested they sell the shack – to notice, and Ollie was too busy glaring at the world.

As much as she didn't want to go to the jetty, she didn't want the questions that would follow if she stayed behind. At some point around dawn, she'd decided she would face everyone like she was fine; it would just have to be the best performance of her life.

And sunglasses would help.

Mum and Dad were so busy sniping at each other they barely said goodbye when she and Ollie left the shack. Her brother stalked ahead, basically radiating a bad mood. After what she'd overheard, she wasn't all that surprised.

'Ollie, wait,' she called, knowing she had to try before they reached the others. Once surrounded by his mates, there'd be no chance he'd listen to anything she had to say.

'What?'

He stopped, but the angle of his body screamed impatience

and he was already looking ahead to where the other kids were gathered. He could pretend all he wanted that he didn't care about the fight with Adele but she knew better. Who knew what he'd do once around the other boys? He wasn't being himself lately but today he was even more wound up, like anything could press him the wrong way and he'd explode.

But as fast as she thought all that, she decided against trying to put it into words.

'Just don't do anything stupid,' she said.

His laugh came easily even if it did have an edge. 'You worry too much.'

'Please,' she said. 'I don't know if those pills were Jason's, but I know you've taken some before.'

'You don't know anything.'

There was something about him that was different. Past being moody, like he wasn't himself. 'Are you on something now?'

'Oh my god, what are you, five?'

It wasn't an answer, but she discovered part of her didn't want to know. 'Be careful.'

His eyes flashed with that temper he tried so hard to hide. 'Or what?'

She scrambled for something to get through to him and landed on his precious reputation and the way he gloried in being the apple of Mum's eye. 'I'll tell Mum.'

He snorted. 'Like I give a fuck. Bitch better not try telling me what to do after what I saw. She's a fucking hypocrite.'

'Tell me.'

'Trust, me, you don't want to know.'

She was left blinking at the raw violence in him as he

stormed off. The ache in her tummy had her wanting to go straight back to the shack, and the safety of her bed. But the others had already seen her.

'Hey, Soph? I hope we can still be friends.' Pip's arm came over her shoulder from behind as he spoke.

She flinched.

He dropped his arm.

It wasn't his fault, but how could she tell him that? When she dared look at him, she could see his hurt. Why had she messed this all up so badly? All she'd wanted was to be even closer to Pip and instead she'd gone and…

No, she wouldn't think about that.

Before he could turn away, she grabbed his hand and laced her fingers through his, even as every cell in her wanted to be left alone. This was Pip. What had happened the night before would not destroy this as well. She could save this one precious thing, no matter what it cost her.

'You scared me,' she said lightly. 'And Ollie's acting odd.'

He squeezed her hand briefly, then fell into step beside her. His familiar presence soothed in a way she could never tell him about, but she hoped he somehow knew.

'Hopefully he and Adele sort it out.'

So, he knew about the fight.

'Hopefully,' she agreed, but she doubted it.

'We're good though?' he asked. 'Aren't we?'

She let herself look at him fully then. His gorgeous features, his kind eyes, the slight lopsidedness of his mouth that she'd only noticed because she'd thought so long about him kissing her. One thing she'd learned over the last few weeks was that she undeniably loved this boy. And she suspected she always would.

Even though, and she accepted it now, there would be no romance in their future.

'Better than good,' she said. 'Best friends.'

His face lit up and he was so beautiful because of it that the part of her that desperately wanted more than that from him made tears sting her eyes.

'Always.'

As they headed across the sand, some of the easiness of before had returned between them. It wouldn't take Pip long to ask her about Jason and she didn't know what she'd tell him. Mostly, she wanted to forget everything about that boy. Every time she thought about Jason and his tongue and his hands pushing at her, the toast she'd had for breakfast threatened to return.

And her brain was still turning over the way Ollie had been so scathing of Mum. That was not like the golden boy, not at all. He'd been more than just mad.

But then they were at the jetty and she was distracted, forcing a smile onto her face and hoping the dark sunglasses hid how much she'd cried the night before.

71

ADELE - THE BRIDE

TUESDAY — THREE DAYS AFTER THE WEDDING

Jason's shack has been gone over by the police and their specialists for evidence by the time I'm allowed to go in a few days after the wedding. I don't know if they found what they were looking for, but it appears strangely undisturbed.

It's hard not to think that he might appear at the top of the stairs at any moment, except that I saw him in the morgue not long after he was found. With Dorothy still being detained by the police despite her lawyer's best efforts, and Laura beside herself with grief, it fell to me as his wife to identify his body. Heart aching, I again try to banish the mental image of his injuries. Anywhere else in Refuge Bay and he might have sunk to the sea bed but instead his body was caught in the currents and thrown onto the jagged rocks at the end of the point.

He still would have drowned though. Once he hit the water after his altercation with Dorothy, and with no immediate help available, he didn't have a chance. The police know that much from the cocktail of laxatives and seasickness medication found in his system as well as the alcohol. Together, those would have left him weak and the heavy material of his expensive suit would have meant that he was quickly dragged under.

Who'd have thought a cheap and nasty suit might have given him a better chance?

I miss him less than a new wife should, but more than I might have guessed. This is not how it was supposed to be. Something I had to tell Rory when he turned up, crying on my doorstep in the early hours of the morning whining about somehow being karmically to blame because he wanted Jason gone.

Pathetic men are not at all attractive.

I find the key for next door where Dorothy said it would be, hanging on a hook in the butler's pantry. She's asked me to check on her place.

The breeze hits me as I walk back out into the main living space and then I see the door to the deck is wide open. I'm sure I shut it, considering I have Laila with me, something else I seem to have inherited responsibility for while Dorothy is locked up. But the little dog is sitting where I left her.

'You could really do something with this place.'

I spin towards the couch where Mum has made herself at home. At my gesture, Laila comes, jumping up into my arms.

'I was just leaving,' I say pointedly.

Mum waves me away. 'Don't mind me, I'm just getting comfortable. This place has a lot of potential. I know a really good interior designer; I could give you their details.' She must see my face because she adds, 'In due time of course, after the funeral and whatnot.'

She's already reminded me three times about how Jason was going to sort out her and Dad's little financial problem.

'I have to check on Dorothy's place. Wouldn't want to

upset her considering she could challenge any will leaving Jason's share in the business to me.'

Now I'm talking in a language Mum can understand.

She jumps up. 'Best to keep on the in-laws' good side. Wouldn't want to end up over the side of a boat.' She titters at her own hilarity.

But at least she leaves.

I head across to the older shack, making sure I lock the door behind me before I let Laila down. Once inside, there's something about Dorothy's style and taste that comforts.

'You remind me of myself when I was your age,' Dorothy had said when I visited her in remand. 'I think we'll work well together.'

I make short work of the list of things she asked me to check and collect a few personal items she needs. I'm on my way out when the 'Secret wedding business' sign catches my eye. Of course, she was making the cake that so worried Jason.

The fridge door gives easily under my hand, the padlock on it, clearly, just for show.

Inside, there is nothing. Nothing at all. She didn't make a cake.

Did she know there would be no need?

72

MELANIE – THE MOTHER

WEDNESDAY – FOUR DAYS AFTER THE WEDDING

So, it turns out they breath test you if you accidentally-on-purpose crash a luxury yacht into a jetty. Who knew drink-driving boats was a thing? Likely because of all the years I've spent trying to get that jetty demolished, they started throwing out terms like 'malicious' rather than 'accidental' public property damage.

Giovanni called in a favour, and I had a lawyer at my side not long after Dorothy, who ended up a few rooms down from me. I didn't even realise Giovanni was fishing on the jetty that morning, or that when he saw me at the wheel of the boat before it crashed he'd guess I'd need help.

There was more buzz down Dorothy's end of the small country police station given the Ellingsworths' status around here and that they had begun to accept that finding Jason alive was unlikely.

Sophie had kept her head and returned the bathroom to a more ordered state so there were no questions asked on that front. She even came to collect me after the police were done with all the questions and paperwork. According to the lawyer, I'll likely get a fine and community service.

All worth it since now they'll have to demolish the whole thing.

I allow myself a small smile while looking out to the water, darker grey below a cloudy sky, finding comfort in its ever-changing familiarity.

Jim blamed the water for what happened.

I knew better. The water might have claimed my son, but it was the jetty and Jason Ellingsworth who were to blame.

There's a tap on the door that leads out to the beach. The tall figure is cast into a silhouette by the sky beyond, their face hidden in shadow.

My heart skips a beat then settles.

Not Jason.

Too big. Too broad. Too alive.

I open the door and it's Pip standing there. 'Sophie in?' he asks.

'Come in.'

Sophie must hear our voices because she appears from the hallway before I can call out, a layer of sand on her blue-painted toenails evidence of our earlier walk together on the beach. I'm not winning any mother of the year awards but I'm trying. Helped by my attending a nearby AA meeting yesterday.

'I'll leave you to it,' I say quickly as I leave the room.

However, hearing Pip mention his sister's name has me straining to listen.

Sophie leans her head around the doorway and I jump.

'I… ah… was just…'

'Being nosy,' she finishes for me but there's a smile teasing her lips. 'If you're going to listen, you might as well join us.'

'Thank you.' I trail her back into the room noticing Pip is still standing not far from where I let him in. I gesture towards the table. 'You two sit down.'

Pip obediently pulls a chair out and sits. Sophie follows suit.

'Coffee?' I ask, wishing, given Pip's star status, I had one of those fancy machines. 'I have a decent ground brew and a plunger.'

'Sounds lovely,' Pip says.

As I potter around the kitchen, making coffee and finding a cake Sophie must have picked up, I listen in to Pip's update.

I'm not surprised that Adele seems to be the one in charge now; it was easy to see that Dorothy approved of her. Nor am I shocked they expect Dorothy to be back home under some sort of bail conditions by the end of the week.

I'm so wrapped up in what Pip's saying, and in playing host that I've set out the afternoon tea before I realise there's anything amiss.

'Mum?' There's a strangled note to Sophie's voice.

I look down at the table. My heart cramps in my chest. I've shifted the puzzle.

For a second I don't breathe, but nothing else happens. I breathe again, properly this time. My son is still in my heart. Swallowing past a lump in my throat, I move the rest of the puzzle aside. 'It's not like I'm ever going to get around to finishing it anyway.'

My voice is light, but Sophie's touch on my hand tells me she understands.

Later, when Pip and Sophie have headed out to some bar, I

hold that corner piece. I don't need to let everything go, but I can give some attention to those left behind. With the jetty and Jason both gone I should feel overjoyed, but something about Dorothy's confession bothers me. Of course, she's saying it was an accident but her revelation about Fiona rang oddly too.

The mayor's body was found where Dorothy said it would be. Jason to blame. Or was he? Could Dorothy have wanted to eliminate Fiona herself in an attempt to save investigations into the company?

Jason and Fiona both gone in less than twenty-four hours. If Dorothy did have something to do with the mayor's death, that would make her a serial resolver of problems.

A serial killer?

I want to laugh at the ridiculousness of it, but I can't. I wonder what I'd find if I investigated exactly what happened to her son, Stephan. She's never been secret about how disappointing she found him. Then, there's her husband.

Funny that the Ellingsworth men have so much bad luck.

Ultimately the only thing that matters to me is that Jason isn't here to hurt anyone else. If I had a drink, I would make a toast to the woman who did what I couldn't.

Now my daughter can get on with her life, and my Ollie can rest in peace.

73

ADELE – THE BRIDE

SATURDAY – ONE WEEK AFTER THE WEDDING

I'm strangely nervous when I knock on the front door of Dorothy's city address even though I've been to the exquisitely renovated, stone-fronted bungalow with Jason for dinner several times. The little dog under my arm begins to squirm and when the door opens, Laila leaps forward and lands in Dorothy's arms.

'Laila,' Dorothy says into her fur. 'I've missed you. Have you been a good girl?'

'Of course she has,' I say.

Dorothy's smile is wide and her eyes clear and I can't help remembering she didn't bother to make the cake at all.

'Come in, dear,' she says.

She's the perfect hostess, offering tea and a freshly made caramel slice, despite the band around her ankle that was part of the conditions of her being released.

Her lawyers agreed to it in order to get her home as soon as possible, but they expect that even that will not last long. They're likely to rule her role in Jason's death an accident, helped, ironically, by the evidence he submitted to the company board describing Dorothy as having dementia.

'How are you?' she asks me.

'Okay,' I say but the waver in my voice betrays me. 'We weren't together long, married only minutes.' I've been repeating this fact to myself every time I catch myself fighting tears. I didn't even want to be married.

A hand placed on my knee breaks me from my mental recriminations. 'He was your husband.'

It's said as though that's enough, but I'm not sure if it is.

The open newspaper on the coffee table gives me the change in subject I need. It's open to a damning expose on the late Jason Ellingsworth – his dodgy business dealings and even darker interactions with various women. Finishing with his being linked with Fiona Lewis' death. Penned by the mayor's sister and the journalist who went undercover with us kids during Ollie's last summer, Kirsty Lewis.

'What about the article?' I ask. 'Did you know it was coming?'

Dorothy sighs. 'I had my suspicions.'

'Couldn't you let the law run its course then? Or his illness?' It's the closest I dare come to saying that I'm not sure Jason's death was an accident.

'Illness?' She guffaws, a shocking sound considering the topic. 'What did he tell you?'

I hesitate, feeling suddenly stupid although I'm not sure why. 'Cancer,' I whisper.

Dorothy shakes her head. 'Oh, you poor girl. He lied. It's something the Ellingsworth men like to do. Pathologically so.' There's no hint of grief or regret but she turns serious.

'He was a blight that needed to be stopped. He's done things, those you think you know and more. Seducing you was a long time in the planning. He always envied that poor Oliver; Melanie was probably right about him being at fault.'

I go to deny it, my own guilt heavy on me, forcing me to his defence, but she silences me with a wave.

'I am the kind of person who takes responsibility.'

I see again the white handkerchief dropped. Each time Jason bending over to pick it up for her. Always wanting to be seen as the gentleman. Wanting her approval.

Being trained just like her little dog.

It's so easy to see it happening again on the boat. Her dropping the white square of cloth to the ground. Him bending. A bump. He'd be over the side easily enough.

She switches to business mode then, talking through details of when and how she expects the control of Ellingsworth Hotels to come to me and what we'll do when that happens.

I'm about to leave when she slides me a small white envelope that's been sitting on the coffee table. I move to open it but she stands and shakes her head. 'When you're alone. My grandson forgets the people who worked for him were originally hired by me, and they liked to keep me in the loop.'

When I get home, I make myself a cup of tea and will my hands to steady as I open it. Three photos fall out onto my lap. All bright colour, crisp and clear. All of me and Rory.

The lurch in my belly has me tasting acid.

Me and Rory smiling at each other over coffee. Kissing in the rain. Pressed against a wall. Clearly, not just friends.

Why would Jason marry me if he had these?

He'd always wanted what Ollie had. A memory hits me,

sneaking into Ollie's room. Imagining our perfect wedding day. *'By the water, near sunrise, with bare feet, and flower crowns. Maybe on a boat?'*

In the end Jason's and my wedding was a modern version of the fantasy Ollie and I played out that night in his bed as teenagers. From the setting to the honeymoon and even the jazz music he'd picked. And now I remember that I'd thought I heard someone outside that night.

Nothing of the ceremony on the boat suggested a thrown-together, last-minute event – and besides, that was never Jason's style. He loved to plan and control to the last detail. He must have planned it all.

Nausea rises in my throat. No wonder Dorothy said he was sick.

My brain's reeling. Not just because of what it means about everything Jason did these last weeks but also what being given the pictures means about Dorothy. A woman who's survived husband, son and grandson.

It's a warning.

74

SOPHIE – SUNDAY JANUARY 30ᵀᴴ

TWELVE YEARS AGO

As Sophie and Pip passed a couple of the old fishermen about halfway along the jetty, Sophie noticed a small crowd gathered near the far end that jutted out into the dark water. As they got closer to the group, a murmur of excitement rippled through them.

'What's going on?' she asked, even though clearly Pip was as confused as she was.

Something made her walk a little faster, like she could smell trouble on the salty breeze. There came the sound of raised voices over a gull squawking and a few of the nearest kids moved apart, revealing her brother in the middle, standing toe-to-toe with Daniel.

'Please let it not be a fight,' she whispered. Ollie might be bigger, but she wouldn't put it past Daniel to carry a blade. And if Ollie was on something he might not be able to protect himself.

Pip grabbed her hand and squeezed it. 'Ollie's not stupid.'

Usually, she'd agree, but not today.

As they drew closer, she saw the two boys were just talking, even though every part of their narrowed eyes, puffed-out chests and tense muscles suggested that could change at any moment.

Daniel jerked his head towards the jetty outcrop. Some of what he said was lost in a gust of wind that whipped the water into little white peaks below, but the final question carried to all.

'Or are you scared?'

Sophie scanned the faces of the other kids, hoping Adele might say something. But she stood with Daniel. And there at her side, where suddenly Sophie realised he'd always wanted to be, was Jason.

Ollie hesitated.

Sophie clenched her teeth to stop herself calling out. Anything she said now would only stoke his rage.

Then Jason leaned close to Adele at his side, so close his lips almost brushed her ear – the sight of it making Sophie's stomach heave – and he whispered something to Adele. Maybe it was coincidence. Maybe it had nothing to do with the gauntlet that Daniel had just thrown at Ollie's feet. But whatever Jason said right then, made Adele laugh.

The sweet pitch of it making Ollie visibly wince.

Sophie wanted to cry out, tell the other girl she didn't need to make Ollie jealous, didn't need to get back at him for the awful things he'd said. Wanted to shake them both and tell them they were so clearly meant to be together.

But they'd hurt each other too much, and no one would listen to her now.

'From the top rail?' Ollie said.

Daniel nodded.

Ollie spun towards the fencing keeping them out.

'Ollie, don't!' Sophie couldn't help it; she was past caring that he'd get mad. She'd never seen anyone jump from the top. It was higher, would be slippery, and he wasn't in his right mind.

Ollie's eyes were wild, his mouth a cruel line baring his teeth. He held her gaze for a microsecond, then without a word he turned away.

'I'll need someone to help me balance.'

Jason stepped forward, bringing Adele with him, eager and making sure there was no time for anyone to come to their senses. No time for Ollie to back out. The two of them squished in behind through the fencing as Ollie climbed the rail, slipping twice on his way up.

All of this before Sophie could halve the distance between them. People were staring at her, but she didn't care. 'Don't,' she cried again, but the wind caught her voice, and her brother didn't seem to hear.

Ollie manoeuvred himself so he faced the crowd, his back to the water. He teetered in a crouch at the top, high above everyone watching. He seemed to wobble up there, like the rough, solid wood beneath his feet was moving with the tug of the currents far below.

Jason, then Adele, gripped an ankle, as he rose to a stand.

'He's definitely on something.'

Sophie heard Pip say what her brain had skirted around, but it came from a distance. She kept moving towards the crowd. If she could get closer, she could still stop this.

'Well, are you going to jump?'

The question came from Jason. Jason whose face made Sophie's skin crawl, whose grin was like he'd just won the lotto and this couldn't be better if he'd planned it. Which he couldn't have, could he?. He couldn't have known Ollie would take the dare.

Ollie glanced down at Adele, but she looked away. His throat worked, then he squared his shoulders and held his hands up in a victory pose, exposing the bronze tanned muscles rippling across his chest.

He pushed his hair out of his eyes.

Took one last look at the admiring faces on the jetty, grinned. Then he looked back to Jason and Adele.

'Now,' he said.

And leapt.

Sophie's gasp of awe and terror as Ollie jumped was lost in similar responses from those who'd pushed to get a better view. No one had successfully jumped from up there. It was the stuff of Refuge Bay legend; only a few had ever tried.

He flipped backwards. Once, then again. A gorgeous arc of athletic youth and power, with a backdrop of a stunning blue sky.

Sophie held her breath.

He was still so high. He should hit the water feet first but the second somersault took him further. Arms and legs loose and extended like he'd lost control. She thought she saw his eyes roll back in his head.

He hit the water.

The back of his skull took the full force of the blow. The ocean swallowed him whole, sending a violent spray of water high into the sky, marking the spot Ollie disappeared.

His dark form sank to where it was even darker still.

And it didn't come up.

'Ollie,' Sophie screamed, 'Ollie, this isn't funny.'

Steps came from somewhere behind her, but they were still

far away. Sophie gripped at the rail, took a step to climb up – maybe she could get down there.

Out of the corner of her eye, Sophie saw Jason. He was part way up on the rails already, concern on his face. But then a slim arm reached out from his other side, gripped his hand in hers, and ever so gently, tugged him back.

Sophie tried to make sense of what she was seeing, but a splash from further along the jetty dragged her attention to the water. There, the old fisherman had jumped in and was closing the distance to where Ollie had been with confident strokes.

He dived below, then briefly popped up before diving again.

As though from some TV show, there were the sounds of people further along the jetty and the beach, calling for someone to get an ambulance, calling for someone, anyone, to help.

Then Giovanni broke the surface, the limp figure of Ollie in his arms almost dragging him back under.

He swam steadily towards where someone had thought to throw in a flotation device, where another adult was in the water to help get Ollie to shore.

'He'll be all right,' Sophie said, catching on a sob. 'He has to be.'

Pip didn't answer, but he stayed with Sophie as she stumbled along above the figures down in the water. Ollie's skin was grey, and he wasn't responding to anything the adults were doing as they tried to get him to safety.

Sophie glanced back over her shoulder. Jason was still next to the rail as though a statue caught in time. Next to him, her hand still holding tight to his where she'd reached out to stop him diving straight in after his friend, stood Adele. Shock made their mouths hang open, and horror widened eyes. Their stunned stillness was stark in the whirl of movement to follow Ollie's body towards the shore.

While everyone else had been listening to Ollie's declaration, Sophie had dropped her gaze to where the two people he was closest to held his ankles for support. And in the moment before he leapt, she would have sworn she saw them share a look and then move as one, adding momentum to Ollie's careful jump. Creating the devastating over-rotation.

Together, they pushed him.

Acknowledgements

I'd like to acknowledge the Kaurna people and the Kaurna Country on which *The Wedding Party* was written.

The beginnings of this idea came from wanting to distract myself one afternoon worrying about my teenage son jumping from a jetty. A 'what if' that took on a life of its own. Ollie, his friends and family are, of course, completely fictional in all their pain and heartaches, secrets and lies.

Although writing a book takes hours alone at a keyboard, getting it to the hands of readers needs a dedicated team. So much thanks to anyone not explicitly mentioned below.

A huge thank you to my editor, Peyton Stableford, for her enthusiasm and brilliant help and encouragement to work this book into its best possible shape. And also to the rest of the wonderful team at Head of Zeus. Thanks to Kay Coleman for the copyedits and Simon Michele for the cover design. Thanks also to the Australian Bloomsbury team for your continuing support. I'm so lucky to work with two great publishers.

Special thanks to Hattie Grünewald for her endless support and brilliant insight. Thanks too, to all the team at The Blair

Partnership for always being in my corner, particularly Jordan Lees.

Thanks again to George S. Patton for your help with police questions. All mistakes are my own, and your advice is much appreciated. Thanks to Nat for connecting us.

Writing friends make showing up at the keyboard so much easier. I've felt so warmly welcomed into the crime and thriller community, and I'm so lucky to be a part of it now on my third book. A particular shoutout to the SA bookish contingent who share events and support each other so well. Voxes and conference catchups with my Writers Camp friends keep me going. Thanks to Emily Madden and Lisa Ireland, and especially to Amanda Knight. You girls are fabulous. And of course, Rach Johns for sprints and emails and chats and reading everything. I owe you so much!

Thanks to the friends who ask about the book-in-progress and get to hear about these characters like they're real people (because they are in my head). Caroline and Rowan, Alison, Amy and Julie, your support means so much.

Refuge Bay is fictional but is inspired by South Australian beaches where I was lucky enough to spend time as a child with family and friends. Thanks so much to the Tuckers and to the Jantzens for having me!

Harriet (the very best dog) and Karma (is a cat) are tremendous writing company. Laila is inspired by my niece's gorgeous girl of the same name, and I hope she loves her starring moment!

I couldn't do this without family. Thank you to Dick, Shirley and Lyn, and remembering Dad and Wendy.

To my big sisters and their families. Particularly to Chloe and Mitch, who never hesitate to help with my questions that come at them at all hours. And to their partners, I promise your weddings into the family are not this book's inspiration. This time Chloe needed to take a few things to the group chat, and I'm very appreciative that they came through! My love and thanks always to Fi and Kirst who aren't a mayor nor a journalist but are wonderful sisters. To Mum – always missed, always loved.

My most heartfelt thanks to all the readers, booksellers, bloggers, Instagrammers, TikTokkers, podcasters and reviewers who supported the release of *The Summer Party* and *The Dinner Party* and have meant that I could keep doing this. I feel so incredibly lucky and grateful! Thank you.

Much love and thanks to my kids, Amelie, James and Claire. You three are everything to me, and I am so very proud of you and the great humans you are becoming. And, of course, to Dave. What can I say? You listen, you read, you support, you believe, and I adore you for all this and so much more. Thank you.

About the Author

REBECCA HEATH studied science at university, worked in hospitality and teaching, but she always carved out time to write. She lives in Adelaide, Australia, halfway between the city and the sea with her husband, three children and a much-loved border collie. Her debut adult novel, *The Summer Party* was released in 2023 by Head of Zeus, followed by *The Dinner Party* in 2024. This is her third adult novel.

Perfect families are only as perfect as their best kept secrets.

Summer, 2000
The Whitlam siblings have it all and sixteen-year-old Lucy only wants one thing – to be close to them. Soon she's lazing around their impossibly large pool, wearing Annabel's expensive clothes and having secret rendezvous with Harry, until at their lavish clifftop party she sees something that could jeopardise it all.

Winter, 2020
One failed marriage later, Lucy is back in town and quickly lured back into the Whitlam's shiny world. But when a body washes up on the beach and someone seems determined to frame her for murder, keeping their secrets this time could cost her everything.

*Now that summer is over,
is she with them or against them?*

FOUR COUPLES.
Summer 1979. In the idyllic suburban neighbourhood of Ridgefield, Australia, during a scorching heat wave, four couples gather for their weekly dinner party.

AN ORDINARY EVENING.
When Frank Callaghan checks on the sleeping children, he finds an empty crib where his four-month-old daughter Megan should be sleeping. The party-goers swear they didn't see anything but each of them has something to hide.

THE BEGINNING OF A NIGHTMARE.
Forty years later, a stranger knocks at the Callaghan's door. She claims to be their missing daughter. And she's holding the blanket she was wrapped in the night she disappeared. Shocked, the Callaghans must finally confront how well they know their neighbours, and ask themselves:

Where has Megan really been all this time?